Behpoin

**What do all those metric prefixes mean? . . .
How do I form the possessive case of
"sisters-in-law"? . . . How can I compose a good
opening paragraph? . . . What's the difference
between *irreversible* and *irrevocable*? . . .
How do I capitalize the names of religious
groups and religious terms? . . . What does
"ISBN" stand for?**

Good writing can be tricky—and it gets trickier every day,
with new developments in usage, new technologies, and
new ideas. This in-depth encyclopedic dictionary offers an
understanding of the timeless basics of good writing—and
an up-to-date look at the changes you need to know about
today.

Berkley Books by Mary A. DeVries

THE ENCYCLOPEDIC DICTIONARY OF STYLE AND USAGE
THE BUSINESS WRITER'S BOOK OF LISTS
THE ENCYCLOPEDIC DICTIONARY OF BUSINESS TERMS

The Encyclopedic Dictionary of
Style and
Usage

MARY A. DEVRIES

BERKLEY BOOKS, NEW YORK

THE ENCYCLOPEDIC DICTIONARY OF STYLE AND USAGE

A Berkley Book / published by arrangement with
the author

PRINTING HISTORY
Berkley edition / June 1999

The Penguin Putnam Inc. World Wide Web site address is
http://www.penguinputnam.com

ISBN: 0-425-16942-1

BERKLEY®
Berkley Books are published by The Berkley Publishing Group,
a division of Penguin Putnam Inc., 375 Hudson Street,
New York, New York 10014.
BERKLEY and the "B" design
are trademarks belonging to Penguin Putnam Inc.

PRINTED IN THE UNITED STATES OF AMERICA

10 9 8 7 6 5 4 3 2 1

PREFACE

THOSE OF US who write or edit material for publication or other purposes know that it should look appealing and sound intelligent. Notice that I said *should,* because producing the best possible document is often far from easy. In fact, few of us can create professional copy—inviting, accurate, meaningful, and consistent—without a little help from our friends: the style guides, grammar books, and word-usage books.

Professional writers understand that it takes a minilibrary just to prepare one document. With that in mind, we set out to make *The Encyclopedic Dictionary of Style and Usage* a blended book—one volume containing the most important style *and* usage information that writers and editors need to know to create a manuscript or produce a printed document. Especially, we wanted to give the *usage* part of *style and usage*—word choice, grammar, and so on—the attention it deserves. All too often this type of book is 90 percent style and 10 percent usage, even though the latter affects reader response as much as capitalization, punctuation, and other points of style.

An A-to-Z encyclopedic-dictionary format proved to be the best way to present the massive detail drawn from the realms of both style and usage. It allowed us to describe more terms than would be possible in a handbook format while also providing more examples than would be possible in a short-entry dictionary format.

Because the book focuses heavily on English grammar

and word choice as well as style, its usefulness has a wider reach than either a style or usage book alone would have. Although it is aimed at writers and editors in traditional book and periodical publishing, its significantly extended coverage will appeal to many others outside of publishing— those who create a variety of written or printed material in business, government, academia, and the various professions.

Whereas longtime professional writers and editors may feel that their English-usage skills are sufficiently polished, not everyone else shares that degree of confidence. In fact, the literature we read every day attests to a noticeable deficiency in this area. For all who may have no doubts about their IQ but do have some questions about their UQ (usage quotient), this book has an abundance of usage terms to complement its points of style. In addition, no dictionary of this type would be complete without explaining the many technical terms that are prevalent in publishing.

Since this is a dictionary, not a handbook, cross-references are used in place of a traditional subject index. One type of cross-reference occurs within the discussion entries. For example, whenever a term mentioned in an entry is also the name of another entry, that term is printed in **bold** type. Also, at the end of many discussion entries are the names of other related entries that you may want to consult for further information.

Another type of cross-reference is the individual cross-reference entry. This type of cross-reference looks the same as a discussion entry and is alphabetized along with the discussion entries. For example, if someone refers to an *overlay proof* and you're not certain what that means, look up the term in the *O* section of the alphabetical entries. There you'll see an individual cross-reference entry directing you to a regular discussion entry titled *color proof,* which you'll discover is another name for *overlay proof.*

As an *encyclopedic* dictionary, the book has entries that provide not only definitions but also discussion and many realistic examples of proper use. When important rules apply to a particular style or usage, those rules are explained.

Often, though, authorities (major dictionaries, noted grammarians, and so on) disagree about points of style or usage. When they do, we point this out and offer a recommendation or solution but leave it up to you to make your own choice.

Here are some examples of the wide range of information that the entries provide:

Rules of capitalization for every imaginable type of material, from *political bodies* to *television and radio programs* to *building and structure names.*

Punctuation guidelines for all the key marks of punctuation, from the *apostrophe* to *ellipsis points* to *quotation marks.*

Essential grammatical do's and don'ts, including all the essential terms of grammar, from *action verbs* to *predicate nominatives* to *dangling phrases.*

Proper ways to handle word division and line breaks in all types of copy, from *title pages and subheads* to *compound terms* to *mathematical expressions.*

Definitions of linguistic terminology that every writer and editor should know, from *morphemes* to *roots* to *syntax.*

Abbreviation guidelines for all sorts of material, from *scholarly* to *numerical* to *scientific and technical terms.*

Important tips for handling confusing prefixes and suffixes, from *ante-/anti-* to *for-/fore-* to *-able/-ible.*

Special rules for italicizing and accenting foreign material, from *personal names* to *Latin terms* to *book titles.*

Examples of questionable language to avoid, from *doublespeak* to *vogue words* to *slang.*

Ways to distinguish between frequently misused terms, from *practicable/practical* to *disorganized/unorganized* to *us/we.*

Proper procedures in handling special types of copy, from *exponents* to *extracts* to *credit lines.*

Examples of acceptable forms for stating in-text citations and references, from *author-date citations* to *endnotes* to *bibliographies.*

Definitions of key publishing terms, from *castoff* to *platemaking* to *f's and g's.*

Lists of numerous signs and symbols, from *emoticons* to *proofreaders' marks* to *Greek letter symbols.*

Proper procedures in organizing the basic parts of a book, from the *half-title page* to the *contents page* to the *index.*

Tips on processing commonly used supplemental material, from *halftones* to *line art* to *statistical tables.*

Writing aids for improving the effectiveness and readability of text material, from *tone* to *parallel structure* to *paragraph development.*

Definitions and other information in the dictionary have been verified in dozens of authoritative sources, especially dictionaries such as the *Oxford English Dictionary; The American Heritage Dictionary of the English Language;* several Merriam-Webster dictionaries, including *Merriam-Webster's Third New International Dictionary* and *Merriam-Webster's Collegiate Dictionary;* the *Cambridge Dictionary of Science and Technology;* and numerous specialized dictionaries of foreign languages, idioms, linguistics, computers, and many other subjects. A wide variety of writing, communication, grammar, and other handbooks were also consulted, as were both specialized style guides, such as *Mathematics into Type,* and general manuals, such as the *United States Government Printing Office Style Manual.* Some of the most interesting and current material that we found wasn't in dictionaries or handbooks but rather was in the many magazine and newspaper articles that we examined. All of these sources provided unlimited opportunities for research, with enough controversy and other surprises to make the work anything but routine.

I appreciate the collective wisdom of all these sources and gratefully acknowledge their influence on our work. I especially appreciate the page-by-page review of the manuscript and the valuable suggestions provided by noted language authority Judith Grisham at Harvard University, Cambridge, Massachusetts. Finally, my special thanks go to E. du Lac and all the others at my home base in Arizona who supplied daily megadoses of inspiration and practical assistance from concept to completion.

A

A.D. Abbreviation for the Latin term *anno Domini*—in the year of the Lord. Publishers usually set the abbreviation in **roman type** with small capital letters (A.D.), but business-people preparing material by computer often use all capitals (A.D.) to avoid additional keystrokes.

The year, which follows the abbreviation, is stated in **numerals:**

A.D. 1023

Compare with **B.C.** For definitions of other systems of chronology (A.H., A.M., A.S., A.U.C., B.C.E., B.P., C.E., and M.Y.B.P.), see **abbreviations of time and days.**

A.M. Abbreviation for the Latin term *ante meridiem*—before noon. Publishers usually set the abbreviation in **roman type** with small capital letters (A.M.), but businesspeople preparing material by computer often use **lowercase** letters (a.m.) to avoid additional keystrokes. The abbreviation *a.m.* should be punctuated to avoid misreading as the word *am*, which is spelled the same.

Words such as *afternoon* or *o'clock* are unnecessary when the abbreviation *a.m.* or *p.m.* is used:

8:50 *a.m.* (*not* 8:50 *a.m.* in the *morning*)

See also **P.M.** and **M.**

a while/awhile Both *a while* and *awhile* pertain to a period or interval, but they are used as different **parts of speech.**

While is a **noun** meaning a period of time. Therefore, when it is written with *a* as two words, *a while* is a **noun phrase** and may be preceded by the **preposition** *for:*

I'll wait for *a while.*

Awhile (one word) is an **adverb** meaning for a short time and is never preceded by *for:*

They practiced *awhile* [not *for awhile*].

This distinction is fading in general usage, and many people use the one-word form in all situations. Nevertheless, grammarians object to the use of *awhile* as a noun and also believe that under no circumstances should *awhile* be preceded by *for.*

abbreviations See **abbreviations in scholarly works, abbreviations in technical and scientific works, abbreviations of names and titles, abbreviations of religious terms, abbreviations of time and days, acronym,** and **initialism.**

abbreviations, list of When a work has numerous abbreviations and many are repeated throughout the work, an author may provide a list of those abbreviations in either the **front matter** or the **back matter.** The list may include abbreviations used only in the text or only in **notes** and **bibliographies,** or it may include both.

When the list consists primarily of numerous text abbreviations, it is often placed on the **verso** page facing the first **recto** text page. When it consists primarily of source abbreviations used in notes and bibliographies, it is often placed in the back matter preceding the **endnotes.** A long list is placed immediately before the first page of notes. A short list may be positioned after the notes heading just before note 1.

abbreviations in scholarly works Both general abbreviations, such as *etc.* (*et cetera:* and so forth), and purely scholarly abbreviations, such as *cf.* (*confer:* compare), are widely used in scholarly literature. (When *cf.* is used in nonscholarly literature, it is usually spelled out as *compare*.)

However, even in scholarly literature, abbreviations should be avoided in running text and primarily restricted to parenthetical comments, **notes, bibliographies, reference lists,** and other such incidental elements.

Most abbreviations used in scholarly material, including Latin abbreviations, are set in **roman type** even though the spelled-out Latin word is usually set in **italics.** These abbreviations tend to be punctuated more heavily than others, such as **abbreviations in technical and scientific works.** They also tend to be written in **lowercase** letters more often than others, such as computer abbreviations.

The following abbreviations are examples of those commonly used in scholarly works (some, such as *et al., ibid., n.d.,* and *repr.,* are also used in nonscholarly citations):

ad loc.	*ad locum:* at the place
b. *or* n.	born; *natus:* born
ca. *or* c.	*circa:* about; approximately
d.	died
e.g.	*exempli gratia:* for example
et al.	*et alii:* and others
et seq.	*et sequentes:* and the following
f. (*pl.,* ff.)	and following
fl.	*floruit:* flourished
f.v.	*folio verso:* on the back of the page
ibid.	*ibidem:* in the same place
id.	*idem:* the same
i.e.	*id est:* that is
inf.	*infra:* below
loc. cit.	*loco citato:* in the place cited
n. (*pl.,* nn.)	note; footnote
n.d.	no date
n.p.	no place; no publisher; no page
N.S.	New Style (dates)
n.s.	new series
op. cit.	*opere citato:* in the work cited
O.S.	Old Style (dates)

o.s.	old series
p. (*pl.,* pp.)	page(s)
pl.	plate; plural
q.v.	*quod vide:* which see
repr.	reprint(ed)
sup.	*supra:* above
s.v. (*pl.,* s.vv.)	*sub verbo, sub voce:* under the word
ut sup.	*ut supra:* as above
v. *or* vs.	versus

See also **abbreviations in technical and scientific works; abbreviations of names and titles; abbreviations of religious terms; abbreviations of time and days; academic degrees; acronym; address, mail; chemical names and symbols; geographical terms;** and **initialism.**

abbreviations in technical and scientific works Abbreviations abound in technical and scientific copy, particularly in expressions of measures or units, such as the **initialism** *BTU* (British thermal unit). **Acronyms,** such as *CAP* (computer-aided production), are also common.

Most technical and scientific abbreviations are written without punctuation or space between the letters. Some organizations, however, include punctuation in **lowercase** abbreviations that might be mistaken for a word that is spelled the same. For example, without a period after the abbreviation *as.* (auxiliary storage), the abbreviation and the word *as* would look the same.

No firm rule exists for capitalization. Many computer abbreviations, such as *CTRL* (control), are written in all capitals, whereas abbreviations of **metric terms,** such as *mm* (millimeter), are always written in lowercase letters; abbreviations of **chemical names and symbols,** such as *He* (helium), are written with an initial capital letter. Since punctuation and capitalization practices differ among organizations, follow the preferred style of your employer or publisher:

ac, AC	alternating current; automatic analog computer

a/d	analog to digital
Cd	coefficient of drag
cos	cosine
cpu, CPU	central processing unit
FTP	file transfer protocol (Internet)
I/O, i&o	input and output
ISDN	Integrated Services Digital Network
sam., SAM	sequential-access method
uv, u-v	ultraviolet

See also **abbreviations in scholarly works; abbreviations of names and titles; abbreviations of religious terms; abbreviations of time and days; academic degrees; acronym; address, mail; chemical names and symbols; geographical terms; initialism;** and **metric terms.**

abbreviations of names and titles A variety of guidelines apply to the abbreviation of a name or title. Sometimes the choice is a matter of a person's or organization's preferred style rather than a universal rule. *John P. Jones* may prefer to be addressed as *J. P. Jones.* The *XYZ Corporation* may prefer that you use its official name of *XYZ Company, Inc.* The proper style for a street may be *120 Hudson Street, NW,* not *120 Northwest Hudson* or *120 Hudson, NW.*

When envelopes are addressed for automated postal sorting, the use of all capital letters, no punctuation, and officially accepted postal abbreviations of states and common words in street names is common:

120 HUDSON ST NW
NEW YORK NY 10018

In general text, though, it is still preferred practice to punctuate names and to spell out state names and common words in street names:

Mr. R. F. Foxworthy lives at 1400 Western Boulevard in Peoria, Illinois.

Personal titles, such as *Mr.,* are always abbreviated and punctuated. Abbreviations of **academic degrees,** such as

Ed.D., are always punctuated, but professional designations, such as *CPA,* are not.

Some abbreviations that are properly included in mail addresses, such as *Inc.* in *XYZ Company, Inc.,* are usually omitted from names in running text. Words that may be spelled out both in a mail address and in running text, such as *Company,* may be abbreviated in footnotes and tabular material, as in *XYZ Co.* If initials are used for an organization's name in running text, the full name should be spelled out on first use and the abbreviation placed in parentheses after the name:

General Services Administration (GSA)

The following examples indicate common practices in abbreviating names and titles:

W. J. McKay *or* William J. McKay (*not* Wm. J. McKay)
AFL–CIO (American Federation of Labor–Congress of Industrial Organizations)
HMO (health maintenance organization)
IBM Corporation
JFK (John Fitzgerald Kennedy)
Litt.D. (*Litterarum Doctor:* Doctor of Letters)
Gen. Roy Adams, General Adams (*military titles are spelled out when no first name is given*)
Ms. Nora Faulkner, Mss. Faulkner and Wright *or* Ms. Faulkner and Ms. Wright
Dr. Lynn Hill *or* Lynn Hill, M.D.
Mr. Winston and Mr. Sloane *or* Messrs. Winston and Sloane
Rev. Timothy Forrestor, the Reverend Timothy Forrestor (*titles such as* Reverend *and* Honorable *are spelled out when preceded by* the)
Mr. James Robertson III, Mr. Robertson (*not* Mr. Robertson III)
Mr. Adam Roche Jr. *or* Mr. Adam Roche, Jr.; Mr. Roche (*not* Mr. Roche Jr.)
The Notebook Corp. *or* The Notebook Corporation (*as preferred by company*)

U.S. policies, the policies of the United States (*country is spelled out when used as* **noun**, *abbreviated when used as* **adjective** *preceding a noun*)

See also **abbreviations in scholarly works; abbreviations in technical and scientific works; abbreviations of religious terms; abbreviations of time and days; academic degrees; acronym; address, mail; chemical names and symbols; geographical terms;** and **initialism.**

abbreviations of religious terms The names of religious organizations, such as a church, are abbreviated the same as other names as described in **abbreviations of names and titles.** However, proper **nouns,** such as *Jehovah,* should not be abbreviated. The names of religions and of sacred works, creeds, prayers, or writings should also be written in full:

Islam   Lord's Prayer
Torah (*or* torah)   Dead Sea Scrolls

The names of psalms or whole books in the Bible, such as *Matthew,* should not be abbreviated in running text. Informally, though, versions or sections of the Bible are often abbreviated:

American Revised Version (ARV)
New Testament (NT)

Also, in notes and parenthetical comments, scriptural references are usually abbreviated:

Gen. 24:17–30:1

The abbreviations accepted by those using the New American Bible (NAB) differ from the ones accepted by those using the Authorized [King James] Version (AV). For example, the abbreviation of Genesis associated with the NAB is *Gn;* the one associated with the AV is *Gen.* Writers and editors, therefore, should be certain that the chosen form of abbreviation—NAB or AV—is used consistently.

See also **abbreviations in scholarly works; abbreviations in technical and scientific works; abbreviations of**

names and titles; abbreviations of time and days; academic degrees; acronym; address, mail; chemical names and symbols; geographical terms; and **initialism.**

abbreviations of time and days When expressions of time are used in formal material, such as a formal invitation, the even, half, and quarter hours are usually written out:

eight o'clock
half past eight

In other cases when other times are mentioned, numerals are used:

10:35 A.M.
7:45 P.M.

See the entries A.M. (*ante meridiem:* before noon), P.M. (*post meridiem:* after noon), and M. (*meridies:* noon) for the rules of spelling and punctuating those abbreviations.

Systems of chronology are usually abbreviated and set in small capital letters. The abbreviations A.D., A.H., A.M., and A.S., identified in the list that follows, should be set before the year, and the others should follow the number:

A.D. 1300
1300 B.C.

The following are ten common systems of chronology:

A.D.	*anno Domini:* in the year of our Lord
A.H.	*anno Hegirae:* in the year of the Hegira; *anno Hebraico:* in the Hebrew year
A.M.	*anno mundi:* in the year of the world
A.S.	*anno salutis:* in the year of salvation
A.U.C.	*ab urbe condita:* from the founding of the city (Rome, 753 B.C.)
B.C.	before Christ
B.C.E.	before the common era
B.P.	before the present
C.E.	common era
M.Y.B.P.	million years before the present

Controversy has evolved concerning the use of B.C. rather than the more multicultural B.C.E. or the use of A.D. rather than C.E. Since both versions—B.C./B.C.E. and A.D./ C.E.—are used, choose the one preferred by your employer or publisher. However, critics of B.C.E. and C.E. point out that many readers will recognize only B.C. and A.D. Proponents, on the other hand, believe that B.C.E. and C.E. are more inclusive and hence a better choice.

In the United States, the traditional way of writing dates without a chronology designation is *August 4, 1998*. The day appears first in the military services, and the month is abbreviated:

4 Aug 98 (army)
4 AUG 98 (navy)

In an all-numeral form, used only informally in the United States, the month is stated first:

8/4/98 (August 4, 1998)

In certain other countries, however, the day is stated first. Hence *8/4/98* may mean *April 8, 1998* in those countries.

Days and months are not abbreviated in running text (*January,* not *Jan.*) but may be abbreviated in **notes** and tabular matter. The usual forms are as follows, with the examples in the second column of each group used only when space is very limited:

Days

Sun.	Su	Thrs.	Th
Mon.	M	Fri.	F
Tues.	Tu	Sat.	S
Wed.	W		

Months

Jan.	Ja	Mar.	Mr
Feb.	F	Apr.	Ap

May	My	Sept.	S
June	Je	Oct.	O
July	Jl	Nov.	N
Aug.	Ag	Dec.	D

See also **abbreviations in scholarly works; abbreviations in technical and scientific works; abbreviations of names and titles; abbreviations of religious terms; academic degrees; acronym; address, mail; chemical names and symbols; geographical terms;** and **initialism.**

abbreviations of U.S. states, territories, and possessions See **geographical terms.**

ability/capacity The **nouns** *ability* and *capacity* are sometimes used interchangeably, but in strict usage they have different meanings. *Ability* refers to a physical or mental power:

Successful managers have the *ability* to motivate their employees.

Capacity refers to a physical measure or to the power to learn or understand:

The jug has a four-gallon *capacity*.
He has the *capacity* to benefit from his loss.

-able/-ible The **suffix** *-able* may be added to certain **nouns,** such as *bend* (*bendable*), or **verbs,** such as *notice* (*noticeable*). In some cases the main word must be altered by adding or dropping one or more letters before adding *-able:*

receive/receiv*able*

The suffix *-ible* may be added to certain verbs, such as *access* (*accessible*), and in some cases the main word also may have to be altered:

defense/defens*ible*

Both *-able* and *-ible* are used in certain words having no matching verb or noun:

amen*able*
feas*ible*

In other cases a word may look as though it includes the suffix *-able* or *-ible,* but in fact the letters do not constitute a suffix:

table
bible

Some words are correct with either *-able* or *-ible,* and dictionaries list the preferred form first:

discuss*ible* [preferred]/discuss*able*

In some cases the choice of *-able* or *-ible* signals a difference in meaning. *Contractable*, for example, means likely to be acquired:

He has a contract*able* disease.

Contractible means capable of drawing together or contracting:

She used contract*ible* glue.

The following are examples of words commonly formed with the suffixes *-able* and *-ible:*

-able	*-ible*
bearable	collectible
changeable	divisible
debatable	edible
educable	feasible
fashionable	implausible
incapable	legible
justifiable	negligible
reliable	permissible
serviceable	reversible
unmistakable	susceptible

about *About* is used as an **adverb,** a **preposition,** and an **adjective** and has numerous meanings—nearly, almost, close to, and so on. Misuse occurs primarily when *about* is used to mean approximately or close to. This meaning is often expressed as the **phrase** at about (at about seven o'clock), which is redundant. Use either at or about:

   at [or about] seven o'clock

absolute word A word that is not subject to comparison. See **comparison of adjectives** and **comparison of adverbs**. Absolute words are already the most that they can be:

   His sculpture is *perfect*.

Some writers and speakers nevertheless use such words comparatively in casual references:

   His sculpture is the *most perfect* I've seen.

However, this usage should be avoided. Something that is truly perfect can be neither more nor less perfect than something else that also is absolutely perfect. However, it can be *less than perfect*.

The following list has examples of absolute words that in general should not be used in comparisons:

absolute	limitless
best	omnipotent
empty	perpetual
extinct	simultaneous
fatal	square
final	terminal
full	ultimate
inadmissible	unanimous
indestructible	unique
infinite	untouchable
irreversible	whole
irrevocable	worst

abstract A condensed version of a longer written work that summarizes its main points. Many abstracts are only one page or less, but others, such as an abstract of a business or government report, may involve a hundred or more pages.

Abstracts are common not only in business and government material but also in a variety of technical and scientific documents. They may be written in regular text-paragraph style, or they may consist of an introductory paragraph followed by a list of essential points. These points can often be gleaned from a document's **introduction** and **conclusion** and from the **head(ing)s** used throughout the body.

abstract noun A **noun** that denotes something intangible, such as *idealism,* rather than something specific or concrete, such as an *automobile.* An abstract noun may refer to the following:

   an action (*research*)
   a condition (*illness*)
   a quality (*loyalty*)
   an idea or concept (*freedom*)
   a relationship (*friendship*)

Compare with **concrete noun.** See also **abstract word.**

abstract word A word, such as an **abstract noun, adjective,** or other word, that refers to something general or intangible:

   theoretical [adjective] science

Careful writers use abstract words only when a more precise word is unavailable or undesirable. For example, the first of the next two comments is less informative than the second comment:

   He *frequently* travels to the East Coast and earns a *lot* of money.
   He travels to the East Coast *twice a month* and earns *$80,000* a year.

See also **vague words.**

academic degrees Capitalize the names or abbreviations of academic degrees or other honors, such as *Ph.D.,* following a name:

Susan A. Kenton, *M.D.*
William R. Marshall, *Doctor of Law*

Lowercase general references (He has a *master's degree*). When a professional title is used, omit the degree:

Dr. Lawrence Pagoda [not *Dr.* Lawrence Pagoda, *Sc.D.*] earned his *doctorate* at Harvard.

When more than one degree follows a name, place the one pertaining to the person's main profession first:

Although she has a law degree, Anita J. Steiner, *M.D., LL.D.,* has practiced medicine for many years.

Always punctuate abbreviations of degrees, and write them without space between the letters:

A.A.	Associate in Arts
B.B.A.	Bachelor of Business Administration
B.S.Ed.	Bachelor of Science in Education
M.B.A.	Master in, *or* of, Business Administration
M.Ed.	Master of Education
D.Th. *or* D.Theol.	Doctor of Theology
S.D. *or* Sc.D.	Doctor of Science

academic years Use **lowercase** letters for the words that designate academic terms or years:

freshman	junior
sophomore	senior

accent Writers and editors are concerned with two types of accent. One involves the particular stress given to a word or words. This type of emphasis is accomplished through the choice of language, the use of **boldface** type or *italics,* the use of a larger or more prominent type size, or the choice of some other form of emphasis or distinctive manner.

Another type of accent involves the marks or symbols that are used with letters or characters to indicate phonetic values different from unmarked letters or characters. See **diacritical marks** for examples of this type of accent.

accept/except Even when writers understand the difference in meaning between the **verbs** *accept* and *except,* carelessness in spelling often leads to incorrect usage that spell-checkers will not detect. *Accept* means to receive, take, agree with, agree or consent to, approve of, or believe:

> They must *accept* responsibility for their actions.

Except means to omit or exclude, make an exception of, or object:

> We will *except* those who apply after the deadline.

As a preposition, *except* means other than or excluding:

> Everything arrived safely *except* one box of glassware.

acclimate/acclimatize The **verbs** *acclimate* and *acclimatize* both mean to adapt to a new environment, situation, or climate. Although the words can be used interchangeably, *acclimate* seems less formal:

> Every time we move we must *acclimate/acclimatize* ourselves all over again.

Since the word *acclimate* has given way to *acclimatize* in the United Kingdom, some authorities predict that the same shift will eventually occur in the United States. Others believe that writers in the United States always tend to prefer the simpler of alternative terms, in this case *acclimate.*

accommodate The **verb** *accommodate* means to make suitable, reconcile, be helpful, allow for, or adapt oneself to. The main problem that writers have with this word is misspelling, incorrectly using only one *m* instead of two:

> The company always tries to *accommodate* [not *accomodate*] its international visitors.

acknowledgment The preferred spelling of this **noun,** referring to the recognition of something, is *acknowledgment* rather than the alternative form, *acknowledgement.*

acknowledgments A statement of special recognition that an author gives to those who assisted in the preparation of or contributed to the author's work. The statement may be included in the **preface** or prepared as a separate section, usually titled "Acknowledgments," that follows the preface. Occasionally, a separate page or section may be placed at the end of the book, preceding the **index.**

The editors' names may appear on the **title page** in a multiauthor work, with the names of contributors, including their professional affiliations and other pertinent biographical data, provided in a separate alphabetical list. Such a list may be titled "Contributors" or "Participants" and placed at the back of the book. See **contributors, list of.**

When the acknowledgments appear as a separate section in the **front matter** after the preface, the pages are numbered in the same style as that used for other front-matter pages, usually with small **roman numerals.** When the acknowledgments appear at the back of the book, they are numbered in **arabic numerals** the same as other pages in the **back matter.**

acronym An abbreviation formed by combining the initial letters of the main words in a name or **phrase,** with the letters pronounced like a word. Acronyms are usually written in all capital letters without periods or spaces between the letters:

ARM	adjustable-rate mortgage
COLA	cost-of-living adjustment/allowance
FEMA	Federal Emergency Management Agency
FORTRAN	Formula Translation (computer language)
PERT	Program Evaluation and Review Technique
PIN	personal identification number
RAM	random-access memory

See also **abbreviations in scholarly works; abbreviations in technical and scientific works; abbreviations of names and titles; abbreviations of religious terms; ab-**

breviations of time and days; academic degrees; address, mail; chemical names and symbols; geographical terms; and initialism.

activate/actuate The verb *activate,* once obsolete, is now back in use, especially in a scientific sense meaning to make active. It is also used generally to mean set in motion:

> The laboratory scientists will soon *activate* the chemical solution.
> A directive was issued to *activate* the military unit.

The less commonly used verb *actuate* also means to put into motion or action:

> They will *actuate* the assembly line tomorrow.

active voice *Voice* indicates whether the **subject** of a sentence is acting (*active voice*) or receiving the action (**passive voice**). The active voice is more direct and forceful than the passive voice:

> She *took* responsibility, and her boss *applauded* her initiative.

In some situations, however, a writer may want to sound less forceful and more passive: An error *was made* (*not* You *made* an error). Or a writer may want to mention only the receiver of the action instead of the doers or actors: The *director* [receiver] *was informed* (*not Someone* [doer or actor] *informed* the director). See the examples in the entry **passive voice.**

Avoid unnecessary shifts from active to passive voice within a sentence or passage:

> *Not:* We *like* [active voice] the scenic route, and it *should be taken* [passive voice] by anyone who enjoys a leisurely drive.

> *Better:* We *like* [active voice] the scenic route, and anyone who enjoys a leisurely drive *should take* [active voice] it.

acts and treaties Capitalize the names of acts, treaties, and other laws or documents, and set them in **roman type** in running text. (When a law or bill is published and cited in **notes** or the **bibliography,** set the title in **italics** in the same style used for the title of a book or other such document.) **Lowercase** general references or short, informal references to an act or treaty:

United States Constitution, the Constitution (U.S.)
Pennsylvania Constitution, the state constitution, the constitution
First Amendment, the amendment
Declaration of Independence
Strategic Arms Limitation Treaty, the treaty
Pact of Paris, the pact
Civil Rights Act of 1964, the act
Medicare and Medicaid *or* medicare and medicaid
Social Security *or* social security

actuate See **activate/actuate.**

acute accent See **diacritical marks.**

adapt/adept/adopt Two of these words—*adapt* and *adopt*—are **verbs.** The other—*adept*—is an **adjective.** Although they all look and sound similar, their meanings are different. *Adapt* means to modify or adjust for a purpose:

The engineers will *adapt* the model to the new specifications.

Adept means expert, proficient, or highly skilled:

She is *adept* at computer programming.

Adopt means to take or accept by choice:

The members can *adopt* the measure by a two-thirds vote.

addendum (plural, *addenda*) The **noun** *addendum* refers to an addition, such as a supplement in a book. Although the singular *addendum* is sometimes used incorrectly with a plural **verb,** a singular verb should be used with *addendum* and a plural verb with *addenda:*

The new *addendum* is ready; the previous *addenda* are out of date.

address, mail Except for the envelopes of formal social invitations, other envelopes or mailing labels should be addressed according to U.S. Postal Service requirements when you want them to be sorted automatically. This form is also widely used among private delivery services.

Use either all capital letters without punctuation or regular capitalization and punctuation for everything on the envelope or mailing label. The preferred order of listing data line by line on an envelope or mailing label is as follows:

Line 1. Account numbers, if any

Line 2. Addressee's name (person)

Line 3. Addressee's name (organization)

Line 4. Attention line, if any

Line 5. Street name and number or postal box number along with the room or suite number, if any

Line 6. City, state, and ZIP Code

Use the standard two-letter abbreviations for states, territories, and Canadian provinces, and use accepted abbreviations, such as *UNIV* (university) and *BLVD* (boulevard), for other data:

ROV: 2197-8-XU
ADAMS CORP
ATTN MS PD BARNES
2134 THIRD AVE SW RM 4A
ELMWOOD IL 61529-7093

However, in the inside address of a letter that accompanies the envelope, capitalize, punctuate, and spell out the name and address in traditional style:

Adams Corporation
Attention Paula D. Barnes
2134 Third Avenue, SW, Room 4A
Elmwood, IL 61529-7093

See also **abbreviations of names and titles.**

adept See **adapt/adept/adopt.**

adherence/adhesion The **nouns** *adherence* and *adhesion* can be used interchangeably to mean the act or quality of sticking to or fusing. The trend, though, is to use *adherence* to refer to a nonphysical, faithful attachment to persons or things and *adhesion* to refer to a physical attachment:

The employee's *adherence* to company doctrine was weak at best.
The *adhesion* of both metal parts using a strong glue was rapid.

adhesion See **adherence/adhesion.**

adhesive binding See **binding.**

adjective One of the eight **parts of speech;** a word that modifies (describes or limits) a **noun** or **pronoun.** An adjective may refer to some quality of the noun or pronoun it modifies (*descriptive adjective*):

Yesterday was a *sunny* day.
That computer program is *complex.*

Or it may restrict the meaning of the noun or pronoun (*limiting adjective*):

It's a *weekly* newsletter.
The class has *twenty* students.

Adjectives have three degrees of comparison: positive (*new*), comparative (*newer* or *more new*), and superlative (*newest* or *most new*). See **comparison of adjectives** for examples.

Some **clauses** function as adjectives by modifying a noun or pronoun:

> The report *that he prepared* [modifies the noun *report*] has an intriguing conclusion.

Certain **compound terms** also function as adjectives. *Temporary* combinations are usually hyphenated before but not after a noun. *Permanent* or well-established combinations need not be hyphenated either before or after a noun:

> The building has *old-style* architecture [temporary compound].
> The building's architecture is *old style* [temporary compound].
> Their *public relations* office is in New York City [permanent, well-established compound].

See also **adjective pronoun** and **predicate adjective**.

adjective clause See **adjective**.

adjective pronoun Also called *pronominal adjective;* a **pronoun** used like an **adjective** to modify a **noun** or other pronoun. Examples are *this, that, these, those, any, each, which,* and *what:*

> *Some* [adjective pronoun] books [noun] are published in numerous editions.

Compare with **demonstrative pronoun, indefinite pronoun, intensive pronoun, interrogative pronoun, personal pronoun, reciprocal pronoun, reflexive pronoun,** and **relative pronoun.**

admission/admittance The **nouns** *admission* and *admittance* can be used interchangeably to refer to the act of letting someone into a place. However, when an entry fee is involved, the word *admission* is more common, and in the case of a confession, it is the only alternative:

They asked about the price of *admission*.
His *admission* brought the case to a swift close.

When permission is involved, *admittance* is the usual choice, and it is also more common on keep-out signs:

He somehow gained *admittance* to the lab without having proper security clearance.

No Admittance!

admittance See **admission.**

adopt See **adapt/adept/adopt.**

adverb One of the eight **parts of speech;** a word that modifies a **verb,** an **adjective,** another adverb, or occasionally a **noun** or **pronoun:**

The two worked *effectively* [modifies the verb *worked*].
She was *very* happy [modifies the adjective *happy*].
The guests stayed *much* longer than usual [modifies the adverb *longer*].
Almost everyone was satisfied with the decision [modifies the pronoun *everyone*].

Adverbs can be made comparative or superlative by adding *-er* or *-est* (*quicker, quickest*) or by placing *more* or *most* before the word (*more often, most often*). In other cases another word must be used to make a comparison (*worse, worst*). See **comparison of adverbs** for examples.

The **suffix** *-ly* can be added to many adjectives to form an adverb:

loud (adjective)/*loudly* (adverb)
bad (adjective)/*badly* (adverb)

However, some adjectives already end in *-ly* and should not be mistaken for adverbs:

kindly gentleman
timely action

Adverbs may be placed almost anywhere in either the **subject** or **predicate** of a sentence as long as the position provides clear, accurate reading and easy comprehension:

The temperature fell *suddenly.*
The temperature *suddenly* fell.
Suddenly, the temperature fell.

However, see **misplaced clause, misplaced phrase,** and **misplaced words.**

A common mistake is the use of an adjective when an adverb is required or vice versa:

He wrote *quickly* [adverb correctly modifies the verb *wrote*].
Not: He wrote *quick* [adjective incorrectly modifies the verb *wrote*].

Some adverbs consist of a **dependent clause** that modifies a verb, adjective, or adverb in the main clause. Often these clauses are introduced by **conjunctions,** such as *because, since, though, when,* and *where:*

He is upset *because of the layoffs* [clause modifies the adjective *upset*].

adverb clause See **adverb.**

adverse/averse The **adjectives** *adverse* and *averse* look and sound similar and are therefore sometimes incorrectly used interchangeably. However, their meanings are different. *Adverse* means hostile, unfavorable, or harmful:

The *adverse* criticism wounded his pride.

Averse means having a feeling of repugnance or distaste or being disinclined:

She is *averse* to long lectures.

advice/advise The words *advice* and *advise* are frequently confused not only because they look and sound similar but also because they both pertain to an opinion or recommendation. However, they function as different **parts of**

speech. The **noun** *advice* refers to an opinion or recommendation concerning some future action:

My *advice* is to concentrate on West Coast sales.

The **verb** *advise* refers to the act of giving an opinion or recommendation:

I *advise* you to concentrate on West Coast sales.

adviser/advisor The **nouns** *adviser* and *advisor* both refer to someone who gives advice. Although either spelling is correct, some dictionaries list the *-er* spelling first. The *-or* spelling is common only in the United States.

affect/effect The **verbs** *affect* and *effect* are frequently confused, and one is incorrectly used as an alternative spelling of the other. However, they do not mean the same thing. *Affect* means to move emotionally or to influence:

His decision will *affect* the way we do business in the future.

As a verb, *effect* means to bring about or cause:

The high speed limit may *effect* higher traffic fatalities.

As a **noun,** *effect* means a result or consequence:

The *effect* of higher speed limits may be higher traffic fatalities.

affectation A pretense, display, or assumed behavior intended to make an impression on others. Writing that is characterized by affectation is more pompous or showy than is necessary. Affectation often clouds the basic facts and thereby diminishes clarity and comprehension.

For examples of language that may be unnecessarily technical, showy, or unclear in other ways, see **abstract noun, abstract word, cliche, euphemism, jargon, pompous language, vague words,** and **vogue words.**

affective meaning See **connotation/denotation.**

affix A word element that is not used alone but must be attached to a **base, stem,** or **root** to form a complete word. See **prefix** and **suffix** for examples of common affixes.

afflict/inflict Although the **verbs** *afflict* and *inflict* have similar uses, careful writers make a distinction. *Afflict* primarily means to bring grievous physical harm or mental suffering to someone:

> We must not *afflict* the other patients with the virus.

Inflict primarily means to impose, deal, or mete out something burdensome, often as a result of aggressive action:

> If their proposed expansion succeeds, the new competition will *inflict* heavy losses on the other firms.

afterward/afterwards The **adverbs** *afterward* and *afterwards* both mean at a later time, but *afterward* is preferred in the United States, and *afterwards* is more common in Great Britain. See **toward/towards** for a similar example.

afterword See **epilogue.**

age Writers and editors have two important concerns in references to age. One is the choice of terms in referring to men and women. For example, females over the age of eighteen should be referred to as *women,* not *girls*, and males should be called *men,* not *boys*. The **euphemism** *senior citizen* is now widely accepted for those age sixty-five and older, although some object to it on the grounds that it is a stereotype.

Another important concern is the decision regarding the use of numbers or words for designations of age. Either style is acceptable as long as it is consistent with the general style adopted for numbers in a particular document. See **numbers** for a description of the principal technical and nontechnical styles:

> six years old *or* 6 years old
> twelve-year-old student *or* 12-year-old student
> midfifties *or* mid-50s

agencies See **associations and agencies.**

aggregation, signs of See **braces.**

agree to/agree with The **verb** *agree* may be combined with
a **preposition** such as *to* or *with* to mean different things.
Although both **phrases** *agree to* and *agree with* refer to a
type of agreement, one cannot logically be substituted for
the other. To *agree to* something is to give consent to it:

> They will *agree to* the contract if we make one small
> change.

> To *agree with* something is to be in accord with it:

> I *agree with* his thoughts about the advantages of tele-
> commuting.

agreement *Agreement* in grammar refers to a correspondence between words or different elements in a **sentence**
in regard to **case, gender, number,** and **person.** See those
entries for examples.

agreements and programs Style formal or official agreements and programs the same as you would style **acts and
treaties.** Capitalize the official names, and set them in **roman type. Lowercase** general or short, informal references
to agreements and programs:

> the Winslow Agreement, the agreement
> the East River Housing Program, the program

Some federal programs, such as Medicare, have become
so well known that they are often referred to generically or
informally as **common nouns** (medicare) and need not be
capitalized in such cases.

aircraft See **craft and vessels.**

alignment Writers and editors are concerned with the
proper alignment of the different elements in a **manuscript.**
In a numbered **list,** for example, each item is usually set so
that the periods after the list numbers are aligned one on
top of another. See also the example of alignment in the

entry **outline.** In **tables,** too, numbers in the column are set so that the decimal points align one above the other. Certain elements in **mathematical expressions,** such as **subscripts** and **superscripts,** are also aligned one above another.

Other parts of a work, such as titles, **head(ing)s,** and **extracts,** are usually indented or aligned consistently throughout a manuscript. When both left and right margins of a text page are aligned flush against the left margin and flush against the right margin, the material is said to be *justified.* See **justification.**

all right/alright Errors are common in the use of *all right* and *alright.* As an **adjective,** *all right* means in proper working order or correct:

Your computer appears to be *all right.*

As an **adverb,** *all right* means adequately or very well:

The plan worked *all right.*
Question: How are you? *Answer:* All right.

As both an adjective and adverb, *alright* is a nonstandard alternative. Although it is common in fiction, business material, and certain casual correspondence, many authorities object to its use.

all together/altogether The **phrase** *all together* (two words) is commonly confused with the **adverb** *altogether* (one word). The two-word version means all in one place or acting together and should be used only if other words can logically intervene:

They were *all together* at the convention [They *all* were *together* at the convention].

Altogether means wholly, completely, or utterly:

They were not *altogether* happy about the new policy.

allegory A literary, dramatic, or pictorial device in which the characters and events are symbolic representations of something else, such as an abstract idea, principle, or force. Justice, for example, is often symbolized by a blindfolded figure and scales. *Allegory* also refers to the story, play, or picture itself in which such symbolic representation is used. In fact, contemporary fiction writers commonly use allegorical devices in novels and short stories to symbolize some aspect of human existence.

alliteration The repetition of the same **consonant** sounds or of different **vowel** sounds, usually at the beginning of words or in stressed **syllables:**

> *a*id and *a*bet
> as *g*ood as *g*old
> *d*umb and *d*umber

Poets have always used alliteration extensively. In addition, politicians and many other writers and speakers regularly use this device to create titles, phrases, slogans, and other sayings that readers and listeners can more easily remember.

allusion/delusion/illusion The **nouns** *allusion* and *illusion,* as well as *delusion* and *illusion,* are sometimes confused. *Allusion* means an indirect reference to something not specifically mentioned or identified:

> ''We all know that management has not always been open to new suggestions,'' he said, with a clear *allusion* to the recently ousted president.

Delusion means the process of deluding, the state of being deluded, or a false belief, especially one with serious implications. It therefore has a connotation (see **connotation/denotation**) of something harmful:

> Jerry is being treated for *delusions* of persecution.

Illusion also refers to a false or misleading mental image, idea, or perception but is a better choice when the erroneous belief is not physically or mentally harmful:

> Mike is under the *illusion* that he'll be a millionaire by the time he's forty.

alphabetization The two principal systems of alphabetizing items are the *letter-by-letter method* and the *word-by-word method.* Computerized sorting programs usually employ a variation of one of these systems.

Even when organizations use one of the two main systems, they may modify some of the general rules. For example, some may treat hyphenated words as separate words in the word-by-word method; others may treat them as a single word.

Many business organizations and scientific and technical groups observe the following guidelines: When alphabetizing *letter by letter,* ignore spaces, apostrophes, and, if desired, hyphens and slashes. Continue the process for each item up to the first significant punctuation, such as a comma, semicolon, colon, parentheses, or period. If two or more items are identical up to the first significant punctuation, consider next the stream of letters following that punctuation:

Letter-by-Letter System

Item	Read as
Ada Midland School	Adamidlandschool
Adams, Benson, and Carlson	Adams, Benson, and Carlson
Adams, Harold	Adams, Harold
Adamsville and Newton (Counties)	Adamsvilleandnewton (Counties)
Adamsville-Arcadia	Adamsvillearcadia
Arcadia, Samuel	Arcadia, Samuel
Arcadia-Lakeville	Arcadialakeville
Arcadia Mines	Arcadiamines
Arcadia/Northern Hills	Arcadianorthernhills
Arcadia Township	Arcadiatownship

When alphabetizing *word by word,* continue the process to the end of the first word. If the next item also has the same first word, continue with the second word and so on. Continue this word-by-word movement up to the first significant punctuation (comma, semicolon, colon, parenthe-

ses, or period). Ignore apostrophes and, if desired, hyphens
and slashes, treating words separated by them as one word.
Also ignore **articles,** such as *the;* **conjunctions,** such as
and; and **prepositions,** such as *of:*

Word-by-Word System

Item	Read as
Ada Midland School	Ada Midland School
Adams, Benson, and Carlson	Adams, Benson, and Carlson
Adams, Harold	Adams, Harold
Adamsville and Newton (Counties)	Adamsville and Newton (Counties)
Adamsville-Arcadia	Adamsvillearcadia
Arcadia, Samuel	Arcadia, Samuel
Arcadia Mines	Arcadia Mines
Arcadia Township	Arcadia Township
Arcadia-Lakeville	Arcadialakeville
Arcadia/Northern Hills	Arcadianorthernhills

The letter-by-letter system is common in general indexing and in dictionaries. However, writers and editors should
use the system preferred by the employer or publisher for
which the material is being prepared.

alright See **all right/alright.**

alter/change The **verbs** *alter* and *change* are often used
interchangeably in regard to modifying something, although
careful writers make a distinction. *Alter* means to modify
or make something different without completely converting
it into something else:

We should *alter* the final clause in the contract to incorporate an additional requirement.

Change also means to make different, but it is preferred
in situations involving the conversion of one thing into
something completely different:

Next year they will *change* [convert] the vacant lot into a tennis court.

altogether See **all together/altogether.**

ambiguity An uncertainty regarding interpretation that is caused by incorrect grammar or careless composition. Consider this sentence:

He loves golf more than his wife.

Does he love golf more than he loves his wife? Or does he love golf more than his wife loves golf?

Other entries describing language that can cause ambiguity include **abstract noun, abstract word, affectation, cliche, dangling gerund, dangling infinitive, dangling participle, dangling subordinate clause, doublespeak, misplaced clause, misplaced phrase, misplaced words, mixed metaphor, slang,** and **vogue words.**

amend/emend The **verbs** *amend* and *emend* sound similar and have similar meanings, although the use of *emend* is more restricted. *Amend* means to correct, improve, or change for the better:

The members want to *amend* the organization's bylaws to allow for more directors on the board.

Emend should be used primarily to refer to the improvement of a literary or scholarly work by critical editing:

The editor will *emend* the error-laden manuscript.

among/between Confusion exists concerning the proper use of the **prepositions** *among* and *between.* Authorities have traditionally maintained that *between* must be used when two people or things are mentioned and *among* when three or more are involved. Some dictionaries, however, note that *between* has always been used in reference to three or more in certain cases. A common solution is to use *among* when referring to a group or collectivity or to mean each with the other:

The differences *among* the twenty participants were obvious.

Talk it over *among* yourselves.

Use *between* in reference to only two entities or when more than two are considered individually rather than as a group:

The campaign pointed out the sharp differences *between* the philosophies of the Republicans and the Democrats.

The agreement *between* Don, Robert, and Ellen makes clear the responsibility of each person.

amount/number Although the distinction between the **nouns** *amount* and *number* is clear, the two are often used interchangeably in general usage. However, *amount* is a better choice in reference to quantity, volume, bulk, or anything else that isn't counted individually (*mass nouns*):

We have a large *amount* of material to review.

Number is a better choice when individual items are mentioned (*count nouns*):

The *number* of students enrolled has increased each year.

Amount is sometimes used when the reference is to a total or a collection, even when individual items make up the total or collection. However, most authorities object to this usage:

The *amount* of sales this month is staggering.
Better: The *number* of sales this month is staggering.

ampersand The character *&*, which stands for the word *and*. Some organization names, titles, and other items use an ampersand:

Anderson Rentals & Property Management

Writers should not alter an official name or title by substituting the character *&* for the word *and* merely to save space. Neither should they substitute *and* for & if & is part of the official name or title.

analogy A comparison between two or more things intended to show similarity. This type of comparison may be used to suggest that if the things being compared are similar in some respects, they will probably correspond in other ways.

Analogy is a useful device for writers who want to compare something complex and difficult to understand to something else less complex and easier to understand:

> The lens that reflects the laser's beams in a broad spectrum of hues is like a stained-glass window that disperses multicolored rays of sunlight.

Although analogy can help explain certain complex information and can enrich discussions, it should be used with restraint. Unnecessary, unimaginative analogies or **similes,** such as *He sings like a bird,* are also stale **cliches.** Compare with **metaphor.**

and/or A short form of writing the phrase *and or or,* used to avoid repeating the word *or.* The form *and/or* is common in certain legal material, but it is usually unnecessary in other writing. Publishers prefer that one or the other be used or that a sentence be reworded to avoid the *and/or* form:

> He will call, write, or do both to let you know the time of his arrival [*not* He will call *and/or* write to let you know his time of arrival].

The entire sentence should be reworded if something else is meant:

> He will call to let you know the time of his arrival, and if time permits, he will also send a confirmation by mail.

and, symbol for See **ampersand.**

anecdote A short story or account of an interesting or humorous incident. For example, someone writing a technical account of the insect life in a particular region might in-

clude a fascinating account of a life-and-death struggle between an army of ants and a large beetle.

An anecdote may be any length that is appropriate for
the topic or document being prepared. Even brief anec-
dotes, however, should be directly related to the general
subject or should serve to enhance or illuminate a specific
point in a document.

Anglicized See **foreign words.**

animals, names of See **biological terms.**

anonymous work Material that was created by an unknown or unacknowledged person. In citing an anonymous
work when the author is unknown, the **note** or **bibliography** entry should begin with the title of the work. It is not
necessary to precede the title with the word *Anonymous:*

Proof of Betrayal (New York: Fiction Press, 1999).

If the author is known but is not listed on the title page,
the name may be given in brackets. If the name cannot
positively be confirmed, a question mark should follow it:

[Marilyn Stark], *Proof of Betrayal* (New York: Fiction
Press, 1999).
[Marilyn Stark?], *Proof of Betrayal* (New York: Fiction
Press, 1999).

ante-/anti- Many people have trouble deciding whether to
use the **prefix** *ante-* or *anti-*. *Ante-* means before or in front
of:

They want to *antedate* the contract [date it before the
actual date of execution].

Anti-, which is much more widely used than *ante-,*
means opposite or against:

She has always been *antigovernment* [hostile to govern-
ment].

Both prefixes are attached to a word without using a hyphen unless the main word is capitalized or if a vowel is repeated:

anti-American
anti-inflammatory

antecedent The word *antecedent* comes from the Latin *ante-* (before) and *cedo* (go)—that which goes before. It means a word, **phrase,** or **clause** to which a **pronoun** refers or a word or phrase that is connected to the **object of a preposition.** In most cases the antecedent of a pronoun is easy to recognize:

Carl [antecedent] wisely invested *his* [pronoun] time as well as his money.
Everybody [antecedent] learns at *his* or *her* [pronouns] own pace.
He is the *person* [antecedent] *who* [pronoun] was just hired.

The antecedents of **prepositions** may not be as obvious. However, with practice they also should become easy to recognize. The antecedent of a preposition may be a **noun,** pronoun, **adjective, verb, adverb,** or an entire phrase. For example, the antecedent in the next sentence is a verb:

They *went* [antecedent] *to* [preposition] work.

See **preposition** for more about the function of prepositions in showing the relation between a preposition's object and its antecedent.

anthology A collection of poems, short stories, songs, or other literary, musical, or artistic works by various authors; any assortment or catalog of items, such as a collection of ideas or comments.

An anthology may consist of new or original work by various authors or material that was previously published and copyrighted. In the latter case, compilers or editors must secure permission from the **copyright** owners before using the material in the anthology.

A source **note** with required copyright information, as supplied by the copyright owner, should be prepared for any copyrighted material used in an anthology. Usually, the information is stated in a **headnote** placed before the text begins or in an unnumbered **footnote** at the bottom of the first page of the particular selection:

> Reprinted from *Socialism in the 1990s,* ed. John C. Huntington (Chicago: Midland Press, 1997), 212–28, by permission of the author and the publisher. © 1997 by The Chicago Center for Political Research.

Previously copyrighted material is usually reprinted verbatim unless selected passages are clearly identified as *adapted* from a copyrighted work, with permission having been secured to make certain changes. New or original material that has never been copyrighted is commonly edited so that contributions from the various authors will be consistent in matters of **style** and **format.**

anti- See **ante-/anti-.**

antithesis The direct contrast of ideas. Antithesis is shown by using a parallel arrangement of words, **clauses,** or **sentences** that are in opposition to or in contrast with each other:

> They promised *wealth* but delivered *poverty.*

Skilled writers often employ antithesis to enliven and enrich their prose.

antonym A word that has the opposite meaning of another word. *Tall,* for example, is an antonym of *short.* Some thesauruses include antonyms as well as **synonyms.** Such works commonly list synonyms first followed by an often smaller group of antonyms:

> **impetuous** (*adj.*): **Syn.** abrupt, ardent, eager, fervid, fiery, forceful, hasty, headstrong, hurried, impulsive, intractable, passionate, precipitous, rash, rushing, spontaneous, swift, vehement, violent. **Ant.** calm, cautious,

circumspect, composed, patient, reflective, sensible, steady, thoughtful, wary, wise.

anxious/eager The **adjectives** *anxious* and *eager* are widely used interchangeably, although careful writers make a distinction. *Anxious* primarily means being uneasy, apprehensive, or worried. Even when it is used to mean eager, it implies an agitated desire or an unsettled sense of eagerness:

> I'm *anxious* about making a good impression.

Eager means having keen interest or desire. Even in reference to impatient expectancy, *eager* suggests a happy, pleasant sensation:

> I'm *eager* to start our vacation.

apostrophe (') The *apostrophe* has five common uses:

> To indicate the **possessive case** of a **noun:** *employee's* car; *Michael's* office.

> To indicate a **contraction** or the omission of letters: doesn't; nat'l.

> To indicate **plurals** of abbreviations: A's; Ph.D.'s.

> To indicate that a letter or word is being referred to as a letter or word: M's; no's.

> To indicate plurals of letters, numbers, and symbols when it might be confusing to use an s alone: a's and b's; 3's and 4's; #'s and %'s.

appendix Supplementary material placed at the end of a chapter, book, or other work. Appendixes in a multiauthor work are placed at the end of each contributor's material. Those in a single-author work are usually placed at the end of the work in the **back matter** just before the **notes, glossary,** and **bibliography.**

Supplementary material may be presented in a single appendix or in various numbered or lettered appendixes:

Appendix 1, Appendix 2, and so on
Appendix A, Appendix B, and so on

Individual appendixes are often titled as well as numbered or lettered. Even when there is only one appendix, the word *Appendix* precedes the title, sometimes on a line by itself:

Appendix

Desktop Publishing Equipment Vendors

An appendix may be set in the same type size as the main text or in a smaller size. The pages are numbered in **arabic numerals,** the same as the regular text pages, and the first page of the first appendix begins on a **recto** page. Subsequent appendixes may begin on either a recto or **verso** page.

Tables and **illustrations** in an appendix are numbered apart from regular text tables and illustrations and apart from those in other appendixes:

Table A.l, Table A.2, and so on
Table B.1, Table B.2, and so on

appositive A **noun** or **noun phrase** that follows and further identifies another noun or noun phrase. When a sentence can function without the appositive and it can therefore be deleted, it should be set off by commas:

Jeanne Clarke, *our new director,* will give the keynote address [there are no other directors so the appositive is not essential].

When a sentence is unclear without the appositive and it therefore cannot be deleted, it should not be set off by commas:

The writer *Paul Hendricks* is one of the guests [the appositive is essential to indicate which writer].

Confusion arises in punctuating appositives pertaining to family members. A basic rule is to set off the appositive with commas if the sentence is clear and can mean only one thing even in the absence of the appositive:

Her husband, *Tim Matthews,* heads the new division [she has no other husband, so the sentence would be clear without the appositive].

If it might be unclear which family member one is referring to, the name should not be set off by commas:

His son Joe is graduating this year, and his son John will graduate next year [the appositives are necessary to indicate which son].

To decide which **case** to use, try substituting the appositive for the noun it modifies:

They gave both of us, *Nancy and me,* an award [they gave Nancy and *me* (not *I*) the award].

appraise/apprise The **verbs** *appraise* and *apprise* are primarily confused because they look so similar, although their meanings are very different. *Appraise* means to evaluate, value, assess, or estimate the worth of:

I've hired someone to *appraise* the lot before we list it for sale.

Apprise means to inform, bring up to date, or give notice to:

We need to *apprise* the manager of the backlog.

apprise See **appraise/apprise.**

apt/liable/likely As **adjectives,** these three words are used interchangeably in casual comments:

He is *apt/liable/likely* to say anything.

However, they are not synonymous when certain distinctions are intended. *Apt,* for example, is the correct choice to mean being fit, able, or qualified:

She is *apt* in computer skills.

Liable is the correct choice to mean being obligated by law or responsible:

Each person is *liable* for his own debts.

Likely is the correct choice to mean having a high probability of occurring or being true:

Snow is *likely* tomorrow.

arabic numerals Sometimes capitalized (*Arabic numerals*), the **numbers** *1, 2, 3, 4, 5, 6, 7, 8, 9,* and *0.* Arabic numerals are used for **page numbers** in the body of a book or other document and in the **back matter. Roman numerals** are used for page numbers in the **front matter.**

around/round The words *around* and *round* both have many meanings and are used as numerous **parts of speech.** *Around,* for example, may be an **adverb,** a **preposition,** and an **adjective.** *Round* may be an **adverb,** a **preposition,** an **adjective,** a **noun,** and a **verb.**

Misuse occurs in casual comments and informal writing when some people drop the *a* from *around* and incorrectly substitute the word *round:*

They live *around* [not *round*] Los Angeles.

article In grammar, *article* refers to two types of **adjectives**—the indefinite articles *a* and *an* and the definite article *the.* The articles *a* and *an* are used when no specific item is mentioned, and *the* is used to indicate a specific item:

a house in town
an agreement between Eileen and Max
the agreement to provide day-care services

The problem that writers and editors have with articles concerns exceptions to the rule that one should use *a* before a **consonant** and *an* before a **vowel.** Generally, use *an* if a word beginning with a consonant has a vowel sound:

an hour
an honor

Use *a* if a word beginning with a vowel has a long *u* or *eu* sound:

a union
a euphorious moment

Also use *a* if a word beginning with a vowel has a non-vowel sound, such as *w:*

a one-time profit
a once-in-a-lifetime opportunity

In journalism, an *article* refers to a nonfiction composition usually intended for publication in a magazine, journal, newsletter, or newspaper. The subject, length, and **style** of an article depend on the requirements of the publication and should be strictly observed by freelance writers.

References to the title of a published article should be set in **roman type** and enclosed in quotation marks:

''The New Economic Indicators''

A citation to an article should follow the required style of the organization publishing the document containing the reference. See **bibliography, notes,** and **reference list** for examples of article citations.

artwork See **illustrations** and **paintings and sculptures.**

as . . . as/so . . . as These two constructions have always been used interchangeably in certain comparisons, formerly with a preference for *so . . . as* in negative expressions:

His work is not *so* good *as* hers.

Nowadays, the form *as . . . as* is more common and is used for both positive and negative expressions:

His work is not *as* good *as* hers.

However, some writers still prefer to use *as . . . as* in positive comparisons and *so . . . as* in negative comparisons.

as regards/in regard to/regarding/with regard to These three **phrases,** which function as **prepositions,** are frequently used interchangeably. Except for *regarding*, they are often needlessly wordy ways of saying "about" or "concerning." Nevertheless, professional writers sometimes use them to vary their comments:

> We received your letter *in regard to* [*about*] the training workshop.

The phrases *in regards to* and *with regards to* are substandard versions of *in regard to* and *with regard to*. Only *as regards* is standard, though wordy.

ascender The part of tall **lowercase** letters that extends above the **x-height,** or above the top of the lowercase letter *x*. For example, the straight vertical lines rising above the main body in the letters *b, d,* and *h* are ascenders. Compare with **descenders.**

ASCII character set See **extended character set.**

associations and agencies Capitalize the full, official names of associations, agencies, and similar organizations. See **conferences and meetings** for the style of writing their conference and convention themes. **Lowercase** general references to an organization:

> American Association of University Presses, the association
> Better Business Bureau, the bureau
> Consumer Product Safety Commission, the commission
> Kiwanis International, Kiwanis
> Small Business Administration, the SBA

In text discussions, lowercase the word *the* preceding a name even if it is part of the organization's official name:

> The new tax code applies to *the* Historical Society.

See also **names, organization.**

assume/presume The **verbs** *assume* and *presume* are used interchangeably when the meaning is to suppose:

I *assume/presume* you know the risks in starting a new business.

In all other cases particular writers observe a subtle distinction. *Assume* is preferred when the meaning is to take for granted or infer without proof, and it is the obvious choice when the meaning is to take upon oneself:

I *assume* that dividends will be paid at the usual time.
He should *assume* responsibility for the error.

Presume is preferred when the meaning is to believe something to be a fact or true in the absence of evidence or proof to the contrary. It is also the best choice when presumptuousness is implied:

The violation is still punishable by a fine, I *presume.*
She *presumes* that she will get a raise even if no one else does.

assure/ensure/insure The last two of these three **verbs** are often used interchangeably to mean make certain:

The new measures will *ensure/insure* that no customer is overlooked.

Insure also refers to insurance coverage:

Please *insure* both packages.

In all other cases in which *ensure* and *insure* are used interchangeably, some organizations prefer the spelling *ensure* and others *insure*. Whereas the spelling *ensure* is used almost exclusively in Great Britain, both *ensure* and *insure* are widely used in the United States.

The remaining verb, *assure,* meaning to convince or guarantee, should be used only in relation to persons. To the dismay of language experts, however, many writers ignore this rule and use *assure* with things:

Questionable: The technology *assures* that quality control will not be a problem.
Better: The technology *ensures/insures* that quality control will not be a problem.

asterisk (*) The star symbol is sometimes used instead of a number or letter to indicate a **footnote** reference. For **note** references in mathematical copy (see **mathematical expressions**), symbols such as * are often preferred over letters or numbers, which might be confused with an **exponent.** Also, in certain reference material authors prefer to separate substantive (discussion) notes from numbered source notes. In those cases the asterisk and other symbols may be used for the substantive notes.

astronomical terms Capitalize the specific names of asteroids, stars, planets and their satellites, constellations, and other celestial bodies:

Earth
Venus
Sun
Moon
Big Dipper
Milky Way
North Star
Alpha Centauri
Ursa Major
Halley's comet

Lowercase general references to a body, including phenomena and general references to the sun, moon, and earth:

a galaxy far away
the solar system
mysteries of the sun, moon, and stars
earth, rain, and fire
the aurora borealis

attributive An **adjective** placed immediately before a **noun** or a noun similarly placed before another noun:

The *colorful* [adjective] catalog [noun] will tantalize shoppers.
The *procedures* [noun] *manual* [noun] is mandatory reading for all trainees.

When the adjective or noun occurs in the **subject** of a sentence, it is said to be *attributive* or in an *attributive position*. When the adjective or noun appears in the **predicate** of a sentence, it is said to be *predicative* or in the *predicative position*.

audience A term applied to both spectators-listeners of a performance or event and readers of printed material. The **style** and usage in a document intended for a particular audience should be tailored to the needs, interests, and comprehension level of the receivers of the message. Audience evaluation, therefore, is an essential step in message preparation preceding other basic steps, such as data collection and composition.

Sometimes a message is targeted to more than one audience, and writers must then take into account secondary as well as primary readers. The *primary audience* consists of the principal readers for whom a document is intended—the ones who are most likely to act on its message. The *secondary audience* consists of any others who may also receive and use the document for some purpose but may not act on it in the same way that the primary readers do. Multiple audiences are common in business. For example, an annual report to the stockholders may also be read by employees, customers, and the general public.

augment/supplement The **verbs** *augment* and *supplement* are used interchangeably to mean increase or expand. However, *augment* primarily means to enlarge, increase, or magnify the size, extent, or quantity of something generally complete in itself:

He took a second job to *augment* his basic income.

Supplement primarily means to add on to something to strengthen the whole or to make up for a deficiency:

Many people must *supplement* their diets with vitamins to make up for poor eating habits.

authentic/genuine The **adjectives** *authentic* and *genuine* are both correctly used to mean being consistent with beliefs or known facts. However, some writers make use of a subtle distinction in their primary senses. *Authentic* primarily means not being fictitious:

> The film's portrayal of that period in history is *authentic*.

Genuine additionally implies that the thing being accepted is not feigned, counterfeit, or dishonest:

> The painting discovered in the attic is a *genuine* Degas.

author-date citations Also called *name-date citations*. Two things characterize an author-date system: first, the use of names and dates for citations in the text, rather than **superscript** numbers as in a **notes** system; and second, the placement of the date of publication near the beginning of a reference-list entry, rather than at or near the end as in a **bibliography** entry:

> Windham, Pauline, ed. 1998. *New Age Politics*. Washington, D.C.: Center for New Age Politics.

For the text citations in an author-date system, the author's last name and the date of his or her work are placed in parentheses at a logical or appropriate place. Usually, the information is placed at the end of a quotation, sentence, or **extract** just before the final punctuation mark:

> Telecommuters must have a sufficient degree of self-discipline to work at an acceptable pace without distractions and interruptions (Pierce 1996).

The word *author* in author-date citations refers to any persons or organizations alphabetized under a certain name in the reference list, including editors, compilers, and others who prepare a work. However, the abbreviations *ed., comp.,* and so on, which follow a person's name in the reference-list entries, are omitted in the text citations.

When there are more than three authors, state only the first person's name followed by *et al.* (and others):

> (Brewster et al. 1977)

When two authors have the same last name and their works were published in the same year, include the first two (or all) names:

(Brewster, Smith, et al. 1977)
(Brewster, Whipple, et al. 1977)

Or add a short title of the work after *et al.:*

(Brewster et al., *Marketing,* 1977)
(Brewster et al., *Sales Strategies,* 1977)

When a work has no author's name but was published or sponsored by an organization, use the organization's name in both the text citations and in the reference-list entries in the position where an author's name would normally be given:

(Avanti Research Institute 1994)

When it is important to refer to a specific page, note, or other element in a work, place that information after the date. When both a volume and page number are stated, use a colon to separate the two. When the volume alone is given, include the abbreviation *vol.* so that the reader won't think it's a page number:

(Avanti Research Institute 1994, 135, fig. A-3)
(Lister 1969, 3:114–20)
(Lister 1969, vol. 3)

When there are successive references within one paragraph to pages or other elements in the same work, cite the name and date only once. Thereafter, use the page number alone within that paragraph:

Research data contradicted earlier findings (Mislan 1995, 242). One critic refuted a release dated only two months earlier (p. 243).

Separate multiple references to different authors by semicolons. It is not necessary to place these citations in alphabetical order in a text reference, but always alphabetize corresponding entries in the reference list:

(Barnes 1974; Hill and Chesterton 1965; Adams et al. 1993)

Use a comma between multiple references to different works by the same author unless page numbers are included. If they are, use a semicolon between the references:

(Major 1987, 1991)
(Major 1987, 320–25; 1988, 100–101)

If two works by an author have the same year, place small letters after the years to distinguish them in both the text citations and the reference list:

(Major 1987, 1991a, 1991b)
(Lewis 1998a, 1998b, 1998c)

See **reference list** for examples of the full data used in the reference-list entries.

author's alterations (AAs) Changes that an author makes in proofs of an author's work. See **page proof.** Because of the additional cost of resetting pages, publishers usually charge authors a percentage of correction costs above that for an allowable number of changes. Therefore, excessive changes in the proof stage are usually discouraged.

To distinguish an author's changes from other changes made during editing or **typesetting,** an author should write and circle the abbreviation *AA* in the margin by any of his or her changes. See also **editor's alterations (EAs)** and **printer's errors (PEs).**

author's proofs See **page proof.**

auxiliary verb Also called *helping verb;* a **verb** that is used with a **principal verb** and helps to complete the meaning of that verb. *Be, can, do, have, may, must, shall*, and *will* are basic auxiliaries. Each one also has other forms, such as *do/does/did* and *have/has/had:*

The track team *is* running today.
She *did* receive your letter.

He *has* learned a lot this year.
Tom *will* report to Mr. Madison.

The helping verb indicates time and **tense:**

She *is* typing today [**present tense**].
She *was* typing yesterday [**past tense**].
She *will* type tomorrow [**future tense**].

Auxiliaries sometimes function alone as principal, or main, verbs. In the first of the following examples, *does* is connected to or helps the main verb *paint* complete the meaning of the sentence. In the second example, *does* is the only verb in the sentence because *painting* is a **noun,** not a main verb:

Yes, she *does* [auxiliary verb] paint [main verb].
Yes, she *does* [main verb] painting [noun].

average/mean/median As **nouns,** these three terms all refer to a numerical value or amount that represents two or more items, although *average* also has other familiar meanings (*average* physical appearance). An arithmetic *average* and *mean* are both calculated by adding a series of figures and dividing by the number of figures in the series:

The *average* or *mean* of 5, 16, 3, 9, and 7 is 8 [the sum of 40 divided by 5, the number of items].

The *median* figure is the middle number in a series of numbers:

The *median* of the series 3, 5, 7, 9, and 11 is 7 [the middle number].
The *median* of the series 3, 5, 7, and 9 is 6 [the average of the two middle items, or 12 divided by 2].

averse See **adverse/averse.**

awards and honors Capitalize the official names of awards, honors, and prizes, but **lowercase** general descriptions:

Oscar nominations, the nominations
National Merit scholarships, the scholarships
Nobel Peace Prize, the prize
Nobel Prize in literature, the prize
Pulitzer Prize in fiction, the prize

See also **military honors.**

B

B.C. Abbreviation for *before Christ*. Publishers usually set the abbreviation in **roman type** with small capital letters (B.C.), but businesspeople preparing material by computer often use all capitals (B.C.) to avoid additional keystrokes.

The year, which precedes the abbreviation, is stated in numerals:

1023 B.C.

Compare with **A.D.** For definitions of other systems of chronology (A.H., A.M., A.S., A.U.C., B.C.E., B.P., C.E., and M.Y.B.P.) and for a discussion of the use of B.C. versus B.C.E. (before the common era), see **abbreviations of time and days.**

back matter Also called *end matter* or *reference matter;* one of the three major divisions in a book, the other two being the main text and the **front matter.** The back matter often includes one or more of the following parts, or sections: **appendix, notes, glossary, bibliography,** list of contributors (see **acknowledgments; contributors, list of**), and **index.** It may also include other material that isn't suitable for the main text, such as a detailed list of abbreviations of reference sources, usually positioned before the notes. See **abbreviations, list of.**

Pages in the back matter are numbered with **arabic numerals** the same as in the main text. Like the first page of a regular text chapter, the first page of each section in the back matter has a *drop folio* (**page number** at the bottom of the page) or no folio. Also, **running heads** are used in the back matter the same as in the chapters of the main text.

Each main part or section in the back matter, such as the appendix section, may begin on a **recto** or **verso** page but usually begins on a recto page. The various subsections, such as individual appendixes within the main appendix section, may begin on either verso or recto pages.

back of/behind/in back of The **phrases** *back of* and *in back of* are both widely used to mean behind:

They are waiting *back of/in back of* [*behind*] the gate.

However, some disagreement exists about whether *back of* and *in back of* are acceptable substitutes for *behind*. At best they are unnecessarily wordy alternatives and should be used only in informal writing.

backbone See **spine**.

bad/badly Although there should be no excuse for confusing the **adjective** *bad* with the **adverb** *badly,* both are commonly misused, usually with *bad* incorrectly being used to mean *badly*. Since *bad* is an adjective, it has to modify (describe) the **pronoun** *he* in the following example:

He feels *bad* [not *badly*].

Since *badly* is an adverb, it has to modify the **verb** *types* in the next example:

He types *badly* [not *bad*].

Therefore, *bad* describes the person *he*, such as his emotional state, and *badly* describes the action *types*, such as how well he types.

The same difference in usage described here—adjective versus adverb—applies to similar terms, such as *sad* (adjective)/*sadly* (adverb) and *poor* (adjective)/*poorly* (adverb).

balance/remainder The **nouns** *balance* and *remainder* are frequently used interchangeably to mean the rest or remainder. However, usage experts object to treating *balance* and *remainder* as **synonyms.** Therefore, use *balance* to refer to a state of equilibrium or a bookkeeping amount:

> We must *balance* the budget.
> The *balance* in her account is $347.95.

Use *remainder* in reference to an arithmetic amount and in most other situations to mean what is left over:

> When 6 is deducted from 14, the *remainder* is 8.
> The *remainder* of the weekend has been set aside for taking inventory.

ballet See **musical works.**

bar graph See **graphics.**

barbarisms Words or expressions that are incorrect, tasteless, or otherwise unacceptable (see **nonstandard English**); the use of such language:

> The professor described many of today's crude **slang** expressions as outrageous *barbarisms.*

bare infinitive See **infinitive.**

barely/hardly/scarcely Most authorities agree that these three **adverbs** can often be used interchangeably to mean by a small margin. However, in certain situations when a particular emphasis is desired, they should not be used as **synonyms.** *Barely* is the best choice to express a narrow or thin margin:

> She *barely* passed the test.

Hardly is preferred to express difficulty:

> We could *hardly* squeeze through the small opening in the cave.

Scarcely is the best choice to express a margin so small as to be almost unbelievable:

I could *scarcely* believe that he walked away from such a violent car crash.

base The simple or basic form of a word to which **affixes** or other bases may be added. For example, *walk* is a basic form to which *-ed* can be added to form the word *walked.* See also **inflection.**

baseline An imaginary line in **typesetting** that connects the bottoms of capital letters: *A̱ḆC̱Ḏ*. See also **point, typeface,** and **x-height.**

because of/due to/owing to Although resistance to using these three **phrases** interchangeably is breaking down, some authorities object to this trend. The **prepositional phrase** *because of* is the most commonly used of the three phrases to mean on account of or by reason of, especially when followed by a **noun** or **noun phrase:**

They canceled the order *because of* [on account of] the delay [noun] in shipment.

However, *the reason is* and *because of* should not be used or connected in the same sentence or thought:

Not: The reason they canceled the order is *because of* the delay in shipment.
Better: They canceled the order *because of* the delay in shipment.
Or: The reason they canceled the order *is* that there was a delay in shipment.

The use of *due* as an **adjective** is appropriate, and the word *due* should be a **predicate adjective** when the expression *due to,* meaning owing to or caused by, is used:

The *cancellation* [noun] of the order was *due to* [predicate adjective] the delay in shipment.

Because of is preferred over *due to* at the beginning of a sentence:

Not: Due to the delay in shipment, the order was canceled.

Better: Because of the delay in shipment, the order was canceled.

Owing to, like *due to,* may be used as a predicate adjective to mean caused by or attributable to, although it sounds more awkward than *due to:*

The *cancellation* [noun] of the order was *owing to* [predicate adjective] the delay in shipment.

Owing to may also be used as a compound preposition (see **prepositional phrase**) meaning because of:

The order was canceled *owing to* the delay in shipment.

The wordy forms *due to the fact that* and *owing to the fact that* can often be replaced by *because* or *since.*

behind See **back of/behind/in back of.**

below/under The **prepositions** *below* and *under* are commonly used interchangeably to mean beneath. However, in many contexts one word is preferred over another. For example, *below* is preferred to mean the opposite of *above:*

The temperature is *below* 50 degrees.

Under is preferred to indicate that something else is overhead or that one thing is on top of another:

The wastebasket is *under* the sink.

It is also more usual to refer to something being done *under,* not *below,* someone's direction.

benefactor/client/customer/patron These four **nouns** are often used interchangeably. *Client* and *customer* are sometimes treated as **synonyms,** and *benefactor* and *patron* also are sometimes substituted one for the other. To be clear, though, writers should observe the following distinctions.

Use *benefactor* to refer to someone who donates primarily financial aid to someone or something:

With his donation of $1 million, the president of ABC Company was the flood victims' principal *benefactor.*

Use *client* to refer to someone who consults or purchases the services of a professional person:

The attorney's *client* was awarded $10,000 in damages.

Use *customer* to refer to someone who purchases or uses a commodity or commercial service:

The *customer* called a pest-control service after discovering termites in the basement.

Use *patron* to refer to someone who supports, protects, or champions a person, group, organization, event, or cause, especially when the recipient has a charitable or artistic character. Also use *patron* to refer to a regular customer, one who supports a commercial establishment through regular patronage:

She is a *patron* of the opera.
As a *patron* of Mario's Italian Bistro, he has lunch there
    nearly every day.

beside/besides The **prepositions** *beside* and *besides* are often confused because they look similar. *Beside* primarily means next to or by the side of:

We parked *beside* the garage.

Besides primarily means in addition to, except for, or other than:

One other person from the office *besides* Tom was on the program.

As an **adverb,** *besides* means moreover, in addition, or also:

Besides, we already covered that topic.

between See **among/between.**

bi-/semi- Many people are confused by the **prefixes** *bi-* and *semi-*, particularly in regard to time: *bimonthly, semimonthly,* and so on. The confusion is not surprising because *bi-* has two meanings, one of which is the same as that of *semi-*. In one sense *bi-* means occurring at intervals of two:

biweekly (once every two weeks)
bimonthly (once every two months)

In another sense both *bi-* and *semi-* mean occurring twice during:

biweekly *or* semiweekly (twice a week)
bimonthly *or* semimonthly (twice a month)

One solution to the problem is to use *bi-* to mean occurring at intervals of two (*biweekly*) and *semi-* to mean occurring twice during (*semiweekly*). However, even if writers follow this rule consistently, readers may not be following the same rule. Therefore, another, more practical solution might be simply to reword such expressions more clearly as follows:

every two months (not *bimonthly*)
twice a month (not *semimonthly*)

bias When bias is evident in writing, it is usually unintentional. Most writing does not discriminate against others because of their race, age, gender, or disability. For example, the term *senior citizen* was coined to replace insensitive terms such as *old people*. However, some people object even to the **euphemism** *senior citizen,* believing it creates a stereotype.

The preferred designation of those with disabilities keeps changing. The word *handicap,* for example, is currently unacceptable, and even the more widely used word *disabled* is unacceptable to those who prefer *challenged* to describe all forms of disability (the *hearing-challenged* boy). Terms that suggest sexual discrimination are of special concern to employers who are working to eliminate offensive language as well as the potential for lawsuits.

In spite of many improvements in eradicating bias from published work, some discriminatory language still exists. The following list has examples of sexist words that some readers may find unacceptable:

   average/common man: average/common citizen, aver-
      age/common person
   chairman/woman: chair, chairperson, moderator, presid-
      ing officer
   fellow worker: associate, colleague, coworker
   husband/wife: spouse
   junior executive: executive trainee
   ladylike: courteous, proper, well bred
   manmade: artificial, constructed, handmade, machine
      made, synthetic
   mother tongue: native language, native tongue

bibliography A list of the references that an author uses in
preparing a particular work, which may consist of more
sources than those listed in **notes.** The list is usually placed
in the **back matter** of a book before the list of contributors
(see **contributors, list of**), if any, or otherwise before the
index. Common titles for this type of list are ''Bibliography'' or, if it includes only works referred to in the
text, ''Selected Bibliography,'' ''Works [or ''Literature'']
Cited,'' or ''References.''

   Regardless of whether a note that corresponds to a bibliography entry is complete, the bibliography entry must
have full source data. This includes the author's name, full
title of the work being cited, and full publication information. See the forthcoming examples. (Entries in another type
of bibliographic list—the **reference list** used with **author-
date citations**—also must include full data; however, the
arrangement of information in a reference-list entry differs
from that in a bibliography entry.) Although the notes section in a work does not require a corresponding bibliography if the individual notes are complete, authors usually
prepare both notes and bibliography when a work has numerous citations.

   The number, type, and location of notes may influence
the way a bibliography is organized. For example, the bibliography may be a single alphabetical list, or the list may
be divided into sections according to an appropriate category, such as subject matter. Some bibliographies have an-

notated entries with the author's comments added after the main source data in each entry. Others are styled as essays in which the entry data are incorporated into text-style discussion paragraphs.

The single-list bibliography is the most common. Entries in it are arranged alphabetically by the last names of authors, editors, and so on. When a person's or organization's name is unavailable, the name of the work is used in alphabetizing.

Although the sources in a notes section are numbered, the entries in a straight bibliography are rarely numbered. The second and succeeding lines in a bibliography entry are usually indented, a style called *flush and hang*. See the forthcoming examples.

When there are successive entries by the same author, a 3-**em** dash is used for the second and succeeding entries, with original works preceding edited, compiled, or translated works. See the forthcoming examples.

Titles of books and other publications are set in **italics,** and article and chapter titles are set in **roman type** with quotation marks:

Abramson, Neville C. *Essays from Below.* 2 vols. Cincinnati: Middle America Printers, 1990.

Abramson, Neville C.; Cline, M. T.; and Oporde, Laura J., eds. *The Letters of Thomas Porter Smith.* 3 vols. Hunter, N.J.: Notebook Press, 1988.

Barkley, Wirth. *DeSteeges Blanc.* Translated by Pamela Merriman. New Orleans: Southern Publishers Institute, 1995.

Crisp, Jeanne. Introduction to *The Failing Law,* by Parker Rogers. Des Moines: Modern American Printers, 1991.

————. "Time Travels." In *Tomorrow Today.* Edited by Eugene Carson III. San Francisco: Oceanside Press, 1984.

[Davis, James J.]. *On Learning Less.* Phoenix: Sun Publishing, 1997.

Downhill from There. Phoenix: Sun Publishing, 1998.

Ishmael, J. K. *Hordes from the Past, Book 2: Asian Invaders.* Reprint, New York: Towers Press, 1979.

————, ed. *An Introduction to the Middle East.* Vol. 2, *The Early Wars,* by Steven Hill. N.p.: Better Publishing, 1986.

————, ed. *The Jasmine Anthology.* Forthcoming.

King, Timothy B. "Another Story." *Port Smith Review* 13, no. 2 (March 1997): 3–11.

————. "The Truth about Webster." *Historical Studies,* vol. 1 (spring 1992).

Koleman, C. V., and Ullman, N. B. "Growing Up Old." *Besters Journal,* January 1996, 21–23.

Milwaukee News. 2 March 1990, sec. 2A, p. 4.

Misner, Mary O. Interview by author. Tape recording. Washington, D.C., 12 August 1984.

Nester, Maxine, ed. Tulane Harman to John Silver. 2 November 1775. In *The Letters of Tulane Harman.* Miami: Eastern College Press, 1994.

Norris, Ellen P. "Working in a Home Office." Paper presented at the annual meeting of the Northern Telecommuters Society, Detroit, Mich., May 1988.

Oregon Research Training Department. "Workshop II Program." Oregon Research Center, Portland, Oreg., 1967. Photocopy.

Parnelli Manuscripts. Parnelli House Collection. Central College Library, Duluth, Minn., n.d.

Riche Dictionary of Economics, 12th ed., s.v. "finance."

United States v Southern Hills, 174 F3d 107, 108 (3d Cir 1960).

U.S. Congress. Senate. Committee on Foreign Relations. *South African Uprising: Hearing before the Committee on Foreign Relations.* 99th Cong., 1st sess., 21 March 1985.

UTEM. Princeton, N.J.: National Library of Political Conferences, 1992–. Available through the National Society of Public Colleges On-Line Database.

Winston, Noreen. "A Study of Affirmative Action from Its Rise to Decline." Ph.D. diss., University of Hawaii, 1995.

"Young Company Ripe for Merger." URL: http:///
www.svc-online.org/newsletr/apr6-99.html.

bills See **acts and treaties.**

binary number A value expressed by some combination
of the two digits 0 and 1. Whereas the decimal system,
traditionally used in manual calculations, has a base of ten,
the binary system, developed for use with digital computers, has a base of two. Therefore, each digit of a **number**
in the decimal system represents a power of ten, and each
digit of a number in the binary system represents a power
of two.

Both systems use a decimal or binary point to express
decimal fractions:

101.5 (decimal)
1010.0110 (binary)

When binary numbers are written in groups of four
digits, insert a space but no punctuation between each
group:

0010 1010

The following table gives the binary equivalent of decimal numbers 0 through 9:

Decimal	Binary
0	000
1	001
2	010
3	011
4	100
5	101
6	110
7	111
8	1000
9	1001

binding The covering around the pages of a book; the process of attaching a **cover** to a book. Books are bound in different ways using different materials depending on the type of book, budget available for production, and other factors. Scholarly books, for example, are commonly bound in hardcover. Familiar book-binding processes are case, adhesive, and mechanical binding. Common materials used in binding are paper, cloth, leather, and plastic.

Case binding, used for hardcover books, is done with a heavy, rigid cardboard covered with cloth, paper, or plastic. Before being bound, the pages are folded into **signatures** of eight, sixteen, twenty-four, thirty-two, forty-eight, or sixty-four pages. They are then *Smyth sewn* (individually sewn through the fold) or *side sewn* (sewn straight through the signatures from one side). Although a side-sewn book is more durable, a Smyth-sewn book has the advantage of being able to open flat.

Adhesive binding, used for paperback books, is done by gluing to the pages a flexible cover stock, which often has a transparent coating. Three common types of adhesive binding are perfect, notch, and burst binding. In *perfect binding* the backs of the signatures are cut off, the surface is roughened, and an adhesive is applied before adding a wraparound cover. In *notch binding* the backs of the signatures are not cut off but are notched and roughened before applying the adhesive. In *burst binding* the backs of the signatures are also not trimmed but are perforated and roughened before adding adhesive.

Mechanical binding, used for notebook- or workbook-style books and manuals, is done by perforating the edges of covers and pages with holes where a device is attached to hold the sheets together. Common processes are the spiral and comb bindings. In *spiral binding* a somewhat rigid plastic or metal spiral is threaded through small, round holes in the cover and pages. In *comb binding* a flexible plastic comb is threaded through rectangular holes.

Other publications, such as magazines and pamphlets, ῾sually bound with saddle wiring or side wiring. In *wiring*, also called *saddle stitching,* two or three staples are inserted through the folds of both pages and cover from the outside to the inside fold. In *side wiring* the staples are inserted along the fold from one side, and the cover is then glued on.

biography An account of one person's (the *biographee*'s) life as written or produced by another person (the *biographer*). The work may be about a historical figure or a living person, and it may be produced with or without the consent of a living subject. However, the authenticity of a work is sometimes questioned when it is done without the consent of the biographee or over the subject's objection. When fictional dialogue, events, and other matters are created and dramatized, the work is called a *fictional biography*.

biological terms The rules for capitalizing and italicizing the names of living organisms are complex. Therefore, those who are preparing a work with numerous biological terms should consult a modern scientific style guide and observe the requirements of the organization publishing the document.

Generally, set both the generic and Latin names of plants and animals in **italics.** Capitalize the genus name, but **lowercase** the species name:

Sanguinaria canadensis (bloodroot)

After first use of the full name (genus + species), the genus name may be abbreviated:

S. canadensis

Set the names of subspecies, such as *syriacus,* in italics:

Ursus arctos syriacus (Syrian bear)

When minor character differences exist in a population, set the words *form* or *variety* (abbreviated as *var.*) in **roman type** following the genus and species names:

Mentha arvensis var. (wild mint)

Capitalize the divisions above the genus (family, order, class, phylum [division], and kingdom), and set them in roman type. The following examples illustrate usage in the various divisions for a dog:

kingdom: Animalia
phylum (division): Chordata
class: Mammalia
order: Carnivora
family: Canidae
genus: Canis
species: familiaris

Also capitalize suborders, and set them in roman type:

Fissipeda (a suborder of Carnivora)

Lowercase English derivatives of scientific names, and set them in roman type:

carnivore (derived from the order Carnivora)

Vernacular, or common, names of plants and animals can be handled in a variety of ways. Many experts recommend using roman type and lowercase letters for common names, capitalizing only **proper nouns** and **adjectives:**

pygmy antelope
river dolphin
golden retriever
blue-point Siamese
Rocky Mountain sheep
Canada thistle
black-eyed Susan
But: jack-in-the-pulpit

Capitalize names that are recognized as special breeds or horticultural varieties, especially if they are or may be patented or trademarked and whether or not they are proper nouns:

Peace rose
Better Boy tomato

Black English Also called *Black English Vernacular* and, more recently, *Ebonics;* a distinctive variety of **nonstandard English** spoken by the majority of blacks in the United States. Although criticized by some as a substandard form of contemporary English or even as **slang,** Black English is widely accepted as an alternative speech pattern traced to West African pidgins and West Indian creoles. (*Pidgin* is a simple spoken language used by people who don't share a native language. *Creole* is a pidginized language that a community adopts as its native language.)

Among the characteristics of Black English are the omission of **plurals,** the omission of **verbs,** the absence of *r*'s and *l*'s, and the use of **double negatives:**

All my *friend*[*s*] sing.
She [*is*] a fine woman.
We[*'ll*] be there.
He *didn't* do *no* work.

Black English Vernacular See **Black English.**

bleed To print so that the inked image appears to run off the page on one or more sides; an **illustration** that runs across one or more margins of a page; a page trimmed so that an illustration appears to run off the edges.

blend word Also called *portmanteau* word; an expression that blends parts of two existing words or combines two separate words into a single blended term. Although blend words are becoming more common, especially in business, they should be used cautiously and avoided with readers that may not recognize or understand the expressions. The following **nouns** are examples of blend words:

advertorial *advertisement + editorial:* A newspaper feature that resembles an editorial but is really a paid advertisement.
Amerenglish *American + English:* The principal form of English spoken in the United States.
bruncheon *breakfast + luncheon:* A variation of

brunch, which is considered by some to be more socially correct than *bruncheon.*

docutainment *documentary* + *entertainment:* A television program that dramatizes factual information so that it is entertaining as well as informative.

expunctuation *expunction* + *punctuation:* The editing or marking of material for deletion in a manuscript.

fuzzword *fuzzy* + *buzzword:* A deliberately imprecise form of jargon, such as *revenue enhancement* (taxes), often used to impress or confuse others.

opinionnaire *opinion* + *questionnaire:* A questionnaire primarily intended to solicit opinions.

prequel *precede* + *sequel:* A literary work set in a time before rather than after that of an existing work.

blind stamping See **embossing.**

blueline See **blueprint.**

blueprint Also called *blues* or *blueline;* a form of proof made from the photographic negatives of text and **illustrations** that are used in offset **printing.** Other forms of photographic prints made from negatives are called *vandykes,* or *brownprints,* and *silver prints.* The purpose of all such proofs is to show text and illustrations in place as they will appear in the final printed copy.

Negative proofs are checked by both an editor and a designer or by others in the publisher's production department. The proofs are examined to see that all text errors found in the **page proofs** have been corrected, that page numbers and **running heads** are correct, and that all text and illustrations are in their proper positions and appear right side up. Each page is also scanned for unwanted marks, scratches, and other blemishes caused by ink or debris on the negatives.

Since changes at this late stage of production are costly, usually only errors are corrected or other essential changes made.

blues See **blueprint.**

boldface Type with dark, heavy letters, such as that used for entry heads and cross-references in this dictionary. Writers and editors instruct **compositors** to set text in bold by drawing a wavy line under the desired word or words.

book parts The main divisions of a book are the **front matter,** text or body, and **back matter.** The front matter may include some or all of the parts listed in this entry. Pages are numbered with small **roman numerals** beginning with the **half-title page,** although the numerals are not printed on any pages preceding the **contents page.**

In the following list, the page—**recto** or **verso**—on which each part usually begins is stated in parentheses.

Half-title page (*recto*)

Series-title page, list of contributors, or blank page (*verso*)

Title page (*recto*)

Copyright and publication data (*verso*)

Dedication or epigraph (*recto*)

Blank page (*verso*)

Contents, table of (*recto*)

Illustrations, list of (*recto or verso*)

Tables, list of (*recto or verso*)

Foreword (*recto or verso*)

Preface (*recto or verso*)

Acknowledgments (*if separate from preface: recto or verso*)

Introduction (*if separate from text: recto or verso*)

Abbreviations or chronology, list of (*recto or verso*)

The text begins with the following parts, after which it may have various recto or verso chapter opening pages, end-of-chapter **notes,** chapter **appendix** opening pages, and other material:

Second half-title page (*recto*)

Blank page (*verso*)

First chapter, part, or other text page (*recto*)

The back matter immediately follows the last chapter or other page of text, and its pages are numbered with **arabic numerals** the same as the text pages. The back matter may include some or all of the following parts:

Appendix(es) (*recto or verso*)

Notes (*recto or verso*)

Glossary (*recto or verso*)

Bibliography (*recto or verso*)

Contributors, list of (*if not in front matter: recto or verso*)

Index(es) (*recto or verso*)

For a description of the important parts in a book, see the individual entries for the various parts.

Bookland EAN bar code A product identification code similar to that found on merchandise in retail stores. It consists of a thirteen-digit number and black-and-white vertical stripes printed on the back **cover** or **jacket** of a book and is used to identify the item and its price and to record the sale.

The **International Standard Book Number (ISBN),** which is printed above or below the vertical stripes, identifies the publisher and the title of the work. An optional five-digit side-bar code, positioned to the right and above the EAN number, may be used to indicate the currency, such as U.S. currency, and the price of the book, or it may be used for another purpose.

books Capitalize the important words in titles and subtitles of books, pamphlets, and collections (see **collective work**

and **anthology**) in running text and citations, and set all parts in **italics.** Also capitalize the titles of series and editions, but set them in **roman type** without quotation marks. **Lowercase** the words *series* and *edition* when they are not part of the title:

> *The Encyclopedic Dictionary of Style and Usage*
> *The Three-Step Vocabulary Builder: How to Super-charge Your Vocabulary in Just Minutes a Day*
> English Throughout the Ages series (*series* is not part of the title)
> Modern Library Edition (*Edition* is part of the title)
> Professional Books (*Books* is part of the title)

Set titles of chapters and the main parts of a book in roman type enclosed in quotation marks. Lowercase common titles such as *preface* (unless the word begins a sentence), and also set them in roman type without quotation marks:

> ''Research Papers,'' chapter 3 in his new edition, has been heavily revised.
> ''Word Usage,'' part 1 in his new book, is highly informative.
> His introduction and glossary are both useful.

Omit the initial *The* in the title of a book or one of its parts in running text if including it will sound awkward:

> They picked up a copy of *The Lost Pillar*.
> Have you read Jenning's *Lost Pillar*?

See also **bibliography, notes,** and **reference list** for the style of writing titles in citations.

The title of a book is set in prominent letters on the **cover** and in display type for the **half-title page** and **title page.** Individual items—title, subtitle, author's name, and publisher's imprint—are usually set on separate lines.

The same type style is commonly used on both the half-title and title pages. However, the display type for the cover or **jacket** may be different from the **typeface** used inside.

Also, the main title on both the cover and the title page is often larger than the subtitle, if any.

The wording of titles depends on the type of book, subject matter, audience, existence of similar titles, and many other factors. Therefore, no universal rule exists, and the publisher and author may work together to select a suitable original title.

boundary/limit/parameter/perimeter As **nouns,** these four terms are used interchangeably—sometimes incorrectly—in the broad sense of a border or outer edge. However, popular use has not changed the need to be selective in certain contexts. *Boundary* is often the best choice to indicate a physical border or a specific limiting physical line:

> The fence marked the *boundary* between the two houses.

Limit is a better choice to stress a point, especially a nonphysical point, beyond which something cannot or may not proceed:

> The new law sets a *limit* on the city manager's authority.

To most authorities the word *parameter* is a mathematical or statistical term that should be used only in technical calculations:

> The *parameters* were varied in the experiment.

Parameter, therefore, should not be used in the sense of a physical border or limiting line as described for *boundary* and *limit.* When it is borrowed from science and used in such general contexts, it tends to sound pretentious. The questionable use of *parameter* as a physical border or line may be attributed to the fact that it looks and sounds like the fourth term in this entry—*perimeter.* This term has a mathematical meaning, too, but can be used legitimately to mean a border or outer line:

> Guard dogs patrolled the *perimeter* of the prison yard.

boxhead The former term for a column **head(ing)** in a **table.** Although many tables are now produced by computer without extensive surrounding rules or boxes, the table heads at one time were enclosed in rectangular boxes and were therefore referred to as *boxheads* or *boxheadings.*

braces { } One of several *fences,* or *signs of aggregation,* primarily used to enclose **mathematical expressions.** Some authorities suggest a preferred order for common enclosures, with **parentheses** on the inside, then **brackets,** followed by braces on the outside:

   { [( )] }

However, authors of mathematical material use different enclosures to mean different things. Editors, therefore, usually leave the enclosures in mathematical **manuscripts** in whatever order the authors have chosen to use them.

brackets [ ] Brackets have four principal uses:

To indicate an error in quoted material by enclosing the word *sic,* meaning so, thus, or in this manner: The machine run [*sic*] continuously.

To enclose a parenthetical comment within material that is already enclosed in parentheses: A method of conduction (movement of positive or negative ions [see *ionic conduction*]) was used previously, although newer technology has supplanted that use.

To enclose **mathematical expressions** in a series of *fences,* usually between **braces** and **parentheses:** { [( )] }.

To enclose certain comments in **manuscript** copy to indicate that they are instructions rather than text to be typeset: [Insert Table 2.7 about here].

breve See **diacritical marks.**

broadside Also called *landscape* in computer terminology; a reference to the position of information on a page such that the page must be turned ninety degrees to read it normally. A **table,** for example, that is wider than the width of a book page may be printed sideways, or *broadside,* on the page. Usually, when material is printed broadside on a page, the left side of the material is positioned at the bottom of the page.

brownprint See **blueprint.**

building and structure names Capitalize the official names of buildings and other structures. When a generic term, such as *bridge* or *building,* is part of an official name, also capitalize the general word; otherwise **lowercase** most general references to a building or structure. Write the names of foreign buildings and structures in **roman type,** the same as the names of English buildings and structures:

U.S. Capitol, the Capitol (U.S.)
Jefferson Memorial, the memorial
Leaning Tower of Pisa, the tower
Empire State Building, the building
Times Square, the square
Westminster Abbey, the abbey
Golden Gate Bridge, the bridge
Palais Royal, the palace

bullets Small, bold dots that are sometimes placed before items in a list instead of numbers, letters, or other symbols:

• Copyright Act of 1989

• Copyright page and notice

• Copyright registration and fee

burning See **printing.**

burst binding See **binding.**

byte A computer term referring to a set of eight binary digits (bits) that as a unit designate a single character, such as a letter. See **binary number.** Each bit is represented by 0 or 1. For example, *0100 0001* represents the letter *A.*

The amount of computer memory is often expressed in terms of kilobytes (1,024 bytes), megabytes (1,048,576 bytes), or gigabytes (1,073,741,824 bytes). Those measures are usually abbreviated as follows: *B* (byte), *K* or *KB* (kilobyte), *M* or *MB* (megabyte), and *G* or *GB* (gigabyte). The term *bit,* however, is abbreviated as a **lowercase** *b.*

C

calendar designations Capitalize the names of days of the week and month. See also **abbreviations of time and days.** **Lowercase** the two equinoxes and solstices and the names of seasons, except when they are personified:

Friday
January
spring
vernal equinox
summer solstice

As we watched in awe, *Winter* stretched her icy fingers across the silent meadow.

callouts Marginal notations that an author or editor writes and circles in the margins of a **manuscript** page to indicate where **tables** or **illustrations** that are prepared on separate pages are to be inserted in the typeset text:

Fig. 1

Fig. 1 about here.

The manuscript page number where the notation is written should then be lightly penciled on the back of the figure or table.

If **galley proofs** instead of **page proofs** are set, the same notations should be circled on the galleys for the **compositor** to use in preparing page proofs.

camera-ready copy The **illustrations, tables,** text, and any other material in a finished form suitable for photographing in preparation for **printing.** Many authors have computers and printers that are capable of producing tables and illustrations ready for the camera without their needing to be redrawn or reset.

can/may Although the **verbs** *can* and *may* are used interchangeably, strict usage dictates that *can* should be used to express ability or the capacity to do something and *may* should be used to express permission:

> If we *may* [have permission to] use your statistics, we *can* [will be able to] finish drafting the report today.

Can is also sometimes used in informal contemporary usage to express permission, especially when it sounds less condescending:

> You *can* use my computer until yours is fixed.

In other cases it may be important to emphasize the permission aspect as a matter of courtesy or for another reason:

> *May* I choose my own topic, Professor Edmunds?

can not/cannot The common negative of the **verb** *can* is *cannot,* written as one word:

> We *cannot* decide what to do.

The term should be written as two words only when another word intervenes. Usually, though, that form of expression is more awkward:

> We *can,* therefore, *not* comply under those circumstances.

Better: Therefore, we *cannot* comply [*or* We *cannot,* therefore, comply] under those circumstances.

The most confusion arises over the idiomatic phrase (see **idiom**) *cannot but,* and some critics question whether this is a **double negative.** However, both *can but* and *cannot but* are standard English, though the usage tends to sound stilted:

We *cannot but* be pleased by the response.

The intervention of *help* between *cannot* and *but* is criticized by some authorities both as a redundancy and as an obsolete form. Nevertheless, the expression has become an established idiom:

We *cannot help but* be pleased by the response.

A less wordy alternative would be to omit *but,* although the statement then implies—perhaps incorrectly—that the feeling of being pleased is beyond one's control.

We *cannot help* being pleased by the response.

The expression *cannot seem* is also widely used informally, though more in speech than in writing:

He *cannot seem* to get started.
Better: He *seems* unable to get started.

Writers striving for a more relaxed writing style are likely to choose the **contraction** *can't* over the full word *cannot.*

canvas/canvass The principal cause of confusing the **noun** *canvas* with the **verb** *canvass* is the similar spelling and pronunciation. However, the meanings are completely different. *Canvas,* for example, refers to a closely woven cloth:

The *canvas* cover is water repellent.

Canvass means to request or solicit something, such as votes, opinions, or donations:

On Thursday we will *canvass* the neighborhood for donations.

capacity See **ability/capacity.**

capital/capitol One of these two **nouns,** *capital,* has several meanings including wealth and business assets. Confusion between *capital* and *capitol* occurs mostly in reference to governmental activity, and in this sense *capital* refers to a town or city that is an official seat of government. It also refers to an important center of commercial activity:

Des Moines is the *capital* of Iowa.
Miami is the tourism *capital* of the Southeast.   •

Capitol has only one principal meaning: the building or buildings where a state legislature or the U.S. Congress meets. The word is capitalized in reference to the U.S. Capitol (the building) in Washington, D.C., but is lowercased in reference to state buildings.

Capitol is sometimes used in error to refer to the town or city seat of government, and *capital* is sometimes used incorrectly to refer to the building where a state legislature or the U.S. Congress meets. To keep the two apart some writers use this **mnemonic:** Many *capito*ls are o*l*d buildings, and *capita*l is used for al*l* other purposes.

capitalization See individual entries, such as **geographical terms** or **television and radio programs.**

capitol See **capital/capitol.**

caps Short for capital, or **uppercase,** letters: CAPITAL. To indicate this style to a **compositor,** draw three lines under each letter to be capitalized.

caps and small caps Short for capital, or **uppercase,** letters and small capital letters (see **small caps**): CAPS AND SMALL CAPS. To indicate this style to a **compositor,** draw three lines under each letter to be capitalized and two lines under each letter to be set in small capital letters.

caption A title or descriptive headline that accompanies an **illustration.** Each important word in the title may be capitalized:

Fig. 1. Sample Edited Page

Or only the first word and **proper nouns** may be capitalized, as in a regular sentence:

Fig. 1. Sample edited page

Most captions are set beneath rather than above an illustration and may or may not be followed by a **legend** (explanation). Sometimes the caption is omitted, and an illustration has only a legend or a figure number followed by a legend. See the example in the entry **legend.**

When a legend follows the caption, the caption ends with a period or colon. See the example in the entry **legend.**

When a figure number precedes a caption, a period or colon follows the number. See the preceding examples.

A caption alone with or without a figure number and without a legend usually has no ending period. See the preceding examples.

cardinal number A **number** used in counting, as in *1, 6,* or *17.* Compare with **ordinal number.**

case The relation of a **noun** or **pronoun** to other words in a sentence denoted by one of three cases. See **nominative case, objective case,** and **possessive case** for examples.

case binding See **binding.**

case fractions See **fractions.**

cases, legal See **legal cases.**

castoff An accurate character count of a **manuscript,** usually prepared by a production department or **compositor,** to determine the number of pages that the book will have when typeset as well as to determine other matters, such as width of line and number of lines per page. The process of casting off, or casting up, is also known as *copyfitting*.

A common method of copyfitting is to divide the estimated total character count by the number of characters per **pica** for the selected **typeface** and type size. This step projects the number of picas for the document.

The next step is to divide the total character count by the number of picas in a typeset line. This step indicates the total number of typeset lines.

The final step is to divide the total number of characters by the number of lines of type per page. This operation forecasts the number of printed pages the manuscript will provide.

Since different elements in a book (**tables, notes,** and so on) are often set in different type sizes, a designer must know not only the total character count but also the count for each element. This information is used in selecting a typeface, sizes of type for each element, size of the type page, and other matters. All of this information affects the cost of production and the pricing of the finished product.

Cataloging in Publication (CIP) The Library of Congress cataloging data, usually printed on the **copyright page** of a book. The data are summarized on the Library of Congress's catalog card and commonly include the name of the author, the title of the book, any special material the book includes, a list of the main part titles, the catalog number, and the **International Standard Book Number (ISBN).**

The CIP data can be obtained from the Library of Congress by sending the library the book title, the **contents page,** the International Standard Book Number (ISBN), and a set of proofs or enough other material for the library to use in classifying the book.

catchphrase A **blend word** formed by combining **catchword** and **phrase;** a phrase or **clause** that catches attention and is widely repeated, especially one that is used as a slogan (see **mottoes and slogans**) for a group or movement:

Read my lips.
Laugh [*or* Cry] all the way to the bank.

catchword In general usage, a memorable name or other word or words that catch attention and are widely repeated, such as *politically correct.* See also **catchphrase.**

In publishing (reference works), a headword, guideword, or **running head,** usually printed at the top of a page to indicate the first or last entry or article on that page.

In library science, a **keyword** in a title, **head(ing),** or text used in indexing and as a guide to locating certain information.

CD-ROM A compact optical disk with read-only memory on which large reference works, software programs, and other text or audio material are stored. Writers and editors with computers that have a CD-ROM drive can access vast electronic reference libraries consisting of encyclopedias, dictionaries, directories, and other useful databases.

cedilla See **diacritical marks.**

Celsius/Fahrenheit The **adjectives** *Celsius* and *Fahrenheit* both refer to a type of temperature scale. *Celsius* is the international name for *centigrade,* a scale that has largely replaced the Fahrenheit scale worldwide.

The *Celsius* scale (after Anders Celsius) registers the freezing point of water as 0 degrees and the boiling point as 100 degrees. Therefore, the scale is divided into 100 equal parts between 0 and 100 degrees.

The *Fahrenheit* scale (after Gabriel Daniel Fahrenheit) registers the freezing point of water as 32 degrees and the boiling point as 212 degrees. Therefore, the scale is divided into 180 equal parts between 32 and 212 degrees.

Follow these formulas to convert from Celsius to Fahrenheit or vice versa:

$$°C = (°F - 32)/1.8$$
$$°F = (°C \times 1.8) + 32$$

censer/censor/censure Although these three terms have different meanings and are used as different **parts of speech,** they are sometimes confused because they look and sound similar. The **noun** *censer*, which is sometimes used incorrectly when *censor* is intended, refers to a vessel used for burning incense:

> The *censer* was decorated with the head of a dragon.

The noun *censor,* which is sometimes used incorrectly when *censure* is intended, refers to someone who examines books and other material before they are released to remove or suppress anything objectionable. In the more widely used **verb** form, *censor* means to examine and remove or suppress:

> He serves as a *censor* [noun] for the political journal.
> Prison authorities *censor* [verb] the mail of inmates.

The noun *censure,* which is sometimes used incorrectly when *censor* is intended, means an expression of strong disapproval or a rebuke. In the more widely used verb form, *censure* means to criticize severely or blame:

> She received the *censure* [noun] within an hour of her
>   provocative speech.
> The society will *censure* [verb] the unruly member.

centigrade See **Celsius/Fahrenheit.**

centuries Spell out and **lowercase** general references to centuries. In titles, however, follow the style of the publisher in matters of capitalization, punctuation, and the use of **numerals** or words:

> The *twenty-first century* will be a time of great techno-
>   logical advancement.
> *The Twentieth Century Dictionary of Proverbs* or *The
>   20th Century Dictionary of Proverbs*

See also **decades** and **eras.**

ceremonial/ceremonious *Ceremonial* is the more widely used of these two **adjectives** and is sometimes used incorrectly when *ceremonious* should be used. *Ceremonial* means concerning ritual or ceremony, especially in regard to occasions:

The president and the first lady paid a *ceremonial* visit
to Spain.

The priest put on the *ceremonial* robes.

Ceremonious primarily means observing or having a
fondness for ritual, ceremony, or formal etiquette:

She always displays a *ceremonious* politeness.

The butler greeted us with *ceremonious* reserve.

Less commonly, *ceremonious* shares the meaning of *ceremonial* as being characterized by ritual or ceremony but
more in a habitual rather than official sense:

Each day the school guard went through the *ceremonious* act of putting on his uniform.

The confusion in usage is understandable since both
terms are concerned with ritual and ceremony. However,
ceremonial is usually a safe choice when an act of formal
ritualistic training or an official occasion is involved. *Ceremonious* is usually a safe choice in situations involving a
precise, fussy attitude or demeanor.

cf. See **footnotes** and **notes.**

chair/chairperson The **nouns** *chair* and *chairperson* are
synonyms referring to the presiding officer at a meeting or
the head of an organized group or entity. *Chair* also refers
to a seat, office, or position of authority.

At one time the term *chairman* was used in reference to
both male and female presiding officers. In an attempt to
avoid sexism (see **bias**) this usage gave way to *chairman*
and *chairwoman* and finally to the neuter *chairperson*. This
last term has recently been shortened to *chair,* although
both *chair* and *chairperson* are acceptable and widely used.
The original term *chairman* still persists in some corporations as the traditional term *chairman of the board.*

change See **alter/change.**

chapters No firm rule exists for the number of chapters
that a work should have or for the size of a chapter. Most

book-length works are organized so that major topics form the basis of individual chapters.

The titles of chapters should indicate chapter content and should be as short and concise as possible. Prospective readers frequently scan the titles on the **contents page** to determine whether a work is of interest to them.

Chapter titles are listed in **roman type** without quotation marks on chapter opening pages and on the contents page. However, they are enclosed in quotation marks in citations.

The first chapter begins on a **recto** page and each succeeding chapter on a new **verso** or recto page. A chapter opening page has a drop (bottom-of-page) folio but no **running head.** Chapters may or may not be numbered, and titles may or may not be followed by subtitles:

The Editorial Function

4   The Editorial Function
     in Desktop Publishing

4   Desktop Publishing (*title*)
     Disk Preparation and Editing (*subtitle*)

Periods after numbers and colons between titles and subtitles are often omitted, as illustrated in the previous examples. Periods or other end-of-line punctuation, except for an essential exclamation point, should also be avoided in display titles.

character count See **castoff.**

charts See **graphics.**

chemical names and symbols The official names of chemical elements are abbreviated in one to three letters, with the first letter capitalized and no space or punctuation between the letters. Names and abbreviations are both set in **roman type:**

Symbol	*Name*
Au	gold
Bi	bismuth
C	carbon

Fe	iron
H	hydrogen
Na	sodium
O	oxygen
Zr	zirconium

The number of atoms in a molecule is set as a **subscript** after the symbol:

H_2O

By international agreement the *mass number* (sum of the number of neutrons and protons in an atomic nucleus) is often set as a **superscript** before the symbol:

^{235}U (international style)
U^{235} (traditional style)
U-235 *or* uranium 235 (alternative style)

chronology, list of When a reader must deal with many dates, events, and names, or when the sequence of events covered in the text is not clear, a chronological list of dates and events is helpful. A list of chronology may be placed immediately before or after the text and may be set up in any way that is practical for the amount of data.

In a common arrangement, dates are given in one column and events in a second column. The dates may consist of months, days, and years; months and years; or years only:

1498   Vasco da Gama reaches India.

1506   Explorer Christopher Columbus dies on May 20 in Valladolid, Spain.

chronology systems See **abbreviations of time and days.**

churches See **religious groups.**

circumflex See **diacritical marks.**

circumlocution A roundabout expression; the use of unnecessarily wordy, indirect, or evasive language:

The company had a *negative sales outcome* [a loss] last year.

This type of undesirable language, also called *periphrasis,* is obscure and unclear and tends to sound pompous and ostentatious.

See also **euphemism** and **pompous language.**

citations See **author-date citations, bibliography, endnotes, footnotes, notes,** and **reference list.**

citations, legal See **legal citations.**

class, socioeconomic See **socioeconomic groups.**

classic/classical In certain contexts, the **adjectives** *classic* and *classical* can be used interchangeably. However, their principal meanings differ. *Classic* is a broader term and primarily means belonging or pertaining to the highest, best-known, or most excellent of a kind or conforming to established standards:

His case is a *classic* example of back-door jurisprudence.

Classical primarily means characterized by the art, architecture, and literature of ancient Greece and Rome or music in an educated European tradition, such as symphony and opera:

William is a *classical* scholar and is especially well versed in ancient Greek literature.

In secondary senses, *classical* also means well known or classic, and *classic* also means of or relating to the ancient Greeks and Romans.

clause A group of words containing a **subject** and a **predicate** found in a **complex sentence** or a **compound sentence:**

We know we've gone beyond the deadline, but *we hope to finish the rest of the work today.*

See **dependent clause, independent clause, nonrestrictive element,** and **restrictive element** for examples.

clause, dangling See **dangling subordinate clause.**

cliche A trite, overused, and often vague or wordy expression. Although many cliches originated as proverbs that represented basic truths, they lost their freshness and impact through repeated use. Most of them now sound dull and unimaginative. In addition, readers in other countries who tend to translate everything literally may be puzzled by sayings such as *fly in the face of* (defy the odds).

However, not everyone objects to cliches. Some believe these expressions are colorful additions to our language and should be recognized for their historical value as a key to the wisdom of previous generations and other cultures. Nevertheless, because the bad points of cliches generally outweigh the good points, writers should avoid expressions such as the following in most writing and substitute clear, precise language:

> **to cross that bridge when one comes to it** To wait as long as possible or until it is necessary to make a decision or deal with a problem.
>
> **the die is cast** The decision has been made and can't or won't be reversed.
>
> **to lay one's cards on the table** To be candid or to reveal what you believe, have, or want.
>
> **to pay through the nose** To pay an exorbitant price.
>
> **to put all one's eggs in one basket** To risk everything on one venture.
>
> **to put on the back burner** To postpone something or hold it in reserve.
>
> **to split hairs** To argue over fine points or trifling matters.

client See **benefactor/client/customer/patron.**

clip art Ready-made electronic or printed art that is in the **public domain** and can be used without permission. Books and computer disks with clip art can be purchased both individually and by subscription. However, a user may be required to limit the number of pieces drawn from any one clip-art book or disk for use in a particular document.

With the right equipment, printed art can be scanned into a document being prepared, or electronic art stored on disk can be copied into the document. Once it is in the computer, a skilled user may be able to alter or manipulate the image to make it more suitable for the user's document.

clipped word A word with either the beginning or end deleted but treated as a complete word:

> phone (tele*phone*)
> dorm (*dorm*itory)
> lab (*lab*oratory)

Since a clipped word is not a true abbreviation, such as *admin.* (*administration*), but rather is a real word in itself, no punctuation is used:

> ad (*not* ad.)

A clipped word should not be confused with a shortened form of spelling:

> nite (night)

Although regularly used clipped words, such as *memo* (*memorandum*), are acceptable in general, informal writing, shortened forms of spelling, such as *thru* (*through*), are not acceptable in any writing. They should be used only as a form of shorthand for private activities, as in note taking.

cognate Related in origin, such as a word in one language being related to another word in a different language; two or more languages that have common ancestors. For example, the English word *mother* and the German word *Mutter* are cognates, and both the English language and the Low and High German languages have a common Germanic ancestry.

cognitive meaning See **connotation/denotation**.

coinage The invention of a new word or **phrase** (see **neologism**); the word or phrase that is coined. Coinages may be formed by adding **prefixes** or **suffixes** to existing words:

*retro*virus

They may also be formed by combining two or more words, as in a **blend word** or a **compound term:**

teleconference
day bed

Some coinages are new meanings for old terms: a relatively new meaning for *bit* is binary digit (traditionally, *bit* meant a small amount or a pointed tool). Other coinages are not only new meanings but are also newly created words, many of which began as **slang** or **jargon:**

digerati (the highly computer literate)

cold stamping See **embossing.**

collaboration Working in cooperation with someone, as with two or more people writing a book together. A **joint work** prepared by two or only a few coauthors may resemble the work of and be handled the same as the work of a single author. In such a work the authors usually share the **copyright.**

Preparation procedures may differ in a multiauthor work in which there are numerous authors. Each person may contribute a chapter and be listed on the opening page of that chapter as the author. Although an individual contributor to a multiauthor work may hold the copyright on his or her own contribution, the copyright for the full **collective work** is usually in the name of the editor or publisher.

When there are many contributors, only the editor is listed on the **title page;** the various authors are often listed separately on a contributors page. See **contributors, list of.**

When there are only two or a few coauthors, they will reach an agreement among themselves concerning the division of labor and split of royalties, the order in which names are listed on the title page, and so on. In citations to the work, the authors should be listed in the same order in which they are listed on the title page.

If only an editor is listed on the title page, the citation should give only the name of the editor, not all the names of individual contributors. However, if the citation is to a contributor's chapter, the name of the author of that chapter should be stated. See **notes** and **bibliography** for examples of a citation to a multiauthor work and its editor and a citation to a contributor's chapter in such a work.

collective noun A **noun** that is singular in form but denotes a class or group of people or things. For example:

congregation	herd
crew	jury
family	multitude
group	team

A collective noun may take either a singular or plural **verb** depending on the meaning. If the noun refers to the group as a single unit, it takes a singular verb. If it refers to the separate people or objects in the unit, it takes a plural verb:

The *committee* [single unit] *is* large.
The *committee* [members] *disagree* about the proposed amendment.

collective work An **anthology** or other collection of individual pieces. In the absence of any transfer of **rights** to the publisher, the author of each contribution continues to hold the rights to his or her piece. See **copyright.** However, the publisher has the right to include the contribution in the collective work.

When a collective work consists of or includes individual pieces that were previously published and copyrighted, the editor will not reword or revise the copyrighted material. However, the editor will edit in the usual manner any material that has never been edited or published. See **copyediting** and **editing.** See also **symposium volume.**

collocation The common association or habitual occurrence together of certain words and usually in a certain order:

to and *fro*
cats and *dogs*

spick and *span*
innocent bystander
cautiously optimistic

colloquial English The **vernacular** form of English; informal, everyday speech, including **slang:**

We're gonna go now.
You got the car keys?

Since the term *colloquial English* has a disparaging connotation (see **connotation/denotation**), the term *informal English* is preferred by many language authorities.

colon (:) The colon has many uses including the following:

After a word or words that introduce a **list** or other special material—The book has three main divisions: front matter, text, and back matter. (Do not use a colon to introduce a list after a form of the **verb** *to be*—*not* The main divisions of the book are: . . .)

To indicate a pause between two closely associated sentences. The first word of the second sentence may or may not be capitalized, as preferred—The article is meant to accomplish several things: Its main purpose is to stimulate further thought about the rise of Eastern philosophy; another purpose is to contrast Eastern and Western philosophy.

After the city/state in book citations: Samuel Hart, *Book Publishing* (Nashville: The New Religion Press, 1998).

After the date in certain periodical citations: Betsy Martell, ''Writing Better E-Mail,'' *Internet Communication* 87, no. 3 (1998): 13–17.

Between the verse and chapter in biblical citations: Ruth 3:2.

After the salutation in a business letter: Dear Ms. Snowden:.

After the hour in clock time: 10:35 P.M.

Between the numbers in a ratio: 2:1.

colophon A publisher's emblem or other device placed on the **title page;** an inscription, now seldom used, that is added to the last page of a specially designed book giving the facts of publication (**design, typography,** and so on).

color proof Also called *overlay proof;* a final-stage pre-press proof in which transparent overlays are used to approximate the various colors that will be printed. A color proof is used primarily to check the position of the overlays, alignment of colors, and so on rather than to evaluate color quality.

Since this type of proof cannot be cut and folded like a **blueprint** (negative proof), it shows only one side. Therefore, a blueprint is also needed to make a final check of the document before it is printed.

columns Text, **tables,** and **illustrations** may be set in as many columns as a page width will accommodate but with an allowance for sufficient space between columns, such as one **pica** space. For example, if a two-column type page is twenty-nine picas wide and the space between the columns is one pica, each column will be fourteen picas wide.

Reference works and certain other books are commonly set in a double-column **format.** Two columns will often allow for more words per page. For example, because double-column lines are shorter than single-column lines, smaller type and less **leading** between lines may be used without adversely affecting readability.

comb binding See **binding.**

combining form A **linguistic** base, or part of a word, that when added to another combining form or to a complete other word will create a new word:

biography (bio + graphy)
electromagnet (electro + magnet)
telescope (tele + scope)

Often a connecting **vowel,** such as *o* or *i,* is needed to link the two parts:

bar*o*meter
hort*i*culture

See also **prefix** and **suffix.**

comma (,) The comma has many uses including the following:

To separate sentences, except very short ones, joined by a **conjunction:** The conference is scheduled for the first of the month, but it will have to be canceled if registrations don't increase.

To set off a **nonrestrictive element** that could be omitted: Our new car, which I love, gets better mileage than our old one.

To set off parenthetical or transitional words: In addition, the workbook is free with an order of $30 or more.

To follow introductory words, except for very short words such as *thus,* and after words ending in *-ly:* Coincidentally, that's where I went to college.

To set off an **appositive:** The head of purchasing, Mr. Davis, is retiring next month.

To set off direct quotations: "That may be true," she said, "but it isn't necessarily logical."

To indicate the omission of words: Her boss is from Buffalo, New York; her husband, from Syracuse.

To separate words in a series: Remember to pack your computer disks, disk labels, and disk mailers.

Before *Inc., Jr.,* and *Sr.,* when the abbreviation is part of the company's or person's preferred style: ABC Company, Inc.; John Ellis, Sr.

To enclose a state when both city and state are given: His office is in Lexington, Kentucky, although he travels most of the time.

To enclose the year following a date that includes both month and day: I began working here on March 3, 1990, after moving from Mobile.

To separate thousands in number amounts: $15,980.

comma fault Also called *comma splice;* the incorrect connection of two **independent clauses** with a **comma** instead of a **conjunction,** such as *and* or *but:*

We had to drive thirty miles in blinding snow, [but] we made it without any problems.

comma splice See **comma fault.**

common/mutual/reciprocal Two of these three **adjectives**—*common* and *mutual*—are often used interchangeably, although they have distinct meanings. *Reciprocal* is sometimes substituted for *mutual,* although those two words also do not always mean the same thing.

Common means shared equally by two or more people and is the best choice in reference to many, especially the community as a whole:

The residents had a *common* goal—to reduce crime by 50 percent in the next year.

Mutual also means possessed in common. In particular, it is the best choice in reference to positive or negative relationships in which something is done to or felt by two persons toward each other:

Harry and Adam share a *mutual* dislike.

Reciprocal means interchanged, given, or owed to each other. It is the best choice in reference to things, especially in regard to something positive that is exchanged:

Heads of the three countries signed a *reciprocal* agreement to exchange technology and promote trade.

Although *mutual* could be used in the preceding example, *reciprocal* suggests an equal exchange. *Mutual* would
be more suitable to describe the similar feelings of the national leaders about the agreement:

> The heads of state had a *mutual* interest in signing the
> *reciprocal* agreement.

In spite of the different shades of meaning or emphasis,
writers continue to use the terms interchangeably, especially the terms *common/mutual* and *mutual/reciprocal*.
Some language authorities, therefore, expect traditional ob-
jections to such loose interchangeability to subside.

common noun One of two main types of **nouns,** the other
being the **proper noun.** A *common noun* is a word that
designates a class or group of objects, ideas, or things:

company	politics
ship	rehabilitation
woman	creativity
river	success

Unlike a proper noun, a common noun is not capitalized.

comp A **clipped word** meaning **compositor;** the person or
organization responsible for setting **manuscript** copy into
typeset form; a short version of *comprehensive layout,* a
designer's accurate drawing of what a printed piece will
look like including the position of text and **illustrations,**
page and type size, and other matters that affect appearance.
Once prepared manually, most page design is now prepared
using a computer and color printer.

company names See **names, organization.**

comparative degree See **comparison of adjectives** and
comparison of adverbs.

compare/contrast The **verbs** *compare* and *contrast* are often confused because both pertain to examining something.
However, the two are used in different ways. *Compare* can
be used when you mean examine for similarity or differ-

ence but is primarily used with similarities. When one is examining like things, *compare* is followed by *with*. When one is examining unlike things, *to* is used:

> We will *compare* her score *with* his.
> "You can *compare* a house *to* a car," he said, "but that wouldn't be very helpful."

Contrast should be used to show only differences, and the verb *contrast* is usually followed by *with:*

> Modern jetliners *contrast* markedly *with* the early planes designed by pioneers in aircraft technology.

comparison of adjectives An **adjective** has three degrees of comparison: positive, comparative, and superlative. By changing the form of the *positive degree* of many adjectives, one can compare two things (*comparative degree*) or more than two things (*superlative degree*).

The comparative degree of a word such as *tall* or *important* can be formed by adding the ending *-er* (*taller*) or the word *more* (*more important*). The superlative degree can be formed by adding the ending *-est* (*tallest*) or the word *most* (*most important*). The comparative and superlative degrees of other adjectives must be formed by using different words: *many* (positive), *more* (comparative), *most* (superlative):

> *Positive:* The copy image of my fax machine is *sharp.*
> *Comparative:* The copy image of my fax machine is *sharper* than his.
> *Superlative:* The copy image of my fax machine is the *sharpest* of the three in our office.

> *Positive:* My fax machine is *temperamental.*
> *Comparative:* My fax machine is *more* temperamental than his.
> *Superlative:* My fax machine is the *most* temperamental of the three in our office.

Positive: He has *many* ideas.
Comparative: He has *more* ideas than she does.
Superlative: He has the *most* ideas of all the students.

However, not all adjectives can be compared. Those that can't be compared include numerals (*one* person); the articles *a, an,* and *the* (*the* boy); and those that are absolute (*unlimited* power). See **absolute word** for additional examples. See also **comparison of adverbs.**

comparison of adverbs An **adverb** has three degrees of comparison: positive, comparative, and superlative. By changing the form of the *positive degree* of some adverbs, one can compare two things (*comparative degree*) or more than two things (*superlative degree*).

The comparative degree of a word such as *near* or *abruptly* can be formed by adding the ending *-er* (*nearer*) or the word *more* (*more abruptly*). The superlative degree can be formed by adding the ending *-est* (*nearest*) or the word *most* (*most abruptly*). The comparative and superlative degrees of other adverbs must be formed by using different words: *well* (positive), *better* (comparative), *best* (superlative):

Positive: He arrived *late.*
Comparative: He arrived *later* than she did.
Superlative: He arrived the *latest* of the three people.

Positive: He wrote *carefully.*
Comparative: He wrote *more carefully* than she did.
Superlative: He wrote the *most carefully* of the three people.

Positive: My machine works *well.*
Comparative: My machine works *better* than her machine.
Superlative: My machine works the *best* of all three machines.

Some adverbs cannot be used in comparisons and must be used only in the positive form. Examples are *before, here, now, very,* and *whenever.*

See also **comparison of adjectives.**

compass directions Points of the compass, such as *northwest,* are not abbreviated in running text but may be abbreviated in certain specialized copy, such as in real estate descriptions:

N, NE, NNE, NNW (*or* N., N.E., N.N.E., N.N.W.)

Compass points following a street name and number in mailing addresses are abbreviated in a similar way, with no periods or spaces between letters:

1800 Joseph Street, SW

compendium (plural, *compendiums* or *compendia*) An **abstract** or short summary of a full text. It may be prepared as a separate document or as part of a large document, such as a large report. When it is part of a report, the more common term is *abstract* or *summary.*

compilation Any work, such as an encyclopedia, an **anthology,** or a report, that is compiled or composed of material drawn from several sources. On the **title page** and in citations, the compiler's name is treated the same as that of an editor:

Alfred K. Lawrence, comp. *Essays on Social Unrest in Modern Times.* Minneapolis: Social Policies Publications, 1989.

complacent/complaisant The principal meanings of these two **adjectives** are very different, but the terms are sometimes confused because they look and sound similar. *Complacent* primarily means self-satisfied or calmly unconcerned:

She may be *complacent,* but the rest of us are worried that we may lose our jobs.

Complaisant primarily means being politely deferential or showing a desire to please:

Have you noticed how *complaisant* she is around her boss now that it's time for salary reviews?

In addition to being confused because they look and sound similar, the terms also may be confused because a secondary meaning of *complacent* is the same as one of the primary meanings of *complaisant*—eager to please. Therefore, to keep the two terms apart, it's helpful to focus on the primary meanings of each.

complaisant See **complacent/complaisant.**

complement In a narrow sense, a word, **phrase,** or **clause** used after a **verb** in the **predicate** of a **sentence** that completes the meaning of the sentence:

Programmers write [verb] *programs* [word complement].
To help others is [verb] *to help yourself* [phrase complement].
The assistant hoped [verb] *that he would be promoted* [clause complement].

In a broad sense, a word, phrase, or clause used to complete the meaning of any other word, such as an **adjective:**

She is [verb] happy [adjective] *that the work is done* [complement].

See also **subject complement.**

complementary/complimentary/supplementary   These three **adjectives** have different meanings, but the first two are nevertheless easily confused. The pronunciation of *complementary* and *complimentary* are the same, and except for one letter, the spelling is the same. Also, *complementary* and *supplementary* have closely related though slightly different shades of meaning and therefore are sometimes used interchangeably.

Complementary means completing something or serving to bring something to completion or perfection:

Singing and dancing have always been *complementary* forms of entertainment.

Complimentary means serving to express or resemble praise, admiration, or congratulations. It also describes something given free or as a favor:

The new play received *complimentary* reviews.
Ned got *complimentary* tickets to the game.

Supplementary describes an addition that makes up a deficiency or strengthens the whole:

The herbs were *supplementary* to his usual nutritious diet of fruits, vegetables, and whole grains.

Although *supplementary* and *complementary* both involve a type of addition, *complementary* often stresses an addition that perfects or completes something previously or otherwise incomplete—an *essential* addition. For example, a song-and-dance act that consists of singing only is obviously incomplete. The dancing aspect is an *essential* addition.

Supplementary stresses not so much that an addition is *essential* or that without it something is incomplete; rather, it stresses that something, usually beneficial, could be or has been added, and it may have been added to something that is already whole or sufficient in itself. A diet may be technically complete, for example, but it could be enhanced with an addition.

complimentary See **complementary/complimentary/supplementary.**

complete predicate See **predicate.**

complete subject See **subject.**

complex sentence A **sentence** that consists of one main **independent clause** and one or more **dependent clauses:**

She was the employee of the year [independent clause] *who was recognized for her initiative* [first dependent clause] and *who was honored at the annual dinner* [second dependent clause].

Compare with **simple sentence.**

compose/comprise The **verbs** *compose* and *comprise* are often confused, although the difference in meaning is clear. *Compose* means to form or make up the constituent parts of something by combining:

The corporation is *composed* of three subsidiaries.

Therefore, the parts (three subsidiaries) *compose* (make up) the whole (the corporation).
Comprise means to include or contain:

The corporation *comprises* three subsidiaries.

Therefore, the whole (the corporation) *comprises* (includes) the parts (three subsidiaries).

compositor Also called *typesetter* or *operator;* a person, department, or organization responsible for setting type. See **typesetting.**

compound, permanent See **compound terms.**

compound, temporary See **compound terms.**

compound-complex sentence A **sentence** that consists of two or more **independent clauses** plus one or more **dependent clauses:**

We must renew our commitment [first independent clause], and we must do it soon [second independent clause], because when too much time lapses [dependent clause], enthusiasm wanes [third independent clause].

Compare with **complex sentence** and **compound sentence.**

compound phrase Two or more **phrases** not containing a **subject** and **predicate** that are connected by a **conjunction,** such as *and* or *but:*

They began the tour *after a disappointing year* but *with great expectations.*

compound preposition See **prepositional phrase.**

compound sentence A **sentence** consisting of two or more **independent clauses,** or **simple sentences,** that are joined by a **semicolon, conjunction,** or **conjunctive adverb:**

A political life is no longer within everyone's financial reach [first independent clause]; *however,* [semicolon followed by conjunctive adverb] dedicated public servants often find another way to serve their community and society in general [second independent clause].

Compare with **complex sentence** and **compound-complex sentence.**

compound terms A word formed by combining two or more other words. See **coinage.** The new term may be written as one word, hyphenated, or written as individual words:

loudspeaker
editor-in-chief
post office

Some terms are *temporary compounds* formed only for a particular sentence or usage. Others are *permanent compounds,* words that are always used together to designate a particular object, idea, or something else:

The *high-level* [temporary compound] talks resumed.
The *word processing* [permanent compound] department is closed for the holiday.

Plurals of compound terms are formed by adding *s* to the most important word:

high schools
fathers-in-law

Possessives are indicated by adding an **apostrophe** and *s* to the last word:

ex-senator's award
notebook's cover

A broad view of compound terms also includes words created with **combining forms.** See **prefix** and **suffix** for additional examples:

agriculture
preexisting

The more common type of compound is formed by combining two or more complete, independent words:

all-important (*adj.*)
attorney general (*n.*)
by-product (*n.*)
catchword (*n.*)
double-check (*vb.*)
everybody (*pron.*)
moreover (*adv.*)
proofread (*vb.*)
stock market (*n.*)

comprehensive layout See **comp.**

comprise See **compose/comprise.**

computer terms Generally, capitalize the official names of hardware (equipment) and software (computer programs), and **lowercase** general terms such as *program*. Also, write names that represent **acronyms** in all capital letters. However, writers, manufacturers, and other suppliers may differ in the way they handle terms in documentation and programming languages. Therefore, follow the style of your employer or publisher:

Macintosh, Mac, the personal computer
COBOL (*C*ommon *B*usiness *O*riented *L*anguage)

Microsoft Word, the word processing program
software, freeware, groupware
on-line (*or* online)
virtual reality
video RAM (VRAM)
Dialog, the database
Game Boy, the game

See also **abbreviations in technical and scientific works** and **Internet terms.**

conciseness Clear, succinct writing is a major objective of skilled writers and editors. Although **wordiness** may be intentional, such as in creating realistic dialogue for a novel, conciseness is usually a virtue in nonfiction or business material.

However, conciseness is rarely a virtue when text is tightened so much that it becomes terse and choppy or that it lacks an essential color or descriptive quality. For example, qualifying **adjectives,** such as *exciting* or *round,* may be needed to help readers imagine or understand a message. Also, **transition** words, such as *in addition* or *moreover,* are needed to help one thought, sentence, or paragraph slide easily into another.

Concise writing may or may not be brief. For clarity or other reasons it is sometimes necessary to elaborate on a topic. But even if additional detail is necessary or desirable, wordiness in expressing the added information is not.

To encourage conciseness in a work, use the **active voice,** which usually involves fewer words than the **passive voice:**

He *said* that the market may rally [active voice].
It *has been said* that a rally in the market may be forthcoming [passive voice].

Eliminate unnecessary words and phrases:

In connection with the request in your most recent letter [unnecessary introductory **phrase**], we will be happy to send the information you requested.

Omit unnecessary **intensifiers:**

quite right
very useful
rather new

Adopt a positive **tone,** which often involves fewer words:

Not: We will be unable to ship your order until May 5.
Better: We will ship your order on May 5.

Choose simple statements over complex ones:

Not: The current or conventional medical treatments do not alleviate the breathing difficulties of patients who are experiencing bronchial-type problems.
Better: Conventional treatments do not help bronchial patients breathe easier.

Avoid unnecessary repetition:

Sales were highest in *the year of* 1998.

See also **redundancy** and **wordiness** for further examples.

conclusion Depending on the document, a conclusion may be as brief as one sentence or paragraph or as long as a separate chapter following the last of the other text chapters. It may be numbered or unnumbered and may begin on either a **verso** or **recto** page.

The conclusion provides an opportunity to summarize the main points in the text; make a final judgment, statement, or decision about the topic and the research; comment on the implications of the study; recommend further steps to take; and briefly refer to or tie in to the opening so that the text is united from beginning to end.

concrete noun A **noun** that denotes an observable or touchable person or thing; the opposite of an **abstract noun:**

administrator
condominium

Among the concrete nouns are count nouns and mass nouns. A *count noun* denotes something that can be counted (two *buildings*). A *mass noun* denotes something that cannot be counted (*gasoline*).

conferences and meetings Capitalize the official names of conferences and meetings, but **lowercase** general references to a conference or meeting:

> Twenty-third Annual Meeting of the National Geography Union, the union's annual meeting
> Republican National Convention, the convention

Enclose a topical conference theme or title in **quotation marks:**

> ''Technology Beyond the Millennium,'' the conference theme

In **bibliographies, notes,** and **reference lists,** treat the papers presented at conferences and meetings like chapters in a book, as in the following bibliography entry:

> Paulson, H. M. ''Medical Technology Today.'' Paper presented at the quarterly meeting of the International Computer Center, Indianapolis, Ind., March 1998.

conflicts See **wars and conflicts.**

conjunction One of the eight **parts of speech;** a word that connects or shows the relation between other words, **phrases, clauses,** and **sentences:**

> We won the contest, *although* none of us expected it.

See **connective, coordinating conjunction, correlative conjunction,** and **subordinating conjunction.**

conjunctive adverb Also called *relative adverb;* a word that functions as both a **conjunction** and an **adverb:**

> accordingly   since

besides	subsequently
furthermore	then
however	thus
indeed	whenever
moreover	where

As an adverb, a conjunctive adverb modifies the **clause** it introduces, and as a conjunction, it joins two **independent clauses:**

However, everyone should be careful.

The deadline for submitting all papers for the book is May 7; *therefore,* we need to schedule reviews to begin by May 12.

When a **coordinating conjunction,** such as *and,* joins two sentences, the word *and* is usually preceded by a **comma.** When a conjunctive adverb, such as *therefore,* links the sentences, it is usually preceded by a semicolon as illustrated in the preceding example.

connective A word or words that connect other words, **phrases,** or **clauses.** Among the major connectives are **conjunctions,** such as *and, but, nor,* and *or;* **prepositions,** such as *at, by, for,* and *to;* **relative pronouns,** such as *who, which, what,* and *that;* and **conjunctive adverbs,** such as *hence, when, where,* and *why.*

connotation/denotation Broadly, the **nouns** *connotation* and *denotation* both refer to a meaning attributed to a word. However, they cannot be used interchangeably because each refers to a different type of meaning.

Connotation, also known as *affective meaning,* is a meaning suggested by or associated with a word or thing but not its primary meaning. For example, the word *cat* has various *connotations,* such as agility, independence, and hunter.

Denotation, also known as *cognitive meaning,* is the direct, primary meaning, or the dictionary definition. For example, the denotation of *cat* is a small carnivorous mammal in the family Felidae.

Writers must be on guard against mixing the two meanings improperly. Using connotations can be a valuable technique in many types of writing, such as in creating a fictional scene that a reader can visualize. But in other cases it can be misleading and prejudicial.

Whether or not a writer has negative feelings about a topic, a reader may respond negatively to certain connotations. Therefore, it is important to avoid tainting basic descriptions and definitions with associated meanings and emotions. For example, *cheap* has connotations of shoddiness and low quality, so if those connotations are incorrect or might mislead the reader, the word *inexpensive* is a better choice.

consensus Two problems are common with the use of the **noun** *consensus.* First, it is frequently misspelled as *concensus,* and second, the commonly added words *of opinion* are redundant. The word *consensus* alone means the opinion of a group as a whole or a majority.

Some authorities believe that the term is used broadly to refer to attitudes other than opinions, such as a consensus of beliefs, and that a qualifying phrase such as *of opinion* or *of belief* is therefore necessary for clarity. However, this is usually clear from the context in which *consensus* is used, and when it is, any added phrase such as *of opinion* is therefore redundant.

consonant A speech sound other than a **vowel;** the letter of the alphabet that represents such a sound. In the English alphabet five letters represent vowels (*a, e, i, o,* and *u*), and twenty-one letters represent consonants (*b, c, d, f, g, h, j, k, l, m, n, p, q, r, s, t, v, w, x, y, z*). In the word *band,* therefore, *b, n,* and *d* are consonants.

contact The **verb** *contact* is often used both socially and in business to mean telephone or consult someone. Although it is widely accepted in this sense, the term is vague and to some has a connotation (see **connotation/denotation**) of being forceful or aggressive. To be clear and tactful, it is important to use more precise language—

telephone, fax, write, E-mail, meet at a specific place, stop at the person's office, and so on.

contemptible/contemptuous The **adjectives** *contemptible* and *contemptuous* were once **synonyms,** but that usage is obsolete. *Contemptible* now means deserving of contempt or being despicable:

> A con artist who preys on senior citizens is *contemptible*.

Contemptuous means feeling or showing contempt or being scornful:

> The ruthless dictator is *contemptuous* of charity and kindness.

contents page The table of contents, commonly titled "Contents," usually follows the **copyright page** or **dedication** page, if any. It is frequently the first page in the **front matter** on which a page number is printed: page v if there is no dedication page or page vi if a dedication page is included.

A contents page lists the titles and beginning page numbers of each part, chapter, or other main section or division in the book (see **book parts**), including the main sections in the front matter and **back matter.** Page numbers for **part pages** may be omitted if a chapter immediately follows a part page. Subheads within a chapter may or may not be included on the contents page:

The name of the author of each chapter is usually included in a multiauthor work. See **anthology, collaboration,** and **collective work.** On the contents page the name is often set in **italics** following the chapter title:

Elements of Communication, *Joan Kingsley*   1

continually/continuously The **adverbs** *continually* and *continuously* are used interchangeably in a broad sense to mean not interrupted. But the slight difference of meaning in a strict interpretation is useful to a writer who wants to distinguish between something repeated at intervals and something unbroken.

Therefore, *continually* is the better choice to mean repeated or recurring over and over at close intervals. In the following example this usage implies a pause, even if momentary, between each beep:

The beep of the fax signal sounded *continually* for nearly two hours until a connection could be made.

Continuously is the better choice to mean unbroken or continuing without interruption. In the following example this usage implies no pause in an ongoing operation, day and night:

The air conditioner runs *continuously* during the summer.

continuation line A continuation, or continued, line may be needed in certain material that is interrupted by other copy or **illustrations** or in tabular matter (see **table**) when it is necessary to guide the reader to another page. For example, *Continued on next page* (or *on page 4*) may be stated at the foot of one page, and *Table 3—Continued* may be placed at the top of the page where the table continues. Sometimes the phrase is placed in **parentheses** or **brackets:**

[*Continued from page 201*]

Continuation lines are common in a long **index** when an entry on a right-hand page is carried to the next left-hand page. Usually, the main **head(ing)** of the entry is repeated on the next page, followed by the word *continued* in parentheses:

reports (*continued*)
    tone 295
    unnecessary 304
    visuals 361–62

Continuation lines are not needed for the text in a book or other document simply because a figure or table intervenes.

continuously See **continually/continuously.**

contract See **rights.**

contraction A shortened spelling of words or **phrases,** such as *it's* and *can't,* that is used frequently in everyday speech and discriminately in writing. The general rule is that contractions are unacceptable in strictly formal writing, such as in a printed invitation or a formal court paper. But they are widely adopted in business letters and other general writing in which a writer wants to use a readable, relaxed style and avoid a stiff, unfriendly **tone.**

contrast See **compare/contrast.**

contributors, list of When there are too many contributors to list on the **title page** of a multiauthor book, a separate page may be used for their names. A very long list of contributors (exceeding one page) is usually placed at the end of the **front matter** just before the main text or in the **back matter** just before the **index.** A shorter list (one page or less) is usually placed on page ii after the **half-title page.**

The list may be titled "Contributors," "Participants," or any other suitable name. Although an alphabetical list of names is the most common form of arrangement, another type of grouping, such as geographical, may also be used.

Regardless of the arrangement, a contributor's name is not inverted:

Joseph C. Parsons (*not* Parsons, Joseph C.)

A list of contributors is not mandatory since each author's name usually follows the title of his or her contribution on both the **contents page** and on the chapter opening page of the contribution. In addition, an unnumbered **note** is often placed at the foot of the chapter opening page identifying the author and the original source of the contribution, if it was first published elsewhere.

See also **anthology, collaboration,** and **collective work.**

convince/persuade Although authorities still maintain a distinction between the **verbs** *convince* and *persuade,* the two terms are regularly used interchangeably. Those who object to such casual usage follow the traditional rule that *convince* means to use evidence or argument to lead someone to understand or believe something, especially the truth of a statement or proposition. With this definition, *convince* is never used with an **infinitive,** such as *to go:*

She *convinced* her colleagues that the plan will do more harm than good [made them believe her reasoning is correct].

Persuade primarily means to use argument and reasoning to lead someone to act on or make a decision to do something. With this definition, *persuade* may be used with an infinitive:

She *persuaded* her colleagues to go to the meeting [led them to take that action].

Under the traditional rule, therefore, one would *convince* someone of the truth in a statement but would *persuade* someone to act or take certain steps. However, since even respected writers sometimes ignore this rule, the distinction between the terms is likely to disappear over time.

coordinating conjunction Also called *coordinate conjunction;* a **conjunction** that connects two words, **phrases,** or **clauses** of equal order or rank:

> He spoke quickly *but* carefully.
> The market for new technologies is expanding, *and* Jim intends to take advantage of it.

The seven coordinating conjunctions are *and, or, but, yet, for, nor,* and *so.* See also **correlative conjunction** for examples of coordinating conjunctions used in pairs. Compare coordinating conjunctions with **subordinating conjunctions.**

copulative verb See **linking verb.**

copyediting Correcting and preparing a **manuscript** for **typesetting** and **printing.** Publishers commonly have a house **style** that is based on a particular style book and is used by copyeditors in their work.

A copyeditor is primarily concerned with technical matters, or *mechanical editing.* When nontechnical work, or *substantive editing,* is required, it may be handled by another editor. Substantive editing frequently involves rewriting, reorganization, or other major work needed to improve the overall document.

Mechanical editing involves correcting spelling, grammatical, and other technical errors; ensuring that capitalization, punctuation, formatting, treatment of **numbers,** and other such matters are handled consistently; verifying that **cross-references,** text citations, and text references to **tables** and **illustrations** (see **callouts**) are accurate; and generally ensuring that the copy conforms to a **style** acceptable to or required by the publisher.

An editor may do the editing manually on a paper copy or electronically on a computer display screen. The manual marking of corrections and other changes is done directly on the manuscript pages, with **queries** and comments for the author circled in the margins or written on small self-adhesive notes (*flags*). Standard marks are used for both copyediting and **proofreading.** See the examples in the entry **proofreaders' marks.**

After the copyeditor's corrections and changes are approved by the author, they are entered on the disk copy. When the editing is done electronically, a revised printout is given to the author for review.

Codes may be added to the disk by the author or **compositor** for **desktop publishing** and other computer-generated typesetting to designate how various elements of a manuscript, such as chapter titles, are to be set (size of type, position, and so on). Manuscript markup, or **type-marking,** is a separate step to be done after a designer has prepared a **design** for the publication, which will include type specifications, spacing, and other matters affecting appearance.

To keep track of the various elements of style and how the author has handled them or how the publisher wants them to be handled, the copyeditor maintains a **style sheet.** This sheet is used to record the first occurrence of a particular style, such as the style of punctuating an abbreviation. Each new usage can then be checked against that first use to be certain that subsequent uses are consistent.

See also individual entries pertaining to specific types of copy to be edited, such as **equations** or **notes.**

copyfitting See **castoff.**

copyright The legal right to exclusive publication, production, sale, and distribution of an original literary, musical, dramatic, or artistic work. After **rights** have been obtained, they may be retained, sold, given away, or licensed to others for their use. See **licensing of rights.**

Information and forms for registration of copyright are available from the Copyright Office, Library of Congress, Washington, D.C. 20559. A filing fee and copies of the work to be registered must accompany the application form.

Recorded works that have been published since January 1, 1978, are protected until 50 years after the author's or last surviving coauthor's death. The copyright period for earlier works is 28 years from the time of publication or, for some unpublished works, from the time of registration. Copyright on a **work for hire** lasts for 100 years from creation of the work or 75 years from initial publication, whichever is shorter. In all cases, renewals for a second term of protection are handled by the Copyright Office.

Since March 1, 1989, it has not been necessary for a work to bear a copyright notice to be protected. However, including such notice may discourage infringement and may be helpful in case of later legal disputes:

© 1998 by Jennifer Stanton

The phrase *All rights reserved* ensures protection under the Buenos Aires Convention, to which the United States and most Latin American countries belong:

© 1998 by Jennifer Stanton. All rights reserved

One may also spell out or abbreviate the symbol for copyright:

Copyright 1998 by Jennifer Stanton. All rights reserved
Copr. 1998 by Jennifer Stanton. All rights reserved

If renewal has taken place, that fact is also noted:

© 1970 by Jennifer Stanton. © renewed 1998 by Jennifer Stanton. All rights reserved

The usual place for publishing a copyright notice is on the **copyright page** following the **title page.** See the copyright page in the front of this book for an example of wording and placement.

See **public domain** for information about works that have not been registered with the Library of Congress; see **anthology** for information about the publication of previously copyrighted material in a multiauthor work; and see **joint work** for information about copyright ownership of works prepared by more than two authors.

copyright page A page following the **title page** in the **front matter** on which various **copyright** information and publishing facts are printed. The copyright page in this book, for example, includes the book title, publisher, printing history, copyright notice and statement, **International Standard Book Number (ISBN),** and the publisher's address.

correlative conjunction Any of the **coordinating conjunctions** used in pairs. Like a single coordinating conjunction, a correlative conjunction links words, **phrases,** or **independent clauses:**

Neither you *nor* I should take credit for Dave's idea.

The following are the main correlative conjunctions:

although . . . yet
as . . . as
as . . . so
both . . . and
either . . . or
if . . . then
neither . . . nor
not only . . . but also
now . . . now
now . . . then
so . . . as (*or* that)
such . . . as (*or* that)
though . . . yet
whereas . . . therefore
whether . . . or

councils, religious See **religious meetings.**

count noun See **concrete noun** and **half.**

country names See **names, country.**

courts See **judicial bodies.**

cover The cover of a document may be hard or soft and may be attached to the pages in one of several ways. See **binding.** A hardcover book has a cover consisting of heavy cardboard covered with cloth, plastic, or treated paper. It also usually has a loose outside paper cover called a book **jacket.** A softcover book has a cover consisting of heavy but flexible paper coated with varnish, resin, or laminate.

The three main parts of a cover are the front, back, and **spine.** The front cover of a hardcover book may or may not have the book title and the name of the author printed on it. Regardless, the spine has the book title or a short version of it, the name of the author (sometimes last name only), and the name of the publisher (sometimes a shortened name or only an emblem; see **colophon**). The back cover is often blank but occasionally contains the **International Standard Book Number (ISBN).**

Printing usually appears on all three parts of a paperback cover. The front cover has the book title, subtitle (if any), full name of the author, and other information, such as a few succinct selling points. The back cover contains a variety of information, such as biographical data about the author, promotional comments about the book and its contents, and the ISBN and **Bookland EAN bar code.**

The cover design of paperbacks and hardcover book jackets typically contains a special display type, artwork, and color **printing.** The copy for the cover and jacket of both hardcover and paperback books is prepared by the publisher, although the author may supply biographical material and other information about the book's content.

See also **books.**

craft and vessels Capitalize the official names of specific craft and vessels, and set them in **italics.** Set abbreviations that precede the name of a craft or vessel in **roman type:**

Spirit of St. Louis (airplane)
Voyager 2 (spacecraft)
Seacroft (ship)
Sputnik II (satellite)
USS *Victory*

Capitalize designations of class or make, but lowercase general references to types of craft or vessels. Set both designations and general references in roman type:

Boeing 747
Concorde
jetliner
space shuttle

Capitalize the names of trains and space programs, and set them in roman type:

California Zephyr
Project Mars

credible/creditable/credulous   These   three   **adjectives** sound similar but have different primary meanings. *Credible* means believable, plausible, or reliable:

Her story is simply too bizarre to be *credible*.

Creditable also means worthy of belief and in this secondary sense is similar to *credible,* the more common term for being believable. However, *creditable* primarily means deserving of praise:

The hastily assembled cast gave a *creditable* performance.

Credulous means gullible or overly willing to believe:

The politician smiled to himself, realizing that he was addressing a *credulous* audience.

See also **incredible/incredulous.**

credit line   An acknowledgment of the source of artwork or another **illustration** along with the permission that was received to use it in a book or **article.** The wording of credit lines may vary and often follows the required wording of the **copyright** owner. If a credit line follows a **caption** or **legend** or contains full reference data, it ends with a period. If it is a brief line standing alone, the end punctuation is usually omitted:

Courtesy of The Pierce Science Library
From a drawing by Martin Seale Langley for the cover
   of *Ryer's Lost Chronicles,* reprinted by permission of

the author from Nora Anne Kilmer, *Life Along the Nile* (New York: Papyrus Printers, 1960).

Reprinted by permission from J. C. Henderson, Jr., *Maude's Diary* (San Francisco: Seaside Publishers, 1985), 61.

Illustration by Mary Marche for Lila P. Frankel, *The Home World* (London, 1907), 30.

Adapted from M. M. Relatte, *Personal Lives of Politicians,* figure 2.1 [if the full publication data is given elsewhere].

Photograph courtesy of the Branson Steele Corporation

Map by Gerald E. Jenson III

Photo by the author

Credit lines stating the source of others' material are usually given even if the material was not previously copyrighted. Original material, such as an illustration, created by the author of the work being prepared does not require a credit line. If no outside source is given, the material is assumed to be owned or created by the author of the text in which it appears.

creditable See **credible/creditable/credulous.**

credulous See **credible/creditable/credulous.**

creeds See **religious works.**

creole See **Black English.**

critique A critical evaluation, review, commentary, or discussion of a topic, especially of a work of art or literature, such as an art show or play; the process of evaluating, reviewing, commenting on, or discussing the topic or material. To the dismay of many authorities, the term is being used generally to mean a description of or report on virtually anything from a horse race to an Easter egg hunt.

cropping Trimming a photograph or picture to select the most desirable portions and to make it fit in a particular space on the page. Photos often contain detail that is not needed or is not suitable for a particular document. The author, editor, or someone else may then insert crop marks in the margins to designate to the printer the area to be reproduced. A grease pencil is used for this purpose to avoid creasing the surface of the photo.

Those who do the cropping of a photograph or picture must also calculate the correct dimensions. This is important so that the area to be used will correspond proportionately after reduction or enlargement to the dimensions of the space that has been set aside for the illustration. See **scaling** for sample calculations.

cross-reference A reference from one part of a document to another part containing related or useful information; the process of providing the reference. Cross-references may be stated in any way that is suitable for the document and acceptable to the author and the publisher. The following are familiar forms:

See figure 4.6.
See also Chapter 3.
Compare with Table 14.

Cross-references within a sentence that are enclosed in parentheses, as illustrated here (see **parentheses**), begin with a small letter and are not punctuated. When they are placed after another sentence, however, they are often set without parentheses but with ending punctuation the same as a regular sentence, as illustrated here: See **sentence.**

Cross-references may be set in **boldface, italics,** or **caps and small caps.** In this dictionary, for example, the cross-references are boldface except for the words *see, see also,* and *compare,* which are set in the regular text **typeface.**

Two common types of cross-references are used in this dictionary: those that are run in with the text (see the example in the second paragraph of this entry) and those that are set as separate entries. See the numerous examples throughout this dictionary. See also examples of **index** cross-references in that entry.

CRT composition See **typesetting.**

cultivated/cultured The **adjectives** *cultivated* and *cultured* are **synonyms** that mean being educated, polished, and refined:

> She is known and admired throughout the community as being a very *cultivated/cultured* person.

However, some writers prefer to use *cultivated* to stress a person's educated quality and *cultured* to stress a person's elegance and grace as well as his or her knowledge of art and culture.

cultural terms Capitalize cultural movements, styles, schools, and so on if they are derived from **proper nouns. Lowercase** most general terms, especially those with an *-ism* ending, unless it is necessary to distinguish a term from the same word used in a general sense:

> Platonic movement, platonic relationship, Neoplatonism
> Gothic movement, gothic novel
> Epicurean movement, epicurean taste
> Scholastics, Scholasticism
> Stoic, Stoicism
> Romanesque
> romantic, romanticism
> Hellenism
> abstract expressionism
> surrealism
> pop art
> art deco

> See also **historical terms.**

cultured See **cultivated/cultured.**

currency See **money.**

cursive type A **typeface** in the style of handwriting or script in which the letters of a word are joined together rather than set as individual, separate letters. This style is used primarily with special material, such as invitations, but is not used for the main text of books, articles, reports, and similar documents. See also **sans serif** and **serif**.

customer See **benefactor/client/customer/patron**.

D

dangling gerund phrase A **verbal** phrase containing a **gerund** that does not refer to the appropriate **noun** or **pronoun** in the main **clause**:

After clearing my desk, the mail had to be opened.

The gerund **phrase** in that example modifies the noun *mail,* which doesn't make sense—the mail didn't clear the desk. Therefore, the sentence needs to be reworded so that the gerund phrase will modify the appropriate noun or pronoun:

After clearing my desk, I opened the mail.

Or the phrase may be converted to a clause:

After I cleared my desk, I opened the mail.

See **dangling infinitive phrase** and **dangling participial phrase** for examples of other dangling phrases. See also **dangling subordinate clause.**

dangling infinitive phrase A **verbal** phrase, often preceded by *to* and used as a **noun,** an **adjective,** or an **adverb,** that does not refer to the appropriate noun or **pronoun** in the main **clause:**

To become successful, a good education is needed.

The infinitive **phrase** in that example modifies the subject *education,* but education doesn't become successful—

people become successful. Therefore, the sentence needs to be reworded so that the infinitive phrase will refer to a person:

To become successful, one needs a good education.

Or the phrase may be changed to a clause to make the reference clear:

If you want to become successful, you need a good education.

See **dangling gerund phrase** and **dangling participial phrase** for examples of other dangling phrases. See also **dangling subordinate clause.**

dangling modifier See **dangling gerund phrase, dangling infinitive phrase,** and **dangling participial phrase.**

dangling participial phrase A **verbal** phrase containing a **participle** that does not refer to the appropriate **noun** or **pronoun** in the main **clause:**

Looking ahead, my schedule appears flexible.

The participial **phrase** in that example modifies the noun *schedule.* However, people, not schedules, look ahead. Therefore, the sentence needs to be reworded so that the participial phrase will modify the appropriate noun or pronoun:

Looking ahead, I see that my schedule is flexible.

Or the phrase may be converted to a clause:

As I was looking ahead, I could see that my schedule was flexible.

See **dangling gerund phrase** and **dangling infinitive phrase** for examples of other dangling phrases. See also **dangling subordinate clause.**

dangling subordinate clause A **dependent clause** in which the **subject** and **verb** are omitted with the result that the dependent **clause** does not refer to the appropriate **noun** or **pronoun** in the main clause:

While out of work, his company paid him full salary.

The subordinate clause in that example modifies *company,* but the company wasn't out of work. Therefore, the sentence needs to be reworded so that a noun or pronoun in the subordinate clause will correctly refer to the subject in the main clause:

While he was out of work, his company paid him full salary.

Or the clauses may be reversed:

His company paid him full salary *while he was out of work.*

See **dangling gerund phrase, dangling infinitive phrase,** and **dangling participial phrase** for examples of other dangling modifiers.

dash (—) A dash has four principal uses:

To set off parenthetical (see **parentheses**) **phrases** or **clauses:** The Model U5000 copier—also known as the U5000 Personal Copier—will fit on most small tables or cabinets.

To set off words that are repeated for emphasis: You have a friendly, relaxed writing *style—a style* that is inviting and easy to read.

To indicate an abrupt change: We can talk further at lunch on the fourteenth—or is it the fifteenth?

To separate an introductory series of words referred to in the main **clause** that follows the series: Capitalization, punctuation, spelling—these are all important elements of style.

Although the dash can properly be used in all of the situations just listed, it should not be overused. Writers sometimes use a dash when a comma or other mark would suffice. Since the visual effect of a dashed line suggests a sharp interruption in a sentence, too many dashes in a paragraph or section of text can make the text seem choppy, harsh, and hard to read.

See also **en** and **em** for other types of dash.

data Although the singular *datum* has all but disappeared from use, some authorities insist that the word *data* is a **plural** form and is properly used only with a plural **verb:**

> The *data are* extensive.

However, in scientific and technical material, the word *data* is often used as a singular **noun** and in such cases takes a singular verb:

> As soon as all the *data* has arrived, we can begin final calculations.

Since disagreement exists about whether or not a singular verb is acceptable, follow the practice of your employer or publisher.

database See **Internet terms.**

dates The traditional style of writing dates is as follows:

> The company was founded on April 11, 1989, in Colorado.
> The company was founded in April 1989 in Colorado.

Some writers place the day first and eliminate the comma, especially in correspondence, although this style is not widely used in general writing:

> The company was founded on 11 April 1989 in Colorado.

An all-numeral system should be avoided because it is not clear whether the day or month is stated first. Most writers in the United States place the month first (*April 11, 1989 = 4/11/89*), but writers in certain other countries state the day first (*April 11, 1989 = 11/4/89*).

In **notes, bibliographies,** and **reference lists,** dates may be spelled out or abbreviated consistently according to the style preferred by your employer or publisher.

See also **abbreviations of time and days, centuries, eras, numbers,** and **years.**

days See **calendar designations.**

dead copy See **page proof.**

dead manuscript See **page proof.**

decades Use **lowercase** letters to refer to decades as words:

the twenties
the sixties

When the reference consists of **numerals,** use an **apostrophe** to indicate the absence of numbers referring to the century. However, omit the apostrophe between the year and *s:*

'20s
'60s

When the number includes both the century and the decade, omit the apostrophe:

1920s
1960s

Write the first two decades of a century as inclusive numbers:

1900–9 *or* 1900–1909 (*not* 1900s)
1910–19 *or* 1910–1919 (*not* 1910s)

See **numbers** for an explanation of the two main styles for writing inclusive numbers. See also **centuries** and **eras.**

decided/decisive For many years the **adjectives** *decided* and *decisive* have been used interchangeably to mean unmistakable (*decided/decisive* victory) or resolute (*decided/ decisive* effort). But skilled writers often take advantage of the difference in primary definitions to express various shades of meaning. For example, the primary meaning of *decided* is definite or unquestionable:

> He had a *decided* advantage when applying for the position of bookkeeper because of his prior experience in an accounting firm.

The primary meaning of *decisive* is being conclusive or having the power to decide:

> The president's speech was *decisive* in persuading the delegates to change their vote.

decimal fractions Set decimal fractions in **numerals** (*2.17*). Use an initial **zero** in scientific copy if the fraction is less than *1.00* but could equal or exceed *1.00*. If desired, omit the zero in nonscientific copy:

> an average of 0.45 (scientific)
> an average of .45 (nonscientific)

Omit the zero in all copy if the quantity could never exceed *1.00*, such as in probabilities:

> $p < .05$

A **comma** rather than a **period** is used to represent the decimal point in Europe:

> 7.1309 (U.S. style)
> 7,1309 (European style)

See also **fractions** and **percentages**.

decimal system See **binary number**.

decisive See **decided/decisive**.

decked heads See **tables**.

deckled edge The untrimmed edge of paper coming from a machine or the rough edge of handmade paper. Some stationery is produced with a deckled edge to give it a hand-made look.

declarative sentence A **sentence** that makes a statement:

I live in New York.

Compare with **exclamatory sentence, imperative sentence,** and **interrogative sentence.**

dedication An author may dedicate his or her book to one or more people. Usually, this dedication appears on a **recto** page by itself immediately following the **copyright page** in the **front matter.**

A dedication may state only the person's name (full name, first name, or initials only, as preferred), or it may also make a brief statement. The word *dedication* and ending punctuation are omitted:

To Paul T. Rider
To Amy, Jean, and Ted
To E.C., without whose help, support, and love this book
     would not have been possible
In memory of V. K. Gillette

A dedication is seldom used in a multiauthor book unless it is jointly made by all of the contributing authors.

defer/delay/postpone These three **verbs** are regularly and correctly used interchangeably to mean keeping something from happening until later. However, some writers observe an important distinction. Use *defer* to mean decide to do something later:

Let's *defer* our decision until we have more information.

Use *delay* to mean impede something or deliberately set something aside:

If we *delay* carrying out the supervisor's unpopular order, she may forget about it.

Use *postpone* to mean put off something until a specified future date, with full intention of resuming it on that date:

Since we no longer have a quorum, we'll have to *postpone* our vote until the next regular monthly meeting.

degrees, academic See **academic degrees.**

deities Capitalize the names of deities, formal references to one supreme God, and designations of revered persons, such as saints.

God	the Lord
Allah	Holy Ghost
El	the Omnipotent
Dagon	Prince of Peace
Vishnu	the Savior
Buddha	Messiah
the Prophet	Christian
Jehovah	John the Baptist
the Almighty	the Blessed Virgin
Lamb of God	the Twelve Apostles

Lowercase the pronouns that refer to deities as well as derivatives, both **nouns** and **pronouns:**

God in his mercy	christological
messianism	the apostle Paul
godly	omnipotence

See also **religious events and concepts, religious groups, religious meetings, religious movements, religious services,** and **religious works.**

delay See **defer/delay/postpone.**

delusion See **allusion/delusion/illusion.**

demonstrative adjective An **adjective** that refers to the thing it modifies. The four demonstrative adjectives are *this, that, these,* and *those. This* and *that* are used with singular **nouns,** and *these* and *those* are used with plural nouns:

This/that computer has a new operating system.
These/those computers have new operating systems.

When the nouns *kind(s), type(s),* and *sort(s)* are included, they should agree in number with the demonstrative adjectives.

This/that kind of computer program is hard to learn.
These/those types of programs are easy to learn.

Compare with **demonstrative pronoun.**

demonstrative pronoun The words *this, that, these,* and
those are used as both **demonstrative adjectives** and demonstrative **pronouns.** Whereas a *demonstrative adjective*
modifies a **noun,** a *demonstrative pronoun* takes the place
of a noun. The **antecedent** of a demonstrative pronoun may
be a noun, **phrase, clause,** or **sentence.** *This* and *that* are
substituted for singular nouns, and *these* and *those* are substituted for plural nouns:

> *This/that* is his proposal.
> *These/those* are the new employees he hired.

Compare with **adjective pronoun, indefinite pronoun,
intensive pronoun, interrogative pronoun, personal pronoun, reciprocal pronoun, reflexive pronoun,** and **relative pronoun.**

denotation See **connotation/denotation.**

dependent clause Also called *subordinate clause;* a **clause**
that cannot stand alone and needs the rest of the sentence
to complete its meaning. A dependent clause cannot be deleted and therefore should not be set off by commas:

> Ms. Hill explained *that we must follow the guidelines
> precisely.*

Compare with **independent clause.** See also **restrictive
element.**

depositary/depository Although the **nouns** *depositary* and
depository are **synonyms** in a secondary sense, they differ
in a primary sense. A *depositary* primarily refers to a person or group entrusted with something for safekeeping or
preservation:

> Mr. Michels will serve as *depositary* for the collection.

A *depository* primarily refers to the place where something is deposited for safekeeping or storage:

> The museum is the *depository* for the collection.

In major dictionaries the second listed sense of *depositary* is a depository, and the second listed sense of *depository* is a depositary. However, the primary distinction must be observed to make clear whether one is referring to a person (*-ary*) or a place (*-ory*).

derivative work An additional work, such as an abridgment or translation of an original book, that is based on an original work. When a publisher agrees to publish an author's work, the contract specifies that certain **rights** are assigned to the publisher. One of them is the publisher's right to make derivative works.

descender The part of **lowercase** letters that extends below the **baseline** of capital letters. For example, the lines extending below the main body in the letters *g, j, p, q,* and *y* are descenders. Compare with **ascender.**

design A plan for the physical appearance and purpose of a publication using graphic techniques. Those responsible for a design evaluate the author's **manuscript** and other parts of the publication to make appropriate decisions about the **cover** and text. Considerations include the size of the publication, paper (stock) to be used, colors, type style and size, **illustrations,** and general **layout** or arrangement of the various elements.

The designer's plan includes a page **format** consisting of lines and boxes drawn manually or by computer. The drawing indicates the placement of illustrations and the size, position, and spacing around text type, titles and **head(ing)s, notes, extracts,** and other elements of the document.

The designer also prepares a *specification sheet*. This sheet lists in detail the information about **typefaces,** type sizes, and other matters that an editor or a member of the production department will need to mark the manuscript for the **compositor.**

desktop publishing A general term describing the relatively low-cost preparation of a typeset document using microcomputers and page-makeup software. Unlike larger, more sophisticated operations, desktop publishing usually does not include related steps in the publishing process, such as **printing,** which are handled apart from the preparation of **camera-ready copy.**

Publishers that have desktop publishing equipment may ask that authors submit disk copies of their **manuscripts** in addition to the traditional paper copies. Depending on the publisher's equipment and software, the author may be required to add codes to the disk copy that identify each element of the document, such as **head(ing)s, extracts,** and **notes.**

See also **typesetting.**

despite/in spite of The **preposition** *despite* and **phrase** *in spite of* both mean notwithstanding. However, *despite* has a connotation (see **connotation/denotation**) of trying to avoid blame:

Despite our best efforts the business failed.

In spite of, although more wordy, may be used in other situations:

We enjoyed the tour *in spite of* the rainy weather.

diacritical marks Diacritical marks, or *diacritics,* are marks that are added to a letter to indicate a special phonetic value or to distinguish between words that are spelled the same but have different meanings:

resume (start again)
résumé (professional summary)

The following are nine frequently used diacritics:

acute accent: *háló* (Hungarian: net)
grave accent: *caffè* (Italian: coffee)
circumflex: *dôr* (Portuguese: pain)
tilde: *mañana* (Spanish: tomorrow)
macron: *dēfendo* (Latin: repel)
breve: *tăranul* (Rumanian: peasant)
hacek: *raž* (Slovak: rye)

diaeresis: *söndag* (Norwegian: Sunday)
cedilla: *française* (French: French)

English dictionaries and some English dictionaries of foreign words contain detailed guides to pronunciation, usually in the front of the book.

diagnosis/prognosis The **nouns** *diagnosis* and *prognosis* are both important terms in medicine with distinct meanings that should not be confused. *Diagnosis* refers to an identification, evaluation, and opinion concerning a disease or injury:

> The doctor's *diagnosis* was based on a thorough examination of the patient's medical history and current symptoms.

Prognosis refers to a prediction concerning the course and outcome of a disease or injury:

> The doctor's *prognosis* that he would have a full recovery was welcome news.

The terms are also used in other professions in similar ways, as in a businessperson's *diagnosis* about what is responsible for the problems in a failing company and the *prognosis* concerning the company's prospects for survival.

dialect A form of speech characterized by a distinct pronunciation, **grammar,** vocabulary, or **idiom.** The dialect may apply to a particular region in a country, such as the North or South, or it may be based on economic or social class, occupation, rural-urban residency, or ethnicity.

Numerous dialects in addition to the familiar regional varieties can be found in the United States. Among the most common ethnic dialects are Hispanic English, Jewish English, and **Black English.**

In general, dialects are all widely viewed as **nonstandard English.** They are therefore inappropriate in business documents, formal material, and most other nonfiction writing. However, they are frequently used in fiction to depict the speech of fictional characters.

dialogue When exact comments and thoughts are quoted in running text, they are set off by **quotation marks ('/'').** See the examples in that entry. A new paragraph signals a change in speakers. In many other situations, though, quotation marks are not used. Indirect comments, for example, are not set off by quotation marks:

> He thought she would say yes.

The stream of consciousness is another comment that is not set off by quotation marks. *Stream of consciousness* is a passage that gives a fiction character's thoughts and feelings as they develop. Also, when the name of the speaker introduces or precedes his or her words, such as in a typescript or playscript, the dialogue is not set off by quotation marks. The person's name is often set in **italics** or **caps and small caps,** followed by either a period or colon:

> *Mrs. Beneke.* I don't understand.
> *Mr. Beneke.* How can I make it any clearer?

> MRS. BENEKE: I don't understand.
> MR. BENEKE: How can I make it any clearer?

See **ellipsis points** for the correct way to handle words omitted from direct quotations, and see **extract** for the use of quotation marks in a blocked or displayed quotation.

die copy The type and other material prepared for the **spine** and **covers** of a hardcover book. The word *die* refers to a device used for cutting and stamping. The die copy, which is prepared by the binder (see **binding**), may consist of names, titles, and ornaments or other symbols. When proofs (see **page proof**) of the die copy are ready, editors check the type and other material for accuracy and position. See also **jacket.**

diaeresis See **diacritical marks.**

different from/different than The question of whether *from* or *than* should follow the **adjective** *different* puzzles many writers. A widely accepted rule, which is not strictly followed, is that *from* is preferred in reference to two persons or things:

My work is very different *from* yours.

However, when a **clause** with a **subject** and **verb** follows, *than* is the correct choice:

My work now is very different *than* it was when I first joined the company.

To use *from* in the preceding clause, the sentence would have to be reworded:

My work now is very different *from what* [or *from how*] it was when I first joined the company.

differentiate/distinguish The **verbs** *differentiate* and *distinguish* are often used interchangeably to mean show a difference. Which term is the better choice in a particular situation depends on the amount of detail that is involved. For example, *differentiate* is preferred when you want to indicate specific technical details:

The two cats were *differentiated* by their colors and the patterns on their coats.

Distinguish, the more widely used term, is usually preferred when you want to point out general or broad differences without specific technical details:

The psychologist said the teenager appeared unable to *distinguish* between right and wrong.

direct object A **noun** or noun equivalent, such as a **pronoun,** that receives the action of a **transitive verb** and often answers the question *what* or *whom:*

I was surprised to learn that he wrote that *book* [noun].
After hearing about the new word processing program, she bought *it* [pronoun].
Although bicycling is fun, we really prefer *running* [**gerund**].
I hope you know *what I mean* [noun **clause**].

The direct object is a **complement** in that it completes the sense of a transitive verb.

directions, compass See **compass directions.**

disability/inability The **nouns** *disability* and *inability* both refer to a lack of ability or power, but the implications of each are different. *Disability* implies a lack of ability or power specifically related to a mental or physical weakness or impairment:

> Because of his *disability* after being injured in the accident, he had to find a less strenuous job.

Inability implies a lack of talent, ability, or power that may or may not be related to a physical or mental disability:

> His *inability* to understand complex computer programs had nothing to do with his poor eyesight.

discover/invent The **verbs** *discover* and *invent* both involve something previously unknown or unfound, but *discover* cannot logically be substituted for *invent*. *Discover* refers to the acquisition of knowledge through observation, planned or unplanned, or through study:

> She *discovered* an herb that completely eliminates fatigue.

Invent is the correct term to refer to the use of ingenuity or imagination to create something previously unknown or not existing:

> He *invented* a detachable lock for cabinets and boxes that have no built-in locking device.

discreet/discrete Because the **adjectives** *discreet* and *discrete* are pronounced the same, one is sometimes incorrectly used when the other is intended. However, their meanings are very different. *Discreet* means characterized by prudence and self-restraint:

The two were so *discreet* that no one realized they were carrying on an office romance.

Discrete means consisting of things that are separate and distinct:

The spreadsheet has twelve *discrete* parts.

discriminatory language See **bias.**

disinterested/uninterested The **adjectives** *disinterested* and *uninterested* are regularly used interchangeably, although some authorities insist that writers should observe the different shades of meaning in their primary definitions. *Disinterested,* for example, primarily means impartial or unbiased:

The judges on the panel were *disinterested* and therefore able to make a fair decision.

Uninterested primarily means indifferent or lacking interest:

We loved the movie, but she seemed to be *uninterested.*

A secondary meaning of *disinterested* is indifferent, the same as the primary definition of *uninterested.* This similarity helps to explain the wide use of the terms as **synonyms,** in spite of the difference in their primary meanings.

disorganized/unorganized Broadly, the **adjectives** *disorganized* and *unorganized* are **synonyms** that mean lacking a system, order, or unity. However, they differ in whether they refer to an existing pattern of organization or the lack of any pattern. For example, *disorganized* is the better choice to describe an existing system that has been disrupted and now lacks order and unity:

The files in his office have become so *disorganized* that we can no longer find anything.

Unorganized is the better choice to describe something that never was organized:

As yet the files in his office are *unorganized* pending a decision about whether to set them up alphabetically or numerically.

Unorganized also describes a group of individuals with like interests who have not yet formed an official organization, such as employees who are not yet represented by a labor union.

display type A type that is larger than text type and is used for titles, subheads, and other lines that are displayed, or set apart from the running text. See **typeface.**

distinguish See **differentiate/distinguish.**

documentation In computer work, the reference material that describes operations and provides instruction in the use of equipment or software; in general, any supporting documents or reference material.

double negative In **nonstandard English,** two negative terms, such as *no* and *not,* used in a single sentence or thought. Often the two terms together equal an affirmative:

I've found that there is *no* job that is *not* hard once you learn proper procedures.

Saying that *no* jobs are *not* hard (not hard = easy) is the same as saying that no jobs are easy. Therefore, the example is equivalent to saying that all jobs are hard once you know proper procedures. However, that doesn't make sense and is not likely to be what the writer meant. One of the negatives should thus be deleted:

I've found that *no* job is hard once you learn proper procedures.

Other, more obvious double negatives, such as "I *won't* do *no* work" or "I *haven't* got *no* time," are not a problem for literate people. However, the less obvious double negatives, such as those in the first example, are sometimes seen in the work of even professional writers.

See also the use of double negatives in **Black English.**

doublespeak Also called *doubletalk;* meaningless language that is deliberately ambiguous or evasive. For example, doublespeak is often used to mislead the public or to avoid revealing facts that might cast an individual or organization in an unfavorable light. Therefore, *bribes* become *sales incentives, taxes* become *revenue enhancements, nuclear waste dumps* become *monitored retrievable storage sites,* and the *firing of workers* becomes the *release of resources.*

Doublespeak often relies on tactics such as abstractions and generalizations that cloak the truth and gloss over revealing details. For example, by stating very generally that a particular governmental expenditure is for *vehicles,* taxpayers are left to wonder about the *kind* of vehicles that were purchased with tax dollars—limousines to chauffeur officials to work, tanks or other vehicles for the military, trucks to transport supplies to governmental facilities, or something else.

When doublespeak is used, one suspects that the person using it has something to hide. However, this isn't always the case. Some people use ambiguous language so frequently that doublespeak becomes a habit and is used even when nothing questionable is involved. See also **gobbledygook.**

doubletalk See **doublespeak.**

down style Another term for a **lowercase** style; a **style** that reflects a tendency toward using less capitalization when there is a choice, such as in abbreviating words and terms. See the examples in the various entries pertaining to abbreviations. Compare with **up style.**

draw-down Also called *roll-out;* a sample of a particular ink printed on a particular paper. When a publisher is uncertain and concerned about the way the printed version of a document will look, it may request a draw-down from the printer before committing to a particular ink or stock.

drawings See **paintings and sculptures.**

drop folio See **page numbers.**

due to See **because of/due to/owing to.**

dummy A usually unprinted sample of a proposed document prepared by cutting and pasting **galley proofs** or other proofs and copies of **illustrations** on sheets that resemble the pages of the document. The sample then serves as a guide to the **compositor** in page makeup. Although a dummy is not needed for relatively simple, straightforward text documents, it can be helpful when a document has a complex format and numerous illustrations scattered throughout the text.

duotone A **halftone** illustration in two tones or colors created from the same original. The effect is achieved by printing two intensities of black and gray or black and one color or two intensities of the same color.

dust jacket See **jacket.**

dust wrapper See **jacket.**

E

e.g. Abbreviation for the Latin term *exempli gratia*—for example. The spelled-out English expression *for example,* not the abbreviation *e.g.,* should be used in running text. However, *e.g.* is sometimes used to introduce parenthetical comments (e.g., such as this one) and in incidental material set apart from the text, such as in a **table.**

each and every A **redundancy** that should be avoided. Although the **phrase** is frequently used for emphasis, either *each* or *every* alone is sufficient:

> We need to reach *each* [or *every*] customer.

each other/one another The distinction between the **pronouns** *each other* and *one another* has all but disappeared in casual writing. Nevertheless, many authorities object to using the terms interchangeably and follow the traditional rule that *each other* should be used in referring to two persons or things and *one another* in references to more than two:

> The two attorneys spoke with *each other* only last week.
> The five employees competed with *one another* for the recently vacated supervisor's position.

eager See **anxious/eager.**

Ebonics See **Black English.**

editing Both writers and editors prepare written material for publication by correcting, revising, adapting, or polishing the material. Professional writers edit their **manuscripts** before submitting them to a publisher, and one or more editors at the place of publication provide more detailed editing along with other steps in production.

See **copyediting** for a description of *mechanical editing* and *substantive editing.* See also individual entries pertaining to specific types of copy to be edited, such as **tables** or **extracts,** and see the individual entries pertaining to various steps in production, such as **typesetting, proofreading, printing,** and **binding.**

edition The original publication of a work or each reissue; the entire number of copies issued at one time; the form in which a document is issued, such as a *paperback edition.* After the first edition of a book has been produced, subsequent editions are usually numbered, such as the *second edition, third edition,* and so on, and the edition number, usually spelled out, is printed on the **cover** or **spine** of the book.

Other terminology may be used if desired, such as *newly revised* or *second revised edition.* In citations, words such as *revised* and *edition* are abbreviated, and the edition number is stated in **numerals,** such as *rev. ed., 2d ed.* or *2nd ed.,* or *3d rev. ed.* or *3rd rev. ed.*

The time may be mentioned in newspaper editions, such as the *morning edition.* Similarly, radio and television programs may include the day, such as the *Monday edition* of the five o'clock news.

Compare with **series.**

editor's alterations (EAs) After a **manuscript** has been typeset, both the author and an editor or proofreader read the **page proofs** or **galley proofs.** If an editor makes changes at that stage, in addition to marking **typesetting** errors, those changes are identified as editor's alterations. The editor usually circles the initials *EA* in the margin of the proof by each change to distinguish it from other changes made by the author. See also **author's alterations (AAs)** and **printer's errors (PEs)**.

effect See **affect/effect.**

effective/effectual/efficacious/efficient Broadly, these four **adjectives** all mean producing or capable of producing a desired effect and, therefore, are widely used interchangeably. Nevertheless, they have important shades of meaning that professional writers should take into account. *Effective,* for example, is the best choice to mean having a definite or desired effect or being operative. Both persons and things can be effective:

> The new policy is *effective* immediately.
> He is an *effective* instructor.

Effectual means capable of producing a desired effect and applies to the action rather than the agent. A thing, therefore, can be effectual, but not a person (although interestingly, a person may correctly be called *ineffectual*):

> His letter was *effectual* in terminating the agreement.

Efficacious means producing or certain to produce a desired effect and applies only to things:

> The homeopathic treatment for his respiratory illness was *efficacious.*

Efficient means being productive with minimum effort or waste and applies to both people and things:

> He developed an *efficient* procedure for recording receipts.
> She is *efficient* in everything she does.

egoism/egotism The **nouns** *egoism* and *egotism* sound similar but differ in their primary meanings. However, their secondary meanings are generally the same, with both referring to conceit and a sense of self-importance. The primary meaning of *egoism* is an ethical doctrine or belief that morality is founded on self-interest or that self-interest is the principal basis for all human conduct:

Tim regularly points to the doctrine of *egoism* to justify his ruthlessly selfish pursuits.

The primary meaning of *egotism* is the tendency to boast and talk about oneself too much:

With his blatant *egotism*, it's little wonder that he bragged about his new job all night.

ellipsis points (...) A series of spaced periods (dots) used in quoted material to indicate omitted words, sentences, or longer passages. The dots should be set on line the same as a regular **period.**

One system uses three spaced dots for any type of omission regardless of where it is located. A slightly more complex system, preferred by scholars and many professional writers, uses three dots for omitted words within a sentence and four dots for omitted copy between sentences (three dots if the end of a sentence is grammatically incomplete). The fourth dot is the period that would normally conclude a sentence. Although there should be a space between each dot in most cases, no space is used between the last word of a sentence and the dot that represents the end-of-sentence period.

In modern works of recent decades, the first word of a sentence that follows another sentence with four dots may be capitalized even if it is not really the first word of that sentence:

Thomas Jefferson agreed. ... The document proved his point.

However, in older works, particularly from earlier centuries, or in legal or scholarly works, the capital letter should be placed in brackets, or the word should be left in the **lowercase** letters of the original:

Thomas Jefferson agreed. ... [T]he document proved his point.
Thomas Jefferson agreed. ... the document proved his point.

When a paragraph other than the first one omits the first sentence(s) of that paragraph, three dots should precede the opening word. See the forthcoming example. Therefore, in certain cases one paragraph may end with four dots and the next one begin with three dots.

The following example repeats portions of the preceding paragraphs and inserts ellipsis points where words have been omitted:

ellipsis points ... A series of spaced periods ... used ... to indicate omitted words ... or longer passages. ...

... A slightly more complex system ... uses three dots ... within a sentence and four dots ... between sentences. ...

In modern works ... the first word of a sentence that follows another sentence with four dots may be capitalized even if it is not really the first word of that sentence. ... In older works ... the capital letter should be placed in brackets, or ... left in the **lowercase** letters of the original. ...

See also **extract** and **quotation marks.**

em A **typesetting** measure equal to the **point** size of the type. For example, a three-point em is three points wide. When a **manuscript** is being prepared for typesetting, paragraph and other **indentions** may be marked in ems. Therefore, in a ten-point type size, each paragraph or other element marked for a one-em indention will be indented ten points.

To indicate a one-em indention, draw a very small square box next to the word to be indented; to indicate a two-em indention, draw two small boxes next to the word; and so on.

A **dash,** which is typed as two **hyphens** (--) in a **manuscript,** is marked to be typeset as a solid-line em dash (—). To indicate this to a **compositor,** an editor will write a capital *M* above the typed dash or write 1/M in fraction style on top of the dash: $\frac{1}{M}$.

A three-em dash is used for the names of authors that are repeated in successive entries in a **bibliography** or **reference list.** See those entries for examples. An editor therefore writes *3M* above the author's typed line on the manuscript copy or writes 3/M in fraction style on top of the line.

A two-em dash is used to indicate missing letters and is set without space before the dash: M——$\frac{a}{M}$.

Compare with **en.**

embossing Forming or stamping a raised image by pressing paper between metal dies that have a relief surface. The process of stamping may be done in various ways. *Cold stamping* is done by inking a metal die. *Hot stamping* is done by placing leaf (metallic foil or plastic film with pigment or metallic powder bonded to it) between the die and the paper and heating the die. *Blind stamping* is also done by heating a die and making an impression but without the use of ink or leaf.

emend See **amend/emend.**

emigration/immigration/migration These three **nouns** all pertain to movement but differ in whether the movement is from or to a particular place. For example, *emigration* is the movement *from* one country or region to another with the intent of settling in the new location. The emphasis is therefore on the place of departure and the movement away from it:

He wrote about the *emigration* of the Germanic tribes from northern Germany to England.

Immigration is the entry *into* a new location in order to settle there. In this case the emphasis is on the place of entry:

She reminded us that Lee McKay's *immigration* to the United States took place before World War II.

Using the distinction of *from* versus *to*, one would say that someone in the process of moving *from* one country *to* another is an *emigrant;* someone who has already moved to the other country is an *immigrant.*

Migration, which is the only one of the three terms that can apply to animals as well as people, also means the movement from one place to another, the same as *emigration.* But unlike *emigration,* it often implies a periodic or seasonal movement, not a permanent settlement in a new region or country:

> The *migration* of the elk across highways to lower-elevation winter pastures creates a hazard for drivers.

eminent/immanent/imminent These three **adjectives** sound the same, and the last two have similar spellings. However, their meanings are very different. *Eminent* means outstanding, prominent, or of high rank:

> The *eminent* scientist Harold Laughlin will be honored at Tuesday's banquet.

Immanent, the least used of the three words, means inherent or remaining within:

> Love is *immanent* in all human beings.

Imminent means about to occur or impending:

> The dark, churning clouds made it clear that a storm was *imminent.*

emoticons Symbols used in personal electronic messages to represent emotion. Some symbols, such as :-), are said to resemble a facial expression if you tilt your head to the left; those symbols are called *smileys.* Others, such as ‹s› (sigh), that don't resemble any facial expressions are called *nonsmileys.*

Different writers may use variations of a particular symbol or completely different symbols to represent a particular emotion. For example, both ‹L› and :D represent laughing. Because others may not use the same symbols that you use, it is important to provide a list of symbols and your meanings to those who receive your personal correspondence. However, this type of emotion and the associated symbols should be avoided in business and social correspondence and should never be used in formal correspondence.

The following are examples of common smileys and nonsmileys:

:-)	basic smiley
;-)	winking
‹g›	grin
‹L› *or* :D	laughing
‹J›	joking
:-o	surprised
:-!	foot in mouth

empathy/sympathy The **nouns** *empathy* and *sympathy* both refer to a response to another's feelings or situation but are **synonyms** only in a broad sense. *Empathy* is a specific identification with another's feelings or situation, with the ability to project one's own feelings to the other person or object:

His *empathy* for her pain left him physically as weak as she was.

Sympathy is a more general term that refers to a mutual understanding of another's feelings or situation based on an affection in the relationship:

Jill's *sympathy* with her best friend's decision to end her marriage was expected.

The **plural** form *sympathies* (condolences) is often used to refer to a message of sympathy or an expression of sorrow and compassion on the misfortune of another:

He sent his *sympathies* [message of sympathy] to Jeffrey as soon as he heard about Helen's death.

en A measure that is one-half the length of an **em.** An en **dash** (–), typed as one **hyphen** (-) in **manuscript** copy, is used between inclusive **numbers** and between words in a compound **adjective** when one of the words is a two-word open compound:

1989–90
1989–
ex-senator–ex-governor Jones
New York–Washington corridor

Editors mark en dashes by writing a capital *N* above the typed hyphen or by writing 1/N in fraction style on top of the hyphen: $\tilde{\text{N}}$.

Compare with **em.**

end matter See **back matter.**

endleaf See **endpaper.**

endnotes The **notes** in a book that are placed in the **back matter** after the **appendix** and just before the **bibliography** or **reference list.** The **notes** are usually organized by chapter with each group of chapter notes preceded by a subhead consisting of the chapter number and, if desired, chapter title:

Chapter 2: Windfall Profits in the 1980s

Notes are usually numbered consecutively beginning with note 1 in each chapter. Each page of notes after the first may have a **running head** consisting of the inclusive text pages where the in-text citations to notes on that page can be found. The running head may also include the chapter number.

See **notes** for examples of the arrangement of data in different types of notes.

endpaper Also called *endsheet* or *endleaf;* folded sheets of heavy paper, half of which are glued to the inside front and back **covers** of a book and the other half of which are glued to the first and last **signatures,** thereby securing the inside pages to the **binding.**

endsheet See **endpaper.**

engravings See **paintings and sculptures.**

ensure See **assure/ensure/insure.**

envisage/envision The **verbs** *envisage* and *envision* are widely treated as **synonyms** meaning to picture or imagine. *Envisage* is the older term and is used more in Britain than in the United States. In a strict sense it means to confront or face:

> She unhappily *envisaged* her disheveled appearance after a sleepless night on the train.

Envision, the more popular term in the United States, strictly means to have a vision but broadly means to imagine or foresee:

> I *envision* a four-block complex of high-end restaurants and boutiques.

Some authorities consider both *envisage* and *envision* too pretentious and prefer words such as *imagine, foresee, picture,* or *visualize.*

epigraph A quotation placed at the beginning of a book or on a chapter opening page that sets a theme for the book or chapter. An author may include both a **dedication** and an epigraph, one of the two, or neither.

If an author has both a dedication and an epigraph, the epigraph may be placed on **recto** page vii. If no dedication is used, the epigraph may be placed on recto page v. Sometimes the epigraph appears on **verso** page vi or on a blank verso page facing the first text page. Although the page containing an epigraph is counted in the numbering of the **front matter,** the number is not printed on the page.

The source of the epigraph (usually, the author and title of the work) is given flush right on the line immediately below the last line of the quotation, often preceded by a dash. When the author of the quotation is very well known, the person's last name only may be sufficient. When the author is not widely known, the person's full name should be used:

> We cannot divide ourselves between right and expedience. Policy must bow the knee before morality.
>
> —Kant, *Perpetual Peace*

> The social system in which a man, willing to work, is compelled to starve, is a blasphemy, an anarchy, and no system.
>
> —Thomas Devin Reilly, *The Irish Felon*

epilogue Also called *afterword;* a short concluding section at the end of a literary work, such as a novel. An epilogue may be set like a separate chapter and may begin on either a **recto** or **verso** page. Usually, the epilogue has no chapter number even when the main text chapters have both a number and title. However, page numbers are printed on the pages of an epilogue in **arabic numerals** the same as in the main chapters.

Compare with **conclusion,** a more extensive type of concluding section used in nonfiction works.

episodes, geological See **geological terms.**

epithet A nickname; a descriptive substitute for or part of the given name of a person or thing. When the descriptive word or **phrase** has become permanently associated with the name, it should be capitalized. When the word or phrase is used within the person's name rather than in place of it, it also should be enclosed in quotation marks:

> the First Lady
> the Great Emancipator
> the Iron Duke
> Alexander the Great
> George Herman "Babe" Ruth
> William Frederick "Buffalo Bill" Cody

Temporary epithets that are not regularly associated with a name should be written with **lowercase** letters:

> *the guru* Edmund Shore
> *the scientist* Donna Madison

See also **appositive.**

epitome An **abstract** or brief summary of a book or article; an example or representative of a type or class:

She is the *epitome* of a truly selfless person.

epochs See **geological terms.**

eponym The person after whom an object or something else is named; the personal name that is the source of another name; a word derived from a person's name:

John B. Stetson: a *stetson* hat
Constantine: city of *Constantinople*
Alexander Garden: the *gardenia* plant
Louis Braille: the *Braille* system

equations Complex equations that contain many **mathematical expressions** require special treatment by a qualified editor and **compositor.** Those who deal with this type of copy should consult a style guide devoted to setting mathematical copy, such as *Mathematics into Type: Copy Editing and Proofreading of Mathematics for Editorial Assistants and Authors,* published by the American Mathematical Society in Providence, Rhode Island.

Generally, letter symbols should be set in **italics** unless marked for **roman type.** Mathematical symbols, such as $>$ (greater than), and Greek symbols, such as μ (**lowercase** Greek mu), should be identified for the compositor by spelling out and circling the name at the first occurrence.

Many equations are set run-in style as part of a text sentence:

Therefore, he easily proved that $a + b = c$.

Very long equations; stacked equations; those with **fractions, subscripts,** and **superscripts;** and any others that merit special emphasis are often displayed, or set apart from the text sentences. Those that will not fit on one line are usually broken before a *verb operator,* such as $<$ (less than), or before a *conjunction,* such as $+$, that follows a *sign of aggregation,* such as the closing bracket]. See the next example.

When an equation is centered, runover lines are aligned on the verb operators unless a runover line begins with a conjunction, in which case the conjunction is aligned to the right of the verb operator in the preceding line. In the following example, the runover line begins with a conjunction (a minus sign); therefore, it is aligned to the right of the verb operator (an equal sign) in the line above, under the letter M:

$$a(x, z) = M[v(b) + u(2)]$$
$$- 4m > l(x) + z(2) - 3.$$

If a displayed equation is not centered, runover lines may be set flush against the right margin, or if there are verb operators in each line, the runover lines may be aligned under the operator in the top line. In the following example the runover line is set flush against the right margin:

$$a(x, z) = M[v(b) + u(2)] - 4m > 1(x)$$
$$+ a/x^3 - w/(b - c)^2 - 3.$$

See **mathematical expressions** for more about signs and symbols in, and the handling of, mathematical copy.

eras Use words for **centuries** but **numbers** for years preceded by or following the abbreviation for eras:

The philosopher was born in 9 B.C. and died in A.D. 54. His son lived well into the *first century* A.D.

See **abbreviations of time and days** for a list of the most commonly used designations of eras.
See also **geological terms.**

errata Lists of errors and corrections included in a printed work. (The singular, which is seldom used, is *erratum.*) A list of errors and corrections is included when errors too serious to ignore are discovered after **printing** but before distribution of the work. The list, called an *errata sheet,* may be supplied on loose pages inserted inside the front cover, or the pages may be bound in with the printed pages of the book.
The errata should include the important errors, their location, and the corrected copy:

Page	For	Read
267, line 6	is considered	is never considered
301, line 20	figure 4	figure 12

Errata are provided only in cases of errors that would seriously hinder reader comprehension. They are not provided for minor problems such as an obviously misspelled word or a missing **comma.**

errata sheet See **errata.**

esquire The title *esquire* originally referred to a young English man born into a socially respected family or to any man of the higher-order English gentry. Eventually, the title was used after the name of any adult male in England.

The title *esquire,* capitalized when used after a name, should not be used when another title is included. Initially, the title was spelled out, but now it is always abbreviated after a name:

James Rowan, Esq. (*not* Mr. James Rowan, Esq. *or* James Rowan, Esq., LL.D.)

The title is rarely used in the United States except among attorneys who correspond with each other. In the United States the title is appended to the names of both men and women attorneys. In England the title is used only with the names of men.

et al. Abbreviation for the Latin term *et alii*—and others. It is used in **notes, bibliographies,** and **reference lists** to avoid stating the names of many (usually more than three) authors. The abbreviation consists of two parts with a period after *al.* It is set in **roman type** and follows the name of the author listed first on the **title page** of a work:

9. Mae Herman et al., *Rhetoric and Composition in the Twenty-first Century* (San Francisco: The English Press, 1989), 101–2.

See also the examples of use in **author-date citations.**

etc. Abbreviation for the Latin term *et cetera* (or *etcetera*)—and others of the same kind. Publishers generally prefer other expressions such as *and so on* or *and so forth.* However, in a parenthetical series or when space is limited, such as in a **table** or **list,** the abbreviation *etc.* is sometimes used.

Originally, the full term *et cetera,* the abbreviation *etc.,* and substitutes such as *and so on* were enclosed by commas in a sentence. In most current usage the expression or abbreviation is treated the same as any other final element in a series after which the concluding comma is omitted:

> The living room, bedroom, hallway, *et cetera/etc./and so on/and so forth*[,] were all damaged by the flood waters.

ethnic In contemporary usage the term *ethnic* applies to any part of a community that has common cultural, racial, religious, or linguistic characteristics. Most names referring to ethnic groups, such as *Hispanic,* are capitalized. See the examples in the entry **peoples.** General designations, such as *black,* based on color, custom, habitat, and so forth are often written in **lowercase** letters. However, authorities differ in their preferences, and some may capitalize certain general designations. Follow the preference of your employer or publisher.

ethnic groups See **peoples.**

euphemism A mild or vague substitute for a term considered to be more harsh, blunt, or offensive. Although a substitute such as *fatigue* for *mental illness* may be less precise and more evasive, writers sometimes justify such use on the presumption that readers will find the substitute less objectionable.

In many cases, though, a euphemism such as *classic* for *pretentious and costly* is an effort to entice or mislead readers. Writers should therefore evaluate terms such as the following examples to determine whether the substitute is thoughtful and sensitive or intentionally evasive and misleading:

Basic Term	*Euphemism*
decline	negative growth
disabled	physically challenged
dishonesty or fraud	irregularity
false accounting	financial engineering
slanted information	managed news
lie	misspeak
poor	disadvantaged
willing to abandon principles	flexible

everybody/everyone When the **pronouns** *everybody* and *everyone* are written as one word, each term means every person, takes a singular **verb,** and refers to a singular pronoun:

> *Everybody/everyone* enjoyed *his or her* [not *their*] gift.

Although both words are correct in this sense, some writers prefer every*one* over every*body* for aesthetic reasons.

When the terms are written as two words, *every one* (followed by *of*) and *every body* are used to mean *each* and are used to emphasize one individual among many:

> *Every* [Each] *one* of the seventeen dancers performed beautifully.
> *Every* [Each] *body* in the morgue showed signs that the plague had reached an advanced stage.

In the two-word phrases *every one* and *every body,* the pronoun *every* functions as an **adjective** modifying *one* and *body.*

exceedingly/excessively The **adverbs** *exceedingly* and *excessively* both mean to an advanced degree but have different shades of meaning or emphasis. *Exceedingly* is the better choice to mean very much or to an unusual degree but not too much or beyond reason:

> Some students said the test was *exceedingly* difficult.

Excessively is the better choice to mean too much or to a degree beyond reason:

I think his language is *excessively* crude and should not be used in a place of business.

except See **accept/except.**

excerpt A passage or segment taken from a longer work; the process of selecting and using the passage or segment. When the chosen material is reprinted in another work, it is styled as an **extract** or run-in quotation. See **quotation marks.**

excessively See **exceedingly/excessively.**

exclamation point (!) An exclamation point has four principal uses:

To indicate strong emotion: That's disgusting!

To indicate words used in exclamation: Stop! No!

To suggest satire or irony: Isn't that *nice*—someone scratched my car! (*Caution:* Readers in other countries may not understand this usage and may take such comments literally.)

To add emphasis to advertising and sales material: Sale! Storewide Clearance!

exclamatory adjective See **interjection.**

exclamatory noun See **interjection.**

exclamatory sentence A **sentence** that expresses strong feeling:

Oh, no, I simply can't believe it!

Compare with **declarative sentence, imperative sentence,** and **interrogative sentence.**

expletive The introductory words *there* or *it,* which are used to introduce a **verb** preceding the **subject** or to represent a **phrase** or **clause** following the verb. An expletive therefore takes the place of the principal subject, which appears in the **predicate:**

> *There* [expletive] were six hundred delegates [principal subject] at the convention.

A principal objection to the use of expletives is that they add unnecessary words to a sentence. For example, the preceding sentence could be rephrased in fewer words as follows:

> Six hundred delegates were at the convention.

Nevertheless, professional writers frequently use expletives to vary their comments. Most authorities recognize this practice and consider it a legitimate alternative, objecting only when it is used excessively.

Expletive also refers to a vulgar expression.

explicit/implicit The **adjectives** *explicit* and *implicit* both describe a type of expression but differ in whether the expression is direct or indirect. *Explicit* means expressed clearly and directly so that there is no misunderstanding:

> The manual gives *explicit* instructions for handling a paper jam.

Implicit also means that something is clearly understood, but it is not directly expressed:

> The prospect of a serious financial crisis was *implicit* in his report even though he avoided mentioning the word *recession.*

Implicit also means unquestioning or having no doubts:

> I have *implicit* faith in her plan.

exponent A **number** or symbol in **mathematical expressions** placed immediately to the right of another number or symbol to denote the power to which that other number or symbol should be raised, such as the **superscript** 3 in the following example:

$$(a + b)^3$$

In that example the number 3 is the exponent and the quantity $(a + b)$ is the base. The expression should be read as "the quantity $a + b$ raised to the power of 3."

When e is raised to a certain power, it is referred to as an *exponential function:*

$$e^{x - y}$$

The preceding expression with a superscript may alternatively be written run in and on line as follows: exp $(x - y)$, with *exp* substituted for *e*. This on-line style may be preferred if the other style using superscripts would appear too crowded set within a sentence.

Writers and editors who deal with complex mathematical copy should consult the latest edition of a dedicated style guide such as *Mathematics into Type: Copy Editing and Proofreading of Mathematics for Editorial Assistants and Authors,* published by the American Mathematical Society in Providence, Rhode Island.

extemporaneous/impromptu The **adjectives** *extemporaneous* and *impromptu* are **synonyms** meaning said or done with little or no preparation. However, professional writers make a distinction. *Extemporaneous* is the better choice to describe an unmemorized speech given from a prepared outline or from notes:

> The speaking engagement was arranged so hastily that his speech was *extemporaneous,* given without benefit of a complete written text.

Impromptu is the better choice to describe something said or done without any advance warning or notice:

> After everyone sang happy birthday, they started prodding him to make a speech, so he nervously gave a few *impromptu* remarks.

extended character set A set of additional characters in computer work that can be used for foreign language, mathematical, graphics, and other characters not represented on the keyboard. For example, with some **word processing** programs you can create the monetary sign for the yen (¥) by pressing the ALT key and certain numerical keys. The yen sign will then appear on the display screen, although it will print only if your printer supports the extended character set.

The extended character set is commonly known as the *ASCII character set,* which includes 256 additional characters. ASCII (pronounced *ask-ee*) is an **acronym** for American Standard Code for Information Interchange.

extract Also called **excerpt;** a passage or segment taken from a longer work and set as a blocked or set-off quotation rather than run in with the text. An extract is usually indented from the left margin and sometimes from both the left and right margins and is set with one or more blank lines above and below the extract. Paragraphing and **indention** should follow the style of the original copy, and omitted words should be indicated with the use of **ellipsis points.**

A quotation may be (but is not required to be) set off as an extract if it runs to more than ten lines or involves more than one paragraph. Shorter passages may also be set off if they are very important and merit special attention. For example, poetry of two or more lines is often set apart from the text.

Extracts that represent direct quotations are not enclosed in **quotation marks** as they would be if set run in with the text. However, dialogue or other quoted words within an extract should be enclosed in quotation marks:

Poet Charles Caleb Colton wrote in *The Lacon* that our *actions* are the only things in which we have any property. As he explained, ''Our actions must follow us beyond the grave: with respect to them *alone* we cannot say that we shall carry nothing with us when we die, neither that we shall go naked out of the world. Our actions must clothe us with an immortality, loathsome or glorious: these are the only *title-deeds* of which we cannot be disinherited. They will have their full weight in the balance of eternity, when everything else is as nothing.''

F

f. (plural, *ff.*) See **index.**

Fahrenheit See **Celsius/Fahrenheit.**

fair use A provision of **copyright** law that allows writers to use the copyrighted work of others, with certain restrictions, without permission of the copyright owners. Since the *exact* limits of fair use are not defined by the copyright law, a user who has any doubts may need legal assistance. Generally, the following four factors must be considered:

1. The purpose and character of the use, including whether the use is for commercial or nonprofit, educational purposes

2. The nature of the copyrighted work, such as whether it is a factual report or a literary work

3. The size and substantiality of the portion to be used relative to the copyrighted work as a whole

4. The effect of the use on the potential market for, or value of, the copyrighted work

Reviewers and critics are among those who rely on the fair use doctrine to quote or reproduce small amounts of material to support points they are making. Those who take advantage of fair use should nevertheless state the source of any passage that is used and quote from it accurately and consistently with the author's intended meaning in the copyrighted work.

fallacy/falsity The **nouns** *fallacy* and *falsity* have a similar meaning but differ in their connotations. See **connotation/denotation.** A *fallacy* is a false notion or invalid inference. Although in a secondary sense it has the quality of being deceptive, it primarily refers to a statement or belief that is based—often unknowingly—on incorrect facts:

> Her belief that there are no homeless people in town is a *fallacy;* she may not have seen any, but I have.

A *falsity* is an untruth; a lie. In a secondary sense it also refers to something arising from mistaken ideas. However, in its primary sense this term has a different connotation and suggests a deliberate misrepresentation or a statement known to be untrue:

> His comment about all the money he made in the stock market last month is a *falsity;* his partner told me privately that he really lost money.

falsity See **fallacy/falsity.**

famed/famous/infamous/notorious These four **adjectives** all have meanings pertaining to a sense of being well known. Two of them—*famed* and *famous*—are **synonyms,** as are the other two—*infamous* and *notorious. Famed* and *famous* are also **antonyms** of *infamous* and *notorious. Famed* and *famous* mean having great fame or being noted or widely known in a favorable sense:

> The *famed/famous* actress announced her retirement today.

Infamous and *notorious* mean having a bad reputation or being widely known in a very unfavorable sense:

> The actor played an *infamous/notorious* villain in the movie.

family names, foreign See **names, foreign.**

family-relationship terms Capitalize a name referring to family relationship, or kinship, when it is used before a **proper name** or in place of the name. **Lowercase** general references to family names if they are preceded by a modifier, such as *her.*

> Thank you, *Aunt* Lara, for the wonderful gift. I'm very lucky to have an *aunt* like you.
>
> Yes, *Mother,* I agree. His *mother* is much more strict than you are.
>
> In his last letter *Uncle* Roger said that his *uncle* (my *great-uncle*) recently had another novel published.

See also **abbreviations of names and titles; names, fictitious; names, foreign; names, personal;** and **personification.**

famous See **famed/famous/infamous/notorious.**

farther/further As **adverbs,** *farther* and *further* are used interchangeably to refer to a distance. In recent decades some authorities have recommended that *farther* be used for physical distances and *further* for nonphysical advancement:

> As he practiced for the marathon, he ran *farther* each day.
>
> She hopes to progress *further* at the Adler Jones Company than she could ever have gone at her previous place of employment.

Not all writers observe this distinction, however, and business writers in particular often use one term—usually *further*—for all situations.

feasible/possible The **adjectives** *feasible* and *possible* both refer to something that can be accomplished or may occur, but each has a slightly different sense. *Feasible,* for example, is a better choice to describe what can be accomplished and suggests the ease with which it can be done:

> His plan to consolidate operations is *feasible,* but I still don't like it.

Possible is a better choice to describe something that may happen or be true:

It's *possible* that we may move to Colorado if Jim is transferred to the Denver field office.

Compare with **viable/workable.**

feedback Technical **jargon** meaning the return of a portion of the output of a process or system to the input. Some writers also use the term to mean a personal response. However, careful writers avoid using *feedback* in a general sense to mean information or evaluation provided by a person in response to something another person said or did:

Not: He asked members of the staff for *feedback* on his proposal.
Better: He asked members of the staff *for their opinions about* [or *to comment on*] his proposal.

fences See **braces, brackets,** and **parentheses.**

few/less In most cases the **adjective** *few* should be used to describe things that can be counted (*count nouns*) and the adjective *less* to describe things that cannot be counted (*noncount,* or *mass, nouns*):

A *few* members of the staff attended the workshop.
The new format involves *less* setup time than the old one.

Less is also used idiomatically (see **idiom**) before a plural **noun** denoting time, amount, or distance when the notion of quantity exists even though something countable is involved:

Her car broke down *less* than five miles from home.

Less is also common when the word *no* precedes it even when something countable is involved:

No less than forty people were at the meeting.

fictitious names See **names, fictitious.**

figure of speech An expression or device in which words are used imaginatively or figuratively to make a point more clearly, colorfully, or emphatically. For examples of expressions and devices that represent figures of speech, see **alliteration, analogy, antithesis, hyperbole, irony/sarcasm/satire, metaphor, oxymoron, personification,** and **simile.**

films See **motion pictures.**

first person See **person** and **personal pronoun.**

first proofs The first set of proofs sent by the **compositor** to the publisher and by the publisher to the author. The first proofs may be either **galley proofs** or **page proofs.**

first serial rights See **rights.**

flags See **copyediting.**

flammable/inflammable/nonflammable These three **adjectives** have caused considerable confusion and need to be used with care. *Flammable* and *inflammable* are **synonyms** meaning easily ignited and tending to burn rapidly:

> Because the bedding was *flammable/inflammable,* it was taken off the market.

Although the word *flammable* is clear to most people, many mistakenly believe that *inflammable* means not flammable. Therefore, authorities recommend that one use *flammable* rather than *inflammable* to describe something that is combustible.

Nonflammable is the only one of the three words that means not flammable or not combustible:

> Since the new bedding is *nonflammable,* it meets required safety standards.

flats See **printing.**

flier/flyer The **nouns** *flier* and *flyer* both refer to a pamphlet or circular usually intended for wide distribution. *Flier* is the preferred form in the United States and *flyer* in England.

flush-and-hang style See **bibliography.**

flyer See **flier/flyer.**

flyleaf A usually blank page placed at the beginning or end of a book in addition to the **endpaper.** Occasionally, the page has a special design or text printed on it.

flysheet A printed sheet, pamphlet, or handbill (advertising) often distributed by hand; not to be confused with a **flyleaf.**

folded and gathered sheets See **folding.**

folding Before **binding** can begin, the *press sheets* (printed sheets) must be folded into **signatures** of eight, sixteen, twenty-four, thirty-two, forty-eight, or sixty-four pages. Additional card or paper inserts are added to a signature separately.

The basic sheets for the signature are first placed in order and then folded in half over and over until only one page is showing and all pages open in the proper sequence. The *folded and gathered sheets* (also called *f's and g's*) are then ready for sewing. See the steps described in **binding.**

folios See **page numbers.** See also the discussion of *inclusive numbers* in **numbers,** and see **back matter, front matter,** and other entries pertaining to parts of a book in which the use of page numbers is discussed.

font A complete set of type of one size and face including all letters, numbers, punctuation marks, accents, and other symbols. See **typeface.**

footer Printing that is placed in the bottom margin of a page, such as a page number, title, or date that is repeated throughout the document. Compare with **header.**

footnotes The **notes** that correspond to reference numbers in the running text may be placed at the bottoms of the pages where the text numbers occur (footnotes) or may be collected at the end of a chapter, book, or article (**endnotes**). Footnotes are most common in scholarly works and are used less and less in other material. In nonscholarly works, end-of-chapter or end-of-book notes are more common, and commentary that might otherwise appear in a discussion footnote (*substantive note*) is incorporated into the regular text discussion.

When footnotes are used, they are numbered consecutively throughout a chapter or article starting with note 1. Each footnote is introduced by a number, letter, or symbol, which is set on line and is often indented paragraph style. The number, letter, or symbol must match a corresponding number, letter, or symbol in the text, which is set as a small **superscript** figure. This text reference figure is placed after most punctuation marks but before a **dash.** End-of-sentence note figures are less distracting to a reader than those placed in the middle of sentences:

> The records were classified under the rules of the new system, although remnants of the old system remained.[1]

Compare this type of text-numbering system to the numberless **author-date citation** system.

Superscript footnote numbers after subheads and article or chapter titles should be avoided. Numbers following a text subhead should be moved to a suitable place in the text discussion. Numbers following a chapter or article title should be deleted and the numbered note replaced by an unnumbered footnote or endnote.

For example, if a note makes a general comment about an entire chapter, it might be set as an unnumbered note preceding the numbered notes of an endnotes section. If a note provides reprint or copyright information concerning a chapter, it might be set as an unnumbered footnote at the bottom of the chapter opening page.

Notes to **tables** and **illustrations** are numbered apart from the text footnotes or endnotes and are positioned after the material to which they pertain.

Footnotes may consist of only source data or only discussion, or they may consist of both sources and comments. When a work requires both types of notes, the source notes consisting only of source data may be set as endnotes; the substantive notes consisting only of discussion may be set as bottom-of-page footnotes. In such cases the endnotes may have corresponding superscript numbers in the text, and the footnotes may have corresponding superscript letters or symbols, such as asterisks and daggers.

A short rule may be placed between the last sentence of text on a page and any footnotes set at the bottom of that page:

---

a. The data for this project were verified by the Altman Research Institute in Atlanta.

When a work does not have a complete **bibliography** or **reference list,** it is very important that the footnotes or endnotes include full bibliographic data the first time each source is cited. Thereafter, a shortened reference may be used. See examples in the forthcoming list. The full data are often repeated in each chapter with each first occurrence in that chapter.

An author's name should be stated exactly as it appears on the title page of the work being cited. When an author's name is known but is not listed on the title page, the name should be enclosed in brackets. After the first use of an author's name, *idem* may be substituted for the name in successive references within a single note.

Various forms can be used to refer to a source more than once without having to repeat the full data each time. For example, *ibid.* can be used to refer to an immediately preceding work. *See also,* followed by a shortened reference, can be used to refer to a prior work other than the immediately preceding work. *Cf.* (scholarly works) or *compare* (general works) can be used to refer to a preceding work that merits comparison with the work presently being cited. All of these expressions are set in **roman type** in footnotes and are not capitalized unless they begin a sentence.

The following examples, which contain the same source data as that used in the **bibliography** and **reference-list** entries, illustrate a common arrangement of information in a footnote. Examples of shortened references, as well as *idem, ibid., see also,* and *cf.,* described previously, are also included. As is true with all forms of citation, consistency is more important to most publishers than the precise form or arrangement of data that an author uses:

1. Many organizations have adopted Watson's theory, but some holdouts are inevitable. Neville C. Abramson, *Essays from Below,* 2 vols. (Cincinnati: Middle America Printers, 1990), 1:5.

2. Neville C. Abramson, M. T. Cline, and Laura J. Oporde, eds., *The Letters of Thomas Porter Smith,* 3 vols. (Hunter, N.J.: Notebook Press, 1988), 2:211–14.

3. Abramson, *Essays from Below,* 1:17.

4. Ibid., 1:13.

5. Wirth Barkley, *DeSteeges Blanc,* trans. Pamela Merriman (New Orleans: Southern Publishers Institute, 1995), 100–109.

6. Jeanne Crisp, Introduction to *The Failing Law,* by Parker Rogers (Des Moines: Modern American Printers, 1991), 311–401; idem, ''Time Travels,'' in *Tomorrow Today,* ed. Eugene Carson III (San Francisco: Oceanside Press, 1984), 92.

7. Abramson agreed in *Essays from Below,* 2:79; see also [James J. Davis], *On Learning Less* (Phoenix: Sun Publishing, 1997), 111–12.

8. [Davis], *On Learning Less,* 114.

9. Not everyone can deal with a concept of this complexity, a point emphasized throughout *Downhill from There* (Phoenix: Sun Publishing, 1998).

10. Cf. Crisp, Introduction.

11. Maxine Nester, ed., Tulane Harman to John Silver, 2 November 1775, in *The Letters of Tulane Harman* (Miami: Eastern College Press, 1994).

12. Ibid.

13. J. K. Ishmael, *Hordes from the Past, Book 2: Asian Invaders* (reprint, New York: Towers Press, 1979), 40–78; idem, ed., *An Introduction to the Middle East,* vol. 2, *The Early Wars,* by Steven Hill (N.p.: Bet-

ter Publishing, 1986), 18–61; see also Barkley, *De-Steeges Blanc,* 416.

14. J. K. Ishmael, ed., *The Jasmine Anthology,* forthcoming.

15. Timothy B. King, "Another Story." *Port Smith Review* 13, no. 2 (March 1997): 3–11.

16. Perhaps, but Davis contradicts himself repeatedly in *On Learning Less;* see pages 21 and 74 for examples.

17. Timothy B. King, "The Truth about Webster," *Historical Studies,* vol. 1 (spring 1992).

18. C. V. Koleman and N. B. Ullman, "Growing Up Old," *Besters Journal,* January 1996, 21–23.

19. Ibid., 22.

20. *Milwaukee News,* 2 March 1990, sec. 2A, p. 4.

21. Mary O. Misner, Interview by author, tape recording, Washington, D.C., 12 August 1984; see also Koleman and Ullman, "Growing Up Old," 21.

22. Ellen P. Norris, "Working in a Home Office," paper presented at the annual meeting of the Northern Telecommuters Society, Detroit, Mich., May 1988.

23. Ibid.

24. Oregon Research Training Department, "Workshop II Program," Oregon Research Center, Portland, Oreg., 1967, photocopy.

25. Parnelli Manuscripts, Parnelli House Collection, Central College Library, Duluth, Minn., n.d.

26. *Riche Dictionary of Economics,* 12th ed., s.v. "finance."

27. Rutherford Marley, the new director, reversed the decision of his predecessor his first day in office. That bold decision set the tone for the rest of the year. King, in "Another Story," 10, said the signs were all present even before Marley took over.

28. *United States v Southern Hills,* 174 F3d 107, 108 (3d Cir 1960).

29. U.S. Congress, Senate, Committee on Foreign Relations, *South African Uprising: Hearing before the Committee on Foreign Relations,* 99th Cong., 1st sess., 21 March 1985.

30. UTEM, Princeton, N.J.: National Library of Political Conferences, 1992–. Available through the National Society of Public Colleges On-Line Database.

31. Ibid.

32. Noreen Winston, "A Study of Affirmative Action from Its Rise to Decline" (Ph.D. diss., University of Hawaii, 1995). Cf. Parnelli Manuscripts and Misner, Interview.

33. "Young Company Ripe for Merger." URL: http://www.svc-online.org/newsletr/apr6-99.html.

for-/fore- Although the **prefixes** *for-* and *fore-* have different meanings, misspellings often occur in words formed with these affixes. *For-* has numerous meanings ranging from prohibit (*forbid*) to apart (*forget*) to neglect (*forsake*) to excess (*forlorn*):

He decided to *forgo* dessert.

Fore- also has several meanings ranging from before (*forewarn*) to the front (*forehead*) to preceding (*forerunner*):

It would be nice if we could *foretell* a decline in the stock market.

for example See **e.g.**

foreign names See **names, foreign.**

foreign words Foreign words that are not completely *Anglicized,* or fully assimilated into the English language, should be set in **italics** and accented according to the style in the country of origin. See **diacritical marks.** If a foreign word is made **plural** for purpose of a discussion in English, the *-s* that is added to the foreign word should be set in **roman type:**

comité (committee): *comité*s

Words that are fully assimilated, such as many of the words of foreign origin appearing in English-language dictionaries, should be set in roman type. Diacritical marks may be, but need not be, omitted. Observe the style of your employer or publisher. The following list has examples of familiar foreign words that need not be italicized or accented:

a la carte	elan
a priori	ex officio
aperitif	facade
bona fide	gratis
cliche	hors d'oeuvres
cloisonne	jardiniere
cortege	naive
crepe	nom de plume
critique	rendezvous
debutante	repertoire

Capitalization, punctuation, and spelling of non-Anglicized foreign words should follow the style in the country of origin:

Ankläger (German: prosecutor)
éducateur (French: educator)

However, titles or names of people, organizations, streets, buildings, and so on are set in roman type:

Carmine G. D'Aloisio
Banco Interamericano de Desarrollo
Centralbahnplatz 2
le Palais du Louvre

A foreign word that is part of an English name should not be repeated in English:

Rio [river] Grande (not *Rio* Grande *River*)
Sierra [mountain range] Nevada (not *Sierra* Nevada *Mountains*)

When foreign words appear in English titles, such as in a **footnote,** the words are capitalized according to the style of the country of origin:

3. James D. Crosse, Jr., *A New Face for l'Académie française* (Chicago: The East-West Press, 1997).

The translation of a foreign word may be enclosed in **parentheses** following the word:

According to the South American tourist, the accident occurred *de noche* (in the nighttime).

foreword An introductory statement in a book written by someone other than the author or editor, sometimes by a prominent person who is qualified to comment on the subject of the work. The foreword, which usually is only a few pages, begins on a **recto** or **verso** page immediately preceding the **preface** in the **front matter.** Page numbers are printed in small **roman numerals** the same as pages in other parts of the front matter.

The name of the person writing the foreword is placed two or more lines below the last sentence flush right or indented slightly from the right margin. The person's title or affiliation also may be given immediately below the name, often in smaller type and set against the right margin.

format The shape and size of a document and the arrangement of its elements on the page to create a desired appearance. An author makes format decisions when preparing the **manuscript,** and a publisher makes format decisions when producing the work. See **design.**

Using a **word processing** program's formatting feature, an author can select a variety of settings, such as those for margins, spacing, **indentions,** tab stops, type styles (bold, **italics, caps and small caps,** and so on), number of columns, and many other factors that together will produce a desired look. The publisher makes similar decisions in conjunction with the design prepared for the document. Both **desktop publishing** and other methods of composition have sophisticated page-makeup features to carry out the format decisions that are made for a document.

See also **typeface** and **typesetting.**

four-color process The **halftone** reproduction of photographs or artwork in full color by using four or more plates, each to print a different color. The four *primary colors* used in process color printing are cyan, magenta, yellow, and black. By combining the three hues and black in varying proportions it is possible to print virtually any color in the spectrum. Black, which technically is the absence of color rather than another hue, is needed to create darker shades.

fractions Write common fractions in nonscientific text as words:

Ned's office is only *one-half mile* from his house.
She prepared the index on *four-by-six-inch cards.*

Use **numerals** if fractions combined with whole numbers are too cumbersome when written as words:

The book has a *5½-by-8½-inch trim size.*

Use numerals for fractions expressing physical quantities in scientific text:

$2\frac{2}{3}$ feet (*or* ft.)
$8\frac{1}{4}$ gallons (*or* gal.)

An author using a **word processing** program writes fractions in running text full size using a solidus, or slash, between the parts (1/6). **Compositors,** however, may set the numbers in a stacked style as *case fractions* (⅙).

See also **decimal fractions, equations,** and **percentages.** See **numbers** for rules about using words or numerals in scientific and nonscientific copy.

fragment, sentence See **sentence.**

front matter Also called *preliminaries;* one of the three main divisions in a book preceding the regular text pages and the **back matter.** The front matter consists of some or all of these parts, positioned in the order listed here:

half-title page

series-title page

list of contributors (see **contributors, list of**)

frontispiece

title page

copyright page

dedication

epigraph

contents page

list of illustrations (see **illustrations, list of**)

list of tables (see **tables, list of**)

foreword

preface

acknowledgments

introduction

list of abbreviations (see **abbreviations, list of**)

chronology

Pages in the front matter are numbered in small **roman numerals** beginning with the half-title page, which is counted as page i. However, the numbers are not printed on the pages until the contents page, which is usually page v or vi. See the various entries indicated in the preceding list for further details about position (**recto** or **verso**), numbering of pages, and content.

See also **endpaper** and **flyleaf**.

frontispiece An **illustration** usually printed on the back side of the **half-title page** (page ii). However, when high-quality reproduction is needed, the illustration may be printed on a separate page of coated paper. This page then has to be *tipped in,* or glued at the inner margin after the half-title page so that the illustration will face the **title page.**

Most books do not have a frontispiece, and page ii following the half-title page is usually blank.

f's and g's See **folding.**

further See **farther/further.**

future perfect tense The **tense** or **verb** form indicating that an action will have been completed at a future time. The future perfect tense is formed by combining the **auxiliary verb** *will have* or *shall have* with the **past participle** form of the main verb.

By noon Thursday she *will have written* her last column for the newsletter.

Compare with **future tense.** See also the other tenses: **past tense, past perfect tense, present perfect tense,** and **present tense.**

future tense The **tense** or **verb** form indicating that an action will occur after the present. The future tense is formed by combining the **auxiliary verb** *will* or *shall* with the main verb.

I *will finish* typing the manuscript this weekend.

Compare with **future perfect tense.** See also the other tenses: **past tense, past perfect tense, present perfect tense,** and **present tense.**

G

galleries See **illustrations.**

galley proof A proof (print) of typeset text sent to the author and to the publisher for **proofreading** and correction before being divided into pages. However, with **desktop publishing** and other computerized forms of **typesetting,** the type can usually be divided into pages (**page proofs**) immediately without first having to prepare galley proofs.

Although most **manuscripts** are set directly in page form, a galley proof may be desirable in complex documents. In such cases it is prepared as long columns of copy, which also may be cut apart and pasted onto separate sheets used to prepare a **dummy.**

After the galley proof has been read by both the author and the publisher's proofreader, the author's corrections and changes are transferred to the publisher's master copy (**master proof**). This set, containing all corrections, is then sent to the **compositor** where the indicated changes are made and page proofs are prepared.

See **proofreaders' marks** for a list of standard symbols used to mark corrections on galley proofs and page proofs.

gender In the English language, **nouns** such as *assembly-man* and *assemblywoman* and **pronouns** such as *he* and *she* are used to designate gender. However, to eliminate sexism (see **bias**), authors and editors have abandoned many of the nouns that denote gender.

For example, an *anchorman* or *anchorwoman* is now

often referred to as an *anchorperson* or simply an *anchor;* philosophers and psychologists refer to the *inner self* rather than the *inner man;* a *girl Friday* has become an *aide* or *assistant;* and a *salesman* or *saleswoman* is more commonly referred to as a *salesperson, salesclerk,* or *sales representative.*

The use of pronouns has also undergone a change. Initially, *he* and *him* were key referents for both men and women:

Each person should understand *his* responsibility.

Then the fairer but more cumbersome *he or she* or *his or her* were introduced:

Each person should understand *his or her* responsibility.

Although this usage is still common and acceptable, many writers prefer to reword sentences and use the plural *their* or *them:*

All people should understand *their* responsibilities.

Some writers have attempted to shorten the *he or she* or *him or her* form by using a slash (*he/she; him/her*). However, authorities consider this form of shorthand to be unattractive as well as unacceptable in most writing.

genuine See **authentic/genuine.**

geographical terms Spell out the names of U.S. states, territories, and possessions when they are used alone, such as in running text. Use the U.S. Postal Service's two-letter abbreviations in mailing addresses. See **address, mail.** Use the traditional form of abbreviation in **tables, notes, bibliographies, reference lists,** and other such incidental material where space is limited. See the forthcoming examples.

A few names have no traditional form of abbreviation and are always spelled out in both running text and citations: Alaska, Guam, Hawaii, Idaho, Iowa, Maine, Ohio, and Utah. The traditional abbreviation of a few other names consists of letters only, although they are punctuated traditionally, unlike the punctuation-free, two-letter postal style: C.Z. (Canal Zone), D.C., N.H., N.J., N.Y., N.C., P.R. (Puerto Rico), R.I., S.C., and V.I. (Virgin Islands). The rest of such names should be abbreviated as illustrated in the following examples:

Traditional	*Postal*
Amer. Samoa	AS
Colo.	CO
Ill.	IL
La.	LA
Nebr.	NE
N.Mex.	NM
N.Dak.	ND
Oreg. *or* Ore.	OR
Vt.	VT
Wis. *or*	
Wisc.	WI

Spell out the **prefixes** of geographic names in running text:

Saint Paul
Fort Wayne
Mount Hope
Port Washington

However, when space is limited, some publishers will allow abbreviations for *Saint* (*St. Louis*), *Fort* (*Ft. Collins*), *Mount* (*Mt. Prospect*), and *Port* (*Pt. Huron*).

See also the points of style in **names, country,** and **names, topographical.**

geological terms Many variations occur in the style of writing geological terms. When authors are preparing extensive works, they should follow the guidelines of the U.S. Geological Survey or consult the latest edition of the *United States Government Printing Office Style Manual.*

Generally, capitalize the **proper names** of geological episodes, epochs, eras, periods, revolutions, and series, but **lowercase** words such as *era* when they are used alone or when following a proper name:

Cambrian period, the period
Paleozoic era, the era
Caledonian revolution, the revolution

Whether words such as *lower, middle,* and *upper* (referring to rocks) or *early, middle,* and *late* (referring to time) should be capitalized depends on the proper name used with it. Consult a detailed guide:

Upper Cretaceous
upper Precambrian
Middle Devonian
middle Oligocene
Lower Mississippian
lower Eocene
Early Jurassic
early Paleocene

Lowercase generic structural terms and the names of minerals, but capitalize structural terms if they are part of a proper name:

anticline
dome
strata
felspar
silica
pyrite
Bighorn Basin
Ozark Plateau

Lowercase glacial and interglacial stages and the term *ice age* when it is used generally. Capitalize it in reference to the Recent or Pleistocene glacial epoch:

third interglacial stage
the Ice Age, or the Pleistocene
an ice age

See **historical terms** for the treatment of prehistoric periods.

gerund A **verbal** noun; a **verb** written with an *-ing* ending and used as a **noun.** A gerund may be the **subject** of a sentence, the **direct object** of a **verb,** a **predicate nominative** or **complement,** the **object of a preposition,** or an **appositive:**

> *Running* [subject] is his favorite sport.
> We enjoy *traveling* [direct object].
> Seeing is *believing* [complement].
> Autumn is a good time for *hiking* [object of preposition].
> Her favorite pastime, *reading* [appositive], contributed toward a marked improvement in her reading speed.

When a **phrase** includes a gerund, it is known as a *gerund phrase* and functions the same as a gerund alone:

> *Writing articles about social problems* [gerund phrase as subject] has made me more compassionate toward society's less fortunate citizens.

See also **participle** for another type of verbal with an *-ing* ending but one used as an **adjective** rather than a noun.

gerund phrase See **gerund** and **noun phrase.**

gerund phrase, dangling See **dangling gerund phrase.**

glossary An alphabetical list of selected terms, often consisting of technical or specialized language, and their definitions. Glossary entries are usually brief, unlike some of the comparatively long entries used in an encyclopedic dictionary.

The glossary in a book is placed in the **back matter** between the **notes** and **bibliography.** It is set like a separate section or chapter, and pages are numbered with **arabic numerals** the same as those in the main text. The opening page may begin on a **recto** or **verso** page.

An entry in the glossary of a handbook about meetings and conferences might resemble this:

> **ad hoc committee** A committee formed temporarily for a particular purpose, such as a committee formed *ad hoc* to examine the proposed sites for a technical conference.

gobbledygook Unclear, pedantic, wordy language. Gobble-dygook may include some or all of the following: **abstract nouns,** other **abstract words, cliches, euphemisms, foreign words, jargon, pompous language, vague words, vogue words,** and **wordiness.** It usually results from an attempt to make something sound important or official.

Gobbledygook is often an extreme version of confusing language and may be so muddled and bombastic that it defies translation into simple, straightforward English:

> The expressed fluidity of the problematic denouement has precipitated a policy of fractional retrenchment pursuant to further access of retrievable data in the feedback.

Although it is by no means obvious what that passage means, it may be something as simple as this:

> Because we were uncertain how to resolve the problem, we decided to wait until we had more facts.

gods See **deities.**

good/well *Good* has eroded the domain of *well* in informal language, especially in reference to state of health:

> How are you? I'm *good,* thanks.

In a strict sense, such usage implies that the person responding is behaving properly or is being moral (I'm a *good* person). The answer ''Very *well,* thanks,'' would more appropriately imply that the person is in good health, which is what the questioner presumably wanted to know.

Although *well* may be used as an **adjective** to describe a person's health (he's not a *well* person), its general use is as an **adverb** meaning ably:

> The company performed *well* [ably] last quarter in spite of the stiff competition.

Good is properly used as an adjective to describe someone or something. However, critics believe it is a **vague**

word that should be replaced by something more specific, such as *fast-paced:*

Wasn't that a *good* movie?

Although *good* is commonly used as an adjective, it should not qualify a **verb:**

He writes *well* [not *good*].
But: He does a *good* job in writing the management
   column.

As language standards become more relaxed, it is likely that *good* and *well* will be used interchangeably in more situations. Nevertheless, careful writers should continue to observe the clear distinction between the two words.

got/gotten *Got* is the **past tense** of the **verb** *get:*

We *get* a sales report each Tuesday.
We *got* a sales report last Tuesday.

The past participle of *get,* used with *have, has,* or *had,* is also *got* or, colloquially, *gotten.* See **colloquial English.** *Got* is often used colloquially to mean owned or possessed or must or might:

Colloquial: He *has got* a new car.
Better: He *has* a new car.

Colloquial: I *have got* to leave.
Better: I *have* to [*must*] leave.

Gotten is often used colloquially to mean obtained or to indicate progression:

Colloquial: Each year she *has gotten* a free pass to the
   show.
Better: Each year she *has received* a free pass to the
   show.

Colloquial: His grades *have* [progressively] *gotten* better
   this year.
Better: His grades *have improved* this year.

In most writing *get* and *got* can be safely used in both the **present tense** and the past tense. However, when the **past participle** (*have/has/had got* or *gotten*) is called for, it is often better to reword the sentence:

We *have* [not *have got*] to make [or *must make*] a decision this week.

We *had received* [not *had got/gotten*] another offer by then.

governmental bodies Capitalize the official names of governmental bodies, including local, state, national, and international offices, groups, and organizations. **Lowercase** general references to the body or to a type of body:

Winslow City Council, the city council, a council
General Assembly of North Carolina, the assembly, the legislature
Federal Aviation Agency, the agency
Bureau of the Census, the Census Bureau, the bureau
Department of Transportation, the Transportation Department, the department
U.S. Congress, the Congress, congressional hearings
U.S. House of Representatives, the House
U.S. government, the federal government, the Clinton administration
United Nations Security Council, the Security Council, the council
British Parliament, the Parliament, a parliament, parliamentary law

See also **political bodies.**

grammar The structure of language; the study of the relationship of words and how they work within a language; the system and rules that describe and define a language and provide a basis for the logical formation of sentences, including word formation, **inflections,** and **syntax.**

The two main divisions of grammar are the **sentence** and the **parts of speech: noun, pronoun, adjective, adverb, verb, preposition, conjunction,** and **interjection.**

Editors and professional writers need to have a working knowledge of the rules and conventions that apply to these two divisions. This understanding is essential to be able to avoid errors, correct those that do occur, and express oneself accurately and intelligently.

grant of rights See **licensing of rights.**

graphics The pictorial representation of data. Computer-generated graphics consist of two principal types: art software, or painting programs, and graph-drawing software, or business graphics.

With *art software* a user can create a variety of shapes and styles of lines, different shapes and sizes of text characters, and various colors and patterns of foreground and background. With *graph-drawing software* a user can display on screen a variety of graphs, or charts, including line graphs (*histograms*), bar graphs, picture graphs (*pictograms*), and pie graphs.

Line graphs have thin lines that connect intersecting points on a grid of vertical and horizontal lines to show the relationship between two sets of numbers or to plot variations in data over time.

Bar graphs have thick horizontal bars that show values or quantities of items. When the bars are vertical, the graph is a *column graph*, although the term *bar graph* is used broadly to refer to both horizontal- and vertical-style graphs.

Picture graphs are a type of bar graph that uses picture symbols instead of a solid bar to represent items or values.

Pie graphs are circular drawings with wedge- or pie-shaped divisions that represent a portion of the whole.

For the treatment and handling of graphics material in documents, see **illustrations, typeface,** and **typography.**

grave accent See **diacritical marks.**

Greek alphabet Letters of the Greek alphabet are often used in statistical and mathematical copy. See **mathematical expressions.** The following list includes the capital and **lowercase** letters of the Greek alphabet:

Name	Character	
Alpha	A	α
Beta	B	β
Gamma	Γ	γ
Delta	Δ	δ
Epsilon	E	ε
Zeta	Z	ζ
Eta	H	η
Theta	Θ	θ
Iota	I	ι
Kappa	K	κ
Lambda	Λ	λ
Mu	M	μ
Nu	N	ν
Xi	Ξ	ξ
Omicron	O	ο
Pi	Π	π
Rho	P	ρ
Sigma	Σ	σ ς[1]
Tau	T	τ
Upsilon	Υ	υ
Phi	Φ	φ
Chi	X	χ
Psi	Ψ	ψ
Omega	Ω	ω

[1]The second character is used in the final position.

guarantee/guaranty/warranty The **nouns** *guarantee*, *guaranty*, and *warranty* are **synonyms** when used broadly or generally to refer to a pledge or promise to assume responsibility for something:

The court required their *guarantee/guaranty/warranty* that the obligation will be satisfied.

Guarantee can be used as a **verb** meaning to ensure that something will perform as stated or that there will be a promised outcome. As a noun, it refers to the particular assurance:

They *guarantee* that the product will save time.
The product has a one-year *guarantee*.

A *guaranty* is not only an agreement to ensure payment of a debt but also the thing that is given as security for the debt:

The car was his *guaranty* for the loan.

Guarantee is the more widely used and is the only one of the two terms commonly used as a verb meaning to promise. *Guaranty* is mostly used in business to designate the fact of giving security, as in a contract of *guaranty*.

Generally, *warranty* (sometimes *warrant*) is an official authorization or sanction but is primarily used as a legal term to mean a guarantee by a seller of goods that the facts as stated are correct, that the product being sold is reliable and free of known defects, and that the seller will repair or replace anything defective in the product within a certain time:

The *warranty* on the humidifier does not cover the removable belt.

The verb form, used like the verb *guarantee*, is *warrant*:

The company *warrants* that the product is reliable.

guaranty See **guarantee/guaranty/warranty.**

H

hacek See **diacritical marks.**

half The **fraction** *one-half* is commonly shortened to *half* in general descriptions:

> *Half* of the envelope was torn and stained.
> The company announced that *half* a million dollars will go to charity.

When *half* is used with a singular or *noncount* **noun,** referring to an item that you can't count, such as *sky,* it should be followed by a singular **verb.** When it is used with a plural or *count noun,* referring to an item that you can count, such as *cars,* it should be followed by a plural verb. The word *of,* although frequently used after *half,* should be omitted if the sentence reads clearly and properly without it:

> At least *half* [of] the country [singular, noncount noun] *is* rural.
> *Half* [of] the students [plural, count noun] *were* cheering while the rest remained silent.

The word *half* is used in many expressions in which the fraction *one-half* is unsuitable or uncommon:

> The invitation gives the time as *half* past seven o'clock.
> She left during the second *half* of the game.
> Is that his *half*-brother?

The **article** *a*, often used unnecessarily before *half,* should be omitted when the sentence is clear without it:

We have [a] *half* an hour to wait.
But: He returned a year and *a half* later.

The singular *half* is used in reference to a division of an item into two parts:

He divided the remaining cash in *half* [not *halves*] and gave the two of us an equal share.
But: He divided the remaining cash into *thirds* [or *quarters*] and gave the three [or four] of us an equal share.

half-title page The half-title page is usually the first page with **printing** in a book. Although the page number does not appear on the page, it is counted as **recto** page i in the **front matter.** Usually, the half-title page contains only the main title of the document. The subtitle, author's name, and most other data are omitted. However, it may include a series title (see **series-title page**) or an **epigraph.**

The back of the half-title page, page ii, is often blank but may consist of a series title, list of contributors (see **contributors, list of**), or **frontispiece.** Occasionally, the title page is spread across pages ii and iii.

halftone A reproduction of artwork or a photograph in which gradations of light are created by photographing the subject through a fine screen to break up the image into very small dots of varying size and density (visible only through a magnifying glass); the process of creating this type of image.

A *halftone screen* is used to transform the image into the tiny dots, with the lightest areas having the smallest dots and the darkest areas having the largest dots. When the halftone is printed, the tiny dots combine to give the appearance of a continuous tone.

See **illustrations** for the placement and identification of halftones and other material in a printed work.

halftone screen See **halftone.**

handle/manage The **verbs** *handle* and *manage* are **synonyms** in a broad sense meaning to control:

> Jim can *handle/manage* stressful situations better than I can.

However, *handle* is the more appropriate choice to mean physical control, operation, or direction:

> Can you *handle* the telephones while I take this package to the mail room?

Manage is the better choice to mean nonphysical control or direction:

> She'll *manage* the office while her boss is out of town.

Both terms suggest the existence of or need for competence and responsibility in control or direction.

hang-and-flush style More commonly *flush-and-hang* style. See **bibliography** and **reference list.**

hardcover See **cover.**

hardly See **barely/hardly/scarcely.**

hardware See **computer terms.**

he/she, him/her, they See **gender.**

header Information, such as a title, date, or page number, positioned in the top margin of a page and repeated throughout a document. Compare with **footer.**

head(ing) The title, subtitle, or other identifying label that introduces certain material. The **contents page** lists chapter titles and sometimes the text subheads within the chapters. Whereas titles on chapter opening pages are often set in a larger display type (see **typeface**), subheads within the chapters are usually set in a smaller and sometimes different type as specified by the book **design.**

Subheads may consist only of words, or numbers may precede the words in some reference works. Double numbers are commonly used, with the first number referring to

the chapter and the second referring to the subhead: 1.1,
1.2, 2.1, 2.2, and so on.

The wording of subheads should be concise and meaningful. It should also be parallel. For example, the main
headings may all consist of two or three words and the
secondary headings one word each:

Parts of Speech
    Noun
    Pronoun
    Adjective
    Verb
    Adverb
    Preposition
    Conjunction
    Interjection

If a few subheads are one- or two-word descriptions and
the others are **phrases, clauses,** or full **sentences,** the subheads are not parallel:

Parts of Speech
    Noun
    Pronouns Everyone Should Know
    Adjective
    Verb: The Action Part of Speech
    The Adverb
    Prepositions
    Different Types of Conjunctions
    Interjection

Aside from illustrating what constitutes a parallel head,
the preceding examples indicate two levels of subheads, a
main head and several secondary heads. Some complex
works may have three or four levels of subheads but seldom
more. Also, the number of levels used within the chapters
may vary. Editors commonly refer to the levels alphabetically, with A being the most important level (A level, B
level, C level, and so on).

Upper-level subheads are commonly set in a bold face
and each on a line by itself. The lowest level subhead may

be set in **italics** run in with a text paragraph and followed by a period (*run-in sidehead*).

The design will indicate whether subheads in the typeset work will be centered, flush left, indented, or run in. However, an author should select a logical pattern for the **manuscript** and follow it consistently. The following is an example of four possible levels of headings:

A level: Centered in bold type

B level: Flush left in bold type

C level: Indented one-half inch in bold type

D level: Run in with a paragraph in italic type

Editors should check that an author has used parallel wording, a consistent capitalization and punctuation style, and a consistent pattern of subhead levels.

Publishers prefer that a work have two or more subheads at each level within a chapter. Therefore, if a particular chapter has one A-level subhead, it should also have at least one more A head in that chapter; if a particular section has one B-level subhead, it should also have at least one more B head in that section. The editor usually circles *A, B,* and so on in the margin by each subhead to indicate to the **compositor** how the particular head should be set.

Authors should capitalize each important word in subheads. For clarity, they also should leave one or two blank lines before a subhead and one blank line after it.

Editors and compositors must watch for bad breaks in a heading. For example, a subhead at the bottom of a page or column should be followed by two or more lines of text. If that isn't possible, the head should be carried over to the next page.

See also **word division** and the style for writing **captions** and column headings in **tables.**

headnote A brief explanation preceding text or other material. For example, a **bibliography** that is divided into sections may need a headnote to explain the organization of entries and to list the titles of the various sections. When a work requires an **errata** page, a note of explanation usually precedes the list of errors. If an **index** includes something that may not be obvious to a reader, such as the way accented letters are alphabetized, an explanation should be given at the head of the index.

helping verb See **auxiliary verb.**

herein/herewith The **adverbs** *herein* and *herewith* are usually redundant, stilted, and unnecessary:

Enclosed *herein* [omit] is my check for $89.95.
Herewith [substitute *Here*] is the proposal I promised.

heteronym One of two or more **homographs** spelled the same but with different pronunciations and meanings.

him/her See **he/she, him/her, they.**

histogram See **graphics.**

historic/historical Although the meanings of the **adjectives** *historic* and *historical* overlap in reference to something from the past, the terms differ in usage. *Historic* means having importance in or influence on history with a strong emphasis on the importance of an event:

The explorer's *historic* trek across Africa is remembered in the recently released movie about his life.

Historical means based on, relating to, or concerned with the character of or events belonging to the past without regard to impact or importance:

The movie includes flashbacks to several *historical* periods and uses costumes appropriate for the times.

The traditional distinction between the two terms is therefore based on whether the term refers to memorable events or merely to something past. Although language authorities prefer to reserve *historic* for events of special significance, writers often overlook the value of making this distinction and use the two terms interchangeably.

historical terms Capitalize most formal historical periods and events, but **lowercase** more recent designations:

Stone Age
Middle Ages
Renaissance
Victorian period
New Deal
Third Reich
Thirteenth Dynasty
Age of Reason
Restoration
Roaring Twenties
Boston Tea Party
Prohibition *or* prohibition
Great Society
Industrial Revolution *or* industrial revolution
Civil Rights Movement *or* civil rights movement
Paleolithic times
cold war
space age
nuclear age
baby boom

See also **centuries, cultural terms, eras,** and **geological terms.**

holes See **illustrations.**

holidays Capitalize the names of religious holidays and seasons and the names of most secular holidays or special days. **Lowercase** general descriptive names:

Christmas
Yuletide
Hanukkah
Yom Kippur
Easter
Good Friday
Ramadan
Halloween, All Hallows' Eve

Fourth of July, Independence Day
Father's Day
Veterans Day
April Fools' Day
Labor Day
V-E Day
election day

See also **calendar designations** and **abbreviations of time and days.**

holy days See **holidays.**

homograph A **homonym;** one of two or more words spelled the same but having different origins, meanings, or pronunciations. The pronunciation in the following examples consists of simple phonetic sounds. Consult a dictionary for more detailed information:

August (AW-gust): eighth month of Gregorian calendar
august (aw-GUST): marked by majestic dignity

conduct (kahn-DUCT): to direct or manage
conduct (KAHN-duct): behavior

intimate (IN-te-mit): marked by familiarity or privacy
intimate (IN-te-mate): to hint at

minute (MIN-it): one-sixtieth of an hour
minute (my-NUTE): tiny

tear (TARE): to pull apart
tear (TIER): drop secreted from eye

homonym One of two or more words spelled or pronounced the same but with different origins or meanings. Homonyms include **homophones** and **homographs.**

homophone A **homonym;** one of two or more words pronounced the same but with different origins, meanings, or spellings:

acclamation: enthusiastic approval
acclimation: process of adapting to

depravation: state of being morally corrupt
deprivation: state of having something kept or taken away

peer: a person of equal standing
pier: a platform extended over water

refind: to find again
refined: marked by politeness or freedom from impurities

troop: group of people, animals, or things, especially military units or soldiers
troupe: group of touring entertainers

honors See **awards and honors** and **military honors.**

hopefully The **adverb** *hopefully,* meaning in a hopeful manner, is widely used by writers and the public in general but is disliked by many language authorities. Those who support its use believe it is as suitable as various other words ending in *-ly,* such as *happily.* Those who object to it prefer that writers reword a sentence to be more precise:

Hopefully [We hope], the two groups have merged.

Sometimes a different placement of the word *hopefully* is enough to make the meaning clear.

The two groups merged *hopefully [with great hope for a successful future].*

Although one can point to occasions when the use of words such as *hopefully* or *happily* may create doubt about the precise meaning, the intent is usually clear. However, critics argue that *hopefully* is a positive prediction of trouble-free operation, and *I hope* is a simple wish that there won't be any further trouble (but without any intent to predict the outcome).

Those who believe that the use of *hopefully* raises legitimate concerns about meaning and those who observe the traditional rules of English usage can best avoid the term. However, there is little evidence that people have any intention of abandoning the term or that they're even aware of any usage problem.

hot stamping See **embossing.**

hyperbole Exaggerated language or overstatement not meant to be taken literally but rather used to emphasize something or to create a certain effect. Often, however, the frequent use of hyperbole has an unintended effect—that of dull, stale prose. See also **cliches:**

> Visit our new custom homes with *tons of amenities* at *rock-bottom prices.*

> See also **figure of speech.**

hypermedia Also called *interactive multimedia*; a **hypertext** system capable of displaying two or more media in addition to text. Writers and editors can control a variety of media with such computer-based programs, including audio, video, still images, animated images, photographs, and text.

hypertext A computer-based retrieval system in which writers and editors can access words and sections in a variety of documents or files without having to close one file before moving to the next one. The World Wide Web is an example of a very large hypertext-style program that links files from around the world and opens them to users who can move from one to another.

hyphen (-) The hyphen has eight principal uses:

> To divide a long word at the end of a line: quantitative.

> To connect **numbers** indicating time spans: 1998-99 (but not *from* 1998-99 or *between* 1998-99).

> To connect **prefixes** with a capitalized **proper noun:** pro-American.

> To divide a prefix from the rest of the word so that it will not be confused with a similar term: re-form (to form again)/reform (to abolish abuse).

To indicate that nouns are of equal rank or status: owner-operator. See **hyphenate.**

To connect the parts of certain **compound terms:** editor-in-chief.

To indicate a temporary compound **adjective** preceding a **noun:** high-income residents.

To indicate a series of compound adjectives preceding a noun: 3-by-5-inch cards; two- to three-story apartments (*suspended hyphen*).

hyphenate A person with dual nationality or mixed background; the designation of someone who performs equal tasks. A hyphen usually connects two terms indicating equal tasks and two terms designating nationalities when one of the two is a **prefix.** When both terms designating nationality are complete words, the hyphen is omitted:

Afro-American, African American
Euro-Asian, European Asian
Russo-Italian, Russian Italian
writer-editor
actor-director

See also **peoples** and **titles, personal and professional.**

hyponym A word whose meaning is included in, implied by, or related to that of another, broader or more inclusive term. *Carmine* is a hyponym of the broader term *red,* and *cricket* is a hyponym of the more inclusive category *insects.*

i.e. Abbreviation for the Latin term *id est*—that is. The abbreviation should not be used in running text. However, when space is very limited, it is sometimes used within **parentheses** and in **footnotes** or **tables.** Even this practice is questionable, though, since many people confuse *i.e.* with **e.g.** (for example). In most cases the abbreviation *i.e.* or the words *that is* can be omitted, or a sentence can be reworded to avoid any need for their use:

> *Not:* The employees were disgruntled over their raise; *i.e./that is,* they expected more than a 5 percent increase.
>
> *Better:* The employees were disgruntled over their raise because they expected more than a 5 percent increase.

ibid. Abbreviation for the Latin expression *ibidem*—in the same place. The abbreviation is used in **footnotes, notes,** and in **author-date citations** in the text to refer to the immediately preceding source that was cited. It is written in **roman type** and followed by a period:

> Johnson criticized Hartley for his socialistic views (McKenzie 1988, 43–44). In later years, though, he softened his view (ibid., 67).

The preceding example is also commonly written using the abbreviation for page (*p.*) instead of *ibid.*: (p. 67).

See **footnotes** and **notes** for an example of the use of *ibid.* to refer to an immediately preceding note.

-ible See **-able/-ible.**

idem See **footnotes** and **notes.**

idiom A combination of words that have a meaning different from their literal interpretation; an expression of a given language, region, or people that cannot be understood from the literal meaning of any part of it.

Idioms are usually understood by anyone fluent in the language of a country, but others inside and outside the country who translate expressions literally are often puzzled by words that cannot be understood logically. Although most people would find it difficult to carry on a conversation without using idiomatic expressions, writers should use expressions such as the following cautiously:

to all intents and purposes In essence; effectively.

generous to a fault Being so excessively generous as to embarrass others.

to be short-handed To lack necessary assistance.

at face value As valuable as it appears.

to keep track of To stay informed about someone or something.

in the pipeline In preparation and not yet complete.

to sandwich between To fit, insert, or squeeze between.

to see eye to eye To be in agreement.

to stand on ceremony To do something according to rules of etiquette or custom.

stands to reason Is the only conclusion possible.

track record The record of one's successes and failures.

The fact that an idiom may be misunderstood by some readers is a major concern, but equally troublesome is the fact that any overused expression will soon become dull and stale. In that respect many idioms are also considered **cliches,** and they should therefore be avoided in most writing.

if/whether The **conjunctions** *if* and *whether* are used interchangeably in informal writing to introduce a **clause** expressing uncertainty. Therefore, the traditional rule that *if* introduces one condition and *whether* alternate conditions is usually ignored more than it is observed. Nevertheless, careful writers make a distinction:

> *If* you look closely, you can see the difference.
>
> We were wondering *whether* [or not] the hurricane affected your town.

Language authorities are concerned that choosing the wrong conjunction may lead to misinterpretation. For example, one can interpret the following two examples in different ways:

> We should let David know *if* he's expected to attend.

The preceding example appears to say that David is unaware he may be expected to attend; therefore, we need to tell him so that he'll know. A different sense is obtained when *whether* is substituted for *if*:

> We should let David know whether [or not] he is expected to attend.

The preceding sentence appears to say that David *is* aware of the event and the fact that he may be attending; he's simply waiting for someone to tell him what to do—go or don't go.

In most cases when *if* and *whether* are used interchangeably, the likelihood of confusion among readers may be slight. However, writers who want to avoid even a slight chance of misunderstanding, which is the goal of all professionals, should keep in mind the fine shades of meaning in the use of *if* versus *whether*.

illegal/illicit/unlawful These three **adjectives** are used as **synonyms** in a broad sense. However, certain distinctions can be made. *Illegal,* which means prohibited by law or official rules, has the narrowest meaning of the three terms:

> Shoplifting is *illegal* in all fifty states.

Illicit can be used as a synonym of *unlawful* in certain contexts but not of *illegal*. It means not sanctioned by custom or law; therefore, an illicit act may or may not be illegal, but it is definitely unacceptable:

> We notice considerable *illicit* [unacceptable] material on the Internet.
> The *illicit* [illegal] drug operations were uncovered by law enforcement personnel last month.

> *Unlawful* means either illegal or illicit or both:

> Gambling is legal in Arizona, but many people consider it *unlawful* [illicit], objecting to it on moral grounds.
> Gambling, which is *unlawful* [illegal] in many states, is punishable by law.

> *Unlawful,* therefore, is sometimes synonymous with *illicit* and other times with *illegal*.

illicit See **illegal/illicit/unlawful.**

illusion See **allusion/delusion/illusion.**

illustrations Broadly, any figure (other than **tables**) used to explain, clarify, or enhance the text discussion. Line drawings, photographs, paintings, maps, charts, and graphs are different forms of illustrations.

The illustrations in a document are printed by *offset lithography* the same as the text. Figures that are printed with the text, such as **line art,** are called *text figures.* Those that are printed separately, such as reproductions of paintings or photographs (see **halftones**), are called *plates.* When a document has sections of such plates, the sections are called *galleries.*

The pages on which figures appear alone usually do not have a printed page number. Nevertheless, any such pages consisting of figures discussed in the text are usually counted in the numbering of the book's pages. Some special illustrations, however, may not have printed page numbers and also may not be counted in the numbering of pages.

Text figures should be positioned as close as possible to the place where they are first mentioned in the text. The text references to these figures should include figure numbers, if any, or otherwise the figure title or description:

As figure 4 indicates, the field office is in a remote location.
See figure 5.17.
Refer to the photograph of a scale-model universe.

The author or editor should circle *fig. 1, fig. 2,* or other identifying designation in the margins on the pages where the figures will be inserted.

Figures may be numbered consecutively throughout the entire document beginning with *figure 1*. Or, in some reference works, especially in multiauthor books, they may be numbered consecutively by chapter beginning with *figure 1* in each chapter. In the latter case double numbers are used: *figure 1.1, figure 1.2, figure 2.1, figure 2.2,* and so on.

Halftones, which may be original photographs, stock photographs, **clip art,** or other continuous-tone pieces, may be mixed in and numbered along with the other text figures. When they are grouped separately, however, they may be numbered separately. Or, more often, they may not be numbered, especially if they are not referred to in the text.

Even when certain illustrations are not numbered along with the other text figures, those illustrations should be lightly numbered (on the backs of the pieces), such as *3a, 3b, 3c,* and so on, to indicate to production personnel their proper order in the document. The same numbers should be written and circled in the margins of the text to indicate correct placement, and those numbers should also be circled in the margins next to any corresponding **captions** or **legends.**

Illustrations must be handled with care to avoid soiling or creasing them. Some may be one-of-a-kind illustrations and not easily replaced if damaged. **Cropping** should be done only with a grease pencil that will not leave creases. See also **scaling.** Instructions are best written on separate self-sticking flags affixed to the backs of the prints or to the margins. For example, an editor may need to instruct a camera operator about size or indicate whether a negative is to be screened. See **halftone.**

Figure numbers or working numbers on the backs of unnumbered prints should be cross-checked during **proofreading** to ensure that the correct illustration is in the correct order and position and carries the correct caption or legend. This information should also be compared with any list of illustrations in the **front matter.** See **illustrations, list of.**

When **page proofs** are prepared, blank pages, empty spaces (*holes*), or blank ruled boxes (*windows*) are left where photographs or other figures are to be inserted later. When **blueprints** are prepared, an editor or other person must check during the final proofreading stage to be certain that each illustration has been printed right side up and that it appears in its assigned space along with the appropriate caption or legend.

illustrations, list of When a work has more than a few **illustrations,** an author may decide to include a list of illustrations in the **front matter.** This list, located on a **recto** or **verso** page following the **contents page,** should be set in the same type size and style as that used for the table of contents. However, when illustrations are closely tied to the text, a list of illustrations may be unnecessary.

When a list of illustrations is desired, though, it is usually titled simply "Illustrations." The list should include all figures identified by number and title in the sequence in which they appear in the document. If necessary, the titles may be shortened versions of the full **captions** or **legends.**

If a document has several kinds of illustrations, the list may be organized in sections under subheads such as "Figures," "Maps," and "Plates." If the illustrations are numbered, those in each section should be numbered separately beginning with 1 in each section.

The page numbers where figures appear in a document are listed to the right of the titles on the list of illustrations in the same style used for pages and titles on the table of contents. If any pages with illustrations were not counted in the numbering of pages in the document, the place for page numbers on the list of illustrations should state something such as "Facing page 121" or "Following page 121."

"Facing page 121" means that a plate is not numbered or counted in the numbering of pages. However, it has been inserted so that it will face a certain text page that does have a printed page number or is at least counted in the numbering of pages.

"Following page 121" means that a *group* of plates were not numbered or counted in the numbering of pages. However, those plates have been inserted so that the group will follow a certain text page that does have a printed page number or is at least counted in the numbering of pages.

Authors often do not prepare lists of illustrations even when they are warranted. However, an editor may believe that a book with photographs and other important artwork should have such a list. In that case the editor may ask the author to prepare the list, or the editor may prepare the list in-house. It is not uncommon for an editor to revise a list prepared by an author or to decide to prepare an entirely new list of illustrations, list of tables, or table of contents.

immanent See **eminent/immanent/imminent.**

immigration See **emigration/immigration/migration.**

imminent See **eminent/immanent/imminent.**

imperative mood The form of a **verb** that gives a command, makes a request, gives directions, and so on:

Remember to take some blank disks with you.
Let me see the Madison file when you've finished.
Follow Highway 139 to the conference center.

See also **indicative mood** and **subjunctive mood.**

imperative sentence A **sentence** that makes a request or gives a command:

Please join us [request].
Close the gate [command]!

Compare with **declarative sentence, exclamatory sentence,** and **interrogative sentence.**

implicit See **explicit/implicit.**

imply/infer Writers sometimes confuse the **verbs** *imply* and *infer,* although the distinction between the two is clear. *Imply* is what a speaker or writer does to suggest something indirectly:

> When the directors say that some kind of payroll reduction is inevitable, they *imply* [*suggest*] that either layoffs or salary reductions will occur.

Infer is what a listener or reader does and means to conclude from evidence or circumstance:

> When the directors say that some kind of payroll reduction is inevitable, employees tend to *infer* [*conclude*] that they mean either layoffs or salary reductions.

impracticable/impractical Broadly, the **adjectives** *impracticable* and *impractical* are used interchangeably to mean impossible to put into practice, and in that sense *impractical* is more widely used than *impracticable.* However, the distinction between the primary senses of the two terms is important. *Impracticable* primarily means impossible to do or carry out:

> Adding help when our income is stagnant is *impracticable;* we simply can't do it.

Impractical primarily means not sensible or realistic even if possible:

> Adding help when we're uncertain whether our income will remain constant is *impractical;* we can do it, but I'm not sure it's wise.

See also **practicable/practical.**

impressions See **reprint** and **year of publication.**

impromptu See **extemporaneous/impromptu.**

in back of See **back of/behind/in back of.**

in order to This **prepositional phrase** is usually unnecessarily wordy and *to* alone will suffice in most cases:

> *In order to* [*To*] understand his actions, you need to understand his objectives.
> I wrote the article *in order to* [*to*] let people know that environmental pollution is all around us.

Some authorities suggest that *in order to* should be used in formal writing and *to* in informal writing. However, even in formal writing, if *to* can logically be substituted, the use of the longer form is still needlessly wordy.

in regard to See **as regards/in regard to/regarding/with regard to.**

in spite of See **despite/in spite of.**

inability See **disability/inability.**

inasmuch as/insofar as The **conjunctions** *inasmuch as* and *insofar as* are each written as two words. They mean to the extent that, but *inasmuch as* is primarily a wordy substitute for *since* or *because:*

> *Inasmuch as* [*Since/Because*] the trip was canceled, we're free to make other plans.

The more narrow *insofar as* is used exclusively to mean to the extent that:

> *Insofar as* the new contract allows, we will also continue our former activities.

inclusive numbers See **numbers.**

incredible/incredulous The **adjectives** *incredible* and *incredulous* both deal with believability. Although their different shades of meaning are slight, they are important. *Incredible* means being so implausible or astounding as to be almost unbelievable and usually applies to things rather than people:

Have you heard the *incredible* story of his ordeal while lost in the desert?

Incredulous means being or acting skeptical or disbelieving and applies to people rather than things:

Did you see the *incredulous* look on her mother's face when Eileen admitted that she was once a drug addict?

If you still have doubts about how to distinguish the two terms, use *incredible* to describe something daring or amazing but probably or possibly true. Use *incredulous* as a response to something too far-fetched to be true.

See also **credible/creditable/credulous.**

incredulous See **incredible/incredulous.**

indefinite adjective An **adjective** that qualifies but doesn't specifically describe the **noun** it modifies. For example, the adjective *blue* in *a blue car* describes the noun *car,* but the adjective *a* in *a car* doesn't describe the noun *car.* Notice that indefinite adjectives include **articles** such as *a* and *an:*

He has *other* ideas about revising the bylaws.
She will join us but will be *an* hour late.

indefinite pronoun A **pronoun** that stands for an object generally or indefinitely:

Do *any* of you want to come?
Everything is expensive in that store.

The following are examples of indefinite pronouns:

all	most
another	neither
any	no one
anyone	none
anything	nothing
each	one
either	other
everyone	several
everything	some
few	someone

many	something
more	such

Compare with **adjective pronoun, demonstrative pronoun, intensive pronoun, interrogative pronoun, personal pronoun, reflexive pronoun,** and **relative pronoun.** See also **reciprocal pronoun** for indefinite pronouns used in **phrases.**

indention Various items are commonly indented in a document. **Paragraphs, extracts, lists, outlines,** displayed **equations, footnotes,** and so on are usually indented from the left margin, and some also may be indented from the right margin. The author of a **manuscript** usually indents these items a standard amount according to the settings of the **word processing** program being used. However, the designer of the document may indicate different amounts of indention. See **design.**

For example, an author may indent extracts and lists a half inch from the left margin, whereas the design specifications may call for the **compositor** to use eighteen points indention from both the left and right margins. See **pica** and **point** for a description of such measurements. See also **em** for an explanation of marking indentions on a **manuscript.**

independent clause Also called *main clause;* a **clause** consisting of a group of words containing a **subject** and a **predicate** that can stand alone and does not need the rest of the sentence to be clear. In a **compound sentence,** for example, each sentence is an independent clause:

Richard designed the attachment [first independent clause], and *the lab will test it tomorrow* [second independent clause].

Compare with **dependent clause.**

index The type of index and number of indexes that are needed depend on the subject matter, the nature of the publication, and the needs of the reader. Most books have one general index that includes references to subjects, **proper names,** titles, and other pertinent material.

However, in some reference works the entries may be organized in two or more indexes, such as in an index of persons (*name index*), an index of literary titles (*title index*), and a general index of all other material (*subject index*). Specialized books may also have specialized indexes, such as the geographic index in an atlas.

Indexes are prepared after a work has been set into pages and the numbering of pages is established. Either the author or a professional indexer will prepare the index. Professional indexers often use computerized indexing programs that automatically set up and sort (alphabetize) entries. See **alphabetization** for common systems.

Some authors also prepare indexes manually. The steps include underlining **keywords** on a set of **page proofs** and transferring those words and all page numbers where the words appear to index cards. The cards are then easily shuffled into alphabetical order before typing the entries.

The capitalization and punctuation style of index entries may vary among publishers and authors, but entries primarily include subject **head(ing)s** and page, section, chapter, or other locator numbers. Main headings are usually **nouns** or **noun phrases.** The keyword in **phrases** is listed first:

plurals, foreign
pronouns, classes of

Subheadings are usually indented and listed beneath the main headings. They may each be listed on a separate line or run in paragraph style. See the forthcoming examples.

Inclusive page numbers should be used to indicate the pages where discussion of a subject continues. See **numbers** for examples of different styles for writing inclusive numbers.

Abbreviations such as *f.* (and the following page) or *ff.* (and the following pages) should not be used. *Passim* (here and there) is rarely used anymore.

Cross-references include direct references to the location

of an entry listed under another name and references to additional entries that have related material:

See page proof
See also galley proof

The following samples illustrate a common capitalization and punctuation style and arrangement of data in index entries. Notice the two examples of entries for *personal pronoun.* The first is set *run-in style,* and the second is set *list style:*

compound personal pronoun, ix, 22. *See also* personal
   pronoun

grammar. *See under specific terms*

personal pronoun, 41–52; case in, 41; compound, 22;
   gender in, 42–43; number in, 42–43; person in, 42–
   43; and relative clauses (*see* clause), 47. *See also* pronouns

personal pronoun, 41–52
   case in, 41
   compound, 22
   gender in, 42–43
   number in, 42–43
   person in, 42–43
   and relative clauses (*see* clause), 47
   See also pronouns

William, Father. *See* Adams, Jonathan

For examples of various arrangements of entries, review the indexes in different types of published works.

indicative mood The form of a **verb** that makes a statement or asks a question:

The two executives are forming a new company.
Are the two executives forming a new company?

Compare with **imperative mood** and **subjunctive mood.**

indirect object A **noun** or noun equivalent that indicates to whom, for whom, or for what the action of a **verb** is done. The indirect object usually occurs before the **direct object** in a sentence:

> She sent [verb] *him* [indirect object] a letter [direct object].
>
> His boss offered [verb] *the customer* [indirect object] free tickets [direct object].
>
> Give [verb] *the plants* [indirect object] some water [direct object].

An indirect object may also appear as a **prepositional phrase.** In that case the indirect object follows the direct object:

> She sent [verb] the letter [direct object] *to him* [indirect object].
>
> His boss offered [verb] free tickets [direct object] *to the customer* [indirect object].
>
> Give [verb] some water [direct object] *to the plants* [indirect object].

The indirect object is a **complement** in that it helps to complete the meaning of a verb.

indirect question See **question mark (?).**

ineffective/ineffectual The **adjectives** *ineffective* and *ineffectual* are **synonyms** meaning not effective, but they have slightly different connotations. See **connotation/denotation.** *Ineffective* means not producing the desired effect and implies a lack or failing associated with a particular endeavor:

> His letter was *ineffective*.

Ineffectual means insufficient to produce a desired effect and implies a broader or more general lack or failing:

> The company tried everything possible to solve its financial problems, but all efforts were *ineffectual*.

An *ineffective* person, therefore, would likely be inadequate in regard to one particular task or quality, whereas an *ineffectual* person might be generally weak in most respects. In spite of this distinction, however, writers tend to use the terms interchangeably and especially to use *ineffective* in all cases.

infamous See **famed/famous/infamous/notorious.**

infer See **imply/infer.**

infinitive A **verbal** that functions like a **noun** or **verb** and is commonly called a *verbal noun*. Occasionally, it also functions as an **adjective** or **adverb**. It is the first principal part of a **verb,** such as *write* (*write/wrote/written*), and is often preceded by *to:*

We asked him *to write.*

It may also be used alone (*bare infinitive*) without *to:*

We practically made him *write.*

An infinitive is an uninflected form (see **inflection**), and it is the form under which verbs are listed in dictionaries.

Although an infinitive has many uses, it is often most easily recognized as the **subject** of a verb:

To cheat [subject of verb *is*] is unacceptable under any circumstance.

It is also familiar as the object of a verb:

She wants *to travel* [object of verb *wants*].

See **split infinitive** for ways to handle an infinitive in which an adverb intervenes between the infinitive sign *to* and the infinitive itself (*to hastily handle*).

The infinitive and its **modifiers** or **complements** are called an *infinitive phrase*. The sign of the infinitive, *to,* is followed by a verb in this type of **phrase:**

They want *to* [sign of the infinitive] *create* [verb] *a new line of products* [complement].

An infinitive phrase should not be confused with a **prepositional phrase** beginning with *to*. Whereas in an infinitive phrase the sign *to* is followed by a verb, in a prepositional phrase it is followed by a **noun** or **pronoun**:

They drove *to* [sign] *the factory* [noun].

infinitive phrase See **infinitive** and **noun phrase**.

infinitive phrase, dangling See **dangling infinitive phrase**.

inflammable See **flammable/inflammable/nonflammable**.

inflection The changed form of a word created by adding a **suffix** or by changing the **base** (the basic part of a word to which something else may be added) to indicate a difference such as in **gender, number, person, mood,** or **tense.** Changes in **nouns** and **adjectives** tend to change the number or gender. Changes in **verbs** tend to change the number, person, mood, or tense.

The word before it is altered is the *uninflected word*. The word after it has been altered is the *inflected word*. For example, if the **present tense** of the verb *call* is changed to the **past tense** *called*, the uninflected word is *call*, and the inflected word is *called*.

inflict See **afflict/inflict**.

informal English See **colloquial English**.

ingenious/ingenuous The **adjectives** *ingenious* and *ingenuous* were once **synonyms** but now have different meanings. Nevertheless, they're sometimes misused because they look and sound similar. *Ingenious* means characterized by inventive skill and imagination:

What an *ingenious* plan!

Ingenuous means unsophisticated, unworldly, or naive:

The *ingenuous* young woman left her rural area for the first time last month.

initialism An abbreviation consisting of the first letter of each main word in a name or **phrase** and pronounced letter by letter. Most initialisms are written in **lowercase** letters without space between the letters. They are most commonly used as a form of shorthand in note taking but are also used in certain tabular material and on business forms, such as a requisition. However, they are inappropriate in general text, especially nontechnical text, or in correspondence:

aac	average annual cost
b/d	barrels per day
eer, EER	energy efficiency ratio
h/f	held for
i&p	interest and principal
lmsc	let me see correspondence
na, NA, N/A	not applicable
nes	not elsewhere specified
rps	revolutions per second
s&l	savings and loan
uv, u-v	ultraviolet
wip	work in process/progress

Compare with **acronym.** See also the various abbreviations entries at the beginning of this dictionary.

initials Publishers generally prefer that authors use their full first names on a book's cover and title page unless an author is known by initials only. When initials are used, two rather than one are preferred. Except for the initials *M.D.*, degrees or affiliations are not printed on the title page.

When initials are used alone to designate a name, as in *JFK*, they are written without space between the letters and without periods. When initials are used with a last name, both spaces and periods are used (some publishers omit the spaces when there are three or more initials):

J. B. Prendeville
H. R. T. Longman *or* H.R.T. Longman

An exception to the preceding rule applies to addressing envelopes for automated sorting. The U.S. Postal Service allows the use of all capital letters with no periods or spaces between initials that are used in place of a first name. See **address, mail.**

When a name with initials must be divided at the end of a line, it should always be divided after the initials or as a last resort between syllables in the first or last name:

M. C. / Cartwright (*preferred*)
Martin C. / Cartwright (*preferred*)
Mar / tin C. Cartwright (*avoid*)
Martin C. Cart / wright (*avoid*)

In alphabetizing **index** or other entries, a name with initials should precede a given name beginning with the same letter:

Donovan, C. Carl
Donovan, Dexter B.
Donovan, S. J.
Donovan, Samuel N.
Donovan, Samuel P.

insofar as See **inasmuch as/insofar as.**

institutions See **names, organization.**

insure See **assure/ensure/insure.**

intensifier Previously called *intensive;* a word such as *really, very, awfully, extremely, somewhat, more, most, best, quite, rather,* or *especially* that adds emphasis to an expression. Both **adverbs** (*perfectly* sensible decision) and **adjectives** (*utter* nonsense) are used as intensifiers.

Although intensifiers may be useful or even necessary to heighten or lower an effect, they tend to be overused and contribute to wordiness. Each usage should be evaluated independently and superfluous intensifiers deleted:

They were attending [a *very*] an important meeting.
It was a [*most*] significant development.

Such manuals are [*somewhat*] helpful.
The delegates had [a *rather*] an enjoyable time.

See also **absolute word** for words that cannot be compared and therefore should not be used with intensifiers such as *more* or *most*.

intensive pronoun A compound **personal pronoun** that is used to emphasize a **noun** or **pronoun** in the sentence. The compound personal pronouns are *myself, yourself, himself, itself, ourselves, yourselves,* and *themselves.*
An intensive pronoun always refers to a noun or pronoun that precedes it in the sentence:

Frank [noun] *himself* [intensive pronoun] designed the set.

Compare with **adjective pronoun, demonstrative pronoun, indefinite pronoun, interrogative pronoun, personal pronoun, reciprocal pronoun, reflexive pronoun,** and **relative pronoun.**

interactive multimedia See **hypermedia.**

interjection One of the eight **parts of speech;** a word used by itself, not as an element of sentence structure, to express strong feeling:

Ah!
Ow!
Wow!
Cheers!

When words that also are other parts of speech, such as a **noun** or **adjective,** are used to express sudden emotion or intense feeling, they have the force of an interjection and are sometimes called *exclamatory nouns, exclamatory adjectives,* and so on:

What!
Mercy!
Good!
Never!

Interjections are used primarily in fiction and should be avoided in business or technical writing and in formal material.

International Standard Book Number (ISBN) An identification number that a publisher assigns to each book. The ISBN, included in **Cataloging-in-Publication (CIP)** data, is printed on the **copyright page** and also on the back of a book **jacket** or the back **cover** of a paperback book.

The various groups of numbers in the ISBN each mean something different. In the ISBN 0-347-473586-1, for example, the first digit indicates that the book was published in an English-speaking country, the second group specifies the publisher, the third group identifies the book, and the last digit (a *check digit*) reveals any error in the preceding group. The ISBN is used as an aid in both ordering and cataloging.

See also **International Standard Serial Number (ISSN).**

International Standard Serial Number (ISSN) An identification number that a publisher of serial publications, such as magazines and journals, assigns to a series of issues. In each issue the same ISSN is printed on the page containing **copyright** data or is specified in instructions for ordering the publication.

The ISSN consists of eight digits, such as ISSN 1234-5678. Unlike the **International Standard Book Number (ISBN),** which indicates the language or country of publication, the ISSN identifies the periodical title regardless of the language or country. However, like the ISBN, the ISSN is also used to facilitate ordering and cataloging.

When a serial publication is also a book, such as a yearbook, both the ISSN and the ISBN are printed.

Internet terms Capitalize all **proper names,** including the official names of systems, programs, databases, networks, and so on. **Lowercase** general references to a procedure, application, and so on.

Transmission Control Protocol (TCP), the protocol
Internet Relay Chat (IRC), the chat service
local area network (LAN), the local network
PSINET service provider, the service provider
Network File System (NFS), the file utility
Eudora E-mail program, the E-mail program
EMACS text editor, the text editor
graphical user interface (GUI), the interface

Like computer language (see **computer terms**), Internet
language includes many **acronyms** and **initialisms.** Internet
communication also includes the use of many *smileys,* symbols that denote emotion. See **emoticons** for examples.

interrogative See **interrogative pronoun.**

interrogative adjective See **relative adjective.**

interrogative adverb An **adverb** used to ask questions.
Words such as *where, when, why*, and *how* are interrogative
adverbs and may be used to ask a direct question or state
an indirect question:

Where is the copy paper?
I wonder *where* the copy paper is.

Compare with the interrogative or **relative adjective** and
the **interrogative pronoun.**

interrogative pronoun Also called *interrogative;* a **pronoun** used to ask a question. The three interrogative pronouns are *who, what,* and *which.* Although the three keep
the same form for all **genders** (masculine, feminine, and
neuter), *who* is used only for persons, whereas *which* and
what may be used for persons, animals, or things.

Who wrote that article?
What is the meaning of that term?
Which is the best computer?

Compare with **adjective pronoun, demonstrative pronoun, indefinite pronoun, intensive pronoun, personal**

pronoun, reciprocal pronoun, and **reflexive pronoun.** See also the use of *who, what,* and *which* as **relative pronouns.**

interrogative sentence A **sentence** that asks a question:

Do you know his telephone number?

Compare with **declarative sentence, exclamatory sentence,** and **imperative sentence.**

intransitive verb A **verb** that does not need an object (see **direct object**) to complete its thought:

The student *read* rapidly.

Like other verbs, *read* could also take an object and in that case would be a **transitive verb:**

The student *read* the book [direct object] rapidly.

An **auxiliary verb,** which connects a subject to its **complement** or a **modifier,** is intransitive:

I *am* happy [modifies *I*].

introduction An introduction may be a separate part in the **front matter** or the first chapter of the main text. Also, chapters and sections within chapters as well as any part of the book, such as the **appendix,** may have a paragraph of introduction or a separate brief introductory section.

A separate introduction in the front matter is styled similar to a **preface** or **foreword.** A separate introduction in the main body of a book is styled like a text chapter. Brief introductory paragaraphs within the regular chapters and any associated subheads are styled the same as other paragraphs and subheads in the rest of the chapter.

When an introduction to a complete document is very short and is not an essential part of the text, it is usually placed on a **recto** or **verso** page in the front matter following the **preface** and **acknowledgments.** Pages are then numbered with small **roman numerals** the same as other pages in the front matter.

A longer introduction that begins the subject of the document, perhaps providing historical background, is essential to the text and is therefore positioned after the front matter beginning with the first (**recto**) text page. Pages are then numbered with **arabic numerals** the same as the other text pages.

An introduction may be titled simply "Introduction," or it may use descriptive language, such as "Introduction to Graphic Design." It also may be the first numbered chapter ("Chapter 1: Introduction to Graphic Design"), or it may be unnumbered, in which case the next (second) chapter is Chapter 1.

invent See **discover/invent.**

irony/sarcasm/satire These three **nouns** all refer to a form of contempt or mockery and therefore are not suitable for straightforward text, such as that of a business or technical document. However, all three forms are used in fiction and in some nonfiction writing when it is certain that the audience will understand the intent.

Although there are different kinds and degrees of irony, in one familiar sense *irony* is an expression of something opposite or different from the literal or usual meaning:

"How lovely—I have a new car and three days vacation, and a snowplow just buried the car in a mountain of snow."

Sarcasm is less subtle or mild than irony. It is a cruel, cutting remark that is intended to ridicule and wound someone:

Everyone laughed weakly at Troy's joke except Ed, who patted him on the back and said: "You're as funny as mud, aren't you?"

Satire is another form of ridicule, but it uses wit, humor, irony, and parody to ridicule, mock, or expose human vice, folly, and stupidity:

In *Catch-22*, the *satire* by Joseph Heller, the characters learned that every time they made a move, it simply caused further problems.

irregular verb A **verb** that forms the **past tense** and **past participle** usually through a change in the word, such as by a change in a **vowel** or by adding *-en* rather than *-ed* to the **stem**. Therefore, whereas the parts of the regular verb *call* are *call, called,* and *have/has/had called,* the parts of the irregular verb *take* are *take, took,* and *have/has/had taken.* The following are examples of the present, past, and past participle of irregular verbs (add *have/has/had* to the examples in the third column):

present	*past*	*past participle*
arise	arose	arisen
be	was	been
break	broke	broken
cost	cost	cost
deal	dealt	dealt
give	gave	given
hide	hid	hidden
lend	lent	lent
rise	rose	risen
steal	stole	stolen

irreversible/irrevocable The **adjectives** *irreversible* and *irrevocable* both mean that it's impossible to change something. However, in strict usage they apply to different things. *Irreversible,* which means impossible to reverse, primarily applies to a general plan, pattern, or course of action:

> The developing country seems to be caught in an *irreversible* trend toward socialism.

Irrevocable, which means impossible to revoke or retract, primarily applies to specific statements, decisions, laws, or actions:

> Since he has already signed the contract, his decision to relocate is *irrevocable.*

irrevocable See **irreversible/irrevocable.**

-ise/-ize/-yze Many people have trouble spelling words with these endings. Certain words must be spelled with *-ise,* including the following:

advertise	exercise
advise	franchise
apprise	improvise
compromise	supervise
devise	surmise
enterprise	televise

The **-ize** ending has been useful in creating many new words, and more words now end with *-ize* than with both *-ise* and *-yze*. However, authorities generally object to some of the words, such as *finalize, prioritize,* and *strategize.* Critics believe that such formations are unnecessary and crude and that *-ize* is being overused to such an alarming extent that it threatens the clarity and validity of **standard English.** Nevertheless, over time a number of words with *-ize* have been accepted into standard English, including the following:

apologize	minimize
civilize	patronize
dramatize	realize
emphasize	specialize
legalize	vandalize
memorize	visualize

British English tends to use *-ise* instead of *-ize: authorise, hospitalise,* and so on.

The *-yze* ending is the least used of the three and is common in only a few words:

analyze
catalyze
paralyze

it See **expletive.**

italics Italic type, *such as this,* is used to emphasize words in running text and to indicate unfamiliar **foreign words** and the titles or names of certain items. Titles that are set in italics include those of books, periodicals, newspapers, films, television series, legal cases, long poems, long musical compositions, paintings, and other works of art.

Names that are set in italic type include specific ships, aircraft, spacecraft, satellites, and the genus, species, and subspecies names of plants and animals.

Refer to specific entries, such as **biological terms, craft and vessels,** and **paintings and sculptures,** for examples of items that should be italicized.

-ize See **-ise/-ize/-yze.**

J

jacket Also called *dust jacket* or *dust wrapper;* the paper or other **cover** wrapped around a hardcover book. Since the cover of a hardcover book is often blank except for the **spine,** the jacket carries the promotional copy, *author's blurb* (brief biographical summary), and other information. Although an author may be given a chance to review the information on a jacket, the publisher is responsible for creating the cover **design** and writing the jacket copy.

The front of the jacket, usually printed in one to four colors, has a special design of **typography** and often **graphics** that appropriately reflects the book's content. The design is intended to be appealing enough to compete successfully with other books in attracting prospective readers.

The back of the jacket usually consists of promotional material, such as a list of special features in the book or the testimonials of prominent readers. It may also have information about the author unless the author's blurb appears on the inside back flap. In addition, the back cover provides the **International Standard Book Number (ISBN)** and the **Bookland EAN code.**

The spine of the jacket carries information similar to that found on the spine of the book itself. Usually, this includes the book title, author's full name or last name only, and the publisher's name and **colophon.**

The inside front flap, which is folded inside the front cover, identifies and summarizes the content of the book. This information may be continued on the inside back flap, which is folded inside the back cover. The back flap also may have a biographical summary of the author. Design credits may be given following the other copy on the back flap.

jargon Specialized language of a trade or profession. In strict usage, authorities distinguish between standard technical language, such as *forthcoming software,* and technical slang, such as *vaporware,* looking upon jargon more as the latter than the former. When jargon is so obscure and abstract (see **abstract word**) that it is incomprehensible and meaningless, it is known as **gobbledygook.**

Business or technical jargon that helps members of a group communicate more efficiently and effectively among themselves may be useful. However, jargon directed to people outside the group who do not understand it is inappropriate.

The following are examples of jargon that should be used cautiously and judiciously:

crosstalk Unwanted overlap of sound or other activity between channels, such as on a telephone line.

flanker A new product similar to another and with a similar name intended to take advantage of the other product's success.

golden handcuffs A contract under which executives will lose important benefits if they leave the company.

greenmail The practice of buying sufficient stock in a company to threaten a hostile takeover, thus forcing management to buy back the stock at a high price if it wants to prevent the takeover.

groupware A broad range of software aimed at increasing productivity through team efforts.

hit A record that has been found in a database.

prosumer An older person who continues to work but without pay.

white knight A corporation that comes to the aid of another corporation that is fighting a takeover.

joint work A single work, such as a college textbook, prepared by two or more authors. The authors of a joint work are coowners of the **copyright** on the work, and in that respect a joint work differs from a **collective work,** such as an **anthology.** In the collective work a compiler or editor usually holds the copyright on the overall work, although a contributor may own the copyright on an individual contribution if it was previously published elsewhere.

journals See **periodicals.**

jr./Sr. A name with the abbreviations for *Junior* and *Senior* should be punctuated as the individual prefers. It is increasingly common for people to omit the comma before such abbreviations (the comma is always omitted before *II, III,* and so on):

Benjamin Sims, Jr. *or* Benjamin Sims Jr.
Benjamin Sims II (*not* Benjamin Sims, II)

Omit the abbreviation when referring to a person by last name only:

Mr. Sims won the election for mayor.
Sims won the election for mayor.

In alphabetizing **index** entries and other material, place the abbreviation for *Jr., Sr., II,* and so on after the given name:

Sims, Benjamin, Jr.
Sims, Benjamin, III

judicial/judicious The **adjectives** *judicial* and *judicious* look similar and both involve judgment, but they have different uses. *Judicial* describes something pertaining to a court of law or the administration of justice:

During her trial, *judicial* proceedings were televised every day.

Judicious means prudent or characterized by sound judgment, whether or not it pertains to legal proceedings or justice:

Management made a *judicious* decision to close the Chicago office.

Although they are not interchangeable, the two terms may be closely associated in some cases. For example, a *judicial* [court] decree may be *judicious* [prudent]. Similarly, a *judicious* [prudent] decision is also a *judicial* decision if it is made by a court.

judicial bodies Capitalize the official names of courts and their divisions. **Lowercase** general references to courts or to courts with descriptive titles, such as *traffic court*. However, capitalize a general reference if it will help to avoid confusion with another similarly worded term:

> United States Supreme Court, the Supreme Court, the Court (*all capitalized only in reference to the United States Supreme Court*)
>
> United States Court of Appeals for the Third Circuit, the court of appeals, the circuit court, the court
>
> Supreme Court of Nevada, Nevada Supreme Court, the state supreme court, the court
>
> New York Court of Appeals, the Court of Appeals (*capitalized to avoid confusing it with the U.S. appeals court*), the court
>
> District Court for the Eastern District of Massachusetts, the district court, the court
>
> Juvenile Division of the Circuit Court of Marion County, the juvenile court, the court

judicious See **judicial/judicious.**

junction/juncture The **nouns** *junction* and *juncture* both mean the act or place of joining. *Junction* is the more widely used of the two to refer to a physical point of joining or meeting:

> Let's meet at the *junction* of Highway 189 and Interstate 40.

Juncture is used in another sense to refer to a point in time rather than a physical location. However, since this usage is not acceptable to all authorities, professional writers should reword sentences to avoid using it:

Not: Events have reached a critical stage, and only one course is feasible at this *juncture.*

Preferred: Events have reached a critical stage, and only one course is now feasible.

justification The **word processing** and **typesetting** procedure of adjusting the space between words in each line so that all lines end at the same position. The left and right margins are therefore aligned when type is justified.

Setting copy justified sometimes creates unattractive ''rivers'' of white space meandering up and down a page. Since such spaces also impede readability, editors, proofreaders, and others who examine typeset copy must watch for this problem and mark it on the **page proofs.** The **compositor** will then reset various lines to break up or eliminate the so-called rivers.

K

keyline An outline showing the places reserved for type, photographs, and artwork drawn on copy prepared for offset reproduction. Whereas a *keyline* is an outline showing where different elements will be placed, a *mechanical* is a board, also prepared for offset **printing,** on which the type and artwork have been pasted in their correct positions.

keyword The main word or an especially descriptive word in a heading or other copy; the word that a reader is most likely to look for in searching for an **index** entry or in using a computerized search feature. Most keywords are **nouns** and less often **adjectives.** For example, the italicized words in the following examples are keywords—the words you would most likely look for or use during a manual or computer search:

Philip James *Bennett*
meeting arrangements
classical *Greek*
mathematical *equations*
the *comma* in compound sentences
list of *abbreviations*

kind of/sort of/type of The **nouns** *kind, sort,* and *type* are **synonyms** referring to a group or number of individuals having common traits or to an example from such group. However, *type* is used more often in referring to a narrow or distinct category (*type* of writer, such as a fiction writer).

Kind and *sort* are both used more than *type* for general or broad categories (*kind/sort* of people, such as an educated people).

Confusion exists over the use of *this* and *that* versus *these* and *those* with *kind of, sort of,* and *type of.* Most authorities consider *kind, sort,* and *type* to be singular, therefore requiring the singular **pronouns** *this* and *that* as well as singular **verbs:**

That kind of plant *is* easy to grow.

Nevertheless, one sees constructions such as *those kind of plants are, this kind of plants are,* and so on. To many, such wording is awkward if nothing else. Regardless of any disagreement about the acceptability of those forms, one rule is not contested. When the plural *kinds, sorts,* and *types* are used, the pronouns and verbs used with them must be plural too:

Those sorts of ideas *are* always useful.

The use of *kind of* and *sort of* to mean rather or somewhat is too informal to be acceptable in professional writing:

Business was *kind of* [rather] slow today

The use of *a* after *kind of, sort of,* or *type of* is **colloquial English** and should not be used:

This *type of* [*a*] keyboard is easy to use.

kinship See **family-relationship terms.**

L

lakes See **names, topographical.**

landscape See **broadside.**

latin terms Omit accents (see **diacritical marks**), but use **italics** for Latin terms that have not been assimilated into the English language or may be unfamiliar to many readers. Capitalize all important words in modern Latin titles the same as you would do for English titles. Capitalize the titles of ancient works and very short works in sentence style, with the first word and proper nouns and adjectives capitalized:

> *ceteris paribus* (other things being equal)
> *Dei gratia* (by the grace of God)
> *non plus ultra* (perfection)
> *sub judice* (under consideration)
> a priori (from causes to effects)
> alma mater (one's school or university)
> ex officio (by virtue of one's office)
> sine die (with no appointed date)
> *Summum bonum* (ancient work: *Supreme Good*)
> *Causa bellum* (short work: *The Cause of War*)
> *Cui Bono?* (modern work: *Who Gains by It?*)

See also **abbreviations in scholarly works, biological terms, foreign words,** and **Latinism.**

Latinism A word, idiom, or other expression characteristic of or derived from Latin that is used in another language. For example, the English word *illegality* is derived from the Latin word *illegalis*. See also **Latin terms.**

latitude and longitude Spell out the word *latitude* and *longitude* in running text:

> *Latitude* is indicated by parallel lines ranging north or south of the equator.
> *Longitude* is indicated by parallel lines formed at right angles to the equator and ranging west or east of the prime meridian in Greenwich (near London), England.

Parallels of latitude and longitude are expressed numerically in degrees, which are divided into minutes, which in turn are divided into seconds. The words *latitude* and *longitude* are abbreviated in numerical expressions, and the numbers are written without spaces:

> lat. 36°20'45" S
> long. 77°24'30" E

When the abbreviations *E, W, N,* and *S* are used, the periods may be omitted after *lat.* and *long.,* or the entire abbreviation may be omitted:

> lat 36°20'45" S *or* 36°20'45" S
> long 77°24'30" E *or* 77°24'30" E

The following are alternative ways of writing the numerical designations. Follow the preferred style of your employer or publisher:

36-20-45 S	77-24-30 E
36°20.75' S	77°24.5' E
36°20'.75 S	77°24'.5 E

latter Use the word *latter* to refer to the second item in a pair when you want to avoid repeating the name of the second item. For clarity, place *latter* as close as possible to the second item:

He's qualified to teach both math and history, but the *latter* is his real love.

When more than two items are involved, refer to the last-mentioned item rather than using the word *latter:*

He's qualified to teach English, math, and history, but *history* is his real love.

The word *latter* can also be used to refer to something near an end:

It was a formal style of writing that was popular in the *latter* part of the nineteenth century.

laws See **acts and treaties** and **laws and principles, scientific.**

laws and principles, scientific Capitalize the proper names in laws, principles, theorems, and so on, but **lowercase** general words such as *law:*

Mendel's law, law of segregation, law of independent assortment
the Peter principle, the principle of incompetence
Einstein's theory of relativity, the theory of relativity

lay/lie The **verbs** *lay* and *lie* are often confused, perhaps because the **past tense** of *lie* is also *lay.* However, the definitions of *lay* and *lie* differ regardless of tense. *Lay,* a **transitive verb** requiring an object, means to put or set down. The principal parts of *lay* are *lay, laid,* and (have/has/had) *laid:*

He *lay* the book [object] on the table.
He *laid* the book [object] on the table.
He *has laid* the book [object] on the table.

Lie, an **intransitive verb** that does not need an object, means to recline. The principal parts of *lie* are *lie, lay,* and (have/has/had) *lain:*

After a sleepless night, she needs to *lie* down for a few minutes.

After having a sleepless night, she *lay* down for a few
minutes.
After having had a sleepless night, she *had lain* down
for a few minutes.

Lie also means to make a false statement. The principal
parts with that meaning are *lie, lied,* and (have/has/had)
lied:

They often *lie.*
They often *lied.*
They often *have lied.*

layout A designer's realistic drawing showing the arrangement of text, **illustrations,** and other material on a page,
including the page and type sizes, the **typeface,** and the
appearance and arrangement of other **design** elements.

leading The spacing between lines of type as measured in
points. The term originated when casting machines using
metal strips created lines of type. Additional space was created by inserting extra metal strips between the lines. Today, computerized equipment and photocomposition
machines using film matrices have special settings to vary
the line spacing.

The amount of spacing used depends on the type of
copy, the **x-height** of the type, and any preference for an
open or tight (dense) look. A common style consists of
about two points of leading between lines of text.
Therefore, if ten-point type has two points leading, the type
instructions will specify *10 on 12* or simply *10/12.*

leaf A single sheet of paper in a book with each side constituting a separate page; the foil or film used in stamping
book covers. See **embossing.**

legal cases Use **italics** for the names of legal cases, and set
the abbreviation for *versus* (*v.* or *vs.*) in either **roman type**
or italics, as preferred. When using a shortened version of
a case name and referring to it as a case, use italics. When
referring to a person rather than to the person's case name,
use roman type:

Endicott Water Co. v. *Henry Benson III*
the *Endicott* case
Benson's case
Benson's trial

See also **legal citations** and **legal terms.**

legal citations Set titles of books in legal citations in **italics,** and shorten very long titles if necessary. Also set article titles in italics, and set journal titles in **roman type.** (Set article titles in nonlegal citations in roman type with quotation marks, and italicize the journal titles.) Use symbols or abbreviations for subdivisions, such as a paragraph, section, or chapter.

As the forthcoming sample entries indicate, the order of listing items in a legal citation differs from that in a nonlegal citation. For example, in a book citation, the volume number precedes the title of the book. In an article citation, the first page number listed is the opening page of the article, and the next number or numbers is the page or pages being cited.

In a citation to a court decision, follow the same procedure for listing page numbers as that used with articles. After the volume and name of the reporter, state the opening page number first followed by the cited page number. State the court and date in parentheses at the end of the citation. In a state court case, cite both the official and commercial reporters.

In citations to constitutions, abbreviate words such as *Constitution* and *Article,* and use the section symbol (§) for the word *Section.*

In each of the following examples, notice that commas are omitted after the book title (first example) and the journal title (second example). The place of publication (city) is also omitted in the first entry. In the second entry, several words in the journal title are abbreviated:

Mason Chantelli, ed., 3 *Legal Maneuvers in Court* ch 1
    at 17 (Legal Publishers, 1998).
Jennifer Garcia, *Federal Merchandising Restrictions*, 8

Northern U of Law Rev 15, 20–24 (1997).
McNeil v Kingston, 27 ND 288, 319 F2d 2232 (2d Cir
   1981).
US Const, Art II, § 3.

Authors and editors who deal with many legal citations
should consult the latest edition of a legal style manual,
such as *A Uniform System of Citation,* published by the
Harvard Law Review Association, Cambridge, Massachusetts.

See also **legal cases** and **legal terms.** Compare with examples of nonlegal entries in **bibliography, notes,** and **reference list.**

legal terms Use **roman type** for English legal terms, derivatives of Latin terms, or Latin words that are fully assimilated into English. Use **italics** for other Latin legal
terms, especially those that are unfamiliar to most readers:

de facto	*amicus curiae*
indictment	*ex post facto*
malfeasance	*habeas corpus*
plenary	*in loco parentis*
summons	*prima facie*
testimony	*res judicata*

See also **Latin terms, legal cases,** and **legal citations.**

legend A descriptive explanation that accompanies a text
figure or plate. See **illustrations.** Whereas a **caption** consists of a title to an illustration, the *legend* consists of a
phrase or one or more descriptive sentences. Informally,
the two terms are often used interchangeably.

An illustration may have a caption only, a legend only,
or both. Often the two appear together and are commonly
placed below the illustration. The caption may be run in
preceding the legend or on a separate line:

Caption: Unidirectional Speaker-Listener Interaction
Legend: Unidirectional communication omits the conventional feedback loop. Instead, as this diagram il-

lustrates, listeners only receive from speakers but do not respond.

If a figure or plate number is used, it precedes both the caption and legend, and the word *figure* is often abbreviated. Sometimes an illustration contains symbols or letters. The legend should then use those same symbols or letters in the explanation, capitalized or in **lowercase** letters, the same as in the illustration:

Fig. 9. Unidirectional Speaker-Listener Interaction: Unidirectional communication omits the conventional feedback loop. Instead, as this diagram illustrates, Listeners B and C receive from Speakers A and B but do not respond.

If people are identified, introductory words such as *Left to right,* followed by a colon, may precede the list of names:

Left to right: Harry Morris, Edna Starr, Michelle Jeuner, Kenneth Short Jr., and Dennis Altman (*president*).

During the production of a document, an editor must check that the correct captions and legends accompany the illustrations and that they appear in the proper order.

lend/loan As **verbs,** *lend* and *loan* are both used to mean providing money on the condition that it be returned, usually with interest. *Lend* is preferred to mean providing, contributing, or imparting anything useful:

If you will *lend* me your talents for a few minutes, we can finish the design.

Loan can be a **noun** as well as a verb, and in both cases it is used only in reference to physical transactions, such as a monetary loan:

The bank *loan* was approved yesterday.

Some writing experts object to the use of loan as a verb (*loan* some money) and prefer *lend* for physical transactions as well as for other types of contribution:

My father agreed to *lend* [not *loan*] us enough to re-model the house.

less See **few/less.**

letter-by-letter alphabetization system See **alphabetiza-tion.**

letters used as letters Use **italics** in most cases for letters referred to as letters:

The *M* in this typeface looks unusually wide compared to other letters, such as *A* or *V*.

Also italicize letters in **mathematical expressions:**

$a + b(x - y)$

Use **roman type** for letters referring to academic grades:

She received straight A's this semester.

Use either roman type or italics, as preferred (but con-sistently), for proverbial expressions:

In a contract you have to dot your i's and cross your t's [or *i*'s and *t*'s].
He's good at minding his p's and q's [or *p*'s and *q*'s].

See also **words used as words.**

letterspacing Writing words with extra space between let-ters:

W o r d   P r o c e s s i n g

Although it is not common, the practice of letterspacing is sometimes used to distinguish a **head(ing)** from other heads. For example, in a work with numerous levels of heads, the author may center the first two or three levels and also use letterspacing for the first one to distinguish it from the other(s).

lexicon A dictionary, vocabulary, or other stock of terms; the total stock of words or **morphemes** in a language.

liable See **apt/liable/likely.**

libel/slander The **nouns** *libel* and *slander* are often used interchangeably in informal situations, but traditionally, the distinction between the two has been clear. *Libel* is a published and *slander* a spoken false statement that damages someone's reputation:

> After reading the unfounded charges against him in the newspaper, Doug asked an attorney about suing the writer for *libel*.
> Only last year Doug sued another person for *slander* after the person said something malicious about Doug at a meeting.

library classification system The system used by a library to classify and arrange books and journals. The most widely used system is the Library of Congress System, which assigns letters to major subject categories, such as Archaeology (CC), Encyclopedias (AE), and local government (JS). The major categories in the Library of Congress System are as follows:

General Works (A's)

Philosophy, Psychology, Religion (B's)

Auxiliary Sciences of History (C's)

History: General and Old World (D's)

History: Western Hemisphere (E's and F's)

Geography, Anthropology, Recreation (G's)

Social Sciences (H's)

Political Science (J's)

Law (K's)

Education (L's)

Music (M's)

Fine Arts (N's)

Language and Literature (P's)

Science (Q's)

Medicine (R's)

Agriculture (S's)

Technology (T's)

Military Science (U's)

Naval Science (V's)

Bibliography: Library Science (Z's)

The older Dewey Decimal System, still used in some small public libraries and in private libraries, assigns numbers to major subject categories, such as General Periodicals (050), Physics (530), and Spanish and Portuguese Literature (860). The major categories in the Dewey Decimal System are as follows:

Generalities (000's)

Philosophy and Related (100's)

Religion (200's)

Social Sciences (300's)

Language (400's)

Pure Science (500's)

Technology/Applied Science (600's)

The Arts (700's)

Literature and Rhetoric (800's)

General Geography and History, Etc. (900's)

licensing of rights Also called *grant of rights*. The contract between an author and publisher describes a variety of **rights.** See also **copyright.** These rights are granted, or licensed, to publishers, authors, or other parties, such as agents. For example, an author generally grants a book publisher the exclusive right to publish a **manuscript** in hardcover or paperback book form in the English language in the United States and its possessions for a designated period. The author may also grant various other rights to the publisher, such as the right to license **reprint** rights to other publishers.

Such licensing of rights is a contractual matter that requires legal assistance to be certain that the terms of licensing each right are clearly defined and so that no misunderstanding will occur between the licenser and the licensee. These terms specify who is granted a license to do certain things, where these things may be done, for how long they may be done, how the resulting royalties will be split among the parties, and so on.

lie See **lay/lie.**

likely See **apt/liable/likely.**

limit See **boundary/limit/parameter/perimeter.**

limiting adjective See **adjective.**

line art Those **illustrations** that have only solid black and white, such as a pen-and-ink or computer-generated diagram consisting only of black lines. Since line art has the same composition as type, a page consisting of line art can be photographed directly for reproduction the same as a page of typeset text. Compare with the continuous-tone image of a **halftone.** See also **graphics** for definitions of common types of line art.

line break To keep lines of text relatively equal in length, **compositors** frequently have to break words at the ends of lines. General dictionaries and spelling dictionaries indicate **syllables** after which a word may be divided. See also **word division.**

Words in other elements, such as titles or headlines, should not be divided. Headings of more than one line should be divided between words rather than within words. See **head(ing)s.**

Other elements can be divided but only at certain points.

Mathematical expressions, for example, require special attention and can be divided only at certain places, such as before a verb operator or conjunction. See **equations** for further explanation.

line graph See **graphics.**

linguistics The science of languages; in formal education, the study of the nature and structure of language. The purpose of linguistics, therefore, is not to specify rules of correct usage but to establish general principles and reliably describe individual languages. Today, numerous linguistic subdivisions exist, ranging from psycholinguistics to computational linguistics, each focusing on the nature and structure of the specific type of language.

linking verb Also called *copulative verb;* a **verb** that connects the **subject** of a sentence to a **predicate nominative** or a **predicate adjective.** Linking verbs include all forms of the verb *to be* (**auxiliary verbs**), such as *am, were, is, are, shall be,* and *had been.* They also include other verbs that do not express action but link the subject to another word. Examples are *become, seem, appear, feel, look,* and *sound.* Some verbs, such as *stay* and *keep,* may be either linking or regular action verbs:

> The gardners [subject] *are* [linking verb] also landscapers [predicate **noun**].
> It [subject] *is* [linking verb] he [predicate **pronoun**] who has the most to lose.
> She [subject] *seems* [linking verb] happy [predicate adjective].
> Your meal [subject] *tasted* [linking verb] delicious [predicate adjective].

list Several points or items in a sentence, paragraph, or larger section may be set apart from the running text as a vertical list. Setting such items apart from the running text can help to enhance readability and add emphasis to the items.

Publishers may have a preferred style for vertical lists

in regard to punctuation, capitalization, and general style. Depending on the nature of the work and the publisher's style requirements, lists may be numbered or unnumbered, or they may be preceded by letters or symbols, such as a **bullet.** Usually, a period and one or more spaces follow a letter or number that introduces a displayed list item. Numbers preceding items that are run in with a text paragraph are set like this—(1)—in parentheses without periods.

The first word of an item and proper **nouns** are capitalized in a displayed list:

One of three *moods* indicates how a viewer perceives a verb's action:

1. Indicative mood

2. Subjunctive mood

3. Imperative mood

A period follows the list items only if one of the items is a complete sentence:

a. The *indicative mood* states or questions a fact.

b. The *subjunctive mood* denotes an action or state as conditional or contrary to fact.

c. The *imperative mood* expresses a command or wish.

Even when the final item completes a sentence, the period is omitted after the last item unless each item ends with a period, comma, or semicolon:

These are a verb's principal *moods,* namely:

• The indicative mood

• The subjunctive mood

• The imperative mood

When items end with commas or semicolons, each item begins with a **lowercase** letter:

Three things can be said about *mood,* namely, that

it indicates the manner in which someone perceives the verb's action;

it signifies a mental state or attitude; and

it is a more common term than its synonym *mode*.

Lists may be set in the same type size and **typeface** as the text type or in a smaller size and different typeface, depending upon the design of the particular document. Extra space is usually placed before and after a vertical list and between each list item. Also, lists are commonly indented from the left margin as much as or more than the text-paragraph **indention.**

list of abbreviations See **abbreviations, list of.**

list of illustrations See **illustrations, list of.**

list of tables See **tables, list of.**

loan See **lend/loan.**

localism A word or expression that is peculiar to a specific geographical region. See **nonstandard English.**

longitude See **latitude and longitude.**

lowercase As a **noun,** small letters (*a, b,* and so on) as opposed to **uppercase,** or capital, letters; as a **verb,** to type or set something in small letters or to change a capital letter to a small letter.

luxuriant/luxurious The **adjectives** *luxuriant* and *luxurious* are sometimes confused because they look and sound similar. However, although they both involve abundance or profusion, their primary meanings are different. *Luxuriant* primarily means characterized by rich or profuse growth, flourishing, or yielding in abundance:

The plants in the greenhouse were *luxuriant.*

Luxurious primarily means fond of or marked by pleasure and comfort:

The houses in that development are *luxurious*.

In a secondary sense *luxuriant* also means luxurious, but to avoid confusion writers should use the terms according to their primary senses.

M

M. Abbreviation for *meridies*—noon. Publishers usually set the abbreviation in **roman type** with a small capital letter (M.) Although the abbreviation is not widely used, writers who prepare material by computer frequently type a capital letter (M.) to avoid additional keystrokes. See also **A.M.** and **P.M.**

macron See **diacritical marks.**

magazines See **periodicals.**

mail address See **address, mail.**

main clause See **independent clause.**

main verb See **principal verb.**

majority See **minority/majority/plurality.**

malapropism The (sometimes ludicrous) misuse of a word, especially the substitution of an incorrect word that sounds similar to the correct word:

> His oldest son has always been *fractions* [*fractious*].
> We hope the *meditation* [*mediation*] will soon put an end to the dispute.
> Did you get the new *pendulum* [*Pentium*] processor?
> Mrs. Landrew has a serious *annualism* [*aneurysm*].

manage See **handle/manage.**

manuscript Abbreviated as *ms.* (plural, *mss.*). Unless specified otherwise in a contract, the author is responsible for providing all internal manuscript copy (**front matter,** text, and **back matter**) but excluding the cover, the **half-title page,** the **copyright page,** and the **running heads.** The author should also secure written permission to reproduce **illustrations** from other sources and to quote from a copyrighted work. See **copyright.**

All manuscript text and back-matter pages should be numbered from page 1 to the last page. The front matter should be numbered separately. Formal **tables** and illustrations should be submitted as separate tables and illustrations manuscripts, with items keyed to the proper places in the text. See **illustrations.** However, brief, unnumbered tables are usually incorporated in the text copy the same as a **list, outline,** or **extract.**

All copy, including separate sheets such as a list of **captions,** must be double-spaced with margins of at least one inch to provide room for an editor to edit between the lines and to make marginal notations. Titles and subheads should be typed with all important words having initial capital letters (but not all capital letters). Displayed elements, such as **extracts** and **equations,** should be indented and displayed, or set apart from the other text paragraphs. **Footnotes** to be set at the foot of text pages must be double-spaced and typed on separate sheets, not at the bottoms of the text pages.

Disk copy must be prepared according to the publisher's specifications, if any. For example, the author may be asked to type codes in front of the various elements to distinguish them during **typesetting.** See also **desktop publishing.**

Occasionally, the publisher may ask the author to prepare a **style sheet.** The author should then list on this sheet special terms to indicate how they have been punctuated, capitalized, and so on throughout the manuscript. The sheet should also include any other special style used by the author, such as the style for writing **numbers,** punctuating and capitalizing abbreviations, or writing **dates.**

For more about the handling of a manuscript, refer to

individual entries such as **copyediting** and **typemarking.** See also entries for specific types of material, such as **illustrations, mathematical expressions, notes,** and **tables.**

mass See **religious services.**

mass noun See **concrete noun.**

master proof The **galley proof** or **page proof** containing all changes or corrections made by both the author and the publisher's proofreader. The author's changes are transferred to the publisher's master set before it is sent to the **compositor** for correction.

mathematical expressions Mathematical copy is often complex and must be edited carefully. In a detailed mathematical work, the author or an editor may prepare a list of all special symbols and characters used in the **manuscript,** and this list is then sent to the **compositor** along with the manuscript to be typeset.

Rather than mark a manuscript heavily, an editor usually identifies certain items only at the first occurrence. For example, the editor may circle instructions such as "All letter symbols ital. unless marked" near the first letter symbol at the beginning of the manuscript or at the beginning of each chapter. The editor will also write out and circle the names of special symbols or Greek letters, such as "greater than," "null set," and "lc [lowercase] Gr. [Greek] eta," at the first occurrence.

An editor of mathematical works must be familiar with the various types of mathematical expressions, including **equations, exponents,** definitions, theorems, signs of aggregation (such as **braces**), and many other elements. The editor must also know how to break equations at the end of a line (see **equations** for examples) and how to punctuate mathematical copy correctly. For example, when **ellipsis points** are used in a series, a comma must both precede and follow the dots. When the dots fall between operators such as a plus or minus sign, no commas are used:

$$x_1, x_2, \ldots, x_n$$
$$x_1 + x_2 + \ldots + x_n$$

Editors should closely scrutinize mathematical work for consistency and any unusual use of certain elements. However, authors may use elements such as braces, brackets, and parentheses in a different order than usual or to mean something different than usual in a particular work. Therefore, editors should query authors rather than correct or change such material. What may seem like a simple correction could alter the author's intended meaning of an expression.

Only editors experienced in handling mathematical expressions should edit complex mathematical works. Most editors of this material use the latest edition of a reliable guide to editing mathematical copy, such as *Mathematics into Type: Copy Editing and Proofreading of Mathematics for Editorial Assistants and Authors,* published by the American Mathematical Society in Providence, Rhode Island.

may See **can/may.**

mean See **average/mean/median.**

measurements See **decimal fractions, em, en, metric terms, numbers, pica, point,** and **spacing.**

mechanical See **keyline** and **printing.**

mechanical binding See **binding.**

mechanical editing See **copyediting.**

medals See **military honors.**

median See **average/mean/median.**

medical terms Capitalize only **proper nouns** or trade names (see **trademark**) and **acronyms** relating to diseases, symptoms, diagnostic tests, pharmaceuticals, and so on. **Lowercase** general words, such as *disease*, and generic terms, such as *aspirin*. Treat the names of infectious or-

ganisms the same as the Latin names of plants and animals
as described in the entry **biological terms.**

> multiple sclerosis, MS
> Parkinson's disease
> Reye's syndrome
> Mendel's laws, the laws of hereditary characteristics
> Schick test
> CAT scan
> Epstein-Barr virus
> influenza, the flu
> a virus, a retrovirus
> diazepam (Valium)
> anesthetic (Novocain)
> *Trichophyton, T. mentagrophytes*
> *Pseudomonas, P. aeruginosa*

metaphor A **figure of speech** in which a word, **phrase,** or
larger passage that means one thing is used to refer to another thing. Whereas a comparison is stated directly in a
simile, usually introduced by *like* or *as* (*slow as a turtle*),
it is implied by association or identification in a metaphor,
without *like* or *as:*

> Put it in the *dead*-letter file.
> Joe can be a *tiger* when he feels betrayed.
> They had been waiting more than a year for a *window
> of opportunity.*
> To everyone's surprise her plan *backfired.*
> If he would take off those *blinders* for a minute he
> would realize what has happened.

See also **analogy.**

meticulous/scrupulous Broadly, the **adjectives** *meticulous*
and *scrupulous* are **synonyms** meaning marked by atten-
tiveness to detail. However, a sharp difference between the
two terms involves their connotations. See **connotation/de-
notation.** *Meticulous* primarily means especially careful
and precise. It is the better choice to emphasize excessive

or extreme attention to small details, usually praiseworthy attention:

As an editor, Fred is *meticulous* in his work and catches more errors than any other editor.

Scrupulous primarily means painstakingly conscientious and principled. It is the better choice to emphasize concern with what is right, moral, or ethical:

Noreen is *scrupulous* in her work and is widely respected as a fair and honest mediator.

metric terms Metric terms are used for weights and measures in the International System of Units (Système international d'unités, or SI). Except for Celsius (see **Celsius/Fahrenheit**), metric terms are lowercased in both the abbreviated and spelled-out forms.

In both scientific and nonscientific writing, numerals are used with the name of the metric unit. In the scientific style, the unit is usually abbreviated. Metric abbreviations are written without punctuation and without any space between the letters:

20 millimeters (*nonscientific style*)
20 mm (*scientific style*)

The basic metric unit for length is the *meter* (m), for weight (or mass) the *gram* (g), for volume the *liter* (l), and for temperature the *degree Celsius* (°C). Time is measured using the English units of seconds, minutes, and hours.

By placing **prefixes** in front of the basic units, new units are formed. Since the metric system is a decimal system based on powers of ten, a particular prefix indicates which power of ten a multiple or submultiple represents:

10^3 (*or* $10 \times 10 \times 10$) = 1000

The following are six commonly used metric prefixes:

kilo- (k) = 10^3 (1000)
hecto- (h) = 10^2 (100)
deka- (da) = 10^1 (10)

deci- (d) = 10^{-1} (0.1)
centi- (c) = 10^{-2} (0.01)
milli- (m) = 10^{-3} (0.001)

Combining a prefix, such as *kilo-,* with a basic unit, such as *meter,* changes the values. For example, based on the preceding list, 1 kilometer = 1000 meters. Therefore, in reverse, 1 meter = .001 kilometer.

The metric system, used in many other countries, has not been fully assimilated into American culture. Although some metric weights and measures, such as the *liter* commonly seen in grocery stores, are familiar, others are seldom used and are less familiar. The *kilometer,* for example, has not yet replaced the *mile* on most U.S. road signs.

migration See **emigration/immigration/migration.**

military awards See **military honors.**

military groups Capitalize the official names of branches of the military service, units, companies, corps, fleets, battalions, and so on. **Lowercase** general or informal references to them:

United States Army, U.S. Army, the army, the armed forces
United States Marine Corps, Marine Corps, U.S. Marines, the marines
United States Coast Guard, the Coast Guard
National Guard, the guard
Royal Air Force, British air force
Allied armies (World Wars I and II), the Allies, Allied forces
Pacific Fleet (World War II), the fleet
Sixth Army, the Sixth, the army
Second Battalion, the battalion
13th Regiment, the regiment
Green Berets, the special unit
U.N. peacekeeping force
U.S. Joint Chiefs of Staff, the Joint Chiefs

See also **military honors** and **wars and conflicts.**

military honors Capitalize the official names of medals, awards, and other military honors, but **lowercase** general references to such types of decorations:

> Medal of Honor, the congressional medal, a medal
> Distinguished Flying Cross, the highest honor
> *But:* croix de guerre *or* Croix de Guerre
> Purple Heart, an award for bravery in combat

> See also **military groups** and **wars and conflicts.**

military services See **military groups.**

minerals See **geological terms.**

minority/majority/plurality These three **nouns** or **adjectives** all pertain to numbers, and two of them—*majority* and *minority*—have more than one widely used meaning. Most people understand the meaning of *majority* and *minority* but sometimes fail to use *plurality* correctly.

Minority is an **antonym** of *majority.* Broadly, it means not many or few, and more narrowly, it means less than half:

> *A minority of* [*not many* or *few*] attendees jeered when the governor spoke, but most people applauded wildly.
> Of the two candidates, Mr. Johnson received *a minority* [*less than 50 percent*] of the votes.

Minority is also a common term describing a political party or group that does not have legislative or other control. In addition, it refers to a comparatively small group of people who differ in some way, such as in race or religion, from the larger population.

Broadly, *majority* is used as a **synonym** for many or most, but more narrowly, it means more than half:

> *The majority of* [*many* or *most*] attendees applauded wildly when the governor spoke, although a few jeered on several occasions.
> Of the two candidates, Mr. Stevens received *a majority* [*more than 50 percent*] of the votes.

Majority is also a common term describing a political party or group that has legislative or other control. In addition, it refers to a comparatively large group of people who are representative of and share the characteristics of the larger population.

Plurality is used when three or more persons are involved in an election and no one receives more than 50 percent of the votes. It refers to the number of votes cast for the leading candidate or the excess of votes received by the leading candidate over those received by the closest opponent:

> If Marilyn received 75 votes, James 65, and Julia 57, each person received less than 50 percent of the total of 197 votes cast. However, Marilyn received a *plurality* with an excess of 10 votes over the second in line, James.

misplaced clause When other words intervene between a **clause** and the word(s) it modifies, the clause appears to modify the wrong word(s):

> Roger just finished mailing the contracts to the three parties *that have a Tuesday deadline*.

The clause in the preceding example appears to modify *parties,* suggesting that the parties have a Tuesday deadline. However, if it's the contracts that have a Tuesday deadline, the clause is misplaced and should be moved near the word *contracts:*

> Roger just finished mailing the contracts *that have a Tuesday deadline* to the three parties.
>
> *Or:* Roger just finished mailing to the three parties the contracts *that have a Tuesday deadline*.

See also **misplaced phrase** and **misplaced words**.

misplaced phrase A **phrase** should be placed as close as possible to the word(s) to which it refers, or it may appear to modify the wrong word(s):

> The house *with the shutters* brought a higher price.

The preceding example suggests that other houses were also for sale, but only one had shutters, and it brought a higher price than the other houses.

If the intended meaning is that there was only one house and it brought more money *with* than *without* shutters, the phrase is misplaced. To avoid an incorrect interpretation, the phrase should be moved closer to the word(s) to which it refers—price.

> The house brought a higher price *with* [than without] *the shutters.*

Whereas a *dangling modifier* (**dangling gerund phrase, dangling infinitive phrase,** and **dangling participial phrase**) does not logically modify any word, a *misplaced phrase* refers to or modifies the wrong word. See also **misplaced clause** and **misplaced words.**

misplaced words When a word, such as an **adverb,** occupies the wrong position in a sentence, it can change the intended meaning. Such words should be placed as close as possible to the other words that they modify. Often it helps to place an adverb *before* the word it modifies. In the following examples the meaning changes depending on the location of the adverb *only:*

> We *only* visited the town [didn't move there or do anything else].
> We visited *only* the town [didn't visit friends or relatives or nearby sites].

See also **misplaced clause** and **misplaced phrase.**

mixed metaphors A combination of two or more unrelated **metaphors** that result in an illogical or foolish statement:

> Each time she *opens a new can of worms* it *makes waves.*
> Since the merger, we've had to spend all our time *putting out fires,* so I hope he doesn't *muddy the waters* with his radical ideas.

Mixed metaphors are a common result of the overuse of **cliches** and other **figures of speech.**

mnemonics A word device, such as a verse, intended to help one remember a particular expression, date, fact, or the spelling of a word. *Mnemonic* may be a **noun** or **adjective,** but *mnemonics* is a **noun.**

The mnemonic must be simple and easier to remember than the other, more difficult thing that one keeps forgetting. Recalling the easy-to-remember device is meant to prompt one to remember the thing that is not so easy to remember. For example, the following mnemonic might help one remember that *scurry* has two *r*'s:

We like to see the squi*rr*els scu*rr*y about.

To remember that *all right* is two words, one could use another two-word example:

He is either *all right* or *all wrong.*

Any type of memory prompt is acceptable, and it may be used not only to remember spelling but to recall anything else, such as a fact. For example, to remember that Ed's birthday is July 11, you might associate it with the 7 [month]-11 [day] stores.

The use of mnemonics has diminished as more writers use spell-checkers. However, spell-checkers do not include all words, and spelling continues to be a problem for many writers.

Since mnemonics is a creative process as well as a memory device, it often appeals to writers and other creative people. Although spelling guides and other books provide already developed mnemonics, users should create their own memory devices using words and ideas they are likely to remember.

mode See **mood.**

modifier A word, **phrase,** or **clause** that describes, limits, or qualifies another word or a group of words. It therefore changes the meaning of a sentence.

A modifier functions as an **adjective** or **adverb:**

Our *old* [adjective] computer is *exceptionally* [adverb] slow.

Six *of us* [adjectival phrase] drove *for two hours* [adverbial phrase].

We noticed that the people *who are homeless* [adjectival clause] wait *where the restaurant deposits its garbage* [adverbial clause].

molly See **spacing.**

money The rules for writing amounts of money in running text should be consistent with the general style of writing other **numbers.** In one style, appropriate for general use, words are used for whole numbers through ninety-nine and for larger round numbers, such as *two hundred.* In another style, more common in scientific and technical work, words are used for whole numbers only through nine or ten; above that, figures are used for all numbers. In either style, amounts of one thousand and above written in figures should include a comma after the number designating thousands:

$3,241, *not* $3241

When a number is spelled out, the currency symbol used with it should also be spelled out. When figures are used for a number, a monetary symbol should also be used:

Nontechnical style: He earned more than *fifteen hundred dollars* in overtime last year but had only *seventy-five cents* left on December 31.

Technical style: He earned more than *$1,500*.00 in overtime last year but had only *$.75* left on December 31.

When fractional amounts are involved, figures with monetary symbols must be used:

They earned more than *$10,531.62* last year.

Very large round numbers with numerous zeros should be written with the words *million, billion,* and so on spelled out even when monetary symbols are included:

The company had sales of more than *$9 million* last year.

When a sentence or paragraph has one large uneven number or a number with a fractional amount that must be expressed in figures, all other amounts in that sentence or paragraph should also be expressed in figures. If some numbers have a fractional unit but others do not, add a decimal and two zeros to the numbers that don't have a fractional unit:

The computer cost $999 last year, but the price has increased to $1,299 this year.
The computer cost $999.99 last year, but the price has increased to $1,299.00 this year.

Currencies of other countries should be handled the same as U.S. currency. However, when an abbreviation is used instead of a monetary symbol, a space is placed between the abbreviation and the figures that follow:

$192.10
DM 192.10
Fr 192.10

Figures may be used in **tables, lists,** and various elements other than running text to conserve space even when the general rule for numbers in running text is to use words.

monosyllable See **syllable.**

mood Previously also called *mode;* the form of a **verb** that indicates how a speaker or writer perceives the state or action of the verb, such as giving a command (**imperative mood**), making a statement (**indicative mood**), or expressing something conditional or contrary to fact (**subjunctive mood**). See the individual entries for examples of the three moods.

morpheme A word or word element that cannot be divided into smaller parts and is considered the minimal meaningful unit of language. Authorities sometimes interpret the term in different ways and with different degrees of complexity, usually focusing on either **grammar** or **semantics.** However, most writers and editors would identify the following parts as morphemes:

    wind = wind
    dogs = dog + s
    turned = turn + ed
    standing = stand + ing
    childishness = child + ish + ness
    postsocialism = post + social + ism

See also **morphology.**

morphology The science and study of the forms and formation (structure) of words, as opposed to **syntax,** which deals with the arrangement of these words into higher units, such as a **sentence.** See also **morpheme,** which refers to individual words and an element or part of a word.

motion pictures Capitalize important words in the titles of motion pictures, company or promotional films, and so on, and set all parts in **italics:**

All the President's Men
Homeward Bound II: Lost in San Francisco
The Giovanni Center for the Blind: A Modern Day Miracle
Computer-Aided Design at Sewall Manufacturing

See also **television** and **radio programs.**

mottoes and slogans Capitalize the important words in mottoes and slogans, and set the titles in **roman type** without quotation marks:

The Twenty-four Hour Store
Just Say No
Live Free or Die
Run 4 Life

A punctuation mark, such as an exclamation point, sometimes follows a motto or slogan, depending on the chosen style of the originator. See also **signs and notices.**

mountains See **names, topographical.**

movements, cultural See **cultural terms.**

movements, political See **political bodies.**

movements, religious See **religious movements.**

ms. (plural, *mss.*) Abbreviation for **manuscript.**

multiauthor work See **anthology, collective work,** and **symposium volume.**

musical works Capitalize important words in the descriptive titles of long musical compositions, such as operas and ballets, and set them in **italics:**

> *La Bohème*
> *Le Nozze di Figaro*
> *Carmen*
> *Swan Lake*

When a work has no descriptive title but rather consists of a numeral or a musical key along with a word such as *symphony* to indicate the form, set the designation in **roman type** without quotation marks. If a descriptive title is also included, place it in parentheses, and set the words either in italics (long composition) or in roman type with quotation marks (short composition):

> Piano Concerto no. 5 (*Emperor*)
> Concerto in C Minor ("Sweet Dreams")
> Fantasy in B Minor
> Beethoven's Fifth Symphony *or* Beethoven's Symphony
>   no. 5
> Sonata in B-flat, op. 21, no. 1

Set the titles of songs and other short compositions in roman type enclosed in quotation marks:

"Star-Spangled Banner"
"Tennessee Waltz"

When a book contains numerous references to musical works, some publishers prefer that no distinction be made between long and short compositions and that all descriptive titles be set in italics. However, even then, designations without descriptive titles and with only numbers or keys should be set in roman type without quotation marks, as described previously.

mutual See **common/mutual/reciprocal.**

N

n See **nth.**

name-date citations See **author-date citations.**

names, country Capitalize the official names of countries and the larger divisions in which they are located. **Lowercase** general references, such as *country:*

> United States of America, the United States, America, the Republic, the Union, the States (country as a unit), the fifty states
>
> Kingdom of Saudi Arabia, Saudi Arabia, the Saudi kingdom, the kingdom, the Arabian Peninsula
>
> England, Scotland, Wales, Great Britain, British Commonwealth, the Commonwealth
>
> Belgium, the Netherlands, Luxembourg, the Benelux countries, western Europe (*but* see **political divisions** for capitalization of central, eastern, and western European political divisions)
>
> the Continent (Europe), *but* the continent of North America
>
> Roman Republic, Roman Empire, the empire
>
> South Africa, the country of South Africa, southern Africa, southern African countries
>
> East Africa, eastern Africa, eastern African countries
>
> Middle East, Mideast, Middle Eastern countries
>
> Eastern [Western] Hemisphere, the hemisphere
>
> the East [West], Eastern [Western] culture

See also **names, topographical,** and **political divisions.**

names, fictitious Capitalize names that denote a fictitious or unidentified person when they are used the same as a real person's name. **Lowercase** most fictitious names when they are used merely as an exclamation or other such expression:

> John Doe (*substituted for a person's name*)
> John Hancock (*a person's signature*)
> Uncle Sam (*the U.S. symbol*)
> jack-of-all-trades (*one who does various tasks*)
> by george! (*an exclamation*)
> johnnycake (*cornbread*)
> *But:* Johnny-come-lately (*a newcomer or latecomer*)

See also **names, foreign; names, organization;** and **names, personal.**

names, foreign In certain parts of the world, such as in Asian countries, the family name is stated before the given name:

Yam Mun Hoh

In that example *Yam* is the family name, *Mun* the middle name, and *Hoh* the given, or first, name. However, businesspeople and Western-oriented residents in many Eastern cultures have adopted the Western style of placing the given name first:

Hoh Mun Yam

When the person has adopted an English first name, it is always stated first:

Richard Yam

In a few countries the family name consists of the father's and mother's family names combined, usually with a **hyphen.** In Spain, for example, the father's family name is stated first and in Portugal the mother's family name first:

Juan Aguilar-Barnuevo (In Spain *Aguilar* would be the father's family name; in Portugal, the mother's.)

Names in Arab countries may consist of the given name, father's name, paternal grandfather's name, and the family name. Therefore, for clarity or to shorten a long string of names, a person may use a prefix, such as *ibn* (son of) or *bint* (daughter of), before the ancestral name.

Abdel-Aziz ibn Saud

A similar policy is followed in certain other parts of the world, although the prefixes may differ. In northern Africa, for example, common prefixes are *ben* and *ould* (son of) and *bon* (father of).

Some names, such as those in Russia, may have different endings for male and female members:

male: Leonid Andreyev
female: Nadia Andreyeva

Regardless of such variations in the use of family names, in **notes, bibliographies,** and **reference lists** one should cite the author's name exactly as it is written on the **title page** of the work. See **particles** for the handling of prefixes, such as *de* and *van*.

See also **names, fictitious,** and **names, personal.**

names, organization Capitalize the names of organizations, such as companies and institutions, including their divisions and departments. **Lowercase** general references to a type of organization or division:

Family Chiropractic Center, Family Chiropractic, the center
Greene Motors Ltd., Greene, the car dealer
Southern Sound Systems, the audio store
Fortune Law Offices, Fortune, the law offices
Xaviar Manufacturing Company, Inc.; Xaviar; the company; the corporation
Consumer Credit Division, the credit division, the division

Purchasing Department, Purchasing, the department
Personnel Office, Personnel, the office

See also **associations and agencies** and **political bodies.**

names, personal Spell out a person's first name unless the
person prefers that you use initials. See guidelines in **abbreviations of names and titles** and **initials.** Use a
woman's maiden, married, or professional name, as she
prefers, and write foreign names exactly as the person
spells, capitalizes, and punctuates the name. See guidelines
in **names, foreign.**

See also **names, fictitious,** and **titles, personal and professional.**

names, topographical Capitalize all important words in the
names of oceans, lakes, rivers, mountains, and so on. **Lowercase** general references to a type of landform, body of
water, and so on, and lowercase words such as *valley* when
they are used descriptively but are not part of the **proper
name:**

Bering Sea, the sea
Bering Strait, the strait
Gulf of Mexico, the gulf
Lake Erie, the lake
Mississippi River, the river
Mississippi and Arkansas Rivers, the rivers
Rio Grande (*not* Rio Grande River), the river
Mississippi River valley, the valley
Rocky Mountains, the Rockies, the mountains
Mount Fuji, Fujiyama (*not* Mount Fujiyama), the moun-
tain
Sonoran Desert, Sonora Desert, the desert
Badlands of South Dakota, the South Dakota Badlands,
badlands topography
Everglades, the swamp region of Lake Okeechobee

See also **geographical terms** and **geological terms.**

nationalities See **peoples.**

nations, names of See **names, country.**

nauseated/nauseous The **verb** *nauseated* and the **adjective** *nauseous* are widely used interchangeably to mean feeling sick. However, many authorities object to this loose application. Because of the considerable disagreement that exists, no firm rule is available. Traditionally, however, *nauseated* has primarily meant feeling sick, and *nauseous* has primarily meant causing nausea:

> The toxic fumes were *nauseous* and caused us to feel *nauseated.*

Some authorities believe that this distinction should be observed. Others note that the distinction has faded, and even professional writers use *nauseous* to mean feeling sick. In fact, *nauseous* is giving way to *nauseating* in the sense of causing sickness. Therefore, the following language is more common in contemporary usage:

> The toxic fumes were *nauseating* and caused us to feel *nauseous/nauseated.*

negative proof See **blueprint** and **printing.**

neither . . . nor As **correlative conjunctions,** the *neither . . . nor* construction is sometimes misused. When *neither . . . nor* is used, a **verb** that follows a singular **noun** should be singular and one that follows a plural noun should be plural:

> *Neither* Alan *nor* his *assistant* [singular noun] *plans* [singular verb] to attend.
> *Neither* Alan *nor* his *assistants* [plural noun] *plan* [plural verb] to attend.

If a sentence is so complex that the preceding noun-verb agreement is not clear, the sentence should be reworded to dispense with the *neither . . . nor* construction. Even when the construction can be used clearly, placement of the word *neither* in a sentence can also cause problems. Usually, the word should appear immediately before the first of the two items:

> *Not:* People who *neither* work in the office *nor* in the plant are the only ones eligible for the contest.
>
> *Better:* People who work *neither* in the office *nor* in the plant are the only ones eligible for the contest.

neologism A new word, expression, or form of usage, such as *virtual reality, politically (in)correct,* and *makeover.* Some new words enter the rolls of a standard dictionary relatively soon after their introduction; others appear only in dictionaries of **slang** or **jargon** for several decades. After that, they either disappear or eventually become assimilated into the general dictionaries.

Neologisms are created in many ways. See **coinage.** Some, such as *telemarketing* (from *telephone/telecommunications* + *marketing*), are formed by blending or combining two existing words. See **compound terms** and **blend word.** Others, such as *NAFTA* (North American Free Trade Agreement), are really **initialisms, acronyms,** or other abbreviations treated as a real word.

Many new words that originate as slang are created when young people give an existing word an opposite or different meaning, such as using *cool* to mean being poised and in control. The same thing happens in business language. For example, the word *handshake* is now technical jargon for a preliminary procedure or establishing a connection.

Writers who enjoy using neologisms should exercise caution. They must be certain that their audience will understand a new word, and when there is any doubt, the term should be defined or replaced with clearly understood traditional language.

networks See **Internet terms.**

new words See **blend word, coinage,** and **neologism.**

newspapers Capitalize the important words in the titles of newspapers and sections that are published separately, and set them in **italics.** However, set article titles within a newspaper in **roman type** enclosed by quotation marks:

Wall Street Journal
New York Times Book Review
"Government Shutdown Imminent," from the Sunday
  Times

An initial **article,** such as *The,* is usually written in roman type and lowercased in running text, although it is considered an essential part of the title in some international newspapers:

We get the *Christian Science Monitor* at the office.
Have you seen *The Times* of London?

The article *The* is omitted in newspaper titles cited in **notes, bibliographies,** and **reference lists.**

nicknames See **epithet.**

no./# The word *number* should be spelled out in running text. In other cases when it is appropriate to abbreviate *number,* such as preceding an identification number on a fill-in form, the abbreviation *no.* is preferred over the sign #. However, some organizations use the sign on business forms, such as purchase orders and packing lists:

credit card no. 12345678
Catalog No. 2101 (*order form*)
Shipped: 2 drill bits #63721 (*packing list*)

no one/nobody There is little to distinguish usage in the **pronouns** *no one* and *nobody* except that some authorities believe *nobody* is less formal and sounds more like **colloquial English** than *no one.* The word *nobody* is always written as one word unless reference is being made to a person's body, usually a corpse:

Shots were fired, but *no body* was found.

nom de plume/pen name/pseudonym These three **nouns** all refer to a name used by an author instead of the person's real name. Only one term—*pseudonym*—can be used to refer to a fictitious name of anyone, whether or not the person is a writer:

The writer used a *nom de plume/pen name/pseudonym* for his first novel.

The actor tried to conceal his true identity by using a *pseudonym.*

nominative case The **case** that denotes a person or thing about which something is said:

The *office* is closed.
He works at home.

A noun in apposition (see **appositive**) is also in the nominative case:

Mr. Hodges, the *owner,* would like to sell the business.

When the person or thing is in the **subject** of a sentence, it is called a *subject nominative.* When it is in the **predicate** but corresponds to the meaning of the subject, it is called a *predicate nominative:*

The *car* [subject nominative] is in the garage.
Most people believe that Roosevelt was a great *president* [predicate nominative].

Compare with **objective case** and **possessive case.**

noncount noun See **half.**

none The **pronoun** *none,* meaning no one or not one, takes a singular **verb** when it is used in reference to one person or thing:

None [*no one* or *not one*] of the members *is* in favor of the proposal.

Some authorities believe that the word *none* may be used in a plural context and in those cases may legitimately take a plural verb. However, not all authorities approve of this usage:

They held several meetings, and *none have* [*all have not*] produced results.

nonflammable See **flammable/inflammable/nonflammable.**

nonrestrictive element A **phrase** or **clause** that provides additional information but is not essential to the meaning of a sentence. Since it can be deleted, it should be set off by commas:

A disk, *sometimes spelled disc,* should be kept free of contaminants.
Our boss, *who has ten years' accounting experience,* was just offered a job with a major competitor.

Compare with **restrictive element.** See also **dependent clause** and **independent clause.**

nonscientific style of writing numbers See **numbers** and **percentages.**

nonsmileys See **emoticons.**

nonstandard English Referred to informally and sometimes unjustly as *uneducated English;* usage and varieties of English that differ from **standard English,** which is the most widely accepted and understood form of English.

Most people who refer to standard or nonstandard English are referring to the written form. Therefore, nonstandard English includes improper punctuation, capitalization, and spelling as well as incorrect grammar, word choice, and pronunciation. **Slang** is a familiar variety of nonstandard English, and other examples are **barbarisms, dialects,** and **localisms.**

nontechnical style of writing numbers See **numbers** and **percentages.**

noon See **M.**

nor See **neither . . . nor.**

notch binding See **binding.**

notes Writers use one of two documentation systems: the note system or the **author-date citation** system. When notes are used to refer to sources of information in a written work, they may or may not be accompanied by a **bibliography.** When a bibliography is not included, the notes must be complete, containing the full facts that would be used in a bibliography. Bottom-of-page **footnotes** with commentary (*substantive notes*) also may or may not be included in addition to the reference notes.

The reference notes in a book may be collected at the end of the book (**endnotes**) or in end-of-chapter sections (notes). In the endnotes of a book, a subhead, usually consisting of the chapter title and number, precedes each group of notes pertaining to a particular chapter. The full collection is titled "Notes" or "Endnotes."

Regardless of whether individual end-of-chapter sections are used or one large, collective group of endnotes is used, notes should be numbered consecutively beginning with note 1 in each chapter. Corresponding numbers in the text are set as **superscripts.** Notes to **tables** and **illustrations,** however, are numbered separately and are placed at the bottom of a table or figure, not in the main notes sections. See **tables** for an example.

The superscript note numbers in the text should be placed *after* most punctuation marks, such as periods, commas, or parentheses, but *before* a dash. If possible, the number should be placed at the end of a sentence. Also, when several note numbers appear together, the individual notes should be combined so that only one number is needed. With a direct quotation, the number is usually placed at the end of the last word and concluding punctuation mark of the quoted passage.

Numbers after chapter titles or subheads should be moved into the running text. A note stating credit or permissions for a chapter or section is often set as an unnumbered footnote at the bottom of the page where the material begins.

The arrangement of data in a note is the same as that described in the **footnote** entry. If bottom-of-page substantive notes are included in a work, the notes sections will include only the notes referring to sources of information, as illustrated in the forthcoming examples. However, if desired, footnotes may be omitted and both commentary and source data may be combined and placed in the notes sections.

Whether or not a notes section has only source data or both sources and commentary, the same procedure described in the entry **footnotes** should be followed in using *ibid.* or shortened references that refer to sources in preceding notes. Also, the same procedure should be followed in using *idem* to designate the immediately preceding author in the same note or in using *see also* and *cf.* (compare) to refer to another source of added interest:

1. Neville C. Abramson, *Essays from Below,* 2 vols. (Cincinnati: Middle America Printers, 1990), 1:5.

2. Neville C. Abramson, M. T. Cline, and Laura J. Oporde, eds., *The Letters of Thomas Porter Smith,* 3 vols. (Hunter, N.J.: Notebook Press, 1988), 2:211–14.

3. Abramson, *Essays from Below,* 1:17.

4. Ibid., 1:13.

5. Wirth Barkley, *DeSteeges Blanc,* trans. Pamela Merriman (New Orleans: Southern Publishers Institute, 1995), 100–9.

6. Jeanne Crisp, Introduction to *The Failing Law,* by Parker Rogers (Des Moines: Modern American Printers, 1991), 311–401; idem, "Time Travels," in *Tomorrow Today,* ed. Eugene Carson III (San Francisco: Oceanside Press, 1984), 92.

7. Abramson, *Essays from Below,* 2:79; see also [James J. Davis], *On Learning Less* (Phoenix: Sun Publishing, 1997), 111–12.

8. [Davis], *On Learning Less,* 114.

9. *Downhill from There* (Phoenix: Sun Publishing, 1998).

10. Cf. Crisp, Introduction.

11. Maxine Nester, ed., Tulane Harman to John Silver, 2 November 1775, in *The Letters of Tulane Harman* (Miami: Eastern College Press, 1994).

12. Ibid.

13. J. K. Ishmael, *Hordes from the Past, Book 2: Asian Invaders* (reprint, New York: Towers Press, 1979), 49–78; idem, ed., *An Introduction to the Middle East,* vol. 2, *The Early Wars,* by Steven Hill (N.p.: Better Publishing, 1986), 18–61; see also Barkley, *DeSteeges Blanc,* 416.

14. J. K. Ishmael, ed., *The Jasmine Anthology,* forthcoming.

15. Timothy B. King, ''Another Story,'' *Port Smith Review* 13, no. 2 (March 1997): 3–11.

16. [Davis], *On Learning Less,* 21, 74.

17. Timothy B. King, ''The Truth about Webster,'' *Historical Studies,* vol. 1 (spring 1992).

18. C. V. Koleman and N. B. Ullman, ''Growing Up Old,'' *Besters Journal,* January 1996, 21–23.

19. Ibid., 22.

20. *Milwaukee News,* 2 March 1990, sec. 2A, p. 4.

21. Mary O. Misner, Interview by author, tape recording, Washington, D.C., 12 August 1984; see also Koleman and Ullman, ''Growing Up Old,'' 21.

22. Ellen P. Norris, ''Working in a Home Office,'' paper presented at the annual meeting of the Northern Telecommuters Society, Detroit, Mich., May 1988.

23. Ibid.

24. Oregon Research Training Department, ''Workshop II Program,'' Oregon Research Center, Portland, Oreg., 1967, photocopy.

25. Parnelli Manuscripts, Parnelli House Collection, Central College Library, Duluth, Minn., n.d.

26. *Riche Dictionary of Economics,* 12th ed., s.v. ''finance.''

27. King, ''Another Story,'' 10.

28. *United States v Southern Hills,* 174 F3d 107, 108 (3d Cir 1960).

29. U.S. Congress, Senate, Committee on Foreign Relations, *South African Uprising: Hearing before the Committee on Foreign Relations,* 99th Cong., lst sess., 21 March 1985.

30. UTEM, Princeton, N.J.: National Library of Po-

litical Conferences, 1992–. Available through the National Society of Public Colleges On-Line Database.

    31. Ibid.

    32. Noreen Winston, "A Study of Affirmative Action from Its Rise to Decline" (Ph.D. diss., University of Hawaii, 1995). Cf. Parnelli Manuscripts and Misner, Interview.

    33. "Young Company Ripe for Merger." URL: http://www.svc-online.org/newsletr/apr6-99.html.

notices See **signs and notices.**

notorious See **famed/famous/infamous/notorious.**

noun The **part of speech** that denotes a person (*woman*), place (*San Diego*), physical thing (*book*), or nonphysical thing (*religion*). The properties of a noun are the **gender** (male, female, neuter), **person** (first, second, or third), **number** (singular or plural), and **case** (nominative, objective, or possessive). See the individual entries for examples. See also **common noun** and **proper noun** for examples of the two principal types of nouns.

noun, abstract See **abstract noun.**

noun phrase A group of words that does not have both a **subject** and a **verb** but does include a **noun:**

    the reorganized *company*
    an unidentified *person*

    Gerund phrases and **infinitive** phrases may also function as nouns. In the following examples such **phrases** occupy the position of the **subject:**

    Notifying everyone by telephone [gerund phrase] would
      be impractical.
    To notify everyone by telephone [infinitive phrase]
      would be impractical.

nth An **adjective** referring to an indefinite number, amount, or power; generally, the highest or utmost. The expression is written in **roman type** in general usage, but the letter *n,* used in **equations** and other **mathematical expressions,** is written in **italics.**

In mathematical copy n originally meant only an indefinite number:

$$a + 1, b + 1, \ldots, n + 1$$

Eventually, the definition was broadened to mean not only an indefinite number but also to any required power. The expression also was adopted in lay usage to mean simply the utmost:

6 to the nth power
She is an intellectual to the nth degree.

nuclear English The name of a proposed core language that would draw on selected elements from natural English. For example, the sometimes misused **verbs** *can* and *may* (see **can/may**) would be replaced by less ambiguous expressions such as *be able to* or *be allowed to*.

An important objective of nuclear English is to develop a controlled or restricted language that will benefit the entire international community, not only the United States and other English-speaking countries. However, some authorities have rejected the idea and do not believe that it will ever gain worldwide acceptance, regardless of any merit it has.

number The grammatical property of a **noun, pronoun,** or **verb** that indicates whether one thing (*singular*) or more than one thing (*plural*) is meant:

Of the three *houses* [plural noun], one *house* [singular noun] just sold.
He [singular pronoun] told me that *they* [plural pronoun] will be leaving on Tuesday.
She *walks* [singular verb] to work, and they *walk* [plural verb] on weekends as well.

The **plural** of nouns is formed regularly or irregularly. The plural is formed regularly by adding *-s* or *-es*. It is formed irregularly by using a different word or by changing an internal vowel. A few nouns are the same in both the singular and the plural:

book/books
match/matches
child/children
mouse/mice
man/men
deer/deer

See **collective noun** for the determination of number and the use of a singular or plural verb with nouns such as *committee*. See also **amount/number** for the proper use of both of those terms.

The singular and plural of pronouns require a different word, except for the pronouns *you* and *your:*

Singular nominative case: I, you, he, she, it
Plural nominative case: we, you, they
Singular objective case: me, you, him, her, it
Plural objective case: us, you, them
Singular possessive case: my (mine), your (yours), his, her (hers), its
Plural possessive case: our (ours), your (yours), their (theirs)

See also **nominative case, objective case,** and **possessive case.**

The singular or plural form of a verb is the opposite of that of a noun. For example, whereas -*s* is added to a noun such as *book* to make it plural, -*s* is added to a verb such as *run* to make it singular:

He *runs* [singular verb] on Saturday.
They *run* [plural verb] on Saturday.

Forms of the verb *to be* (see **auxiliary verb**) require different words to indicate singular or plural:

She *is* [singular verb] well educated.
They *are* [plural verb] well educated.

For a description of the other properties of nouns, pronouns, and verbs, see **case, gender, mood, person, tense,** and **voice.**

numbers The two common styles of writing numbers are the scientific (*or* technical) and nonscientific (*or* nontechnical) styles. In the *nonscientific style,* spell out numbers *one* through *ninety-nine* and large round numbers, such as *three hundred,* and use figures for all other larger numbers. When a large number appears in a sentence or paragraph, also use figures for the smaller numbers in the same category:

> The employee had to drive *thirty miles* to work each day or could walk *one mile* to a bus stop.
> The book has *one thousand definitions* and *450 pages* of which *60* are back-matter pages.
> The high-rise building has *twelve hundred windows.*
> Of the attendees, *three-fourths* were men.

In the *scientific style,* spell out numbers *one* through *nine* or *ten,* as preferred, and use figures for all larger numbers. When a larger number appears in a sentence or paragraph, also use figures for the smaller numbers in the same category:

> The employee had to drive *30 miles* to work each day or could walk *1 mile* to a bus stop.
> The book has *1,000 definitions* and *450 pages* of which *60* are back-matter pages.
> The high-rise building has *1,200 windows.*
> Of the attendees, *3/4* were men.

In either style, scientific or nonscientific, figures are used for the following numbers:

Decimal amounts: $1,732.96
Cumbersome fractions: 8½-by-11-inch paper
Measures or designations that are expressed with an abbreviation or symbol: 142 km, 29°C, 114%, 2:35 P.M.
Mathematical expressions: $p < .01$
Monetary amounts in which a sign is used: £165

Years, numbers designating chronology, and so on: A.D.
1800
Names or titles in which the official wording uses figures: 123d Artillery Division, 10 Webster Avenue

Figures are also used in both styles if there are so many
numbers in a paragraph that it would be too difficult to read
all of them as words.

When very large numbers have many **zeros,** the words
million or *billion* may be used instead:

The company had *$3 million* in sales.
The country's population had reached *100 billion* by
1982.

When words are used for numbers, fractions and **compound terms** are hyphenated. When figures are used, the
hyphen is omitted:

thirty-two and one-eighth miles *or* 32⅛ mi. (*or* miles)
two-foot-high table *or* 2 ft. (*or* foot) high table

Inclusive numbers (from first to last) written as figures,
such as years or **page numbers** (*folios*), may be abbreviated
in different ways depending on the preferred style. In one
style, illustrated in the first column of the following examples, the two numbers are hyphenated with only the
digits that change included in the second number. In another style, illustrated in the second column, all digits are
used in the second number if the first number ends in two
zeros, and all digits are used for numbers under one hundred:

65–6	65–66
100–2	100–102
101–7	101–7
349–85	349–85
1200–14	1200–1214
2732–33	2732–33
14090–192	14090–192

In both styles, when a century changes in the designation of years, all digits in the second number must be retained:

1990–99	1990–99
1990–2000	1990–2000

Figures or words should be used consistently throughout a **manuscript,** according to the preferred style of writing numbers. One exception is that figures may be used for small numbers in tabular matter even if the main style is to use words in the text. Another exception is that a number at the beginning of a sentence must always be spelled out even if it would otherwise be written as a figure.

See the individual entries that comment on the use of numbers in specific types of material: **amount/number, average/mean/median, binary number, cardinal number, centuries, decades, decimal fractions, equations, exponent, footnotes, fractions, list, mathematical expressions, metric terms, money, no./#, notes, ordinal number, page numbers, percentages, roman numerals,** and **word division.** See also the various **back-matter** and **front-matter** entries for information about the numbering of pages in a book.

numeral adjective An **adjective** that modifies a **noun** denoting something that can be counted (*count noun*). *Cardinal adjectives* describe a precise quantity. See **cardinal number:**

one person
fourteen trucks
six ideas

Ordinal adjectives describe the degree or order of something. See **ordinal number:**

second edition
first year
third degree

numerals Words, symbols, or a group of words or symbols that represent a number. Two systems of numerals are used in the United States: **arabic numerals** and **roman numerals.**

nut space See **spacing.**

O

object See **direct object, indirect object, object of a preposition,** and **objective case.**

object of a preposition The **noun** or **pronoun** that follows a **preposition,** such as *of* or *to,* in a **prepositional phrase.** The preposition shows the relation of the object to other words in the sentence:

Please take the package to [preposition] *the mail room* [object of *to*].

objective case One of the three **cases** (objective, nominative, possessive) of **nouns** and **pronouns** that indicates their function and their relation to other words in a sentence. The objective case is the case of the *object.* See **direct object, indirect object,** and **object of a preposition.**

A noun is in the objective case when it is the object of a **verb** or **preposition:**

The writer tried [verb] *the new program* [object of *tried*] for [preposition] *a week* [object of *for*].

The form of a noun is changed only in the **possessive case.** It's the same in the objective and **nominative cases:**

car (nominative or objective case, depending on its use in the sentence)
car's (possessive case)

A pronoun is in the objective case when it is the object of a verb, **verbal,** or preposition or when it is used in an **appositive** to refer to a noun that is an object:

Mr. Kingsley called [verb] *him* [object of *called*].
Meeting [verbal] *her* [object of *meeting*] was the highlight of our visit.
The company distributed the profits among [preposition] *them* [object of *among*].
The company hired two lawyers [noun that is object of *hired*], Charles and *me* [appositive referring to noun/object *lawyers*].

The form of some pronouns is changed in all cases:

he (nominative case)
him (objective case)
his (possessive case)

Compare with **nominative case** and **possessive case.**

oceans See **names, topographical.**

official/officious The **adjectives** *official* and *officious* are sometimes incorrectly used interchangeably, perhaps because they sound similar. *Official* means relating to an office or position of authority:

His *official* duties as major begin on Monday.

Officious means characterized by an excessive and often annoying desire to please or offer unwanted help:

Her *officious* manner at work is annoying everyone.

offset lithography See **illustrations** and **printing.**

one another See **each other/one another.**

one-half See **half.**

onomatopoeia The formation or use of a word that imitates the natural sound of the object or action being identified:

beep	murmur
buzz	sizzle

| cuckoo | slurp |
| ding-dong | wham! |

operas See **musical works.**

operator See **compositor.**

or See **and/or.**

oral/verbal Although the meaning of *oral* is clear, the meaning of *verbal* is not always understood. Writers are sometimes uncertain whether it is a **synonym** or **antonym** of *oral.* The answer is that both **adjectives** can refer to spoken words; in fact, *verbal* has been used interchangeably with *oral* for centuries. However, there is an important distinction. *Oral* means spoken rather than written, and *verbal* primarily means pertaining to words rather than ideas or actions. Only in a secondary sense does *verbal* refer to something spoken rather than written.

Therefore, although one may correctly use either *oral* or *verbal* to mean spoken words, a better solution is to use *oral* when you want to stress spoken words, *written* when you want to stress written words, and *verbal* only when you want to make clear that you're referring to something communicated by words rather than in another way, such as by pictures, music, or actions:

> She sent a *written* message last week to confirm that she will make an *oral* presentation on Tuesday.
> He has strong *verbal* [word/language] skills but lacks physical coordination.

ordinal number A **number** used to indicate order or position in a series, as in *first* (*1st*), *sixth* (*6th*), or *seventeenth* (*17th*). The ordinals *second* and *third* may be expressed by adding *-nd* or *-d* alone, as preferred (*2nd* or *2d; 3rd* or *3d*). Compare with **cardinal number.**

organization names See **names, organization.**

orient/orientate The **verbs** *orient* and *orientate* are **synonyms** meaning to locate in relation to compass points, to determine one's bearings, to lean or move toward a view or position, or to make someone familiar with certain facts.

Although both terms are correct in any of these senses,
publishers usually prefer the shorter version:

> He tried unsuccessfully to *orient* himself to a different
> lifestyle in New York.

outline **A list** that has both main items and one or more
levels of subitems. **Roman numerals,** letters, and **numbers**
are used to introduce items in the different levels.

No firm rule exists concerning whether roman numerals,
letters, or numbers should be used for a specific level. However, writers often begin with capital roman numerals at
level one followed by capital letters at level two, then numbers at level three, and finally **lowercase** letters at level
four. If further levels, or subdivisions, are needed, one can
start over with roman numerals, letters, and numbers, only
this time using lowercase for the letters (*a, b,* and so on)
and roman numerals (*i, ii,* and so on) and placing them in
parentheses. See the forthcoming example.

The roman numeral, letter, or number introducing each
new level should be aligned under the first word in the
preceding level:

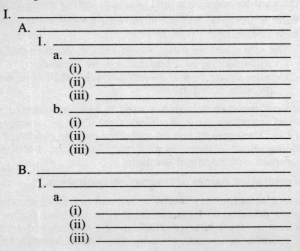

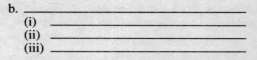

b. _____
   (i)   _____
   (ii) _____
   (iii) _____

Using any such combination of roman numerals, letters, and numbers, one can subdivide items almost endlessly. However, the greater the number of subdivisions, the more complex and difficult to follow an outline becomes.

Even when a writer wants to develop a detailed outline with many levels for personal use, such as to use as a guide during research, it may be unwise to create something overly complex for publication. Therefore each outline intended for publication should be evaluated carefully in regard to the complexity of the subject and the understanding of the primary **audience.**

overlay proof See **color proof.**

owing to See **because of/due to/owing to.**

oxymoron An expression consisting of two or more opposite or contradictory terms. Oxymorons have often been used effectively in poetry and other types of fiction, but the form is inappropriate for most other uses, such as in business documents:

  bittersweet
  deafening silence
  cruelly kind
  cheerful pessimist
  gloomy optimist
  quiet rage
  clever stupidity
  mindless understanding

P

P.M. Abbreviation for *post meridiem*—after noon. Publishers usually set the abbreviation in **roman type** with small capital letters (P.M.), but businesspeople preparing material by computer often use **lowercase** letters (p.m.) to avoid additional keystrokes. Since *a.m.* is best punctuated to avoid confusion with the word *am,* the abbreviation *p.m.* also should be punctuated.

Words such as *afternoon* or *o'clock* are unnecessary when the abbreviation *a.m.* or *p.m.* is used:

4:15 *p.m.* (*not* 4:15 *p.m.* in the *afternoon*)

See also **A.M.** and **M.**

page numbers The page numbers (*folios*) in a book are positioned in the top or bottom margin, often in the left corner (**verso** page) and right corner (**recto** page), according to the book's **design** and depending on the placement of the **running head.** See the placement of numbers in this book for an example. Regardless of the location, chapter opening pages and other beginning pages, such as the opening page of an **appendix,** have *drop* (bottom-of-page) *folios.*

Page numbers in the **front matter** are set in small **roman numerals.** Those in the text and **back matter** are set in **arabic numerals.** Some pages do not have a number printed on them but are counted in the numbering of pages. In the front matter, for example, the **title page, half-title**

page, series-title page, copyright page, and any blank **verso** pages following them are counted in the numbering but have no printed numbers. Some full-page illustrations inserted *between* text pages not only may have no printed numbers but also may not be counted in the numbering of pages. See individual entries, such as **illustrations,** for further information about page numbers.

In a book the numbering of text pages (pages in the main body) is consecutive beginning with number 1 at the second half-title page, if any; the first **part page,** if any; the first text page of the **introduction;** or chapter 1. The blank page after a second half-title page or after the first part page is counted as page 2. Therefore, when a book has either a half-title or part page, followed by a blank page, the first page with running text that includes a printed folio will have the number 3 printed on it.

If a work has more than one volume, the consecutive numbering of the first volume may be continued with the second and succeeding volumes. Or each additional volume may start over with page 1.

page proof A copy or print of typeset text that has been set in pages. The pages may be *first proofs* or *second proofs,* depending on whether **galley proofs** were prepared first.

Page proofs are read against the author's copyedited **manuscript** by both the publisher's proofreader and the author. At this point the copyedited manuscript is known as *dead manuscript* or *dead copy,* and no further editing or revision is made on the manuscript copy. Changes are made only on proof.

The proofs retained by the publisher after **typesetting** are called the *master proofs* or *master copy,* and those sent to the author are the *author's proofs* or *copy.* After an author has read and corrected the author's copy, he or she returns the pages to the publisher, where the author's corrections are transferred to the master set. The master copy is then sent to the **compositor,** where the combined author's and publisher's corrections are made in the typeset text.

Compare with **galley proof.** See **proofreaders' marks** and **proofreading** for the procedure in correcting and marking page proofs.

paintings and sculptures Capitalize the important words in the titles of paintings, drawings, engravings, sculptures, and other such works of art, and set them in **italics.** Set traditional but unofficial titles in **roman type:**

van Eyck's *The Arnolfini Wedding* (painting)
Modigliani's *Beggarman* (painting)
Hopper's *Lighthouse Hill* (painting)
Mona Lisa (painting, traditional title)
Lion God of Kush (engraving, traditional title)
Michelangelo's *Moses* (sculpture)
Rameses II (sculpture, traditional title)

paper See **stock.**

paragraph The text of a **manuscript** should be developed to guide readers through each individual paragraph and from one paragraph to another. A *topic*, or *lead*, **sentence** introduces the point or points of a paragraph, and the succeeding sentences in the paragraph develop the thought further. The **transition** from one sentence to another within a paragraph or from one paragraph to another should be logical, orderly, and smooth. To avoid choppiness and to contribute to readability, authors should use transition words, such as *however, in addition,* or *therefore,* where appropriate.

Well-written paragraphs help the reader easily understand the author's comments and move through succeeding comments at a comfortable pace, without long pauses to handle cumbersome text. Therefore, a single paragraph should not be excessively long. For example, a reader will more easily digest and remember the information in a five-sentence paragraph than that in a ten- or fifteen-sentence paragraph. In addition, a paragraph should not be laden with too many facts or statistics for a reader to assimilate comfortably.

An author needs general composition skills to create an inviting and readable work. A well-written text will be essentially free of errors and grammatically correct. It will be clear and precise and will avoid jarring shifts of **tense** and **voice.** Although **redundancy** is annoying and can hinder readability, judicious repetition or reminders of key facts in preceding paragraphs can give the document greater **unity** and coherence.

Text paragraphs are indented (see **indention**) except for the first paragraph of a chapter, which may begin flush left. In a manuscript, however, even the first paragraph is indented. A single displayed paragraph, such as an **epigraph,** may be set indented or flush left, depending on the document's **design.**

The text paragraphs are all set in the same type size and with the same **leading.** However, paragraphs in other material, such as the paragraph representing a **legend** beneath an **illustration,** may be set in a different size and with different leading or even in an entirely different **typeface.** All of these matters are indicated in the **design** prepared by the publisher for a document.

parallel structure See **sentence.**

parameter See **boundary/limit/parameter/perimeter.**

parentheses ( ) Parentheses have many important uses, including the following:

> To enclose incidental or nonessential comments or other material within a sentence or between sentences. Omit an ending period within the parenthetical comment if the comment is positioned within another sentence: A decline in the market is inevitable (others may disagree), but careful investors can take steps now to prepare. (History reveals that not all will do this.)

> To enclose numbers or letters preceding items in a run-in or displayed **list:** The three requirements are that we (1)

cosponsor the meeting, (2) provide the publicity, and (3) operate the registration desk.

To enclose figures after **numbers** expressed in words, such as in a legal agreement: Five Thousand Four Hundred Dollars and Fifty Cents ($5,400.50).

To enclose material in **mathematical expressions:** $2a(xy) + 3c(xy)$.

part/portion/share Broadly, the **nouns** *part, portion,* and *share* are **synonyms** meaning a division or segment of the whole. Specifically, each refers to a particular type of division. *Part* is the most general and the most widely used of the three terms. Also, it is the only one that is suitable in certain contexts:

Part of the problem is that we're shorthanded.

Portion is preferred to mean a part that is given or assigned for a purpose or to a specific person or persons:

Your *portion* of the work, stuffing the envelopes, shouldn't take very long.

Share, unlike the others, implies or emphasizes an equitable portion:

His *share* of the estate is in a trust fund.

In spite of these subtle differences, the three terms can be and are used interchangeably in broad or general comments.

part page A page preceding major parts, or divisions, in the text of a book. When chapters can be grouped into two or more divisions, each group may be preceded by a part page with a general title.

For example, part 1 in a grammar book may be titled "Parts of Speech," and the eight chapters discussing the main **parts of speech** may be arranged after an introductory part page. Part 2 may be titled "The Sentence" and may be followed by several chapters discussing different types of **sentences.** The **typeface** and type size used for the part number (if any) and the part title may be different from that used for numbers and titles on chapter opening pages.

The number preceding the title on a part page may be an **arabic numeral** (*1*), a word (*One*), or a **roman numeral** (*I*). Or the part page may have only a title without a part number.

The first part page in a book precedes the first page of text. It is a **recto** page and is followed by a blank page. If a book does not have a second **half-title page,** the first part page is counted as page 1 of the main text, although the page number is not printed on the page. The blank reverse side of the first part page is then counted as page 2.

A number and title or title only may be all that is listed on a part page. Or the page may list all chapter titles in that part, along with chapter opening page numbers, in a format similar to that of a **contents page.** The page may also have a displayed quotation beneath the part title. Occasionally, it includes a paragraph of text briefly summarizing the content of the chapters in that part.

When the **back matter** in a book consists only of numerous **tables** and other reference material, it may be preceded by a final part page with a reference-oriented title, such as ''Reference Section'' or ''Reference Library.'' Sometimes the final part page is titled ''Appendix'' if only appendix material follows in the back matter.

participial phrase See **participle.**

participial phrase, dangling See **dangling participial phrase.**

participle A **verbal** adjective; a **verb** form that functions as an **adjective** and may appear in the position of an **adjective** or as part of a compound verb. As a verbal, it may take a **modifier** or **complement.**

The three participles commonly used as adjectives are the *present participle, past participle,* and *perfect participle:*

They told an *encouraging* scenario [present participle modifying *scenario*]

The theory is *compelling* [present participle modifying *theory*].

The manager, *called* out of town, will have to handle the problem when he returns [past participle modifying *manager*].

Having finished the report, she went to lunch [perfect participle modifying *she*].

A *participial phrase* is a participle and its modifiers or complements. For example, in the two preceding examples the participle is part of the larger participial phrases *called out of town* and *having finished the report*.

Compare with the other two types of verbals, **gerund** and **infinitive.** See also **dangling participial phrase** and **past participle.**

particles The **articles, prepositions,** and other **prefixes,** such as *de, la,* and *Van,* that are part of English and non-English names. Since spelling, capitalization, and punctuation practices vary widely in the use of particles, authors and editors should observe the preferred practice of the person whose name is being used. In **notes, bibliographies,** and **reference lists,** the author's name should be written exactly as it appears on the **title page:**

Francis *De* Angelis *or* Francis *de* Angelis

When referring to someone by last name only, retain or drop the particle according to the person's preferred practice:

von Fredricks *or* Fredricks

See also **names, foreign,** and **names, personal.**

parts of speech The traditional classification of words that have certain functions in **sentences, clauses,** and **phrases** or when used alone. For example, if the traditional function of a word is to describe something, it is the part of speech known as an **adjective.** For definitions and examples of the eight parts of speech, refer to the individual entries: **adjec-**

tive, adverb, conjunction, interjection, noun, preposition, pronoun, and **verb.**

party, political See **political bodies.**

passim See **index.**

passive voice *Voice* indicates whether the subject of a sentence is performing the action (**active voice**) or receiving the action (*passive voice*). In the less direct and forceful passive voice, the **verb** consists of a form of the verb *to be* (see **auxiliary verb**) combined with the **past participle** of the main verb.

Whereas the active voice states what the subject is doing, the passive voice indicates what is being done or what is happening to the subject:

The speech [subject] *was given* by Ms. Carson.

The passive voice tends to make a statement sound weaker and therefore may cause the speaker to appear timid or uncertain. Although writers generally want to sound firm and confident, they may at times prefer a gentler approach. For example, the passive voice is less intimidating and accusatory when used to point out someone's error or weakness:

An error *was made* on page 4 [*not* You *made* an error on page 4].

Or a writer may want to mention only the receiver of the action instead of the doers or actors:

The company [receiver of action] *was formed* only last year [*not* The incorporators (doers) *formed* the company only last year].

Regardless of whether the passive or active voice is the better choice for a particular comment, writers should avoid needlessly shifting from active to passive or vice versa within a sentence or passage. See the example in the entry **active voice.**

past participle One of three principal forms of a **verb,** the other two being the **present tense** and the **past tense.** The past participle of a **regular verb** is formed by adding -*d* or -*ed* to the present tense:

> They *call* every day [present tense].
> They *called* every day [past tense].
> They *have called* every day [past participle].

The past participle of an **irregular verb** is formed in various ways, such as by changing a **vowel** (*ring/rang/rung*) or by adding -*en* (*drive/drove/driven*):

> He *writes* every day [present tense].
> He *wrote* every day [past tense].
> He *has written* every day [past participle].

The past participle form is combined with *have, has,* or *had* to form the perfect tenses: **present perfect tense, past perfect tense,** and **future perfect tense.** See also the other three basic **tenses: present tense, past tense,** and **future tense.**

past perfect tense The **tense** of a **verb** used to denote the earlier of two past actions. It consists of the **past participle** form of the **principal verb** combined with the **auxiliary verb** *had:*

> Marcia finished her work after Paul *had completed* his assignment [*had completed* precedes *finished*].

Compare with **future perfect tense, future tense, past tense, present perfect tense,** and **present tense.**

past tense The **tense** of a **verb** used to denote something that took place in the past. It is the second of the three main verb forms—**present tense,** past tense, and **past participle.** The past tense is formed by adding -*d* or -*ed* to the present tense of **regular verbs** or in various other ways in the case of **irregular verbs,** such as by a change in the **vowel** (*sing/sang/sung*) or by changing the entire word (*go/went/gone*):

Ms. Kennedy *stayed* [from the regular verb *stay*] for the presentation.

Mr. Solomon *began* [from the irregular verb *begin*] by making a brief speech.

Compare with **future perfect tense, future tense, past perfect tense, present perfect tense,** and **present tense.**

patron See **benefactor/client/customer/patron.**

pen name See **nom de plume/pen name/pseudonym.**

people/persons The **nouns** *people* and *persons* both refer to a number of individuals and can be used interchangeably in many cases. In fact, most authorities have given up expecting *people* to be used only as a **collective noun** designating a nonspecific, large number of people and *persons* to refer only to a specific, usually limited number. Nevertheless, careful writers continue to observe that distinction:

People would like to have lower taxes but are reluctant to give up the services and benefits paid for by the taxes.

Many *people* attended the concert.

Only eight *persons* applied for the transfer.

peoples Capitalize the names of specific peoples of the world, including nationalities, races, tribes, and ethnic groups. Omit the hyphen in most compound names, such as *Italian American,* unless one of the two parts is a **prefix.** **Lowercase** most general names or titles referring to color, habitat, and so on:

American Indian, Native American (*Indian*), *but* native American (*anyone born in the United States*)

the Navajo tribe

African American, *but* Afro-American

Arab

Hispanic

Eurasian

aborigine

highlander, *but* Highlander of Scotland

Caucasian
Oriental person, *but* oriental culture
blacks *or* Blacks and whites *or* Whites

See also **religious groups.**

percent/percentage See **percentages.**

percentages Set the numbers representing percentages in figures unless the amount begins a sentence. Write *percent* (one word) as a word in nonscientific copy and as a symbol in scientific copy:

> *Fifty-two percent* of the questionnaires have been mailed [first word in a sentence].
> Nearly *52 percent* of the questionnaires have been mailed [nonscientific copy].
> Nearly 52% of the questionnaires have been mailed [scientific copy].

Usually, when no number is specified, use the word *percentage* before the **preposition** *of.* When a number is specified, use *percent:*

> The *percentage* of new employees who soon leave the company after being employed increases each year.
> After being employed, *33 percent* of the new employees soon leave the company each year [nonscientific copy].
> After being employed, *33%* of the new employees soon leave the company each year [scientific copy].

When *percentage* is preceded by *the,* it takes a singular **verb:**

> The *percentage* of students taking history *is* down.

When *percentage* is preceded by *a,* the verb is singular or plural depending on the number specified by the **noun** in the *of* **phrase:**

> A large *percentage* of the buildings [plural] *were destroyed.*

A large *percentage* of the building [singular] *was destroyed.*

In both scientific and nonscientific copy, the symbol % may be used for *percent* or *percentages* in column **head(ing)s** and in the bodies of **tables** and **lists**. However, the word rather than the symbol should be used in the main title. The symbol may be used in parenthetical subheadings, if preferred:

Table 4

Percentage of Residents Who Voted
in National Elections Since 1980

Table 16

Changes in Personal Income Since 1950
(% Increase per Decade)

Table 16

Changes in Personal Income Since 1950
(*Percent* Increase per Decade)

perfect binding See **binding**.

perfect participle See **participle**.

performance rights See **rights**.

perimeter See **boundary/limit/parameter/perimeter**.

period (.) The period has many important uses, including the following:

To end a sentence: The customer will call back.

To follow first and middle initials preceding a last name: A. C. Goldberg (*but* Mr. X).

To conclude certain abbreviations or to separate the letters in some abbreviations: et al., ibid., Ph.D.

To follow numbers or letters in displayed **lists** or **outlines** when no **parentheses** are used:

1. Punctuation
2. Capitalization

To indicate an omission in quoted material (see **ellipsis points**): ''We must follow the schedule . . . and other requirements.''

periodicals Capitalize the names of periodicals, such as magazines and journals, including the titles and subtitles of **articles,** short stories, essays, and other material inside the publication. Set the name of the publication in **italics,** and set the name of the selections inside in **roman type** enclosed by quotation marks:

Newsweek
the article ''Downsized but Not Out''
the short story ''Angels in My Kitchen''

Capitalize and italicize the word *magazine* when it is part of the official name of a periodical, but set it in **lowercase** letters in roman type when it is not part of the title:

Weight Watchers Magazine
Entrepreneur magazine

When the introductory article *The* is part of an official title mentioned in running text, set it either lowercased and in roman type or capitalized and in italics, as preferred:

She reads the *Nation* [or *The Nation*] regularly.

periods, geological See **geological terms.**

periods, historical and cultural See **historical terms.**

periphrasis See **circumlocution.**

permissions Authors who include material from another copyrighted source must request permission to use the material in their documents. The **copyright** owners may or may not charge the requesting author a fee for this use.

Upon receiving permissions from all sources, the author should incorporate the **credit lines** supplied by the copyright owners into the author's **manuscript.** When it is time to submit the manuscript to the publisher, the author should include the various forms and letters granting permission. Since permissions usually apply only to the **edition** currently being prepared, the author must repeat this process with each successive edition, **reprint,** and so on.

When an author wants to use unpublished material owned by others and the material does not mention a specific publisher, it may be necessary to locate private parties or heirs of deceased owners. If the Copyright Office at the Library of Congress in Washington, D.C., has no record of ownership, a librarian or archivist may be able to help the author determine ownership of **manuscripts** or other papers being held in their facilities.

See also **fair use** and **rights.**

perquisite/prerequisite *Prerequisite,* which is used as both a **noun** and **adjective,** is sometimes misused for the **noun** *perquisite,* perhaps because the two words look and sound similar. However, their meanings are very different. A *perquisite,* referred to informally as a *perk,* is a payment or benefit received in addition to a salary:

She especially likes her new job because of the many *perquisites* [perks].

Prerequisite means being required as a precondition or the thing that is the precondition:

Keyboarding skill is a *prerequisite* for employment as a computer operator.

person A property of **nouns, pronouns,** and **verbs** that indicates who is speaking (*first person*), spoken to (*second person*), or spoken of (*third person*):

I, David, like to write letters [first person].
You, David, like to write letters [second person].
He, David, likes to write letters [third person].

The form of a pronoun must be changed to indicate first, second, or third person:

First person (speaking): I/me/my/mine, we/our/ours/us
Second person (spoken to): you/your/yours
Third person (spoken of): he/his/him, she/her/hers, it/its, they/their/theirs/them

The form of the verb that is used must agree with the first-, second-, or third-person **subject** in a sentence. Most verbs, however, use the same form for all persons except the third-person singular:

I/We don't have that information [first person singular or plural].
You don't have that information [second person singular or plural].
He/She doesn't have that information [third person singular].
They don't have that information [third person plural].

See also the other properties of different **parts of speech: case, gender, mood, number, tense,** and **voice.**

personal names See **abbreviations of names and titles** and **names, personal.**

personal pronoun One of the main classes of **pronouns.** Personal pronouns are used to indicate the *first person* (person speaking), *second person* (person spoken to), and *third person* (person spoken of). See **person** for a list of personal pronouns and examples of their use. Compare with **adjective pronoun, demonstrative pronoun, indefinite pronoun, interrogative pronoun, reciprocal pronoun, reflexive pronoun,** and **relative pronoun.**

personification The act of giving something human qualities or form; a person or thing typified or exemplified (*Uncle Sam*). Personification has long been a device of poets and other fiction writers.

Capitalize the act or thing being personified, and set it in **roman type** without quotation marks:

On those dark days when Reticence comes to call, she lingers too long, like Winter's coal-blackened snowbanks in a frosty New England town.

persons See **people/persons.**

persons, titles of See **titles, personal and professional.**

persuade See **convince/persuade.**

photocomposition See **typesetting.**

photomechanical typesetting See **typesetting.**

phototypesetting See **typesetting.**

phrasal preposition See **prepositional phrase.**

phrasal verb See **verb phrase.**

phrase Two or more words that do not have both a **subject** and **verb** but are used as a **part of speech.** Compare with **clause.** For examples and definitions of specific classes of phrases, see **compound phrase, gerund** [phrase], **infinitive** [phrase], **noun phrase, participle** [participial phrase], **prepositional phrase,** and **verb phrase.** See also **dangling gerund phrase, dangling infinitive phrase, dangling participial phrase,** and **misplaced phrase.**

pica A **typesetting** measurement; one pica is equal to twelve **points** or about one-sixth of an inch. The length of a line of type and the type page, or text page, are both specified in picas. Therefore, various other measurements, such as the space allotted for an **illustration,** must also be indicated in picas.

The *type page* refers to the printed area of a page, including **running heads, page numbers,** and lines of text type. The *trim size* refers to the entire page of the final product including margins, after trimming the folded and sewn sheets. Whereas the type page is specified in picas, the trim size is specified in inches.

pictogram See **graphics.**

picture graphs See **graphics.**

pidgin See **Black English.**

pie graph See **graphics.**

place names See **geographical terms** and **political divisions.**

plagiarism The act of using and putting forth another's ideas or words as one's own without crediting the real source. The use of material specifically sold for reproduction, such as **clip art,** without crediting the source may also be considered plagiarism. Editing or modifying an image scanned into a computer does not exempt an author from a charge of plagiarism or, in the case of copyrighted material, infringement of **copyright.** Authors should therefore seek permission to use another's illustrations or to quote verbatim and should credit sources even in general paraphrasing of another's original words or expressions.

planets See **astronomical terms.**

plants, names of See **biological terms.**

plate proof See **printing.**

platemaking See **printing.**

plates See **illustrations** and **printing.**

plays Capitalize important words in the titles of plays, and set them in **italics. Lowercase** the various elements or parts of plays, and set them in **roman type:**

> *Cats*
> *Hamlet*
> *Pygmalion*
> *The Glass Menagerie*
> act 2, scene 1, line 14

plurality See **minority/majority/plurality.**

plurals The plural of most **nouns** is formed by adding *-s* or *-es* to the singular:

computers
books
telephones
boxes
taxes
businesses

The plural of other words is formed in various ways, such as by a change in the spelling of the singular. The rules for forming plurals are complex and laden with numerous exceptions. Consult a dictionary when there is any doubt about correct spelling:

half/halves
photocopy/photocopies
motto/mottoes *or* mottos
policy/policies
foot/feet
child/children
proofreaders' mark/proofreaders' marks
handful/handfuls *or* handsful
parenthesis/parentheses
alumnus/alumni
addendum/addenda
attorney general/attorneys general *or* attorney generals
no./nos.
km/km
p./pp.
Mr. and Mrs. Barnes/the Barneses

See also **possessive case** for guidelines on making plural nouns possessive.

poems Capitalize important words in the titles of poems, but **lowercase** references to elements or parts of a poem. When a work mentions only a few titles, set long poems in **italics** and short poems in **roman type** enclosed by quotation marks. However, when a work refers to numerous poems, set all titles in italics.

Capitalize lines from poems exactly as they are capitalized in the original. When two or more lines are run in with the text rather than set apart as an **extract,** separate the lines with a solidus, or slash, and leave a space on either side of the slash:

> *Don Juan* (long poem)
> *The Ancient Mariner* (long poem)
> "The Growth of Love" (short poem)
> "Wind, Moon, and Tides" (short poem)
> sonnet 6, canto V, stanza 44
> Said Byron in "To Thomas Moore": "And, whatever sky's above me, / Here's a heart for every fate."

point A **typesetting** measurement in which one point is equal to 0.0138 inch, or about ¹⁄₇₂ of an inch, and twelve points equal one **pica.** The point is used to measure spacing in text, such as the **leading** between lines of type and the size of a particular **typeface.** The point size of a typeface refers to its vertical size from the lowest point to the highest point of the various letters. See **ascender** and **descender.**

Text is usually set in a type size of eight to twelve points. Display type, such as that used for a chapter title, is commonly set in a size of fourteen points or greater. However, because of the different styles of type and the varying length of ascenders and descenders, sizes also vary depending on the design of the typeface. Therefore, a ten-point size in one type style may not precisely equal a ten-point size in a different style.

political bodies Capitalize the **proper names** of political groups, but **lowercase** general references to a type of organization. Because of the different styles of treating certain names, especially generic words such as *party* that are used with a proper name, follow the preferred style of your employer or publisher:

> Republican Party *or* Republican party, the party, a Republican, republicanism
> Communist Party, the party, communism, a Communist *or* communist
> Nazi Party, Nazism, a Nazi *or* nazi
> Labour Party, the British party, the party Labourites in

England (spelled *labor* and *laborites* when pertaining to groups in the United States)

South Pacific Forum, the forum

Nonaligned Movement, the movement of the nonaligned bloc

See also **governmental bodies.**

political divisions Capitalize the **proper names** in political divisions, including words such as *District* when they are part of the formal name. **Lowercase** words such as *district* when they are general references to a type of political division:

Central Europe (World War I political division), *but* central Europe (geographical division)

Eastern and Western Europe (post-World War II political division), *but* eastern and western Europe (geographical divisions)

Mayotte, the territorial collectivity of France, the territorial collectivity, the territory

Province of Quebec, Quebec Province, the Canadian province, the province

Arizona Territory, the territory of Arizona, the territory

Commonwealth of Massachusetts, the commonwealth, the Bay State *or* Old Colony (*nicknames*), the state

state of Michigan, Michigan State, Great Lakes State *or* Wolverine State (*nicknames*), the state

city of Prescott, Prescott city, the city

county of Yavapai, Yavapai County, the county

the township of Madison, Madison Township, the township

Tenth Congressional District, the congressional district, the district

Sixth Ward, Ward 6, the ward

Third Precinct, the precinct

See also **names, country.**

polysyllable See **syllable.**

pompous language Complex words that are used in place of clear, simple words primarily to impress others. Professional writers must strive for variety in word choice and would not be able to write at length using only one-**syllable** words. Nevertheless, the overuse of needlessly complex language may lead readers to view the writing as pretentious:

Pompous Expression	*Alternative*
circa	about
conflagration	fire
customary channels	usual way
effectuated	made *or* did
functionalization	use
instrumentalities	means *or* way
obfuscate	confuse
obviate	prevent *or* do away with
promulgate	announce *or* declare
vicissitude	change

portion See **part/portion/share.**

portmanteau word See **blend word.**

positive degree See **comparison of adjectives** and **comparison of adverbs.**

possessions, U.S. See **geographical terms.**

possessive case The **case** of a **noun** or **pronoun** that denotes ownership, possession, or relationship. The possessive case of many nouns is indicated by adding an apostrophe and *s* to the singular form or an apostrophe alone to the plural form:

magazine/*magazine's* theme
magazines/*magazines'* themes
one week/one *week's* vacation
two weeks/two *weeks'* vacation
attorney/*attorney's* defense
attorneys/*attorneys'* conversation

sister-in-law/*sister-in-law's* decision
sisters-in-law/*sisters-in-law's* decision

However, if the singular already ends in an *s* sound, consider the pronunciation of the word. If the possessive creates a new syllable that is not difficult to say, add an apostrophe and *s*. If the extra syllable is difficult to say, add only an apostrophe:

boss/*boss's* office
bosses/their *bosses'* attitude
corp/the *corp's* policy
corps/the *corps'* policies
Mr. Jones/Mr. *Jones's* car
the Joneses/the *Joneses'* houses
Mr. Phillips/Mr. *Phillips'* letter
the Phillipses/the *Phillipses'* telephone calls
Moses/*Moses'* journey
New Orleans/*New Orleans'* atmosphere
appearance/for *appearance'* sake

Different words are used to make singular **personal pronouns** and the **relative pronoun** *who* possessive:

I: my/mine
you: your/yours
he: his
she: her/hers
it: its
we: our/ours
they: their/theirs
who: whose

The possessive of some **indefinite pronouns** is formed the same as the possessive of a noun:

anyone's guess
another's problem
someone's money

See also **nominative case** and **objective case**.

possessives See **compound terms** and **possessive case**.

possible See **feasible/possible.**

postpone See **defer/delay/postpone.**

practicable/practical The **adjectives** *practicable* and *practical* are **synonyms** only in the sense of being useful or usable. In other respects *practicable* differs from *practical*. For example, it also means possible or feasible:

> Combining the two departments may not be *practicable* [possible].

> *Practical* means sensible or realistic as well as useful:

> His suggestion is both interesting and *practical* [sensible].

> See also **impracticable/impractical.**

prayers See **religious works.**

predicate One of the two main parts of a **sentence;** the part of a sentence that makes a statement (see **verb**) about the **subject:**

> The book *will be released* [verb] *in September.*
> Ms. Hill *designed* [verb] *the subroutine.*

The main word or words in the predicate are the verb or **verb phrase,** which is known as the *simple predicate.* All of the words that are in the predicate are referred to as the *complete predicate.* In the preceding example, the verb *designed* is the simple predicate and *designed the subroutine* is the complete predicate. Compare with **subject.**

predicate adjective An **adjective** that modifies the **subject** but is positioned after a **verb** in the **predicate** of a **sentence:**

> The district [subject] is [verb] *large* [predicate adjective modifying *district*].

A compound predicate adjective is usually written open (without hyphens):

The speaker is *well known* [predicate adjective modifying *speaker*].

predicate nominative A predicate **noun** or noun equivalent located in the **predicate** of a **sentence** and used to complete the meaning of the **verb** and identify or describe the **subject.** A predicate nominative, which always follows a **linking verb,** must agree in **case** with the subject:

Roger [subject] is [linking verb] an astute *businessperson* [predicate nominative referring to subject *Roger*].

The most qualified people [subject] are [linking verb] the business school *graduates* [predicate nominative referring to subject *people*].

predicate noun See **predicate nominative.**

preface A statement in the **front matter** of a book that is written by the author and introduces and describes the work, including its purpose, scope, and other pertinent facts. If the **acknowledgments** of help or special material used in the work are not set as a separate section, the preface may conclude with this information.

Since the preface is part of the front matter, the pages are numbered in small **roman numerals.** Unlike the **foreword,** which concludes with the name of the person who wrote it, the preface omits the name if it is clear who wrote it. In succeeding **editions,** a new preface is placed before the one for the previous edition (when both are included). A preface, which may be one page or several pages long, often begins on the first **recto** page immediately after the **contents page.**

prefix An **affix,** such as *de-* in *deactivate,* placed before a word or the main part of a word. Most prefixes are affixed without a hyphen unless the prefix is connected to a **proper noun.** Writers have always used prefixes to expand their vocabularies and create new words (see **coinage**), but the practice especially increased throughout the twentieth century:

a-/*a*cross
baro-/*baro*meter
bio-/*bio*sphere
circum-/*circum*vent
dis-/*dis*mantle
ex-/*ex*-senator
geo-/*geo*metric
il-/*il*logical
kilo-/*kilo*gram
mid-/*mid*-America
pseudo-/*pseudo*linguistic
tele-/*tele*commute

Compare with **suffix.**

preliminaries See **front matter.**

preposition A **part of speech** that relates a **noun** or noun equivalent to other words in a sentence; a word, such as *with,* that shows the relation between its object (see **object of a preposition**) and its **antecedent:**

He drove [antecedent] *to* [preposition] the theater [object of preposition].

That is the train [antecedent] *for* [preposition] Boston [object of preposition].

The preposition and the word or group of words following it in the preceding examples (*to + the theater; for + Boston*) are called **prepositional phrases.** See also that entry for a definition of *phrasal,* or *compound,* prepositions.

The preposition *to* is sometimes confused with the **infinitive** *to* since *to* is both a preposition and the sign of the infinitive. However, when *to* is a preposition, it is followed by a **noun** or noun equivalent, such as the nouns *theater* and *Boston* in the two preceding examples. When it is the sign of the infinitive, it is followed by a **verb** form (*to* [sign of infinitive] *run* [verb] a business).

The following are examples of commonly used prepositions:

about	of
across	on
around	over
before	since
between	under
concerning	up
except	with
in	without

Some words used as prepositions are also used as other parts of speech. *Since,* for example, also functions as an **adverb** and a **conjunction.**

prepositional phrase A **phrase** consisting of a **preposition,** its object (see **object of a preposition**), and any **modifiers** of the object:

> The mail was delivered *to* [preposition] *our* [modifier] *office* [object of preposition].
> The court order fell *under* [preposition] *his* [modifier] *jurisdiction* [object of preposition].

A prepositional phrase should not be confused with a *phrasal preposition* (also called *compound preposition*), which is a two- or three-word phrase that has the force of a regular one-word preposition:

> according to
> along with
> apart from
> because of
> due to
> in addition to
> in spite of
> on account of
> out of
> with regard to

A phrasal preposition is used in a prepositional phrase the same as a one-word preposition. In the following example, *According to* is a phrasal preposition used in the prepositional phrase *According to Mr. Bradford:*

According to Mr. Bradford, the project has been postponed indefinitely.

prerequisite See **perquisite/prerequisite.**

prescribe/proscribe The **verbs** *prescribe* and *proscribe* may look similar, but their meanings are very different. *Prescribe* means to set down as a guide, assert, or order:

Practitioners of alternative medicine frequently *prescribe* herbal treatments.

Proscribe means to condemn, forbid, or banish:

The sheriff's department will *proscribe* so-called cruising by teenagers after 10 P.M.

present participle See **participle.**

present perfect tense The **tense** of a **verb** used to denote action completed at the present time or at the time of speaking. It consists of the **past participle** form of the **principal verb** combined with *have* or *has:*

The company *has finished* its first full year of operations.

Compare with **future perfect tense, future tense, past perfect tense, past tense,** and **present tense.**

present tense The **tense** of a **verb** used to denote habitual action or action presently taking place or to express a general truth. The present tense is the first of the three main verb forms—present tense, **past tense,** and **past participle:**

He *takes* pleasure in helping others.

Compare with **future perfect tense, future tense, past perfect tense, past tense,** and **present perfect tense.**

press proof See **printing.**

press sheets See **folding** and **signature.**

presume See **assume/presume.**

pretentious language See **pompous language.**

primary audience See **audience.**

primary colors See **four-color process.**

principal/principle The words *principal* and *principle* are two of the most often confused words in use today. Whereas *principal* is both a **noun** and an **adjective,** *principle* is a noun only. At one time both words meant first or highest, but eventually, the definition widened. Today the noun *principal* refers both to a sum of money and to someone who holds a high-ranking position:

> The *principal* and interest amount to $400 a month.
> Ms. Carstairs is the new school *principal*.

As an adjective, *principal* means first, foremost, main, or highest:

> Their *principal* objective was to outsell all competitors.

The more limited noun *principle* refers to a rule, standard of behavior, truth, law, or doctrine:

> He has a mind that readily grasps the *principles* of physics.

principal verb Also called *main verb;* a **verb** that expresses action or state of being by itself or that is the main acting verb in a **verb phrase** that also includes an **auxiliary verb:**

> We *make* important decisions as a team.
> We *will* [auxiliary verb] *make* [principal verb] important decisions as a team.

principle See **principal/principle.**

principles, scientific See **laws and principles, scientific.**

printer's errors (PEs) The **typesetting** errors made by a **compositor.** These errors have been called *printer's errors* since the days when a compositor and printer were the same person or firm. The initials *PE* may be written and circled in the margins of a **page proof** or **galley proof** next to errors made by the compositor. See **author's alterations**

(AAs) and **editor's alterations (EAs)** for the sources of other errors that should also be noted on the proofs.

printing The most common method of printing documents today is *offset lithography.* However, the term *printing* also refers to the process of making computer *printouts* of **manuscripts** in **word processing** or of making **page proofs** in **desktop publishing.**

Preparations for printing final copy on an offset press may include preparing negatives from camera-ready text and **illustrations** and making printing plates from the negatives. The finished, corrected text prepared by a **compositor** is considered camera-ready copy. Illustrations may be prepared separately and pasted manually onto cardboard illustration boards (*mechanicals*) ready for photographing, or they may be created by computer already in camera-ready form.

For further information about the preparation of text and illustrations for photographing, see **color proof, cropping, desktop publishing, illustrations, halftone, reproduction proof (repro), scaling,** and **typesetting.**

Some printing operations omit the negative stage and transfer images onto plates directly from camera-ready text and illustrations. Other processes involve creating plates directly from electronic images rather than from camera-ready material. But in a traditional operation, negatives are produced from camera-ready text and illustrations and then are assembled in preparation for platemaking.

When negatives are prepared in the traditional way, they are affixed to large plastic sheets called *flats.* During a process known as *stripping,* the flats are cut away to expose the areas of the negatives that will be printed. These stripped flats are then exposed on a light-sensitive paper (a process called *burning*) to create a *negative proof,* such as a **blueprint,** that can be cut and folded to resemble the finished document. Although changes at this late stage in production are costly, the negative proof nevertheless provides a final opportunity to discover and correct errors before printing plates are made.

Platemaking involves a different type of photographic process. Once again the flats are used, this time to expose a thin metal plate (also called *burning*). This exposed area then attracts the ink that will be printed on the paper used in the finished document.

The traditional offset printing process for large-quantity printing includes fitting the metal offset plates that were made, usually from negatives, onto a cylinder of the press. Both ink and a colorless solution are then applied to the plate. (A different plate is made for each color to be printed.) Whereas the area exposed during platemaking will attract ink, the unexposed area will attract the colorless solution. Therefore, only the inked area will print black or a color on the paper selected for the document.

Printing operations may include making a *plate proof*, an impression of a plate that can be checked one last time before printing begins. Or operations may include a limited run of the job to provide a *press proof* of the document, a printed proof that can also be checked one final time before the rest of the copies are printed.

Generally, the last proof that authors see is the **page proof.** Negative proofs, such as a blueprint, and plate or press proofs are checked only by the publisher's production department.

See **folding** and **binding** for information on postprinting activities.

proceedings See **symposium volume.**

prognosis See **diagnosis/prognosis.**

programs See **agreements and programs.**

programs, computer See **Internet terms.**

progressive form See **shall/will.**

pronominal adjective See **adjective pronoun.**

pronoun A **part of speech** consisting of a word such as *I, them, who,* or *each* that is used in place of a **noun.** Pronouns have the same properties as nouns: **case, gender, number,** and **person.**

The main types of pronouns are the **adjective pronoun, demonstrative pronoun, indefinite pronoun, interrogative pronoun, personal pronoun, reflexive pronoun,** and **relative pronoun.** See those entries for definitions and examples of use.

proof See **blueprint, galley proof, page proof,** and **reproduction proof (repro).** See also the description of *plate proofs* and *press proofs* in the entry **printing.**

proofreaders' marks During **proofreading,** editors and **compositors** use standard marks to indicate errors and changes on **manuscript** copy, **galley proofs,** and **page proofs.** Authors and others who read and correct proofs should use the same marks. See the chart of proofreaders' marks for examples.

proofreading After **manuscript** copy has been typeset, the author and publisher are given **galley proofs** or **page proofs** for proofreading. Using **proofreaders' marks,** both the author and the publisher's proofreader mark corrections in the margins of the typeset pages next to the line containing an error.

Within the line of type, a slash is drawn through any incorrect letter, or an incorrect word or line is crossed out. The corrected letter, word, or line is then written in the margin next to the crossed-out material. When no error has occurred but new information is being supplied, a caret should be inserted in the text at the point where the new information is to be inserted:

$$\underline{x}/ \qquad \text{the text made clear}_{\wedge}\text{view} \qquad hish$$

If a correction or new information is too extensive to add in the margin, it should be written on a separate sheet and keyed to the place on the proof where it is to be inserted. For example, the sheet might be marked ''Insert A on page 211,'' and a circled letter A would be written at the appro-

PROOFREADERS' MARKS

Mark	Meaning	Example
	Delete	bookss
	Delete & close up	boooks
stet	Let it stand	line art.
no ¶	No paragraph; run in	chapter. Therefore
#	Add space	tothem
out, sc	Something missing; see copy	Be four hours
sp. out	Spell out	2 files
	Close up	be gin
[	Move left	[the line
]	Move right	] the line
tr.	Transpose	edtior
//	Line up; align	call the office
¶	New paragraph	hold. It

Mark	Meaning	Example
?	Question to author	1899
?	Insert question mark	Correct
!	Insert exclamation point	Right
/=/	Insert hyphen	new style
⸺/⸺	Insert quotation marks	I know.
;	Insert semicolon	mine yet
:	Insert colon	the following
﹀	Insert comma	1, 2 and
⊙	Insert period	in time
∨	Insert apostrophe	its true
h	Change to h	hardware
caps	Set in capital letters	Now
lc	Set in lowercase letters	NOW

Mark	Meaning	Example
bf	Set in boldface type	Now
ital.	Set in italics	Now
s.c.	Set in small capital letters	Now
c.s.c.	Set in capitals & small capitals	Now
✓✓✓	Correct spacing	h o m e
⏝	Indent paragraph	Yes, we
rom.	Change to roman type	*italic*
✓1	Set as superscript	A1
1	Set as subscript	A1
⟦/⟧	Insert brackets	1999
⟨/⟩	Insert parentheses	1999
1/M	one-em dash	too—until

priate place in the margin of page 211 along with the words
"Insert A from page 211a here."

Proofreaders read the typeset copy against the edited
manuscript copy. Any deviation should be marked on the
proofs and the author queried (see **query**) if anything is not
clear. The following are examples of errors that proofreaders may find:

Typographical errors

Inconsistent or incorrect spelling, capitalization, punctuation, use of **italics, grammar,** treatment of **numbers,**
and other usage.

Incorrect **word division**

Missing or transposed letters or other material

Improper **spacing**

Improper forms of citation

Incorrect use of **quotation marks**

Incorrect **indentions**

Improper paragraphing, **sentence** structure, use of
head(ing)s, and so on

Incorrect numbering of **tables** and **illustrations**

Missing or confusing copy

Incorrect **running heads** or **page numbers**

Each manuscript may have problems unique to it depending not only on the type of document, such as a mathematical work, but also on the compositor and the quality
of **typesetting.** Proofreaders must therefore be alert to unusual errors as well as common mistakes.

proper name A **proper noun** representing the full, formal
name of a specific person, place, thing, concept, action, or
quality or group of such things. Important words in a proper
name are always capitalized.

George Washington Memorial Bridge
American Theological Library Association
Minneapolis and Saint Paul, Minnesota
Superswitch 2000 NT Server
the Peter Principle
Pure Food and Drug Act

Some grammarians treat *proper names* and *proper nouns* as **synonyms.** Others consider *proper name* to be a broader and more inclusive term. As such it includes not only simple one- or two-word nouns but also groups of words that name someone or something, such as the organization name Fund to Protect Endangered Species of the World and the book title *Encyclopedic Dictionary of Style and Usage.*

Compare with **common noun.**

proper noun A word or words that name a specific person, place, thing, concept, action, or quality. A proper noun is always capitalized:

Neil
Food-Mart
Mona Lisa
Thursday
Halloween
Nevada

Some grammarians distinguish between *proper noun* and *proper name.* They believe that **proper name** is a broader category including groups of words constituting a name or title. See the explanation in that entry. Other authorities make no distinction between the two terms, and in this dictionary the terms have been used interchangeably.

Compare with **common noun.**

proscribe See **prescribe/proscribe.**

proved/proven The **verbs** *proved* and *proven* are alternative forms of the **past participle** of *prove.* The form *proved* is also the **past tense** of *prove,* meaning to establish truth or validity through argument or evidence:

> They *proved* [past tense] beyond a reasonable doubt that he could not have committed the crime.
>
> They *have proved/proven* [past participle] beyond a reasonable doubt that he could not have committed the crime.

As a past participle, *proved* is the older form and is usually listed as the preferred form in dictionaries. However, *proven* is widely used as a past participle in legal contexts.

Proved is not used as an **adjective,** but *proven* is more common as an adjective meaning tested than as a verb:

> She has a *proven* ability as a manager.

pseudo-/quasi- As **prefixes,** *pseudo-* and *quasi-* should not be used interchangeably to mean similar. As an **adjective** and a word in itself, *pseudo* means purporting to be something other than the real thing, a sham, or apparently similar (*pseudo* science fiction). As a prefix, *pseudo-* means false or deceptive:

> As hard as he tries, he's still no more than a *pseudointellectual.*

As an adjective and a word in itself, *quasi* means resembling but doesn't have the connotation (see **connotation/ denotation**) of being falsely or deceptively similar (a *quasi* contract). As a prefix, *quasi-* means partly or somewhat but, again, without the implication of being false or deceptive:

> The department is a *quasijudicial* body with limited legal authority.

pseudonym See **nom de plume/pen name/pseudonym.**

public domain The status of works that are not protected by patent or **copyright.** A work that is in the public domain may be used by others without permission of the originator. However, authors who use **illustrations** from or quote from such works should nevertheless indicate the source.

Since legally copyrighted works need not bear a copyright notice, it is often difficult to tell whether a work is in the public domain. In those cases an author can best assume that it may be protected by copyright and that permission to use any part of the work is therefore required.

Federal government publications are always in the public domain, and writers sometimes borrow heavily from them. Other works that may be in the public domain include those for which copyright has expired and some published before 1978 without a proper copyright notice. However, a writer should investigate to be certain that a copyright was never renewed or is definitely not valid. This information is on record in the Copyright Office of the Library of Congress in Washington, D.C.

Certain types of information as well as documents are also in the public domain. Ideas, facts, procedures, titles, names, formats, and so on are not protected by copyright law. Nevertheless, if those things are used in the original treatment or wording of one author, another author must not duplicate that original way of expressing them.

See **copyright** for the term of protection and procedure in registering a work.

publishing agreement See **rights.**

publishing history See **year of publication.**

punctuation See individual entries, such as **dash** and **quotation marks.**

purposefully/purposely The **adverbs** *purposefully* and *purposely* are general **synonyms** meaning deliberately or with a specific purpose. The only subtle distinction that is sometimes made concerns a desire to emphasize determination, especially strong or ruthless determination. If that emphasis is needed, *purposefully* is the better choice:

> She *purposefully* [deliberately and with strong determination] plotted to discredit her rival for the promotion.

> He *purposely* [for a specific reason] enrolled early in the word processing class, knowing that it would soon fill up and registrations would close.

Q

quad See **spacing.**

qualitative/quantitative It is not clear why the **adjectives** *qualitative* and *quantitative* are sometimes confused because the words themselves make it easy to tell the difference. *Qualitative* pertains to quality and *quantitative* to quantity:

> The department will undertake a *qualitative* analysis of the product's attributes.
> The lab will undertake a *quantitative* analysis of the amount of alcohol in the product.

quasi- See **pseudo-/quasi-.**

query A question directed to an author, editor, or **compositor** about something in a **manuscript** or on **galley proofs** or **page proofs.** Queries may be written on flags and affixed to the appropriate page or may be indicated by circled notations with a question mark next to the line containing the material in question.

Discrepancies in facts, confusing statements, questionable dates, and other such problems should be queried rather than changed by an editor. However, technical errors, such as inconsistencies in capitalization or punctuation, need not be queried; rather, an editor should make such corrections routinely as part of the **copyediting** process.

question, indirect See **question mark (?).**

question, rhetorical See **rhetorical question.**

question mark (?) The question mark has three principal uses:

> To indicate a direct question: Is the Avery file in your office? (Use a period after an *indirect question:* I wonder if the Avery file is in your office.)

> To indicate uncertainty about a fact or statement: We purchased that machine in February 1997(?) when we expanded the department.

> To indicate questions in a series: Was the purpose of his announcement to clarify his position? To stimulate thinking about this subject? To promote a conservative approach?

quotation marks ('/'') Quotation marks have three principal uses:

> To enclose words quoted verbatim: As he explained, ''The new procedures will affect every employee.'' See also **dialogue.**

> To enclose a word used in a special sense the first time it is used: Benson is one of many legislative ''shapeshifters'' who are described in this chapter.

> To enclose the titles of articles, chapters, television and radio episodes, short poems and songs, and unpublished works: His dissertation is titled ''The Fall of Nineteenth-century Civility.'' See individual entries such as **poems** for more examples.

Both single marks (') and double marks ('') are used in quoted material. When one quoted passage enclosed in quotation marks has another quotation within it, the internal quotation is enclosed in single marks:

> The authors agree with Stedham: ''We believe, as Stedham indicted, that 'loyalists are in short supply these days.' ''

In an **extract,** which is not enclosed in quotation marks, the single marks should be changed to double marks:

The author agreed with Stedham:

> We believe, as Stedham indicated, that "loyalists are in short supply these days."

When quoted material runs to more than one paragraph and is not set off as an extract, quotation marks are placed at the beginning of each paragraph but only at the end of the last paragraph.

Periods and **commas** are placed inside the marks and **colons** and **semicolons** outside the marks. **Exclamation points** and **question marks** are placed inside the marks only if they are part of the quoted material:

"His actions made his position very clear," the professor remarked, "but his words seem contradictory."

As she said, "The trend is unmistakable"; however, trends can be reversed.

The manual describes "two key factors that must never be ignored": education and on-the-job experience.

Who said "We are one"?

"Join us today!" he shouted.

See **ellipsis points** (...) for the proper indication of omitted words in quoted material.

quotations See **epigraph, extract,** and **quotation marks** (**'/''**).

R

races See **peoples.**

radio program See **television and radio programs.**

ragged right A **typesetting** expression that describes copy set with an uneven, or unjustified, right margin. Compare with **justification.**

re- The **prefix** *re-* is always attached to words without a hyphen unless it is necessary to indicate a different meaning:

> reform (rehabilitate)
> re-form (form again)
>
> recollect (recall)
> re-collect (collect again)
>
> recount (narrate)
> re-count (count again)
>
> recreation (leisure activity)
> re-creation (created again)

reaction/reply/response These three **nouns** are often used interchangeably, although only *reply* and *response* primarily mean an answer. Therefore, most authorities accept interchangeability in the use of *reply* and *response* but object to the use of *reaction* as a **synonym.** In strict usage, *reaction* is a response to stimuli or the state resulting from that response:

Her *reaction* to the drug was severe.

Reply, which can also be used as a **verb** (please *reply*), means a response when used as a noun, especially a written or spoken answer to something:

We expect to receive a *reply* to our letter today.

Response is the act of replying or the reply itself and is often the better choice when the emphasis is on the character of the reply:

His *response* to our suggestion was positive.

In a secondary sense, *response* also means a reaction to a specific stimulus. However, in most cases one should use *reaction* in a scientific context and *response* or *reply* in a nonscientific context.

reciprocal See **common/mutual/reciprocal.**

reciprocal pronoun An **indefinite pronoun** used in the **phrases each other/one another.** The **pronouns** are called reciprocal because the action of one word in the phrase is connected to and affects the other:

They talk to *each other* every day.

Compare with **adjective pronoun, demonstrative pronoun, indefinite pronoun, intensive pronoun, interrogative pronoun, personal pronoun, reflexive pronoun,** and **relative pronoun.**

recollect/remember The **verbs** *recollect* and *remember* are generally accepted as **synonyms,** although some authorities make a distinction. *Recollect* and *remember* both mean to recall to mind, but *recollect* is the better choice to stress a serious and deliberate effort to recall something. *Remember* also means to recall to mind but only secondarily means to recall with effort. In its primary sense it is more suitable in situations involving spontaneous recall:

After weeks of mentally retracing our steps, I finally *recollect* what happened just before the accident.

Oh, yes, I *remember* that storm.

recto The right-hand page in a book or the front side of a **leaf.** Compare with **verso.** See also individual entries such as **contents page** for information about whether a section or part of a book begins on a recto or verso page.

redundancy Authorities often distinguish between unnecessary repetition and useful or at least allowable repetition. The former consists of superfluous repeated words that mean the same thing or that needlessly reinforce each other:

advance warning
blue *in color*
close proximity
deeds *and actions*
final conclusion
large *in size*
the month of December
spell out *in detail*
successful triumph

Another type of repetition is also unnecessary, but its occurrence is more understandable. Certain scientific terms and foreign words may be unfamiliar to a writer, so repetition occurs unintentionally. Nevertheless, careful writers will strive to avoid this. In other cases a writer may believe that certain readers do not know a foreign or technical term and that repetition is therefore necessary or helpful. However, even in these situations the writer could spell out the unfamiliar letter or term on first use rather than resort to unnecessary repetition:

HI*V virus* (*V* = virus)
CI*S commonwealth* (*C* = commonwealth)
pirouette turn (*pirouette* = turn)
*the l'*Académie (*l'* = the)

Certain *intentional* repetition is defended on the grounds that it serves an important purpose. Many writers effectively use such deliberate repetition for emphasis or clarity, and those who want to explain a complex idea or stress an important point may intentionally repeat it using different words or sometimes the same words. For example, the point of the preceding sentence can be repeated or reinforced by adding a follow-up sentence:

> This technique of restating facts is therefore a valuable tool for writers who want to emphasize or reinforce an idea or fact.

Some forms of repetition are used with the hope that readers will focus on the words being repeated because the writer wants the reader to remember those words—and the associated message. Such repetition has been used to capture attention in many types of writing from literary works to political speeches to advertising copy:

> *Review:* He plays a *kind* but *vulgar* crook. What makes people remember his *kind* heart and forget his *vulgar* mouth? Are audiences finally ready to accept a *kind* but *vulgar* protagonist?
>
> *Campaign speech:* So I say to you today: *Don't accept less* from your government! *Don't accept less* for your children! *Don't accept less* for your elderly parents! And *don't accept less* for your country! Vote for Robert C. Perkins, and I promise that if I'm elected, *I won't accept less* for you!
>
> *Ad:* Why is the 4D XL link the *best* buy? Because it offers the *best* network performance, the *best* access technology, and the *best* applications support. You can't help but agree that the 4D XL link is the *best* value in town.

See also **conciseness** and **wordiness.**

reference list A list of references, similar to a **bibliography,** that an author compiles to correspond to **author-date citations** in the text. The list is usually placed in the **back matter** of a book before the list of contributors (see **contributors, list of**), if any, or otherwise before the **index.**

Entries in a reference list must have full source data including the author's name, complete title of the work being cited, and full publication information. See the forthcoming examples.

Reference lists are usually arranged alphabetically by author, editor, compiler, and so on since the text citations are made by name and date. When there are successive entries in the list by the same author, a three-**em** dash is used for the second and succeeding entries, with original works preceding edited, compiled, or translated works. See the forthcoming examples.

Books and other publications are set in **italics,** and article and chapter titles are set in **roman type** with quotation marks. The arrangement of data in an entry and the **indention** of successive lines after the first line (*hang-and-flush style*) are the same as in a bibliography entry, with one exception. Whereas the date is given at the end or later in a bibliography entry, it immediately follows the author's name in reference-list entries. The same data used in the examples of **bibliography** entries are used in the following list so that you can compare the position of the dates:

Abramson, Neville C. 1990. *Essays from Below.* 2 vols. Cincinnati: Middle America Printers.

Abramson, Neville C.; Cline, M. T.; and Oporde, Laura J., eds. 1988. *The Letters of Thomas Porter Smith.* 3 vols. Hunter, N.J.: Notebook Press.

Barkley, Wirth. 1995. *DeSteeges Blanc.* Translated by Pamela Merriman. New Orleans: Southern Publishers Institute.

Crisp, Jeanne. 1991. Introduction to *The Failing Law,* by Parker Rogers. Des Moines: Modern American Printers.

————. 1984. "Time Travels." In *Tomorrow Today.* Edited by Eugene Carson III. San Francisco: Oceanside Press.

[Davis, James J.]. 1997. *On Learning Less.* Phoenix: Sun Publishing.

Downhill from There. 1998. Phoenix: Sun Publishing.

Ishmael, J. K. 1979. *Hordes from the Past, Book 2: Asian Invaders.* Reprint, New York: Towers Press.

———, ed. 1986. *An Introduction to the Middle East.* Vol. 2, *The Early Wars,* by Steven Hill. N.p.: Better Publishing.

———, ed. Forthcoming. *The Jasmine Anthology.*

King, Timothy B. 1997. "Another Story." *Port Smith Review* 13, no. 2 (March): 3–11.

———. 1992. "The Truth About Webster." *Historical Studies,* vol. 1 (spring).

Koleman, C. V., and Ullman, N. B. 1996. "Growing Up Old." *Besters Journal,* January, 21–23.

Milwaukee News. 1990. 2 March, sec. 2A, p. 4.

Misner, Mary O. 1984. Interview by author. Tape recording. Washington, D.C., 12 August.

Nester, Maxine, ed. 1994. Tulane Harman to John Silver. 2 November 1775. In *The Letters of Tulane Harman.* Miami: Eastern College Press.

Norris, Ellen P. 1988. "Working in a Home Office." Paper presented at the annual meeting of the Northern Telecommuters Society, Detroit, Mich., May.

Oregon Research Training Department. 1967. "Workshop II Program." Oregon Research Center, Portland, Oreg. Photocopy.

Parnelli Manuscripts. N.d. Parnelli House Collection. Central College Library, Duluth, Minn.

Riche Dictionary of Economics, 12th ed., s.v. "finance."

United States v Southern Hills. 1960. 174 F3d 107, 108 (3d Cir).

U.S. Congress. Senate. 1985. Committee on Foreign Relations. *South African Uprising: Hearing before the Committee on Foreign Relations.* 99th Cong., 1st sess., 21 March.

UTEM. 1922–. Princeton, N.J.: National Library of Political Conferences. Available through the National Society of Public Colleges On-Line Database.

Winston, Noreen. 1995. "A Study of Affirmative Action from Its Rise to Decline." Ph.D. diss., University of Hawaii.

"Young Company Ripe for Merger." 1999. URL: http://www.svc-online.org/newsletr/apr6-99.html.

reference matter See **back matter.**

references See **author-date citations, bibliography, endnotes, footnotes, notes,** and **reference list.**

reflexive pronoun A compound **personal pronoun** that is the object of the **verb** and indicates who or what received the verb's action. The compound personal pronouns are *myself, yourself, himself, herself, itself, ourselves, yourselves,* and *themselves.* A reflexive pronoun always refers to the same person in the subject:

> The dancer injured *herself* [refers to subject *dancer*] yesterday.

Compare with **adjective pronoun, demonstrative pronoun, indefinite pronoun, intensive pronoun, interrogative pronoun, personal pronoun, reciprocal pronoun,** and **relative pronoun.**

regarding See **as regards/in regard to/regarding/with regard to.**

regular verb A **verb** that forms the **past tense** and **past participle** by adding *-d* or *-ed* to the **present tense,** or the *simple form* of the verb. In a few cases the *-d* or *-ed* ending is changed to *-t*. In the following examples the first word is the present tense, the second is the past tense, and the third is the past participle:

> add/added/(*have/has/had*) added
> love/loved/(*have/has/had*) loved
> build/built/(*have/has/had*) built

Compare with **irregular verb.**

relative adjective A **relative pronoun** used as an **adjective.** The relative pronouns are *who, whose, whom, what, that,* and *which.* When a pronoun such as *whose,* the possessive form of the relative pronoun *who,* modifies the

noun that follows it, the pronoun functions as an adjective and is called a *relative adjective:*

He's the person *whose* [relative pronoun] store windows [noun] were shattered by the gas explosion.

relative adverb See **conjunctive adverb.**

relative pronoun A **pronoun** that substitutes for a **noun** and links a **clause** to its **antecedent**—the noun or pronoun to which the relative pronoun refers. The relative pronouns are *who, whose, whom, which, that,* and *what*:

This is the file [antecedent] *that* [relative pronoun] was missing.

A *compound relative pronoun* consists of a relative pronoun combined with *-ever* or *-soever:*

Whoever [substitutes for a subject noun] finishes first will win the competition.

Compare with **adjective pronoun, demonstrative pronoun, indefinite pronoun, intensive pronoun, interrogative pronoun, personal pronoun, reciprocal pronoun,** and **reflexive pronoun.**

religions See **religious groups.**

religious events and concepts Capitalize the names of most historically important religious events and concepts:

Creation
Crucifixion
Resurrection
Second Coming
Last Supper
Exodus
Diaspora (of Jews)
Hegira (Mohammed's)
the Christian church (concept, not institution)

See also **deities, religious groups, religious meetings, religious movements, religious services,** and **religious works.**

religious groups Capitalize the names of religious groups, such as churches, religions, denominations, sects, and orders, including the buildings in which the groups gather. **Lowercase** general references to a church, an order, and so on:

> Roman Catholic Church, Catholicism, a Catholic church, Catholics
> Mormon Church, Church of Jesus Christ of Latter-day Saints, Mormonism, a Mormon church, Mormons
> Buddhism, the Buddhist temple, Buddhists
> Hinduism, the Hindu temple, Hindus
> Islam, Islamic religion, Muslims
> Reformed Church in America, a Reformed church, the Third Reformed Church of Des Moines, Iowa
> Orthodox Church, the Greek Orthodox Church, an Orthodox church
> Temple Beth Sholom, the temple
> Concordia Seminary, the Protestant seminary
> Independent A.M.E. Denomination, the denomination
> Pentecostal Assemblies of Jesus Christ, Pentecostal Assemblies
> Missionary Church Association, the association
> Quakers, Society of Friends, Quakerism, the Quaker sect
> Sisters of Mercy, the order

See also **deities, religious events and concepts, religious meetings, religious movements, religious services,** and **religious works.**

religious meetings Capitalize the official names of religious meetings, such as councils and synods. **Lowercase** general references to a meeting:

> Second Ecumenical Council, the council
> World Council of Churches, the council's first assembly in Amsterdam

Lutheran Synodical Conference of North America, the
Synodical Conference, the conference
Synod of Dort, the synod

See also **conferences and meetings, deities, religious
events and concepts, religious groups, religious movements, religious services,** and **religious works.**

religious movements Capitalize the **proper names** in specific religious movements of special importance. **Lowercase** general references to a movement:

Advent movement, Adventist movement, the movement
American Lutheranism, the liberal Lutheran movement
Amish Mennonite movement, the Mennonite movement,
the movement
Protestant Reformation, the Reformation, the epochal
movement

See also **deities, religious events and concepts, religious groups, religious meetings, religious services,** and
religious works.

religious services Capitalize references to the eucharistic
sacrament, to Mass in general, and to certain elements of
the Holy Communion. **Lowercase** general references to a
type of service, to individual masses, and to most objects
used in services:

the Divine Liturgy
the High Mass (general celebration)
Tuesday's high mass at noon (individual celebration)
the Sacrament in Holy Communion
the rosary
bar mitzvah, bas mitzvah
confirmation
vesper service

See also **deities, religious events and concepts, religious groups, religious meetings, religious movements,**
and **religious works.**

religious works Capitalize the important words in the titles of sacred works as well as creeds, confessions, and prayers, and set them in **roman type** without quotation marks. **Lowercase** most adjectives derived from the names of sacred works, but see exceptions in the following list:

> King James Bible, the Bible, biblical
> Revised Standard Version
> Old Testament
> Scripture(s), scriptural
> the Gospels, the synoptic Gospels
> Torah *or* torah
> Koran *or* Qur'an, Koranic *or* Qur'anic
> Talmud, talmudic
> Dead Sea Scrolls
> Bhagavad Gita
> Ten Commandments
> Sermon on the Mount, the sermon
> the Lord's Prayer, the prayer
> Apostles' Creed, the creed
> Augsbury Confession, the confession

See also **deities, religious events and concepts, religious groups, religious meetings, religious movements,** and **religious services.**

remainder See **balance/remainder.**

remember See **recollect/remember.**

repetition See **redundancy.**

reply See **reaction/reply/response.**

reprint The same publisher or a different publisher may reprint a published work. When a publisher no longer wants to reprint a work or revise it for another **edition,** the rights to reprint the work may be sold or licensed to another publisher. See **rights** and **licensing of rights.**

However, when a publisher does reprint a work one or more times, the reprintings, or new *impressions,* of the original edition are indicated in the publishing history. This information appears after the copyright notice on the **copyright page.**

Usually, no substantial changes are undertaken in a work to be reprinted, although minor corrections may be made. When substantial revision is undertaken, the work is considered a revised edition rather than a reprint. Whereas a revised edition would usually require a new or amended author-publisher contract, new **permissions,** and so on, a reprinting takes place without preparing and producing a new **manuscript.**

See also the example of a reference entry for a reprinted book in **bibliography, notes,** and **reference list.**

reproduction proof (repro) The final camera-ready proof of typeset material from which negatives are made in preparation for offset **printing.** Since repros are prepared for photographing, they must be handled with care to avoid creasing them or contaminating them with dust, ink, or other blemishes that would show up in printing. The author does not see repros, but they are checked by the publisher before returning them to the **compositor** or sending them to the camera department to be photographed.

Only serious errors should be corrected at this stage, and anything noted on a repro should be lightly written in the margin in light blue pencil. Unintentional marks that do appear must be covered with correction fluid or corrected by computer and another repro page printed.

See also **typesetting.**

response See **reaction/reply/response.**

restrictive element A **phrase** or **clause** that is essential to the meaning of a **sentence.** Since it cannot be logically omitted, it should not be set off by commas:

The window *by his desk* is cracked.
The editor *who has the most experience* should handle
   that manuscript.

Compare with **nonrestrictive element.** See also **dependent clause** and **independent clause.**

revered persons See **deities.**

revolutions, geological See **geological terms.**

rhetorical question A question that does not require an answer and to which none is expected. Rather, the question is often posed to make a point and to encourage a listener or reader to answer it mentally. This type of question can usually be rephrased as a statement:

> Isn't it interesting that metaphysics answers many questions left unanswered by traditional science?

> It's interesting that metaphysics answers many questions left unanswered by traditional science.

rights The privilege or permission to do or not do something as described in a publishing agreement between an author and a publisher. The agreement, or contract, establishes the right of the publisher to publish the author's work in a certain form, sell it, and license rights (see **licensing of rights**) for the work in a certain geographical area, such as in the United States and its possessions and in certain other countries and territories in which the work may be translated. In conjunction with this, the agreement specifies the share of revenue to be assigned to the various parties.

Other rights, called *subsidiary rights,* are also granted to the publisher, and these rights in turn may be licensed to others. Again, the agreement specifies how the resulting revenue will be divided among the parties.

The subsidiary rights that are usually granted to the publisher include the following:

> The right to license others to reprint the work

> The right to license book club editions of the work

> The right to serialize portions of the work in magazines or newspapers after publication of the work (*second serial rights*)

> The right to license others to condense the work and include it in **collective works,** such as an **anthology**

The right to allow others to quote from the work up to a specified number of words

The right to license others to publish and offer the work as a premium, or gift

The rights that an author retains, depending on the agreement negotiated by the author or an agent, may include the following:

The right to publish English-language editions of the work in England and other Commonwealth countries, except in Canada

The right to license foreign-language translations

The right to publish excerpts in magazines and newspapers before the full work is published (*first serial rights*)

The right to produce movies, videocassettes, and so on (*performance rights*)

The right to make audio recordings, such as tapes and compact discs

The right to adapt the work for databases and computer software

rivers See **names, topographical.**

roads See **streets and roads.**

roll-out See **draw-down.**

roman numerals The **numerals** formed with letters of the alphabet, such as the following capital and **lowercase** letters one through ten:

I	i
II	ii
III	iii
IV	iv
V	v
VI	vi

VII	vii
VIII	viii
IX	ix
X	x

Roman numerals are used for **page numbers** in the **front matter** of a book. The other pages in a book, such as the main text and the **back matter,** have **arabic numerals.**

roman type The regular type style used for the text of books, articles, and so on, as opposed to **italics.** For example, this sentence is set in roman type. See also **typeface.**

romanize See **transliteration.**

root The element or part of a word that contains the main component of meaning. A full word is formed by adding **prefixes, suffixes,** inflected endings (see **inflection**), and so on to the root.

The element that is the root in the following words is italicized:

*arch*ive	*myth*ical
dia*gnose*	*opt*ician
hemi*sphere*	*pract*ical

round See **around/round.**

run-in sidehead See **head(ing).**

run-in style See **index.**

running feet See **running head.**

running heads The title or words usually set at the tops of the pages but sometimes at the bottoms (*running feet*) to indicate the chapter, section, dictionary entry, or other material that is printed on that page. The heads are never used on chapter and other opening pages, **part pages,** or **front matter** display pages, such as the **title page** or **copyright page.** Although running heads are not mandatory, they are helpful in textbooks, scholarly works, and reference books.

Usually, **verso** pages have one type of running head and

recto pages another type. For example, one chapter might have the title of that chapter on verso pages and a subheading applicable to the particular page on recto pages. An **appendix** in the **back matter** might have the appendix number or letter on verso pages and the appendix title on recto pages. A dictionary might have the name of the first entry of the page on verso pages and the last entry of the page on recto pages.

The choice of running heads for a particular work is made by the publisher. However, both the publisher and the author should verify the accuracy of running heads on **page proofs** during **proofreading.** The publisher is responsible for checking the accuracy of running heads on later proofs, such as **blueprints.**

S

sacred works See **religious works.**

saddle stitching See **binding.**

saddle wiring See **binding.**

salable/saleable The **adjectives** *salable* and *saleable* are variant spellings of the term meaning suitable for sale. The shorter version, *salable,* is usually listed in dictionaries as the preferred form, with *saleable* as an alternative:

> Our car is old, but it is still *salable/saleable.*

sample pages When sample pages of a work are requested before **typesetting** begins, the **compositor** prepares a variety of samples using the **design** specifications and **layout** prepared for the work. The samples will show how the various elements of the work, such as text, titles, **extracts, tables,** and **notes,** will look when set in page format. The editor reviewing the pages may request changes, or the editor may approve the samples as prepared, in which case typesetting can begin.

sans serif A **typeface** that has no *serifs*—lines that finish off the main strokes of a letter, such as those you see on a capital *T* or *M* in this book. (The word *sans* is French for without.) Compare with **serif.**

sarcasm See **irony/sarcasm/satire.**

satire See **irony/sarcasm/satire.**

scaling Determining the portion of an **illustration** that can be proportionately reduced (or enlarged) to fit a particular space allotted to it. For example, if a two-by-four-inch space on a page has been set aside for a photograph, one must select a portion of the original photograph that will reduce proportionately to fit that space. With an eight-by-ten-inch glossy photograph, one possibility would be to select a four-by-eight-inch portion that would reduce proportionately to fit the two-by-four-inch space. However, a five-by-nine-inch portion or other odd size would not reduce proportionately to fit a two-by-four-inch space. Authors and editors sometimes use scaling instruments that indicate alternative sizes.

See **cropping** for procedures in marking the area of a photograph to be used.

scarcely See **barely/hardly/scarcely.**

schools, cultural See **cultural terms.**

scientific and technical terms See **abbreviations in technical and scientific works, astronomical terms, biological terms, Celsius/Fahrenheit, computer terms, geological terms, Internet terms, medical terms, metric terms,** and **names, topographical.** See also individual entries pertaining to technical publishing terms, such as **leading, point,** and **scaling.**

scientific style of writing numbers See **numbers.**

script See **cursive type.**

scrupulous See **meticulous/scrupulous.**

sculptures See **paintings and sculptures.**

second person See **person** and **personal pronoun.**

second proof See **page proof.**

secondary audience See **audience.**

see also See **footnotes.**

selected bibliography See **bibliography.**

semantics The study or science of meaning in language and the relation between linguistic symbols and their meanings, especially connotative meanings. See **connotation/denotation.**

semi- See **bi-/semi-.**

semicolon (;) The semicolon has four principal uses:

To separate a **compound sentence** that is not connected by a comma and a **conjunction:** *Homographs* are spelled the same but differ in meaning and pronunciation; *homophones* sound the same but differ in meaning and spelling.

To separate heavily punctuated **independent clauses** when at least one of the clauses has several commas: The three applicants are well educated, well trained, and known to be self-starters, the three essential requirements; but even so, the personnel manager wants to solicit further applications.

To separate a series of items that already have commas: She had lived in Sioux Falls, Iowa; Fort Wayne, Indiana; and Clearwater, Florida.

To separate **clauses** or **sentences,** one of which is introduced by an **adverb** that functions like a conjunction: We debated but did not decide the issue of buyer-seller relations; consequently, the subject will be renewed at our next workshop.

sentence A complete unit of thought consisting of both a **subject** and a **predicate.** A sentence may range in length from one word to several hundred words, although the latter would be considered overly long and complex. In a one-word sentence such as ''Stop!'' the subject is implied:

[You] stop!

When a sentence does not have both a subject and predicate and does not express a complete thought, it is called a *sentence fragment:*

He stopped today to say that . . .

When parts of a sentence are equal in rank or importance, they should have a *parallel structure*. For example, a **noun** in one part should be parallel to the comparable noun in the other part, a **verb** in one part should be parallel to a verb in the other part, and so on:

> *Not:* My assignment is *researching* the topic and *to write* the article.
>
> *Better:* My assignment is *to research* the topic and *to write* the article.

The principal types of sentences in terms of sentence structure are the **simple sentence, compound sentence, complex sentence,** and **compound-complex sentence.** See those entries for definitions and examples.

Sentences can also be described according to the way a thought is expressed. The four principal types of sentences classified in this way are the **declarative sentence, exclamatory sentence, imperative sentence,** and **interrogative sentence.** See those entries for definitions and examples.

sentence fragment See **sentence.**

series A succession of issues or volumes with related subjects. Books that are part of a series have their own title as well as the title for the series. The series title is set in **roman type** without quotation marks. See **series-title page.** A series may or may not have numbered volumes or subsidiary numbers:

> 7. Madeline Seymour, *The Other Pyramids,* Mayan Civilization, ed. Jason Thorpe, vol. 1, no. 5 (New York: American Press, 1987).
> 9. Peter Duvall, ed., *The Century Theory,* Breckmore Institute, American Chronology Bulletin 161 (San Francisco, 1961).

Journals may also begin a new series of volumes or issues. In citations the series identification is placed between the journal title and the volume or issue number:

5. Nancy Kilmore, "The 'Wright' Way," *Essays from the Maryvale Sociological Society*, 3d ser., 12 (March 1972): 316–41.

Compare with **edition**.

series, geological See **geological terms**.

series-title page A book in a **series** may include a separate page listing the series title and other information. If this is desired, the series title, volume number, and sometimes the series editor and titles of books in the series already published may be listed on **verso** page ii. Although the series-title page is counted in the numbering of **front-matter** pages, the page number is not printed on the page. If the series title is not listed on a page by itself, it may be included on the **half-title page, title page,** or **copyright page.**

serif One of the short, fine lines that extend from the top and bottom points of the main strokes of a letter, such as the tiny finishing lines in the letters *E* and *R*. Compare with **sans serif**.

service mark See **trademark**.

services, religious See **religious services**.

sexism See **bias** and **gender**.

shall/will The **auxiliary verbs** *shall* and *will* are combined with a **principal verb** to form the **future tense** (*he will write*), and they are combined with *have* and the **past participle** of a verb to form the **future perfect tense** (*he will have written*).

Shall and *will* are also combined with a form of the verb *to be* plus an *-ing* form of the principal verb to create a *progressive form* (*he will be writing*). As its name suggests, a progressive form is meant to show that action is progressing.

Traditionally, *shall* was used in the first person (*I shall*) and *will* in the second and third persons (*you will, he will*) to express *simple futurity*, or anticipation of what will likely happen or what one is likely to do. To show determination or promise, the opposite pattern was used, with *will* in the first person and *shall* in the second and third persons. However, this usage is seldom observed anymore, except in formal situations. In most writing *will* is now more common for the first, second, and third persons, both for simple futurity and to show determination or promise (*I/you/he/*and so on *will*):

> According to the enclosed letter, *I/you/he/she/we/they will find* that the instructions are easy to follow.

The same rules apply to *should* (past tense of *shall*) and *would* (past tense of *will*) but with a couple of additional considerations. *Should,* meaning ought to, is used to express obligation, and *would* is used to express customary action:

> You *should* [ought to] read that book.
> They *would* [customarily] read for one hour every evening.

share See **part/portion/share.**

ships See **craft and vessels.**

short stories See **periodicals.**

should See **shall/will.**

sic An **adverb** meaning so or thus, often used in quoted material to indicate that something, such as a misspelling or an incorrect term, is repeated exactly as it appeared in the original. Although writers who quote others need not point out all unusual terms or spellings, when they do want to point out something, *sic* should be set in **italics** and enclosed in **brackets** after the word or words in question.

By using *sic* in the following example, the writer is pointing out that the spelling *Shangrila* is not the spelling used on Hilton's novel (*Shangri-La*):

> As Mason said, "James Hilton described this type of utopia in his novel *Shangrila* [*sic*]."

Rather than use *sic* to point out a misspelling, it is more helpful in some cases simply to place the correct word or letter in brackets:

"The market took an [a]cute turn in 1997."

side sewn See **binding.**

side wiring See **binding.**

signature A large sheet with pages of a book printed in multiples of four and folded into a group of pages ready to be sewn, trimmed, and bound. The larger the press, the greater the number of pages that can be contained in a single signature. Therefore, depending on both the size of a book and the size of the press, a signature may consist of four, eight, sixteen, thirty-two, forty-eight, or (if the paper is not too heavy to fold) sixty-four pages.

The *press sheet* (printed sheet) that forms a signature must be printed on both sides and have all pages on the sheet arranged, front and back, so that after folding they will be in proper order. To convert a flat sheet into a signature, it must be folded repeatedly until only the top page of the signature can be seen and all the other pages are in proper sequence.

To create a larger signature, one signature may be placed inside another. For example, one signature of eight pages—four pages on the front and four on the back—can be folded and inserted into another folded sheet of eight pages to form a sixteen-page signature.

See **binding** for the final steps in trimming and attaching the individual signatures and adding a **cover.**

signs and notices Capitalize the important words in signs, such as road signs, and capitalize notices written in **sentence** form the same as any other sentence. Use **roman type** without quotation marks:

No Parking
Low Water Bridge
Do Not Cross When Flooded

Effective immediately the door of the restroom by the Spa Center will bear the sign Employees Only.

See also **mottoes and slogans.**

silver print See **blueprint.**

simile A **figure of speech** in which one thing is compared to another unlike thing. The other thing is usually introduced with the word *like* or *as.* Like **metaphors,** similes are used to dramatize, clarify, or illustrate something:

When the sun slipped behind the mountain, darkness came instantly *like someone flipping off a light switch.*
The driver who caused the accident fled the scene *as though the devil himself were pursuing him.*
He is as graceful around the house *as Bigfoot.*
Walking across the museum's polished marble floors is *like walking across a newly glazed ice-skating rink.*
She has about as much depth *as a hologram.*

simple futurity See **shall/will.**

simple predicate See **predicate.**

simple sentence A **sentence** that consists of only one **independent clause** and contains only a **subject** and a **predicate.** However, the subject or predicate may have various **phrases** or **modifiers:**

Kevin and Iris [subject] designed a brochure with a detachable entry form for the seminar [predicate].

Compare with **complex sentence, compound sentence,** and **compound-complex sentence.**

simple subject See **subject.**

slander See **libel/slander.**

slang A form of **nonstandard English** often coined (see **coinage**) by certain groups, such as high school students, to form their own vocabulary:

awesome amazing; great
bad excellent; powerful
blown away overwhelmed
hammered intoxicated
scrub cancel

Many slang terms are short lived, although a very small percentage of them, such as *tailgate* (drive too closely behind another car), linger in general vocabularies.

Some slang terms are also crude and offensive and are therefore used only by certain groups in society. Other terms, such as *straw boss* (foreman), are created as part of the **jargon** of an industry or profession. However, unlike some technical or professional jargon, such as *Web browser,* terms such as *straw boss* are not used to label new technologies or procedures, exchange information, or facilitate communication. Rather, such slang is intended to fortify the users' social identity, often while opposing or mocking conventional authority.

Although slang is largely a spoken language, writers and editors must guard against any unintentional use of it in written material.

slash See **solidus** (/).

slogans See **mottoes and slogans**.

small caps Short for small capital letters, or capital letters that are set as **x-height** letters: SMALL CAPS. To indicate this style to a **compositor,** draw two lines under each letter to be set as small caps.

smileys See **emoticons**.

Smyth sewn See **binding**.

so/so that Controversy exists over whether *so,* which functions as various **parts of speech,** may be used alone to mean in order that or whether *so that* is required. Some authorities point out that professional writers regularly use *so* alone to mean in order that and believe the usage is here to stay. Others maintain that *so* alone should be used only as a **conjunction** when *in order that* cannot logically be substituted:

> They scheduled the program for late Friday afternoon *so that* [in order that] it would be easier for employees to leave work early.
>
> She wants to see the play, *so* [not *so that*] let's get an extra ticket for her.

so . . . as See **as . . . as/so . . . as.**

so-called When the **adjective** *so-called* is used before a **noun** to mean commonly called, it should be hyphenated and set in **roman type.** The expression that follows should also be set in roman type without quotation marks:

> Those so-called antiques can be bought in any discount department store.

socioeconomic groups Use **lowercase** letters for single and **compound terms** denoting socioeconomic groups or classes, and hyphenate the compound terms used as **adjectives** before a **noun:**

> Many job openings for *blue-collar workers* were listed in Sunday's paper.
>
> The workers in the plant are mostly *blue collar.*
>
> That neighborhood has mostly *upper-middle-class families.*
>
> The families in that neighborhood are mostly *upper middle class.*

softcover See **cover.**

software See **computer terms.**

solidus (*/*) Also called *virgule* and *slash.* The solidus, not to be confused with the backslash (\) on computer keyboards, has many uses, including the following:

> To separate lines of poetry run in with the text: We joined her in celebration / Of life's small victories.

To separate the numerator and denominator in **fractions:** 3/4.

To separate letters in certain abbreviations: b/o (back order).

To mean *per* in certain abbreviations: rev./sec.

To separate items in identification numbers: J/U-1473/96.

To indicate time spans when a hyphen (more common) is not used: 1998/99.

To indicate terms of equal weight as, for example, certain entry heads in this dictionary: libel/slander.

soluble/solvable Although the **adjectives** *soluble* and *solvable* can be used interchangeably to mean possible to solve, the primary meaning of *soluble* is easily dissolvable:

All the ingredients are easily *soluble.*
That problem is easily *solvable.*

solvable See **soluble/solvable.**

songs See **musical works.**

sort of See **kind of/sort of/type of.**

spacecraft See **craft and vessels.**

spacing The two types of spacing that editors are concerned with are vertical spacing between lines (see **leading**) and lateral spacing in **indentions** and between words, **mathematical expressions, sentences,** columns, and so on. Writers who submit **manuscripts** on disk usually leave only one space after periods, colons, and other characters. In addition, they indent elements only the standard amount of their computer programs, such as one-half inch.

The **compositor** indents and spaces according to the **design** specifications. A large space in **typesetting** is called a *quad,* usually an **em** quad (or *molly*) equal to the width of the **point** size of type. An **en** quad (or *nut space*) is half that width. However, other technical measurements and systems of spacing may be used depending not only on the design specifications but also on the particular method of typesetting being used.

spanner heads See **tables.**

spanner rules See **tables.**

specification sheet See **design.**

spelling Writers and editors commonly follow a particular dictionary in the spelling of words and expressions. Writers also rely heavily on spell-checkers to verify the accuracy of spelling in their documents.

Alternative spellings are available for many terms, such as **usable/useable,** and general dictionaries list the preferred spelling first. However, writers who have spelling difficulties may also want to refer to a spelling dictionary or to a list of commonly misspelled words published in an office or writing handbook. For examples of correct or preferred spelling, refer to individual entries in this dictionary, including the various **abbreviations** entries at the beginning of the work.

spine Also called *backbone;* the back portion of a book where the pages are bound together and where the front and back **covers** are joined to the back of the book. The spine is usually printed with the title of the book, the name of the author (often last name only), and the name of the publisher (sometimes a shortened name) or the publisher's emblem. See **colophon.** The back portion of a book **jacket** usually contains the same information as that printed on the spine of a hardcover book.

The **typeface** used for the spine and the front and back covers depends on the cover **design.** It need not be and often is not the same as the typeface used on the book's interior pages.

See also **binding** and **signature.**

spiral binding See **binding.**

split infinitive An **infinitive** phrase in which a word or **phrase,** especially an **adverb,** intervenes between the parts of the infinitive:

> to quickly run
> to hastily prepare
> to carefully proceed

The controversy over the correctness of splitting infinitives is waning. Most authorities now acknowledge that professional writers regularly split infinitives, and in some cases a statement would lose its rhythm and effect if an infinitive were not split. One of the best known examples is the opening line of *Star Trek* episodes—"*to boldly go* where no man has gone before"—which would lose its rhythm and impact as "*to go boldly* where no man has gone before."

Nevertheless, authorities have not relented entirely. Some point out that the reverse is often true—that splitting an infinitive sometimes creates a more awkward passage. They therefore suggest that writers at least should not split infinitives unnecessarily:

> *Not:* The instructor asked the students *to clearly think* before writing their answers.
> *Better:* The instructor asked the students *to think clearly* before writing their answers.

sports terms Capitalize the names of sporting events, organizations, teams, and so on. **Lowercase** general references to each item:

> National Football League, the NFL, the league
> New York Giants, the Giants, the team
> Olympic Games, the Winter Olympics, the Olympics, the games
> Chrysler-Plymouth Tournament of Champions, the tournament
> Jim Thorpe Trophy, the trophy, the award

Sr. See **Jr./Sr.**

stages, geological See **geological terms.**

standard English A form of English that adheres to the conventional rules of **grammar,** spelling, and punctuation. It is the language taught in schools and used by writers and other professionals. It is therefore the opposite of **nonstandard English,** which is not consistent with conventional rules.

Although some authorities believe the term *standard English* cannot be clearly defined, others easily list what it is and is not. For example, it is said to be a form widely used by educated writers and speakers that is free of regional or local characteristics and other such deviations from conventional patterns.

states, U.S. See **geographical terms.**

stationary/stationery The **adjectives** *stationary* and *stationery* are widely misused because they are pronounced the same and except for one letter are spelled the same. However, their meanings are very different. Whereas *stationary* describes something not moving, *stationery* refers to writing paper and supplies:

> The mobile homes to the left are mobile, but the one on the right is *stationary.*
> If the area code changes, we'll have to order new *stationery.*

stem The main part of a word, or its **root** plus a word element, such as a **vowel,** connected to it before a word ending is added. See **inflection, prefix,** and **suffix.** For example, the root *card* plus the element *io* form the stem *cardio* to which the suffix *-gram* can be added: *cardiogram.* The root *foc* plus the element *us* form the stem *focus* to which the word ending *-ed* can be added: *focused.* See also **morpheme.**

stet See chart in **proofreaders' marks.**

stock The paper used in **printing.** Paper is available in various weights, textures, and colors and may or may not be recycled paper. The selection of paper for publications depends on many factors, from the nature of the document to budgetary restrictions. In addition, certain papers are more suited than others for various uses.

Offset text papers, for example, are used for endpapers, whereas *book papers* are used for the pages of books and periodicals. *Newsprint* is common in newspapers, catalogs, and the small mass-market paperbacks seen in grocery stores and discount stores. *Cover stock* is usually a heavier paper and may have a slick, coated finish.

The appearance of paper is affected not only by factors such as weight and texture but also by the way each side is finished. Although more expensive paper may appear the same on both sides, less expensive paper may not. In less expensive paper, the top, which is called the *felt side,* may feel smoother than the bottom, which is called the *wire side* because the bottom slides along a so-called wire during the papermaking process.

An old system known as *basis weights* is used in the United States to identify the relative weights of paper. To compare weights, the sizes of different types of paper must be taken into consideration. For example, a standard (basis) sheet of book paper is twenty-five by thirty-eight inches, whereas a standard sheet of cover stock is twenty by twenty-six inches, or about half as large.

Under the basis weight system, a standard quantity—five hundred sheets (one ream)—of fifty-pound book paper in its standard size will weigh fifty pounds. A ream of fifty-pound cover stock in its smaller standard size will also weigh fifty pounds. Therefore, since the cover sheets are much smaller than the book-paper sheets, an individual sheet of fifty-pound cover stock in fact weighs more than an individual sheet of fifty-pound book paper.

strategy/tactics The **nouns** *strategy* and *tactics* are widely used interchangeably, although there is a significant difference in meaning. *Strategy* refers to a broad plan or design to accomplish something:

The company's *strategy* is to drive out the competition before it gains any more of the market share.

Tactics should be used in relation to the specific steps taken in pursuing a certain strategy.

The company's *tactics* included vigorous advertising and lower prices than those of the competition.

stream of consciousness See **dialogue.**

streets and roads Capitalize local, state, and national highways, but capitalize words such as *street, center,* and *square* only when they are part of an official street name. Observe local customs in spelling out **numbers** or using **numerals.** Some communities use numerals for street numbers of *ten* and above, and others use numerals for all numbers. Regardless, it may be necessary to spell out numbers if running building and street numbers together would cause confusion. An alternative, though, is to place a hyphen, with a space on either side, between building and street numbers:

U.S. Route 66
Interstate 40, I-40
County Road 69
130 Central Park East
One [*or* 1] Morton Circle
Nine [*or* 9] Adams Square
710 Southern and Hillside Avenues
528 Sixth Street [*or* 528 - 6 Street *or* 528 6th Street]
18 North 44 [*or* 44th] Street

stripping See **printing.**

structural terms See **geological terms.**

structures, names of See **building and structure names.**

stub See **tables.**

style The distinctive treatment used in a work in matters of spelling, capitalization, punctuation, abbreviation, use of numbers, and so on. Professional writers usually have their own styles of writing that include not only matters such as capitalization but also aspects such as **tone,** formality, word choice, level or complexity of language, and viewpoint.

When a publisher has certain house rules in regard to technical points, such as the use of numerals or words for numbers above ten, copyeditors may make appropriate changes in an author's work so that it will conform to house style. In all other matters, though, copyeditors should not modify an author's distinctive style of writing. They should, however, ensure that the author has used it consistently.

As copyeditors proceed through a **manuscript,** they usually prepare a list of the author's use and treatment of various factors, such as spelling of certain terms or the arrangement of data in **notes.** See **style sheet** for examples. See also **format.**

style sheet A written record of capitalization, spelling, and other distinctive treatment of words and elements in a **manuscript.** Editors maintain a style sheet while **copyediting** a manuscript, and some authors maintain such a record while writing it. The person maintaining the sheet records the first occurrence of a particular **style,** such as a hyphenated **compound term,** and thereafter checks to be certain that subsequent usage is consistent.

A style sheet, which may consist of several pages, has a number of headings under which an editor records the special usage. For example, one page may have a section for recording the style used for **numbers** and **dates,** with other sections for recording the style used for abbreviations, punctuation, and material in **tables.** Another page may have sections for recording examples of the style used in **bibliographies** and **notes,** as well as a miscellaneous section for recording special usage not listed elsewhere, such as the style for writing **captions** and **equations.** One or more pages may have alphabetical sections, *A* through *Z,* where the editor records special terms beginning with each letter of the alphabet.

Usually, the editor notes after each item only the first

page where a particular style or usage occurs. However, if the editor is uncertain whether another style should be adopted, every page where the usage occurs should be recorded. It will then be relatively easy to find each prior occurrence and make any change decided on later. A list of items recorded under the letter *A* might resemble this:

A

all-important (adj) 2
ASCII (n) 1
<u>ancien régime</u> (n—ital) 17
accommodate (v) 48
Abu Rahman 63

See individual entries, such as **acronym** and **Latin terms,** for examples of specific styles.

styles, cultural See **cultural terms.**

subject The word or words that indicate what or whom a **sentence** is about; the part of a **sentence** that indicates its topic. A subject is always a **noun** or noun equivalent, such as a **pronoun.**
    A *complete subject* is the entire group of words that indicate the topic, including words that modify the main subject. A *simple subject* is the particular word in such a group about which something is said. In the following example the word *president* is the simple subject, and the entire group of italicized words is the complete subject:

> *The newly elected president* immediately called a meeting of the directors.

Compare with **predicate.**

subject complement A word that describes another word or words, completing the sense of a **verb.** The **complement** may be a **direct object** or **indirect object,** a **predicate adjective** or **predicate nominative,** or an **object complement:**

They elected Jim *mayor* [object of *Jim,* completing the sense of the verb *elected*].

subject nominative See **nominative case.**

subjunctive mood The form of a **verb** that expresses something imagined, conditional, doubtful, contrary to fact, and so on. **Conjunctions** such as *if, though, that, unless,* and *till* are commonly used in this mood:

If Ms. Altman were here, she would know the answer.
Unless you're certain, we can't continue.
Had I been available, I would have accepted the assignment.

Compare with **imperative mood** and **indicative mood.**

subordinate clause See **dependent clause.**

subordinating conjunction Also called *subordinate conjunction;* a **conjunction** that connects a **dependent clause** with the main **clause** in a **sentence.** The conjunctions commonly used to connect the clauses are *that* and *whether* or *whether . . . or:*

Stan thinks *that* they will accept his proposal.
We wonder *whether* Ellen will decide to attend the academy.

Compare with **coordinating conjunction** and **correlative conjunction.**

subscript A character or symbol written slightly below adjacent letters or numbers, such as H_2O. Compare with **superscript.**

subsidiary rights See **rights.**

substantive editing See **editing.**

substantive notes See **footnotes** and **notes.**

suffix An **affix,** such as *-ment* in *management,* attached to the end of a word or the main part of a word. Writers have always used suffixes as well as **prefixes** to expand their vocabularies and create new words (see **coinage**), but the practice has especially increased during the twentieth century:

-able/predict*able*
-chrome/poly*chrome*
-ence/depend*ence*
-fold/ten*fold*
-gon/para*gon*
-graph/poly*graph*
-ile/percent*ile*
-ite/suburban*ite*
-logy/physio*logy*
-or/react*or*
-ty/senior*ty*
-wide/nation*wide*

See also examples in the entry **-able/-ible.**

summary See **abstract** and **epitome.**

superlative degree See **comparison of adjectives** and **comparison of adverbs.**

superscript A character or symbol written slightly above adjacent letters or numbers, such as $x + y^2$. Compare with **subscript.**

supersede To take the place of. *Supersede* is frequently misspelled *supercede*, possibly because other words, such as *intercede,* are spelled with *-cede.* Also, a few words, such as *proceed,* end in *-ceed.* However, only *supersede* ends in *-sede:*

In March the new 2000 series will *supersede* the previous 1000 series.

supplement See **augment/supplement.**

supplementary See **complementary/complimentary/supplementary.**

suspended hyphen See **hyphen.**

syllable A unit of language that consists of a single sound. A syllable may be either a division in a word or a complete word. Words of one syllable (*man*) are called *monosyllables*. Words of more than one syllable (*woman*) are called *polysyllables*.

Many dictionaries mark syllables with a centered dot between the syllables, as illustrated in the following examples. When a word must be divided at the end of a line, it should be divided after one of the syllables. See **word division.** Pronunciation, however, does not necessarily duplicate syllabic division. Notice the difference in some of the following examples. The pronunciations, which are given in parentheses following the syllabic divisions, are phonetic approximations:

bead (beed)
com•mut•er (keh-mew-ter)
e•van•gel•i•cal•ism (eeh-van-jell-eh-keh-liz-em)
in•ter•rog•a•to•ry (in-teh-rog-eh-tor-eeh)
or•tho•chro•mat•ic (or-tho-kro-mat-ik)
sub•ur•ban•ite (seh-bur-beh-nite)
u•ni•ver•sal•ize (you-neh-vur-seh-lize)

symbols The rules for writing symbols, such as %, are generally the same as those for writing abbreviations, such as *mm* (millimeter). Spell out symbols in running text in nontechnical material, but use the symbols if desired in technical material. Generally, spell out the numbers accompanying symbols when the symbols are also spelled out, but use numerals when the symbols are written as symbols. However, even in nontechnical copy, write the number designating percent as a numeral. See **numbers** and **numerals** for further information:

Nontechnical	*Technical*
twelve degrees	12°
fifty dollars	$50
fourteen inches	14" *or* 14 in.
But: 24 percent	24%

See also **chemical names and symbols, equations,** and **exponent.**

sympathy See **empathy/sympathy.**

symphonies See **musical works.**

symposium volume The papers of various discussion-type **conferences and meetings** are known as *proceedings,* or *symposium proceedings,* when they are published in book form. The symposium's title, location, date, and name of the planning committee or sponsor are sometimes printed on page ii, the back of **half-title page** i.

Like a **collective work** or **anthology,** a symposium volume typically has a compiler or editor and numerous authors of individual papers, which are treated the same as individual chapters in another kind of multiauthor work. The editor is usually a member or appointee of the organization sponsoring the symposium and may also be one of the contributors to the volume.

Although contributors of papers are given a deadline, they do not always submit their papers at the same time. The publisher therefore may need to schedule **copyediting** and **typesetting** in stages to ensure publication by the meeting date or by another date selected for release of the volume.

Citations to published proceedings papers are treated like citations to chapters in any other multiauthor book. See **bibliography, notes,** and **reference list.** If the editor of a symposium volume is identified on the **title page,** he or she should also be included in the citation. If a citation is to a particular paper, the author of that paper should be stated first:

3. Karen Martinson, ''Document Conferencing Tomorrow,'' in *The Second Electronic Age,* Proceedings of the Twenty-third Annual Meeting and Technical Conference of the Portsmith Computer Association, ed. Bernard J. Fiske, Jr. (Concord, N.H.: Bascombe Printers, 1997).

See **anthology** and **collective work** for information on **copyright** of multiauthor works and the handling of previously published material.

synods See **religious meetings.**

synonym One of two or more words that have the same or nearly the same meaning, such as *abstract* and *summary*. See **antonym,** the opposite of *synonym,* for an example of a thesaurus entry that includes both types of words.

syntax The study of or the pattern that explains how words, **phrases,** and **clauses** are combined to form a grammatically complete **sentence.** Compare with **grammar.**

systematic/systemic The **adjectives** *systematic* and *systemic* are both related to the word *system*—elements that together form a complex whole. In that sense *systematic* means characterized by a system, and it also means being methodical.

The files have a *systematic* arrangement.
They dealt with the problem in a careful and *systematic* manner.

In the same sense *systemic* means relating to a system or affecting the whole. However, it is primarily used in a scientific context:

They used a *systemic* weed killer to destroy the weeds in the gravel driveway.

T

tables Like **illustrations,** tables may be included in a **manuscript** to support a text discussion. When they are used, they should be mentioned at the appropriate place in the text, such as "see Table 1." In addition, the author or editor should write and circle instructions about location in the manuscript margins, such as "Table 1 about here."

Tables may be numbered consecutively throughout the text, or they may start over with number 1 in each chapter or appendix. In the latter case double numbers are used to indicate both the chapter or appendix number or letter and the table number: Table 1.1, Table 1.2, Table A.1, Table A.2, and so on.

Table titles should be brief and should identify the nature of the information in the table. Subtitles, which are often enclosed in parentheses, may be included to designate how the information is presented:

Sales by Region, 1998–1999
(in Millions of Dollars)

The column headings are arranged below the table title. The first column on the left, or the *stub,* should be singular. The other column headings may be singular or plural. Like the table title, the column heads may also have subheadings. Authors who prepare tables manually should leave at least one space above and below the column headings. Software that provides table setup will automatically arrange and provide space around all elements.

When there is more than one level of heading (*decked heads*), a line (*spanner rule*) is usually placed between each top head (*spanner head*) and the two or more column heads below it:

Building	
Height	Feet

Decimal points and commas in statistics should be aligned in the columns. When symbols such as monetary designations or the percent sign are listed, and when the column headings and table subtitle do not indicate the type of figures being presented, the sign should be included in the first row of figures:

20.5%	13.9%
16.7	14.1
32.0	27.8
29.2	30.7
15.4	8.6

Footnotes following the table body may include the source note, one or more general notes, and individual footnotes pertaining to items in the columns, or table body. See the forthcoming example of a table with notes. However, footnote numbers should not be placed in or after table titles; rather, an unnumbered general note should be used when a comment pertains to the table title or to the table in general.

Superscript numbers, letters, or symbols corresponding to those used with the footnotes should be inserted at the appropriate places in the table body. However, source notes and general notes have no corresponding numbers, letters, or symbols. See the forthcoming example. When the data in table columns are primarily numerical or statistical, it is less confusing if the footnotes are identified by letters or symbols instead of numbers.

Usually, a bottom rule is included to signal the conclusion of data in the columns, or the end of the main table body, and the footnotes are placed immediately after the rule. Authors preparing manuscripts manually should leave an extra space between the table body and the footnote section as well as a space between each note.

The forthcoming example of a statistical table has only four columns and fits vertically on the page. However, when a table has so many columns that it will not fit vertically on a page, it may be turned sideways with the left column against the bottom margin. See **broadside.** When a table must be continued on the next page, the column headings should be repeated with a continued line above the headings, such as *Table 4, continued.*

Rules may or may not be used with a table, as preferred. However, a table with many headings and columns may be easier to read when rules enclose the column headings and separate the table body from the footnotes, as the model in this entry illustrates.

Table 1

Alabama Cities of 100,000 or More Population, 1980 and 1990

(with ZIP Codes)

City	ZIP Code*	1980	1990
Birmingham	35203	284,413	265,347
Huntsville	35801	142,513	159,880
Mobile	36601	196,263	200,452
Montgomery	36104	177,857	187,543

Source: Adapted from data collected in the 1990 Decennial Census, U.S. Department of Commerce, Bureau of the Census, Washington, D.C.

Note: Similar data for places throughout the United States are published in various almanacs, such as *The World Almanac and Book of Facts.*

*The ZIP Codes are for general delivery only. Consult a ZIP Code directory for the various codes assigned to specific street addresses.

See also **continuation line,** and **tables, list of.**

tables, list of When a technical work has more than a few brief **tables,** an author may decide to include a list of tables in the **front matter** on a **recto** or **verso** page following the list of illustrations (see **illustrations, list of**), if any, or otherwise after the **contents page.** A list of tables should be set in the same type size and style as that used for the table of contents.

When a list of tables is desired, it is usually titled simply ''Tables.'' It should include all tables identified by number and title in the sequence in which they appear in the document. However, the titles used on the list may be shortened versions if the full titles used on the tables are very long. Page numbers on which the tables appear are listed to the right of the titles in the same way as on the contents page.

tactics See **strategy/tactics.**

tag question A question added to a statement in very casual, informal speech or writing:

> It's easy to learn, *don't you think?*
> That's a challenging assignment, *isn't it?*

Since people in other countries may find tag questions difficult to understand, such sentences should be rephrased for an international audience:

> Isn't it easy to learn? [*Or* It is easy to learn.]
> Isn't that a challenging assignment? [*Or* That is a challenging assignment.]

tautology A term used primarily in scholastic fields; the repetition of a word, **phrase,** or **clause,** as in *free gift.* See **redundancy.**

technical style of writing numbers See **numbers** and **percentages.**

television and radio programs Capitalize the titles of television and radio programs or episodes, and set them in **roman type** enclosed by quotation marks. However, set the title of a continuing series in **italics:**

the program "The Mystery of Ludlow Castle"
the series *Star Trek: Voyager*
the episode "Cyberkiller"

tense The form of a **verb** that indicates when an action or condition occurs. The three basic tenses are the **past tense, present tense,** and **future tense.** The three additional *perfect* tenses are the **past perfect tense, present perfect tense,** and **future perfect tense.** See those entries for definitions and examples.

territories, U.S. See **geographical terms.**

text figures See **illustrations.**

that/which/who Only the first of these three **relative pronouns,** *that,* is used to refer to persons, animals, and things. *Which* is used to refer only to animals or things, and *who* (or *whom*) is used to refer only to persons. Also, *that* is used in restrictive **clauses** and *which* or *who* in nonrestrictive clauses:

Have you seen the manual *that* [not *which*] was on my desk [restrictive clause].
The dog regularly vies with the cat in popularity, *which* is not surprising [nonrestrictive clause].
Mr. Mason, *who* used to be my boss [nonrestrictive clause], was recently promoted to the position of general manager.

That is often used carelessly without a clear indication of what it refers to:

That [**pronoun** alone] may be worth considering.
Better: That [**adjective pronoun**] new funding proposal may be worth considering.

The **phrase** *that is to say* is needlessly wordy and should be omitted or changed to another, shorter word or phrase:

The company expects to enhance production with new technology; [*that is to say*] it especially hopes to become more competitive through modernization.

See also **nonrestrictive element, restrictive element,** and **who/whom.**

theorems See **laws and principles, scientific.**

there See **expletive.**

these See **this/these.**

they See **he/she, him/her, they.**

third person See **person** and **personal pronoun.**

this/these Both of these terms are used as **adjectives** and **pronouns.** The principal criticism about them concerns their use as pronouns alone, rather than as **adjective pronouns,** when it is not clear from a pronoun alone what *this* or *these* refers to:

> *Pronoun: This* is [*These* are] hard to understand.
> *Adjective: This* book is [*These* books are] hard to understand.

See also **that/which/who** for a similar problem concerning *that.*

tilde See **diacritical marks.**

time See A.M., P.M., M., A.D., B.C., **abbreviations of time and days, calendar designations, centuries, dates, decades, eras, historical terms,** and **year of publication.**

tipped in See **frontispiece.**

title page The title page is **recto** page iii in a book in which a **half-title page** precedes it. Although it is counted in the numbering of the **front-matter** pages, the page number is not printed.

The information on a title page may include the book's full title and subtitle; the number of the edition, such as the Second Edition; occasionally, the year of publication; the full name of the author, editor, compiler, or translator; the full name of the publisher and possibly its **colophon;** and the city in which the publisher is located.

The subtitle, if any, is often printed in a smaller type

size than the title and is set on a separate line with no colon
separating the two. The **typeface** and placement of the various lines on the title page are determined by the **design**
prepared for the book. Often the type used on a title page
is different from that used on the **cover** or **jacket** of the
book.

titles See **abbreviations of names and titles** and **titles,
personal and professional.** See also individual entries pertaining to specific types of titles, such as **musical works,
plays,** and **tables.**

titles, personal and professional Capitalize personal and
professional titles used before a name, but **lowercase** titles
used in place of a name. Abbreviate most professional titles
only before a full name, and spell out the title when it is
used with a last name alone or, in the case of *Reverend* and
Honorable, when it is preceded by *the.* Always abbreviate
Dr. and personal titles such as *Ms.* whether they are used
before a full name or before a last name alone:

Pope John Paul, the pope
President [*or* Pres.] Joel Frankel Jr., President Frankel,
   the company president
Senator [*or* Sen.] Arnold Devlon, Senator Devlon, the
   senator
Commander [*or* Comdr.] Mary Farnelli, Commander
   Farnelli, the commander
the Right Reverend Paul Seintmas, Right Reverend [*or*
   Rt. Rev.] Paul Seintmas, Right Reverend Seintmas,
   the reverend
Dr. Lois Castell; Dr. Castell; Lois Castell, M.D.; the
   doctor
Professor [*or* Prof.] Adrianne Warner, Professor Warner,
   the professor
Mr. Donald Billingsley III, Mr. Billingsley
Mr. David Sheck and Mr. Joel Conklin, Messrs. David
   Sheck and Joel Conklin, Messrs. Sheck and Conklin
Ms. Donna Siegel, Ms. Siegel
Ms. Erica Lewis and Ms. Ursula Rawson, Ms. Erica

Lewis and Mrs. [*if preferred*] Ursula Rawson, Mss. Erica Lewis and Ursula Rawson, Mlle Lewis and Mme Rawson (*French*)

See also **abbreviations of names and titles, academic degrees,** and **esquire.**

tone The way that writing or speaking sounds, such as formal or informal, flowing or abrupt, warm and friendly, or cold and unfriendly. Generally, except when authors in the United States are preparing very formal material, such as a formal social invitation, they want to sound interesting, friendly, cooperative, and conversational. They want to avoid the appearance of sounding harsh, unfriendly, unbending, condescending, or unconcerned about the reader. They want their writing to be grammatically and stylistically correct (see **style**) and want it to flow smoothly from sentence to sentence and paragraph to paragraph. See **transition.** See also **conciseness** and **wordiness.**

Writers must evaluate both the audience and the purpose of a communication before adopting a tone that matches their objectives and the needs of the reader. For example, readers in other countries usually expect more formality than is common in most social and business writing in the United States.

topic sentence See **paragraph.**

topographical names See **geographical terms; geological terms;** and **names, topographical.**

toward/towards The **prepositions** *toward* and *towards,* meaning in the direction of, are alternative spellings. Although either word is correct, the spelling *toward* is more common in the United States and *towards* in England:

We drove *toward/towards* the column of smoke on the horizon.

See **afterward/afterwards** for another example of alternative spellings.

trademark A name, symbol, or device that identifies a product or service and indicates that its use is restricted to the holder of the trademark. Trademark names are always capitalized, and the companies that have trademark names also use small **superscript** letters in their advertising to indicate this status. *TM* refers to a product and *SM* a service. When the product or service is registered with the U.S. Patent and Trademark Office, the symbol *R* is used:

Deoderm™
We-Care-Health-Care^SM
Band-Aid®

Writers should capitalize trademark names in running text but need not use a symbol with the names since the capitalization indicates that the product or service is protected. However, unless a discussion requires reference to a specific brand name, writers should use the generic term for general references:

Trademark Name	*Generic Term*
Coca-Cola	soft drink
Dacron	polyester
Kleenex	tissues
Plexiglas	acrylic plastic
Realtor	real estate agent/broker
Xerox	copier/photocopier

See **copyright** for the protection of literary and artistic works.

trains See **craft and vessels.**

transition Writers and editors are concerned with the smooth flow of words and ideas both between sentences and between paragraphs. A smooth and logical transition makes the copy easier to read and understand. The smoothness of transition is achieved in part by using transition words, such as *for example, therefore,* and *also.* Such expressions help one thought glide into another and eliminate the choppiness that would otherwise characterize abruptly ending and beginning sentences.

Another effective way to make a thought glide from sentence to sentence is to repeat key words from a previous sentence. For example, the key word *glide* has now been used in three successive sentences. **Pronouns,** such as *that* or *these*, can also be used to refer to a word or idea in a prior sentence, thereby linking the two statements or thoughts.

Various other transition techniques, such as a series of numbered points (*first, second, third,* and so on) used to introduce successive sentences, can also be employed successfully. In fact, professional writers regularly use any such technique to move the reader forward through new sentences while maintaining a connection to the previous sentences.

Just as the previous examples of transition techniques involve the smoothness of movement, others affect the logical transition between sentences and paragraphs. A logical transition is primarily achieved by putting one's thoughts in a proper sequence. To ensure that a clear progression is followed, professional writers often work from an **outline** that lists topics and subtopics in proper order from **introduction** to **conclusion.**

However, proper sequence alone isn't enough. The same techniques used to glide from sentence to sentence are also needed to move smoothly from paragraph to paragraph. For example, the opening sentence of a new paragraph may repeat key words or ideas from the previous paragraph. Or the lead sentence may summarize the essence of the prior paragraph. Or transition words, such as *similarly* and *moreover,* may be used to start the new paragraph.

Other techniques may also be used, such as the question-answer technique. In this case a paragraph ends with a question that will be answered in the next paragraph. All of these techniques—and any others suitable for the particular document—should be used to develop smooth and logical transitions between sentences and paragraphs.

See also **paragraph, sentence,** and **unity.**

transitive verb A **verb** that needs a **direct object** to complete its meaning. The word *transitive* indicates that the action passes from a doer (**subject**) to the receiver (direct object):

> Mrs. Parker [subject] *sent* [transitive verb] the letter [direct object].
> We [subject] *called* [transitive verb] our friend [direct object] from the restaurant.

Compare with **intransitive verb.**

transliteration The process of converting the signs or characters of one language into those of another language, as for example in the transliteration of Chinese characters into the English alphabet. Different systems are used to transliterate (also called *romanize*) languages such as Chinese, Arabic, Hebrew, and others that do not use Latin characters. For further information consult a guide such as the *ALA-LC Romanization Tables: Transliteration Schemes for Non-Roman Scripts*, published by the Library of Congress in Washington, D.C.

treaties See **acts and treaties.**

tribes See **peoples.**

try and/try to Grammarians have traditionally opposed the very informal use of the **phrase** *try and* as a substitute for *try to:*

> *Try to* [not *try and*] attend the conference.
> To be fair, let's *try to* [not *try and*] understand his point of view.

type of See **kind of/sort of/type of.**

typeface The size and style of a complete set, or **font,** of type. Each typeface has a distinctive design. For example, it may appear formal or informal, modern or traditional, heavy or light, condensed or open, and so on.

Typefaces used with personal computers and in various

methods of **typesetting** have different names, such as *Courier*. The typeface used in this dictionary is Times Roman.

See also **cursive type, desktop publishing, em, en, leading, pica, point, sans serif, serif, spacing, typemarking, typesetting, typography,** and **x-height.**

typemarking After the **copyediting** of a **manuscript** has been completed and a **design** has been prepared for a work, an editor will further mark the manuscript for composition. When an author provides a disk copy, codes may have been typed before certain elements, such as subheads, to indicate how they should be set (**typeface,** type size, and so on).

An editor will additionally mark instructions on the manuscript relating to the **typography, leading, indentions,** and so on. Such instructions are taken from the list of design specifications prepared for the work. Copyeditors also may do minor typemarking, such as coding the different levels of subheads as *A, B,* and *C.*

See also **typesetting.**

typesetter See **compositor.**

typesetting Most book, magazine, and newspaper typesetting is done by various *photocomposition,* or *phototypesetting,* methods. These methods use a computer-style keyboard for entering the text, a computer processor for handling (storing and retrieving) the information, and a typesetter (machine) for transferring the images onto paper or film.

One such method, *CRT composition,* is fully electronic. It generates type images on a cathode-ray tube (CRT) that transfers the images to photosensitive paper or film. A more advanced computerized typesetter, the *laser imagesetter,* uses a laser beam to project images onto photosensitive paper. An older photocomposition method, *photomechanical typesetting,* sends flashes of light through a film matrix to project images onto a light-sensitive medium. All of such computer-assisted forms of typesetting have largely replaced the older so-called hot-metal methods in which metal type was cast by hand or machine.

The typesetting for a work may be handled by an outside firm that specializes in photocomposition or by an in-house publishing system. Many publishers have their own **desktop publishing** systems that function like **word processing** programs but have many added features, such as page makeup.

Page proofs of text set by one of the modern computerized systems, whether an in-house system or an outside service, usually consist of photocopies or printouts of the typeset text. Making corrections noted on the page proofs is relatively easy with the advanced systems. Changes are simply made on screen, and the system's page-makeup feature adjusts the affected pages automatically.

See **copyediting, design, typemarking, proofreading, printing,** and **binding** for other steps in production. See also **typeface** and **typography.**

typography Broadly, the style and arrangement of printed text. Typography is sometimes used interchangeably with terms such as *type, typeset text,* and *text composition* that are related to the appearance and use of type in **typesetting.**

Typography, referring to type, should not be confused with *topography,* referring to a description of a place or region. See **names, topographical,** for the latter.

U

umlaut See **diacritical marks** (diaeresis).

under See **below/under.**

uninflected word See **inflection.**

uninterested See **disinterested/uninterested.**

unity Professional writers bring unity to their work by focusing on one main topic and developing that topic without digressing into unrelated areas. Subtopics must therefore be extensions of the one main topic, not additional topics competing for attention with the main topic.

An especially useful tool in developing unity of thought and purpose is a carefully prepared **outline.** By listing subtopics according to level of importance on the outline and by placing all items in a logical sequence, the various parts of the subject form a logically interconnected whole. Moreover, the parts are organized in a direct route from beginning to end toward the intended objective. A carefully prepared outline thereby keeps a writer on an appropriate course and provides the type of discipline in thought and organization that is necessary for a cohesive work.

Just as a carefully prepared outline is a valuable tool to use in developing unity, carefully worded transitions provide the necessary links between the various sentences and paragraphs of the work. The outline, therefore, is the framework, and the elements of transition are the individual connectors that tie together the components of the structure. See **transition** for examples.

unlawful See **illegal/illicit/unlawful.**

unorganized See **disorganized/unorganized.**

unpublished works Documents such as dissertations, theses, symposium papers, and business reports may be prepared not for publication but for a single purpose or limited audience. For example, **manuscripts** or computer printouts are considered unpublished works until such time that they are produced, disseminated, and copyrighted. See **copyright.**

In referring to unpublished works in running text or citing them in reference **notes,** set the title in **roman type** enclosed by quotation marks. For examples, see **bibliography, notes,** and **reference list.**

up style Another term for an **uppercase** style; a **style** that reflects a tendency toward more capitalization of terms, such as *Halley's Comet* rather than *Halley's comet* or *the Queen of England* rather than *the queen of England.* Compare with **down style.**

uppercase As a **noun,** capital letters (*A, B,* and so on) as opposed to **lowercase,** or small, letters; as a **verb,** to type or set something in capital letters or to change a lowercase letter to a capital letter.

us/we The **pronouns** *us* and *we* are frequently confused in two situations—as the **subject** of a sentence and as the **object of a preposition.** The **nominative case** *we* is required when the pronoun is the subject or precedes a **noun** or **noun phrase** in the subject. If you omit the nouns in the following examples, it will be clear why *we* is the correct usage:

> *We* students have our own student government [not *Us* have our own student government].
> *We* two editors may be transferred to the West Coast

office [not *Us* may be transferred to the West Coast office].

The **objective case** *us* is required when the pronoun follows a **preposition.** This will be clear if you reword the sentence to see how *us* versus *we* sounds:

> For *us* students it's important to have our own student government [*not* For *we* it's important to have our own student government].
> The caution is meant for *us* who are unfamiliar with the equipment [*not* The caution is meant for *we*].

In some sentences the **verb** is implied, so the nominative case *we* is required for the subject of the verb:

> He is as excited as *we* [are excited].

When the first pronoun in a sentence with an *as* or *than* comparison is in the objective case, use the objective case *us* for the second pronoun too:

> The director gave *her* [objective case] more assignments than *us*.

usable/useable The **adjectives** *usable* and *useable* are alternative spellings of the term meaning fit for use. Dictionaries usually list *usable* as the preferred spelling and *useable* as a variant.

usage The customary way that words, **phrases, clauses,** and so on are used in speech and writing; the way that the elements of language are used to create meaning, including elements such as spelling, punctuation, grammar, pronunciation, word choice, and any other factor that affects customary practice in writing or speaking.

The entries in this dictionary pertain to all of the principal elements of language that affect and define usage. Refer to individual entries, such as **split infinitive** and **us/ we,** for examples. See also **grammar, nonstandard English, standard English, style,** and **syntax.**

use/utilize The **verbs** *use* and *utilize* both mean to employ or make use of. The shorter form, *use,* sounds less pretentious and is therefore preferred in most cases:

We *use* [not *utilize*] the television mostly on weekends.

However, when the intent is not only to make use of something but also to find a practical or profitable use for it, *utilize* properly suggests more than simple use. Even critics of **pompous language** usually agree that *utilize* is legitimate in this sense:

After all we've spent on developing the formula, we simply must *utilize* [find a practical/profitable use for] it in future projects.

V

v./vs. See **legal cases.**

vague words Although there may be occasions when one does not want to be specific, in most situations it is desirable to be as clear and precise as possible. Professional writers therefore try to avoid words such as *good, bad,* and *nice* that are too general or vague for the reader to be able to form a clear picture or opinion.

See also **abstract word, cliche, gobbledygook, idiom, jargon,** and **vogue words.**

vandyke See **blueprint.**

verb A word that expresses action (*run*) or state of being (*is*). Verbs are classified in various ways, such as **transitive verbs** and **intransitive verbs, principal verbs** and **auxiliary verbs,** or **regular verbs** and **irregular verbs.** Verbs also have properties, such as **voice, mood, tense, person,** and **number.** See the individual entries for further explanation and examples. See also **verb phrase.**

verb phrase The combination of an **auxiliary verb** and a **principal verb,** even if the two are separated by intervening words. The entire **phrase** is usually referred to simply as the **verb:**

> He *should agree* with us.
> I *will call* you tomorrow.
> It *might have been done* before this.

We *may* possibly *stop* in New York.
Could she *have written* the anonymous article?

verbal See **oral/verbal.**

verbal noun See **infinitive.**

verbals Verbs that are used as other **parts of speech.** The
three types of verbals are the **gerund,** used as a **noun;** the
infinitive, usually preceded by *to;* and the **participle,** used
as an **adjective:**

Hiking [gerund] is my favorite pastime.
We need *to understand* [infinitive] the problem before
    we can solve it.
An *illustrated* [participle] brochure would be more eye-
    catching.

vernacular The everyday, common form of spoken native
language of a country, region, or locality. The vernacular
is usually distinguished from a more formal, refined written
language. The term is also sometimes used loosely to mean
nonstandard English, such as **dialect, slang,** and **jargon.**
Black English, for example, is a form of nonstandard English that is sometime called *Black English Vernacular.* See
also **cliche** and **idiom.**

verso The left-hand page in a book or the back side of a
leaf. Compare with **recto.** See also individual entries such
as **contents page** for information about whether a section
or part of a book begins on a recto or verso page.

versus See **legal cases.**

very See **intensifier.**

vessels See **craft and vessels.**

viable/workable The **adjectives** *viable* and *workable* are
used interchangeably to mean **practicable.** See **practica-
ble/practical.** However, the primary sense of *viable* is capable of living biologically:

The doctors judged the life of the fetus to be *viable* outside the womb.

The primary sense of *workable* is capable of being handled or put into operation:

We believe we've developed a *workable* solution to the problem of long cafeteria lines.

The two terms are therefore distinct and pose no problems in their primary senses. Confusion arises only when *viable* is applied to any concept or plan, the same as *workable*. In that sense *viable* is an overused **vogue word** that should be avoided:

Vogue: Jason's promotional plan is a *viable* alternative.
Better: Jason's promotional plan is a *feasible/practicable/workable* alternative.

videlicet A Latin term, abbreviated as *viz.,* meaning that is or namely. It is sometimes used in scholarly work to introduce examples or a list, especially a list of items that compose a whole. However, like the more general abbreviation **i.e.** (that is), it is usually unnecessary and should be avoided in most writing. If it is necessary to introduce a list of items, expressions such as *the following list* or *these three examples* are preferred.

virgule See **solidus** (/).

vis-à-vis An overused French expression primarily meaning face to face with or, in the United States, in relation to. As a commonly used (Anglicized) foreign term, the grave accent over the letter *a* may be omitted if desired, and the term need not be italicized. However, since it is overused and generally considered pretentious, writers should substitute simple English:

The professor discussed word formation *vis-à-vis* [in relation to/based on/using] Greek and Latin roots.

viz. See **videlicet**.

vogue words Words and expressions that are currently popular and fashionable but, because of overuse, soon become stale and are often short lived. Such words tend to sound pretentious (see **pompous language**) and tend to be less clear and precise than basic English. Some also may qualify as **jargon, slang,** or **cliches.** Like **jargon** and **slang,** vogue words also may be **standard English** terms that are given a new or opposite meaning, as in *green,* now associated with environmental issues:

   born-again Converted in any sense, from born-again Christians to born-again liberals/conservatives.
   -free A **suffix** for anything omitted, such as in a product, from cholesterol to gluten.
   input Anything that is contributed, from money to ideas.
   palpable Obvious.
   quantum leap A sudden, spectacular increase or advance.

See also other forms of **nonstandard English,** such as **abstract words, cliche, euphemism, gobbledygook, jargon, pompous language, slang,** and **vague words.**

voice The property of a **verb** that indicates whether the subject is performing the action (He *wrote* the book) or is receiving the action (The book *was written* by him). The two voices of verbs are the **active voice** and the **passive voice.** See those entries for definitions and examples.

volume See **symposium volume.** See also citation examples in **author-date citations, bibliography, footnotes, notes,** and **reference list.**

vowel A distinctive speech sound indicated in writing by the five classic vowel letters *a, e, i, o,* and *u.* Phonetically, other letters may also have a vowel sound, such as *y* (when substituted for *i*) and *w* (when used in certain words such as *won*). However, in written material, all letters of the English alphabet other than the five vowel letters are considered **consonants.**

W

warranty See **guarantee/guaranty/warranty**.

wars and conflicts Capitalize the formal names of wars, battles, and conflicts, but **lowercase** general references to such events:

> Civil War (American), the war
> Spanish civil war, the civil war
> American Revolution, the Revolutionary War, the Revolution, a revolution
> Battle of Gettysburg, the battle
> the Crusades, religious wars
> World War II, the Second World War, the world war, the war
> Korean War, the Korean conflict
> Desert Storm, the Gulf War, the war

> See also **military groups** and **military honors**.

we See **us/we**.

well See **good/well**.

whether See **if/whether**.

which See **that/which/who**.

white space Usually, a reference to the space of margins and the open areas between blocks of copy and **illustrations**. Contemporary designers aim for sufficient white space to enhance readability and avoid a cluttered, heavy appearance. White space also may refer to the rivers of white space in a section of text that is justified. See **justification.**

who See **that/which/who.**

who/whom The **pronouns** *who* and *whom* have been troublesome to many writers throughout time. *Who* is used much more widely than *whom,* even when the latter would be the grammatically correct choice. Usually, the routine substitution of *who* for *whom* is simply an error, although some writers and even some authorities believe that the error should be overlooked in sentences in which *whom* would sound too formal and pretentious.

The traditional rule is that *who* is used in the **nominative case,** such as in the position of a **subject,** and *whom* is used in the **objective case,** such as in the position of the **object of a preposition** or the object of a **verb.** The rules are easy to apply in relatively simple sentences:

Who is at the door [subject of verb *is*]?

She asked *whom* we visited [object of verb *visited:* We visited *whom?*].

By *whom* were you interviewed [object of preposition *by:* You were interviewed by *whom*]?

In more complex sentences additional thought may be needed to decide whether *who* or *whom* is correct:

Who do you believe will win the election [*Who* is the subject of the verb *will win: Who* will win the election]?

We greeted the three people from Germany *whom* last Tuesday our boss had called and invited to the assembly [*Whom* is the object of the compound verb *had called and invited:* Our boss had called and invited *whom?*].

One of the most common errors is characteristic of telephone and other greetings and therefore makes its way into office handbooks and training manuals. Although *who* is usually substituted incorrectly for *whom,* in this case *whom* is incorrectly substituted for *who:*

> *Who* [not *Whom*] shall I say is calling [*Who* is required because it is the subject of the verb *is calling: Who* is calling]?

whose/who's Writers should not confuse *whose* and *who's,* and most misuse is likely a result of carelessness. *Whose* is the possessive form of *who,* and some writers also use it as the possessive form of *which,* although the words *of which* are often a better alternative:

> Unfortunately, he is a leader *whose* charisma exceeds his common sense.
> The book, *whose* thesis is not clear, is worth reading for its political insights. *Or:* The book, the thesis *of which* is not clear, is worth reading for its political insights.

Who's is a **contraction** used informally for *who is* or *who has:*

> *Who's* [Who is] that person leaving Ms. Shelby's office?
> *Who's* [Who has] called the telephone repair service?

widow A short line of type, such as the last line of a paragraph, that is carried over to the top of the next page or column; less commonly, a very short line at the end of a page or column or, as a result of end-of-line **word division,** a short word ending, such as *-er,* carried to a line by itself.

    Compositors usually reset a sentence or sentences to avoid beginning a page or column with a very short line of type. Depending on the publisher's requirements, they may or may not reset copy to avoid a short word ending.

will See **shall/will.**

windows See **illustrations.**

-wise A **suffix** meaning in the manner or direction of:

> clockwise
> lengthwise

More recently, the suffix has been attached to virtually any word to mean *with reference to*:

computerwise
profitwise
religionwise
weatherwise

Authorities frown on the latter vague and sometimes foolish-sounding usage. Although writers are frequently urged to use concise language, this loose use of *-wise* is an example of ineffective and undesirable word economy:

Not: Our company has always been successful *saleswise*.
Better: Our company has always been successful in generating sales.

with regard to See **as regards/in regard to/regarding/ with regard to.**

word, absolute See **absolute word.**

word, abstract See **abstract word.**

word division Writers preparing and printing **manuscripts** by computer or submitting documents on disk usually let the computer adjust each line without dividing words at the end of a line. However, **compositors** must frequently divide words at the end of a line in justified type. See **justification.** Compositors setting type and editors and proofreaders checking **page proofs** are therefore concerned with proper word division and observe certain rules. See also **line break.**

For example, divide words between **syllables** (usually indicated by centered dots in dictionary entry heads):

syl•la•ble
vow•el

However, don't divide words of only one syllable or separate a one-letter syllable from the rest of the word:

heat (*not* he-at)
done (*not* do-ne)

aboard (*not* a-board)
studio (*not* studi-o)

Also, don't divide abbreviations or contractions:

NAFTA (*not* NAF-TA)
haven't (*not* have-n't)

Don't separate an *-ed* word ending unless the *-ed* is a syllable:

talked (*not* talk-ed)
But: defeat-ed

If possible, don't divide the names of persons except after **initials,** as described in that entry.

Also, if possible, don't divide numbers, but if they must be divided, do so only at a comma:

24,634,-963 (*not* 24,63-4,963)

In other cases when it is appropriate to divide a word, leave a syllable of at least three characters (including the hyphen) on the top line and three (including a period or other punctuation) on the bottom line:

ad-vent
in-dent
consequent-ly,
check-up.

Divide a solid **compound term** between the two terms, and divide a hyphenated compound term at the hyphen:

farther-most (*not* far-thermost)
under-current (*not* un-dercurrent)
air-condition (*not* air-condi-tion)
sister-in-law (*not* sis-ter-in-law)

Divide words with **prefixes** between the prefix and the rest of the word, and divide words with **suffixes** before the suffix:

pre-science (*not* presci-ence)
equi-distant (*not* equidis-tant)

change-able (*not* changea-ble)
phrase-ology (*not* phraseolo-gy)

When possible, divide at a one-letter syllable located within a word after the syllable (compositors often ignore this rule):

apolo-gize (*not* apol-ogize)
simi-lar (*not* sim-ilar)

Divide between two adjoining vowels that create two sounds, but don't divide between two vowels that create one sound:

patri-otic (*not* patrio-tic)
situ-ation (*not* situa-tion)
ac-quaint (*not* acqu-aint)
neu-tral (*not* ne-utral)

Even when compositors follow these basic rules of word division, it may be inappropriate to divide words for other reasons. For example, having more than two consecutive hyphens against the right margin creates a jarring, dashed appearance. Dividing the first or last word on a page also looks unattractive and may hinder readability. Therefore, editors and compositors need to view a page in terms of appearance and avoid word division that may be technically correct but is unattractive or disruptive to the reader.

word processing Most **manuscripts** are prepared by computer with word processing software. Such programs enable authors to save their copy on disks that can be sent to the publisher for use in **desktop publishing.**

With computer-generated manuscripts, a writer can check the work for spelling and grammatical errors through the use of spell-checkers and grammar-checkers. Special program features also help a writer format the work consistently, prepare **tables** and **graphics,** and print out extra paper copies or make extra disk copies with minimal effort.

For more about the use of computers in publishing, see **desktop publishing** and **typesetting.** See also **printing.**

word-by-word alphabetization system See **alphabetization.**

wordiness Some writers go to the extremes of using too few or too many words. Finding the right balance is not always easy to do, although it is easy to see. Using too few words creates a sense of abruptness, choppiness, and coldness. Overzealous writers and editors sometimes strive for strict word economy that destroys the smooth flow of words and ideas, a natural or conversational flow that makes written text easy and enjoyable to read.

The opposite is also true. Undisciplined writers and editors allow excessive words that serve no useful purpose. They are not needed for a clear progression of thoughts, for a conversational tone, or for a smooth transition between sentences and paragraphs. This type of wordiness is as counterproductive as excessive conciseness.

The use of too many words that mean the same thing is a familiar type of wordiness. However, some forms of repetition are intentional, and an editor must learn to recognize when an author is using this type of repetition. For example, repetition that serves a useful purpose in reinforcing thoughts and helping the reader remember something should never be deleted. On the other hand, repetition that simply repeats **synonyms** unintentionally should be omitted:

> aid and abet (aid *or* abet)
> brief moment (moment)
> end result (result)
> month of August (August)
> refuse and decline (refuse *or* decline)
> renovate like new (renovate)

Another familiar type of wordiness consists of needlessly long phrases. Often, a more concise version can be substituted without destroying the smooth flow or conversational quality of the writing. Although writers may intentionally and legitimately use certain so-called longer phrases, such as *in regard to* (*regarding*), to vary their comments, excessive use of long phrases will hinder, not enhance, readability:

a sizable percentage of (many)
an example of this is the fact that (for example)
as of this date (now)
come to a decision as to (decide *or* decide about)
had occasion to be (was)
in compliance with your request (as you requested)
in spite of the fact that (although)
in the not-too-distant future (soon)
notwithstanding the fact that (although)
perform an analysis (analyze)
the question as to whether (whether)
within the realm of possibility (possible *or* possibly)

See also **redundancy**, and compare with **conciseness.**

words from proper names Words derived from **proper nouns** are sometimes used as **nouns, adjectives,** or **verbs.** No firm rule exists concerning the capitalization of these terms, although most are written in **lowercase** letters. Consult a current dictionary, or follow the preferred style of your employer or publisher:

brussels sprouts
china (dishes)
india ink
kraft paper
manila envelope
pasteurize
roman type
venetian blinds

See also **proper names** and **trademark.**

words used as words Use **italics** in most cases for words referred to as words (in a few specialized fields, the words may be enclosed in single quotation marks):

A *palindrome* is a word that reads the same backwards as it does forward: *noon.*

Use the article *the* to refer to a specific item or person: *the* copier in my office.

The **plurals** of words used as words are usually formed by adding *-s* alone, unless reading might be difficult without an apostrophe:

ones and twos
yeses and nos
do's and don'ts

See also **letters used as letters.**

work for hire A legal classification for work by someone who is paid to create it. For example, an employee, as part of his or her employment responsibilities, may create a newsletter for the employer. A freelance writer, artist, or photographer may perform certain work on another person's document. In such cases the person doing the work or making the contribution is considered an "employee," and the person or company hiring the contributor is considered the "employer" as well as the "author" or "editor" of the work and the **copyright** owner.

Certain commissioned work may also be identified in a contract as a work for hire. This type of work includes contributions to journals, motion pictures, translations, educational test materials, atlases, forewords to books, and illustrations.

A work-for-hire contract differs significantly from a royalty contract in the method of payment. A writer, artist, photographer, or other person hired to create certain work or contribute certain material is usually paid a fee for his or her time or contribution but does not receive royalties.

Copyright on a work for hire lasts for 100 years from creation or 75 years from initial publication, whichever is shorter. See **copyright** for the term on a royalty work.

workable See **viable/workable.**

would See **shall/will.**

WYSIWYG An **acronym,** pronounced *whiz-ee-wig,* for "What you see is what you get." It refers to a feature of **desktop publishing** programs in which the text and graphics displayed on the computer screen look exactly the way they will appear when printed.

X

x The letter x is a widely used mathematical symbol ($x + y$) and is also used in a nontechnical sense to indicate an unknown quantity (X dollars). It is the typed symbol used in place of the word *by* (4 x 6) and is typed next to a number to specify magnification (2x lens).

In a **manuscript** an author usually types a **lowercase** x for *by* or to represent magnification and a capital X is to indicate an unknown quantity.

See also **equations, exponent, mathematical expressions,** and **x-height.**

x-height A type measurement in which the height of the **lowercase** letter x is used to express the height of the body (minus **ascenders** and **descenders**) of all lowercase letters. Small capital letters (see **small caps**) are also printed in the x-height of lowercase letters. See also **baseline.**

Y

year of publication The year of publication is stated on the **copyright page** of a book as the **copyright** date. See the example on the copyright page in the **front matter** of this dictionary. The copyright date of subsequent **editions** is also listed on the copyright page.

The *publishing history* of a book is often printed after the copyright notice. It may include the year of original publication (first edition) followed by the number and date of the current edition and the number and date of subsequent reprintings (see **reprint**), or *impressions*. The impressions may be identified by a line of numerals below the publishing history. One group of numerals indicates the years of publication beginning with the first or last year at the right, such as *1996* in the following example:

00 99 98 97 96

Another group of numerals indicates the new impressions. The current impression, read from the right, is the first impression:

5 4 3 2 1

When the second printing occurs, the number 1 is deleted, and the number 2 then appears on the right and so on with each subsequent printing:

5 4 3 2

-yze See **-ise/-ize/-yze.**

Z

zero In typing the numeral *0*, writers must be careful not to use the capital letter *O* (''oh''). General references in running text should be spelled out (*zero*), but if the figure is one of two or more other numerals being cited and is referred to as a digit, the number should be used (*0*):

Because of the snowstorm, Jim said he had *zero* [not *0*] sales on Wednesday.

The digits *0* [not *zero*], *5,* and *7* were repeated three times, in varying order, in the new password code.

Mary A. DeVries, a former periodical and book editor, is the author of more than fifty reference books, including the *Prentice Hall Style Manual*, *Practical Writer's Guide*, and *Complete Word Book*. She lives in Arizona.